BEH

Brandon stepp
angle so he co
anyone inside
canvas in a different stage of completion. A glance was
enough to tell Brandon that both were masterpieces.

His eyes widened as Teresa entered the room and
stepped up to one of the canvases. She selected a
brush from a crockery jar and began laying bruised blue
shadows onto a tumult of glowering storm clouds. Brandon
stepped back, feeling as weak as if he were recovering
from a serious disease. Could it be that his lovely Teresa
was a painter . . . an artist . . . a forger?

THE
MASTER'S
TOUCH

Lynda Trent is actually the award-winning husband-
and-wife team of Dan and Lynda Trent. After dating for
only a short time, they were married in 1977, and then
began their new career together.

Formerly a professional artist, Lynda actually began
writing a few months before she met Dan, who worked
for NASA for seventeen years before turning to writing
full-time.

The Trents have written a total of twenty-five novels,
and when asked how they manage to write together,
Lynda says, "We only use one pencil."

The Master's Touch

LYNDA TRENT

AN ONYX BOOK

NEW AMERICAN LIBRARY

NAL BOOKS ARE AVAILABLE AT QUANTITY DISCOUNTS WHEN USED
TO PROMOTE PRODUCTS OR SERVICES. FOR INFORMATION PLEASE
WRITE TO PREMIUM MARKETING DIVISION, NEW AMERICAN LIBRARY,
1633 BROADWAY, NEW YORK, NEW YORK 10019.

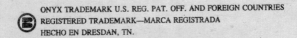

ONYX TRADEMARK U.S. REG. PAT. OFF. AND FOREIGN COUNTRIES
REGISTERED TRADEMARK—MARCA REGISTRADA
HECHO EN DRESDAN, TN.

SIGNET, SIGNET CLASSIC, MENTOR, ONYX, PLUME, MERIDIAN
and NAL BOOKS are published by NAL PENGUIN INC.,
1633 Broadway, New York, New York 10019

First Printing, March, 1989

1 2 3 4 5 6 7 8 9

PRINTED IN THE UNITED STATES OF AMERICA

Prologue

Venice, Italy, 1837

Teresa Verdi studied the blank canvas on her easel. She knew she was supposed to fill it with the still-life objects her grandfather had carefully arranged for her to copy, but at fourteen she was full of rebellion. She frowned at the artful disarray of polished apples, grapes, a silk drapery, and a half-empty bottle of wine. For six years she had painted apples and flowers and bottles; she was disgusted with this limited range of subjects. Her grandfather, Antonio Verdi, was a capable teacher and an accomplished artist in Venice, though he wasn't considered quite a master, and as yet had no wealthy patron. To be selected as one of his students was an honor among the young men who came to him seeking lessons.

At the moment Antonio was away from the house he shared with Teresa, her father, and her uncle, but on his return he would expect to see some progress. Nevertheless, Teresa put down her brush and took one of the apples from the arrangement. As her strong white teeth crunched into the juicy fruit, she strolled to one of the windows and looked out.

Because of the crowded conditions in Venice, the windows in their home, as in most buildings, had been made large to let in as much light as possible. Through the glass panes she watched a black gondola glide by on the gray-brown surface of the Grand Canal several feet below the window. The gondolier sang out a warning as he approached the blind intersection ahead, and even through the closed window she could hear the noise of the crowd. At one time her family had been among the wealthiest in Venice, and had occupied the entire building. They had been close friends with the Giustiniani family, and with the descendants of the Manin family, who had numbered among their ancestors the last doge of Venice. Now the Verdis were among the growing number of *scudati*, the impoverished nobility. Aside from the accomplishment of a distant cousin named Giuseppe Verdi, who was having a degree of success with the operas he wrote, Antonio had often said his sons were the last hope for family pride. He had taught them all he could and hoped that someday one of them would surpass his own artistic achievement. However, Salvatore's work still lacked that special something that makes a painting come alive, and Mario's great technical skill suffered from a lack of creative genius.

Teresa pushed open the window, admitting a breeze into the studio. She inhaled deeply of the familiar scents of fish, salt air, and the mustiness of the polluted canal, which contrasted sharply with the pungent, ever-present aroma of painting oils and turpentine. Sunlight glittered off the rippling water in the wake of one of the many gondolas that transported people and commodities throughout the city. Venice had always been home to Teresa and she loved it. As the breeze billowed her cape of black hair, her caramel-brown eyes studied the ever-changing scene from the window. An idea came to her, and as she considered the thought, the excitement brought a rosy tint to her pale cheeks. Teresa left the window only long enough to get her easel and unwieldy box of paint powders and oil. With quick strokes she began blocking out the picture she would paint.

By the time the lowering sun was casting deep purple shadows over the water, she had her canvas covered and was building up the layers of sepia and white underpainting. When the studio door opened, bringing her attention back to her own surroundings, she turned and hid the brush behind her.

"Teresa! What are you doing over there?" her grandfather bellowed in exasperation. "And where is the still life you were supposed to paint?"

Although she knew her grandfather loved her, she shrank under his intimidating gaze. Then she saw that her beloved father had entered as well, and a hopeful smile came to her lips. She swallowed against the lump in her throat and admitted the truth. "I've chosen another subject, Grandpapa."

Antonio Verdi's bushy gray eyebrows met above his prominent nose. "Oh? And who gave you leave to do this?"

Teresa's eyes cut to her father's, silently imploring his aid. Salvatore stepped closer and looked over his daughter's shoulder, but said nothing. Teresa frowned. She had hoped for praise, but knew he could not go against his father. Later he would tell her what he thought of the result of her disobedient act. Teresa looked back to her grandfather, not knowing how to answer his question without seeming disrespectful.

"You ate the still life," her grandfather reproved as he pointed at the apple core on the windowsill. "How can you ever hope to learn if you eat the subject matter? None of my students would dare such a thing! What do you have to say for yourself?"

"*I* decided I should paint the canal," she offered in her own defense. "And I ate the apple because I was hungry."

Salvatore spoke at last. "Papa, you're right. She is wrong for not doing as you instructed, but come see what she has done. I think you'll be pleased."

Antonio strode across the studio and stood beside his son. His sharp black eyes narrowed as he studied the canvas. "It is good," he admitted. Then, "But no. This is not for you to be doing, *cara mia*." He took her hand in both of his, lovingly but firmly. "You must learn discipline," he said. "No one will want a picture of this canal. They see it every day."

"But, Grandpapa, it's so pretty. I'm tired of still lifes. I want to paint things that interest me."

"Teresa, we have gone over this again and again," the old man said. "An artist must have discipline." He spaced the words for emphasis. "No one cares for pictures of canals. Especially not one with bits of fruit peel and other debris floating in it." He jabbed his finger at the accurate representation of the canal she had captured on her canvas.

"The peels and things were there, so I painted them," she argued, unable to keep the rebellion of her spirit from her tongue. "Canaletto painted what he saw. Why can't I?"

"That was a hundred years ago," Salvatore put in. "Styles have changed, *bambina*. Art is to improve on nature, not merely to duplicate it."

Her frown deepened. "I like my picture, and I want to finish it. Someday I may be as famous as Canaletto and everyone will want my canal picture."

Antonio put his arm around his granddaughter. "Be reasonable. A few years from now you will have a husband and babies to care for. To be a master like Canaletto or Titian or Tintoretto is impossible for you."

Teresa pulled away from him. "Why, Grandpapa? Look at my canvases!" She waved her hand at the drying racks of canvases in the darker end of the studio. "Even my stupid paintings of fruit and flowers and dogs are good!"

"You might work a bit harder on your humility," her father observed.

"I've heard both of you say I'm better than Carlo Sebastiano, and he's the most promising of all your students."

"Carlo is a *boy*," Antonio reminded her. "No woman may be a master. Why, it's a contradiction in terms." He smiled to tease her out of her foolishness. "Be a good girl now, and don't eat the still life—paint it."

Teresa turned to her father for support, but Salvatore nodded sadly in agreement. "He's right. You know he is. I've told you this myself."

"It's not fair!"

"Who told you life must be fair?" Antonio asked. "Everyone has his place, and *there* is where fairness lies. Can I have a baby? Could I give it milk? Yet I don't cry out against the unfairness of it."

"That's not the same thing!"

"A woman cannot be a master painter," Salvatore said. "What would your mother say if she could hear you, rest her soul?"

Teresa, who had no memory at all of the mother who had died when she was born, looked unconvinced. "Perhaps she would have agreed with me. I've seen her sketches, and they, too, are good."

Antonio responded. "Yes, *cara mia*, for a *woman*. Not for a master painter. There has never been one and there never will be. But I don't want to discourage you from painting. You are talented, and may still attain some success. Look at Rosalba Carriera. She was extremely popular and traveled widely throughout Europe doing her portraits."

"Pah!" Teresa spat with contempt as she crossed her arms. "Her work simpers! It conforms! All the faces are the same! And she used pastels, not oils. I want to do better than that."

"For a girl who has yet to sell even so much as a sketch, you have high ambition," her grandfather rebuked, his patience wearing thin.

"Who has seen my work to buy it?" She paced to the table and back again. "Are people so hungry for art in Venice that they knock on doors and ask if anyone inside has paintings to sell?"

"What would you have me do," her grandfather roared. "Go to San Marco and open a booth for you? Demand that the Doge's Palace hang your work in the rooms of state?"

Salvatore hastily stepped between his irate father and

even angrier daughter. "Let us end this. There is no reason to disagree. Teresa cannot be a man, and to be a master, she must be. It's that simple. Why argue over it?" He smiled at his daughter as if the truth should win out, but she continued to scowl. "We can compromise, I think. Teresa will finish her picture of the canal; then she will paint the still life."

Teresa knew she was defeated, but she hated to give up. "I will finish the canal, and *maybe* I will do a still life. Or maybe I will paint the Ramano sisters sewing in their courtyard!" When her grandfather's brows knit, a triumphant grin spread across Teresa's face. She would do as her father suggested and paint the still life after she finished the one of the canal, but she didn't want to give in too easily. Afterward she would paint the Ramano girls.

Before her grandfather could continue the argument, she tiptoed up and kissed his cheek, then winked at her father and hurried out of the studio. After painting the entire day, she had a ferocious appetite.

1

Teresa moved aside her curry-hued skirts and leaned over her father's newest canvas. As she studied the precise brush strokes, she frowned. Grandpapa had been dead a year, and her father was still suffering from a deep depression. His work, what little there had been, was proof of that.

She straightened and looked around the studio. Nothing here had changed following Antonio's passing, except that the drying racks at the far end of the room no longer contained the works of promising young students. There were no students at all, for Antonio Verdi had been the artist of renown, not his son. Salvatore tried to carry on his father's work, but he lacked the fire, the secret song that could change a painting into a masterpiece. He was good, but greatness continued to elude him.

Pensively Teresa walked around the cluttered studio with its familiar smells of linseed oil and turpentine. She felt as if her entire life had been spent here. The canvases were the diary of her childhood and youth. She was twenty-two now, and approaching spinsterhood, but her biggest concern was not the lack of a mate. It was that—because she was a woman—she was not allowed to paint what she felt in her soul.

She swished her skirt away from her father's newest canvas. She should have been born a son. Then she could carry on the Verdi name with pride! Again she

11

turned back and studied the painting he considered finished. She knew what it lacked. To her eyes the omissions were obvious: a broader line here, a bolder stroke there, a layer of vermilion wash over the vivid scarlet. These observations came to her as naturally as the air she breathed, but to Salvatore they were as elusive as moonbeams. When he saw such subtleties in another's painting, he appreciated their value, yet he couldn't recognize their absence in his own work.

The door opening behind her drew Teresa's attention. It was her father. "It's you, *cara mia,*" he said. "I wondered who was in here."

"Who else would it be, Papa?"

Salvatore ran his hand through his unruly graying hair and looked at her with the dispirited expression she had seen so often of late. "Who indeed. Who would come to Antonio Verdi's studio when the master is gone?"

"Papa, you have to pull yourself together. This melancholy is ruining you."

Salvatore crossed the studio to the canvas he had completed only a few days before. For several moments he looked at the painting in silence; then, without meeting Teresa's eyes, he said, "This is my best this year, no? I feel certain Carmelo Di Palma will agree to exhibit it."

"Of course he will," Teresa said with more conviction than she felt. The owner of the prestigious Di Palma Gallery had refused to take the last picture her father had shown him, even though before Antonio's death, Salvatore's paintings had hung alongside his father's. The rejection had been a crushing blow, both to Salvatore's fragile ego and to his dwindling pocketbook, but both he and Teresa knew if he ever resorted to showings in a lesser gallery, he would be finished with Di Palma. Another refusal now would surely seal his fate.

Salvatore's face lined with worry as he scrutinized his latest work. "I just can't seem to do it," he muttered to himself. "I never realized how much I relied on Papa to point out the finishing touches."

Cautiously Teresa moved to his side and said, "I can almost hear him saying 'a broader stroke here.'" Her capable hands gestured over the canvas. "'A vermilion wash there.'"

Salvatore shook his head, not letting her broad hints soak in. "It's no use. Without him I am nothing. Even Mario is reduced to teaching art classes to anyone with lire enough to pay—Mario, who is better than I am. No, Teresa, I cannot do it. Signor Di Palma will refuse this one too."

"You must try, Papa! How else can we live?" She tried to keep the exasperation and concern from her voice.

"There is your mother's sister in Florence. We could go there and ask to become one of her household."

"Accept charity? From Aunt Rosa? Papa! She would drive us both mad in a month's time. You know how she is!"

Salvatore shrugged and stroked his mustache. "You're right. We should see what Carmelo Di Palma says first."

She watched him leave the studio, his shoulders slumped in defeat and his steps were as heavy as those of a man twice his age. Anger sparked her eyes, and she looked back at the painting. She had told him what the picture needed, and he wouldn't listen!

Resolutely she covered her silk gown with her paint-stained smock and took out her palette. With practiced movements she tapped out a bit of powdered vermilion, then added oil to create a transparent glaze. After mixing the paint to the desired consistency, she hesitated for a moment, then put her brush to her father's canvas. The painting was one of two ladies sunning on their *altana* high above the canals. Their titian-blond hair was spread over the brims of their open-crowned hats so the belvedere's sunlight would bleach it. One had her rounded arm poised as if she were greeting someone passing on the street below. The composition was good; it was the painting that was at fault.

Teresa applied the glaze over the too-vivid scarlet dress, then added purple shadows, subduing the color to a hue more in keeping with the lady's obvious station in life. She mixed a sienna paste and corrected the angle of the chimney pot and steps.

As she cleaned her brushes she critically viewed the painting. New subtleties of color and shadings lent a depth it had lacked before. Her strokes were bolder than her father's and added a strength the picture had needed. The lady with the upraised arm no longer simpered but commanded.

Taking care not to touch the wet canvas, Teresa put it in the box-shaped portfolio she used to carry paintings to the gallery. To present Di Palma with a wet canvas was chancy, but she didn't dare let her father see what she had done.

As she let herself out the street side of the ancient building where her family had lived for many years, she heard the chatter of their renters coming from what had once been her family's private sitting rooms. Had it not been for the income from the tenants, she and her father couldn't have lasted even a year. Other fine houses in the area had also fallen on hard times, as evidenced by the clothing that flapped in the breeze from their carved marble windows. Teresa paused as a gang of small boys ran unchecked across the small patio where the Verdis' once-peerless garden had been. Then she rounded the squat well with its crumbling emblem of Crusaders and stepped out into the street.

Although there were no horses to dodge here, for horses were forbidden on all the narrow streets in the city, Teresa was always cautious about walking these streets alone, especially after dusk. Gaslights were an innovation on the larger streets and along the canals, but they hadn't yet been installed on the small cul-de-sacs such as this one, and after dark the more unsavory of Venice's population began to move about in the shadows. Teresa walked briskly, not letting her eyes meet those of the wastrels who lounged in the ocher shade of the entrances to buildings or alleyways. She knew she would have time today to conduct her business and return home before dark, but only if she didn't tarry.

Once she turned onto the wider, more crowded street that led to the gallery, she slowed her pace a bit. The jostling crowd was always preferable to the calculating eyes of the men nearer her house.

The gallery stood near the Piazza San Marco and on the same side of the square as Quadri's Café, an establishment frequented almost exclusively by Austrians, and it was the occupying Austrians who had money to buy art. Although Venice had not been sacked by her victors during all these years, much of her art had been acquired by Austrians and sent home to their palaces.

As Teresa passed Florian's Café on the opposite side of the square, where the Venetians congregated, several soldiers in Austrian uniform drew near her. She kept her eyes on the sidewalk ahead while tightening her grip on the portfolio. Soldiers were rarely a threat, but with the recent increase of resentment between them and the Venetians, she was uneasy. Although they passed by her without incident, she could feel their eyes on her until she crossed the square and stepped into the gallery. She thought of the days of her grandfather's youth, which he had spoken of so fondly, when the famed Venetian Carnival lasted for six months of the year, every year, and when no one was molested in the streets. Teresa wondered whether he had exaggerated or if the patina of age had merely softened the memories. She couldn't imagine an unoccupied Venice. The soldiers had been here since her grandfather was a boy.

As her eyes adjusted to the lighting of the interior of the gallery, she began to peruse the paintings that Di Palma had on display, each strategically placed to prevent sunlight from fading the colors. Teresa was relieved that the gallery appeared to be empty. If Signor

Di Palma were to reject the painting she had brought for his inspection, she would rather it not happen in front of anyone.

She went to the counter near the back wall and laid down the unwieldy portfolio. As she untied the strings that secured it, Carmelo Di Palma poked his head around the corner from the back room. When he recognized her, his professional expression faded. "Oh. It's you again. What do you have there?"

"Papa has sent you another painting." She gave him her most winning smile. "I'm sure you'll be pleased."

Di Palma didn't look convinced. "Your papa? Not your grandpapa?"

"You know we've already sold all of Grandpapa's paintings that we are willing to part with." She removed the cover and began to take out the canvas.

"A moment," Di Palma said. "I'll be back. I was busy wrapping a pastel." He disappeared around the corner.

Teresa's smile became a frown. She could remember a time when Di Palma would have dropped everything to see a Verdi canvas. But that was when the canvas was signed "A. Verdi," not "S. Verdi."

When she looked again to the front of the gallery, she noticed she wasn't alone. A tall man stood in the front corner as if he had been gazing out at the street. When their eyes met through the forest of easels, Teresa felt her pulse quicken in her throat. His eyes were the first thing she noticed. They were as deep and clear a green as the needles on a pine tree, gentle and intelligent, and framed in the blackest of lashes. His lean face had a bone structure that the artist in her admired at once. His hair was thick and nearly as dark as her own, but with ruddy highlights where the rays of the sun touched it.

He smiled, and her heart seemed to skip a beat. Casually he walked over to her, his movements as lithe as an athlete's. Teresa couldn't stop staring at him. He stopped only a few feet from her. She tilted her head up to look at him, and her lips parted unconsciously. Before her was a man such as she had never seen before!

At once she realized she was staring, and she looked away in confusion as embarrassment flooded over her. What was she thinking of to stare at a stranger in that way!

He seemed to realize that he, too, had been staring, because he also looked away. Awkwardly they glanced back at each other at the same time. A blush colored Teresa's cheeks.

"Forgive me for being so rude," he said in a deep voice with a curious accent to his Italian.

"No, no, the blame is mine."

"Allow me to introduce myself. I'm Lord Brandon Kincaid of London."

Her eyes returned to his. "You're English?"

"Yes." Again the smile lifted his lips and he prompted, "And your name?"

"I'm Teresa Verdi. Antonio Verdi's granddaughter."

"Oh? I've heard of him," Kincaid said as he moved to the counter. "Is this one of his paintings?"

"No." She found she was staring again, and more briskly she added, "No, this is a painting of my father's."

He lifted the canvas out of the portfolio and turned it to the light. "It seems to be still wet."

She gave him an expressive shrug. "Papa's paintings sell so quickly, he can't afford the time to let the paint dry." She glanced at the door to the back room, relieved to see no sign of Di Palma. Nothing would please her more than to sell this canvas without having to go through Di Palma and paying him a commission. "He is very popular, my papa."

"I can see why," the man said. He took the canvas nearer the window and studied it. "This is good. Very good indeed. How much is he asking for it?"

Teresa swallowed hard and her hands went cold. Taking a deep breath, she named a sum that was higher than he would ever have received through the gallery.

He glanced at her as if he were amazed, and she

instantly wished she had not been so greedy. Then, to her surprise, he said, "I'll take it. To tell you the truth, *signora,* I had expected to pay more."

For a minute Teresa thought he was teasing her, but his eyes were quite serious. "Not *signora, signorina,*" she said. "I'm unmarried."

His smile broadened, and he turned his attention fully on her. "I see. Do you speak English? I'm afraid my Italian isn't very proficient."

"Yes, I speak English." Prompted by honesty, she added, "Did you understand the price I quoted you? If not . . ."

"Lire I can understand. Money is the same in all languages." His smile included her, though she wasn't too sure what he meant. Was he as rich as that?

"Would it be possible for me to meet your father?" he asked.

"Yes, of course."

"Does he have other canvases he might part with?" He looked back at the one he held. "This use of color, the turn of this lady's arm—these aren't touches to be found every day."

Teresa glanced at the canvas. Those were the areas she had worked on. "Papa has others to sell." She jerked her chin haughtily in the direction of the back room and spoke with greater volume, hoping Di Palma would overhear. "We do not bring all our paintings *here,* where we are asked to wait."

"I'm afraid the waiting's my fault. I bought a pastel and he's packaging it for me to take back to England. Forgive me for inconveniencing you."

"If Di Palma had not been occupied, you might never have seen Papa's *Ladies on the Altana.* It is fate."

"Yes," he agreed slowly as his eyes searched her face. "It is indeed fate."

Teresa felt a strange excitement flow through her. Usually she hated to have anyone stare at her, but with this man, the experience was pleasant, almost too much so. To cover her confusion, she turned back to the portfolio and said, "If you will put the painting back, I will see that it's properly wrapped for its journey."

"When may I see the others? This evening?"

"Oh, no!" she exclaimed. "That is, Papa is still in mourning for the death of his father."

"I'm sorry. I thought . . ."

"Grandpapa has been gone a year, and officially our mourning is over, but Papa is still melancholy."

"Yet he is is able to turn out a work like this? I'm impressed. But I don't want to intrude at such a time."

After a moment's consideration, she said, "Come to our palazzo tomorrow afternoon. Say at two o'clock." She tied the portfolio together and put it under her arm.

"Where do you live?" he asked quickly as she started toward the door. "How can I find you again?"

For a moment his question sounded personal, but then she reminded herself that his interest was only in the art, not in her. "Have a gondolier bring you to the Verdi palazzo." She waved her hand carelessly. "Everyone knows where we live."

Before he could reconsider, she left. To have him come by water was an inspiration, she told herself. That side of the house was much grander than the street side. The tenants seldom dried their clothes there for fear they might drop them into the canal.

Her steps were quick as she headed for home. Lord Kincaid, he had said his name was. She spoke it aloud, and the words felt deliciously foreign in her mouth. She had never met an English lord before. She wondered what he was lord of, or was the term "lord over"?

Long fingers of shadow stretched down the street and up the houses on the opposite side. Because Venice's narrow streets were like brick canyons, dusk slipped quickly into night, and overhead the sky was already turning the dark blue-purple of a butterfly's wing. In the shadowy doorways of the tall houses, unkempt men and slatternly women lounged. Teresa was sad for the depths to which her beloved Venice was sinking, but she was too wise to linger unprotected in the street and contemplate the city's downfall.

When she reached her house, she hurried across the enclosed patio to her door, pausing only briefly to wave to the children of their tenants who played on the steps that climbed the outside of the building. Because space was so dear in the crowded city, few people spared room inside for stairs. The steps made it easy, however, to rent the upper floors and still retain the privacy of those below.

Inside, Teresa was cheerfully greeted by old Saberio Valore. He and his wife, Catherina, had served Verdis all their lives, and their families had done the same before them. Now only Catherina and Saberio were left of all the large and efficient staff. They considered the house to be their own ancestral home of sorts and had been willing to stay on for a pittance.

"Where is Papa?" Teresa asked as she removed her bonnet.

"He's gone to his bed," Saberio said with a shake of his head. "He said he felt bad and hardly ate his supper, which, I might say, you missed."

"Don't scold me," she teased back. "I have news that will brighten even Papa. His painting has already sold!"

"No!" The old man's mouth dropped open. "The new one?"

"Yes. An Englishman bought it, and he paid dearly for it. Not only that, he wants to see more."

"Catherina, come here!" When his wife appeared, Saberio said, "Tell her. Tell her what you told me, for she will never believe it from me."

When Teresa repeated her news, the woman's concerned face brightened with the unexpected good fortune.

"It sold so quickly! And for so much! Our fortunes have turned. I knew they would. Is Salvatore not a Verdi?" She patted Teresa's cheek. "Come to the kitchen. I have kept a plate warm for you."

"I can't eat, Catherina. I have too much to do."

"Not eat? You're too skinny now! I'll set out your plate," she said with determination as she turned away.

"Don't argue," Saberio advised. "In the end you'll lose. I should know."

Teresa knew he was right. With a resigned smile she followed the old woman to the kitchen. Catherina put a rice dish and a fresh melon on the table. "I made *risotto* and this is fresh *melone*. Eat. No one wants a woman too narrow to cast a shadow."

"I'm not that thin," Teresa protested.

"If you don't eat, you will be."

Teresa finished as quickly as she could, leaving the table before Catherina could insist that she follow her meal with a sweet.

She went to her room and changed into her oldest dress—the one she usually wore when she painted. Going back to the studio, she took several of her father's canvases from the rack, and studied each one critically to see how it could be improved. Then she put the first one on the easel and took out her paints.

By dawn Teresa ached all over, but she had a dozen altered canvases in the drying rack ready to show the Englishman. After she scraped her palette clean and wiped her palette knife, she cleaned her brushes and stood them in a jar to dry with the bristles up, then hurried to her room.

As she closed her bedroom door behind her, she heard the Valores coming out of their room. With the last of her energy Teresa put on her nightgown and crawled into bed.

Minutes later Catherina opened her door. "Are you going to sleep all day? I have breakfast cooking."

"I want to sleep late today," she said in a tired voice.

"You aren't getting sick, are you? It's not like you to sleep late." Catherina came to the bed and felt Teresa's forehead.

"I'm fine. Just sleepy."

"Then sleep. When I was a girl, ladies slept until

noon or later. Now that we're coming back to good times, you should sleep as late as you please."

As Teresa drifted into sleep, she hoped she hadn't raised Catherina's spirits for nothing. Foreigners could be unpredictable, and this Lord Kincaid might never show up. She should have had him pay in advance, she thought as sleep overtook her.

"Teresa!! What has happened to my paintings!"

Her eyes flew open and she rolled over to see her angry father standing in her doorway. Sleep left her at once. "I can explain, Papa!"

"No! You can never explain this!" Salvatore raised both his hands as if to beseech heaven. "Why? Why have you done this thing? All my canvases have been altered!"

"Not all of them." She grabbed her wrapper and slipped it on as she slid out of bed. "I had hoped to talk to you before you saw them."

"Talk!" Salvatore said as he left her room and strode toward the studio. "You have ruined me and you want to talk? What would your mother say?"

She caught up with him in the studio. Nervously she tried to smooth her long black hair as she said, "Something wonderful has happened! You have sold your *Ladies on the Altana*!"

"This?" He thrust his palm at the canvas from the portfolio. "This is not mine. Some person left it here. It is not mine."

"Papa, don't be like that. Of course it's yours." She caught his hand, but he shook her away.

"These are not mine either! Not anymore! Why, Teresa? Why would you do this?"

"Listen to me." She again grabbed his hand, and this time refused to release it. "I said the painting has sold! To an Englishman. *And* we don't have to pay Di Palma a commission because he never displayed it."

"What did this Englishman do? See the portfolio

under your arm and buy it sight unseen? Even an Englishman is not so stupid!"

"Of course not. I took it to Di Palma's and he saw me open it and bought it while Di Palma was in the back room. And he's not just an Englishman, he's nobility—Lord Kincaid."

"Kincaid? What kind of a name is Kincaid? Does he have no first name? Where is his money?"

She hesitated. "He will bring it this afternoon when he comes for the painting."

"Hah! So you haven't even seen his money, and yet the painting is sold? I thought you were smarter than to fall for that! But why have you painted on my canvases?" His voice rose, and Teresa lifted her chin to keep it from quivering.

"He bought the painting *after* I had worked on it, and he asked to see more in the same style."

Salvatore stared at her, his mouth agape. "After? Not before?"

"I took it wet to the gallery."

"Wet!" He glared at his daughter as if he were trying to determine what punishment might be severe enough. "You let a wet canvas leave the studio?"

"Aren't you going to ask what he paid?"

"What he *said* he would pay, you mean? How much?"

When she told her father what the Englishman had agreed to pay, Salvatore looked even more doubtful. "And you believed this? My father's paintings perhaps, but not mine. No, he will never show up, and my paintings are ruined!"

Tears stung Teresa's eyes. "Ruined? How can you say that?"

Salvatore propped one of the canvases on an easel. It was a street scene with vendors selling flowers from carts. Now that his shock was passing, he could see that the painting wasn't ruined, just changed a bit. Where the young vendor's expression had been cheeky, it was now imploring, beneath bold eyes. With a few additional brush stokes, Teresa had shown the years of privation the young man had endured in his tenuous survival.

"They aren't ruined." Teresa repeated tearfully.

He lifted the painting of a fisherman hauling in a day's catch. The composition was his, but now the fishes' scales glistened as if they really were fresh from the sea, and crystalline drops of water dripped from the nets. He could almost smell the sea salt and the pungent odor of the fishing boats.

"Papa, speak to me!"

"They aren't ruined," he admitted grudgingly. Then he demanded, "But why did you do it? You know never to tamper with someone's art."

"I saw them with Grandpapa's eyes," she answered miserably. "I saw what he would have done, so I did it."

Thoughtfully Salvatore regarded his daughter. She hadn't meant to do harm, and she had, in fact, improved them. On the other hand, he couldn't allow her to do this. "You're a woman. You presume too much."

"It sold." She went to him and gazed beseechingly up at him. "I didn't do it to hurt you. I meant only to help."

"And what will happen when I try to sell another picture and my style doesn't match these? I will be called a forger. These look more like Papa's paintings than like mine!"

"No, no, the style isn't quite the same as Grandpapa's. No one will accuse you of anything. And once your melancholy has lifted . . ."

"Never have I painted in this style." Salvatore paced the width of the studio and back again. "I must either not sell these or not paint in my own style. Teresa, what have you done?"

"I could help you. Add a stroke here, a shadow there. Together we—"

"Together!" he exploded. "You expect me, Salvatore Marco Giovanni Verdi, to play the apprentice while you play the master?" His face reddened alarmingly.

A knock on the formal entrance sounded throughout

the house. Teresa jumped and clasped her wrapper to her throat. "Sweet Mary! What time is it?"

"Time! What do I care for time?"

"It must be Lord Kincaid. Talk to him, Papa, while I dress." She ran from the studio as she called over her shoulder, "And be nice."

She heard Salvatore's roar but kept running. Too much depended on this sale. She could smooth her father's ruffled feathers later.

She kicked her door shut and dressed as quickly as she could, her hair flying about her shoulders as she dashed about the room, pulling on petticoats and stockings and the first dress she reached. With trembling fingers she brushed her hair and knotted it expertly in a bun at the nape of her neck. As soon as she tied her shoes, she ran back to the studio.

At the closed door she came to a halt and pressed her palms against her stomach. Drawing a steadying breath, she opened the door and stepped in as if she had come there in the most leisurely fashion.

Brandon Kincaid looked up from the canvas he was admiring when she entered. All night he had told himself the illusory light of Venice and its romantic canals and statuary had bewitched him into remembering the woman he had seen in Di Palma's gallery as more beautiful than she actually was. Now he saw he had underestimated her. She wore a garnet dress trimmed in flounces of ecru lace. Her hair was raven black and looked as if it were barely tamed into the neat bun. Her almond-shaped eyes were not quite brown and not quite amber, while her skin was the rich cream that only true brunettes could boast.

"Your father was showing me some of his other canvases," Kincaid said.

"Was he?" She smiled a bit nervously, and he wondered if his presence made her even a fraction as excited as hers made him. Probably not, he decided. Women, or at least ladies, didn't share men's baser instincts. His fiancée had told him so on numerous occasions.

He pointed at the slippery-looking scales of the fish in the net. "This is remarkable. I've never seen anything so well done."

"My father . . ." Salvatore began, but he couldn't finish.

"No, not even him. I'm familiar with Antonio Verdi's work, but yours far surpasses it."

Teresa avoided her father's piercing stare.

A man of action, Lord Kincaid said decisively, "You're just the man I've been searching for. I'm prepared to offer you a house on my estate on the outskirts of London and a comfortable income. In return, you will paint for me, and when the canvases sell, I'll give you a generous percentage."

"London!" Teresa gasped.

With a smile Kincaid said to Salvatore in the best Italian he could manage, "I'm asking to be your patron."

"Patrono!" Salvatore exclaimed. He rounded on his daughter with a glare. "I couldn't possibly accept!"

"Why not? I've taken the liberty to ask around, and I know you're not appreciated here. Venice belongs to the memory of your father. London can belong to you."

"Papa?" Teresa said hesitantly. "Perhaps—"

"No!" Salvatore snapped. To the Englishman he said, "Teresa should never have shown you that painting, or have taken it from the studio!"

"Papa, think what you're saying!" She made a gesture at the canvases that had never sold.

"Are those more back there?" Kincaid asked as he took the liberty of stepping to the back and pulling out first one of the paintings Teresa hadn't retouched, then another. "No, I see these were done by one of your students."

For some reason, this made the Italian man glare even more at his daughter, and Brandon Kincaid wondered if the man were in the habit of mistreating her.

She looked frightened, and he was surprised at the protectiveness this awakened in him.

"Papa, I think we should go to England," she encouraged.

"How can you suggest such a thing, Teresa? Think what you're saying!"

"But to have a *patrono*, Papa. For years you've dreamed of an offer like this!"

"I know you must be reluctant to leave your home," Kincaid said, "but I assure you that I will see to it that you'll be well provided for. My country house is called Hawthorn Manor and is enclosed by parks, forests, and meadows, yet London is an easy ride. On the lands I have a small cottage of rustic design but with every convenience. Naturally I will supply you with whatever servants you require, and I will do all in my power to make your name known throughout England."

Both Teresa and Salvatore stared at him, speechless.

"Forgive my forwardness," Lord Kincaid continued, "but my name may not have yet reached Venice. In England I'm considered a connoisseur of art."

"You're *that* Kincaid?" Salvatore gasped.

Teresa's eyes grew rounder.

"I believe we may both benefit from the arrangement," the Englishman concluded.

"Papa," Teresa murmured as she tugged at his sleeve, not taking her eyes from Brandon Kincaid.

"Quiet, *cara mia*, I'm thinking." He stroked his chin as if he were sizing up the Englishman. "No. No, I can't do it."

"Papa!" she implored. "Think what you're turning down!"

"You think what you're asking me to do!" he snapped at his daughter. "How can we consider this?"

Kincaid waited patiently. He could tell that Salvatore Verdi was more tempted than his words had implied. "Perhaps I should mention that the living I would settle on you is such that you would never have a want." He casually named a price, and by the expression on the

Italian's face, he didn't think he would have to increase his offer.

Again Teresa whispered, "Papa?"

Salvatore looked at her in a strange way. "How can we do this?"

"How can we not do it?" she countered.

Salvatore drew in a deep breath and said in a rush, "We accept. You are my *patrono*. I hope you don't live to regret it." He paused. "Naturally my daughter will accompany me."

"Of course." Brandon Kincaid smiled at Teresa and said, "I never considered that she might not."

2

Teresa first saw Hawthorn Manor in April, when wild crab apples made pink-and-white clouds among the hedgerows, and primroses, violets, and anemones carpeted the woodlands. Hawthorn sat on a flat expanse of impeccably tended lawns with a crescent of parkland behind it. Its mellow red bricks had aged to a rosy patina and green moss limned the gray slate roof. Off to the right were formal gardens and hedges. The paving blocks of the front courtyard were outlined by the creeping thyme that grew in the spaces between the stones.

"Do you think this is the right place?" Teresa asked her father. "It's so big! And look at these grounds!"

"I told the coachman the directions Lord Kincaid gave me."

She was almost afraid to get out of the carriage. Since she had left Venice, the sights she had seen were beyond her imaginings. London alone had been enough to occupy her thoughts for weeks. Now this. "When he said it was a country house, I imagined something like the Salernos' villa outside Padua. But their villa would fit into the courtyard here!"

Salvatore's face showed concern as he said, "I hope we have not made a grave mistake in coming here. A man who lives such as this! What will he say if he finds out you altered my paintings?"

"Hush, Papa. What if someone here can understand Italian?"

The coachman had climbed down and was opening her door. Teresa let him hand her out as if she were accustomed to a retinue of such servants. Above the creaking sounds of the carriage springs and horse harness, she heard the lilting song of a bird. She smiled at her father and said, "It's so lovely here! No crowds, no smells from the streets."

"Venice is your home. Don't forget it," he reminded her from habit as he looked around.

A tall man with silvery hair came out of the front door. With him was a younger man. Teresa watched as they approached, wondering who they were and how she was supposed to greet them.

The older man bowed slightly and said, "Welcome to Hawthorn. My name is Fitch; I'm the butler. This is the head groom, Jesse Holcolm. He will transfer your trunks to one of our vehicles and take you to the cottage. Lord Kincaid is in London at the moment, and as he was uncertain of your time of arrival, he asked me to greet you on his behalf and see to it that all your needs are met."

"Thank you," Teresa said, vaguely disappointed that their handsome benefactor hadn't welcomed them himself.

As they were speaking, a carriage emblazoned with the predominantly red Kincaid coat of arms—a sable stallion rampant on a field of gules—rolled up beside the public conveyance. The younger man transferred their baggage, and after the butler paid the public driver, he handed Teresa and her father into the carriage. By comparison with the merely serviceable appointments of the hired carriage, this one was exquisite. The cushioned seats were covered with soft leather that had been dyed the color of red wine. The walls were of carved oak, and the red velvet curtains over the windows were drawn back with red tassels. Below one seat was a covered brazier for coals to make winter travel more comfortable. On the back wall hung a large carriage clock. Teresa raised her eyebrows at her father to show how impressed she was. He pretended to take in all the opulence as a matter of course, but Teresa knew he was impressed as well.

The matched team of black horses drew the carriage forward. Beneath the rumble from the wheels, Salvatore said, "We should confess it all to Lord Kincaid and go back home where we belong."

"Nonsense. He's already paid our way here, and has made a cottage ready for us. We can't leave now." She caressed the glove-soft leather of the seat. "Besides, I don't want to go."

"We'll come to a bad end here. I can feel it! I may never see Venice again."

"Of course you will, Papa. I had thought your melancholy was lifted."

"It was. What you see now is my guilt. We are here under false pretenses. What if Lord Kincaid has us arrested? A Verdi in prison!"

"He contracted for an artist, and he got two for the price of one. Besides, he will never know."

Salvatore frowned. "I don't know how I let you talk me into going through with this. The Verdi name is old and proud and has never before been touched by scandal."

"Nor will it be now," she said firmly. "If I were your son and not your daughter, there would be no problem."

"But you are my daughter. And there is a problem." He put his hands on his knees and gave her a disapproving frown. "There is only one thing to do. I will paint the pictures and present them to him. Perhaps he will not see the difference."

"You know he will! This is Lord Brandon Kincaid, the renowned art critic. We must do as we planned in Venice."

Salvatore shook his head dismally. "My poor father. I thank God he didn't live to see this day. To think I must have my paintings finished by another hand, and by a woman's at that."

"Be glad you have my hands," she said a bit tartly.

She was growing tired of hearing how inferior she was. "Catherina told me the butcher and the fishmonger were becoming angry with you over their unpaid bills. What if we had had to sell our palazzo?"

He looked unconvinced. "People always make noises when one owes them money."

"This way we owe no one. Saberio and Catherina will take care of our home in Venice just as they always have, and we will have money and all this fresh air and space."

"To hear you talk, a person would think you weren't Venetian."

"Venice is where my roots are, Papa, but I like for my head to be in the fresh air and sunshine."

The carriage circled the house and continued on through the extensive park, where tall oaks stretched their leafy boughs over the grass and wildflowers, forming a shade spangled with sunlight. Ahead, beyond a copse of tall white willows that looked silvery against the darker oaks, was a cottage nestled among hedges and a riotous flower garden.

Teresa's eyes grew round as the carriage stopped in front of it. "Papa, look! It's like a fairy-tale house!"

The cottage was narrow but deep, making it look smaller at first glance than it really was. It was made of stucco, and the thatched roof overhung the eaves like the forelock of a pony. The walls were a pale yellow-cream and the shutters had been painted a cheerful blue. Each window box was filled with flowers that made a rainbow of color. The small walk that led to the tiny porch circled to the back of the house, where more willows lined the banks of a quiet stream.

Teresa didn't wait for the coachman to hand her out. She hurried up the short walk, but before she could reach the door, it opened and a young woman and a teenage boy came out. The woman bobbed a curtsy and said, "Welcome to the cottage, Miss Verdi. I'm your maid and cook, Katie Banning. This here is the foot-boy, Hal Lunn."

When Salvatore reached Teresa's side, the woman again made her short speech, complete with curtsy. He looked at Teresa as if to say they could never pull off their deception with two servants in the house, but Teresa ignored him.

The inside of the house was as clean and neat as the outside had been. Bleached oak covered the floors, and the front parlor was papered in a pale yellow with rows of tiny rosebuds. The furniture looked comfortable, though not quite new, as if it might have come from Hawthorn's attics.

Behind the parlor was a hallway that led to two bedrooms, one obviously intended for a man, the other for a woman. "Lord Kincaid has certainly been busy these past few weeks," Teresa observed to the maid.

"Aye, Miss. That he has."

The back room jutted off at an angle from the front of the house, and Teresa saw at once that it was meant to be the studio. Light poured in through windows on three sides of the room, and it had no furniture except for a small table, newly sawn drying racks, and several easels.

Salvatore nodded begrudgingly. "It is good."

"Good? Papa, it's perfect." She went to a back window and looked out at the placid waters of the stream. "Look out here. You can pretend it's a canal."

He refused to smile at her teasing. In Italian he said, "We must leave while we still can. I'm telling you, this is wrong!"

Teresa turned to the maid and footboy. "Can you speak Italian?" she asked.

"No, Miss," the girl replied. "Not a whisper. Nor can Hal. You'll not be replacing us because of it, will you?"

"No, I merely wondered." To her father she said in rapid Italian, "The time to back out is long past. If we were going to do that, we should have stayed in Venice. Please be reasonable, Papa. This could make your fortune and your name."

"It's a matter of pride, not money." His expression was solemn.

Teresa looked back out the window and ran her fingers over the smooth wood of the windowsill. Most of the buildings she had ever known were centuries old. This one was so new. "Who lived here?" she asked the maid.

"No one, Miss. It were part of the folly. When he came back from Venice, Lord Kincaid had this big room added."

"No one has ever lived here?" Teresa repeated in surprise. "Then why was it built?"

"It were part of the folly, as I said. A hermit's cot. The neighboring estate, Smythfield, has a 'Roman ruin' that's no older than this here cottage. There's crumpled walls and toppled-over columns and some headless statues with no arms at all. 'Tis fair enough to unnerve a body. That's why they're called follies. There's no rhyme nor reason to 'em."

"How strange." Teresa, who had lived amid ancient ruins all her life, couldn't comprehend anyone wanting to create a ruin for no reason; and with housing at such a premium in Venice, the cottage built for no one to occupy seemed even more unusual.

"There's no understanding the gentry, Miss," Katie confided. Then she recalled she might be speaking to a member of it, despite the woman's strange accent, and she added, "No offense, Miss."

Teresa smiled to show she harbored no resentment, and headed back to the front to be sure that each trunk was sent to its proper room. With that done, she went to her room to unpack.

Her bedroom was smaller than the one in Venice, but it was large enough for comfort. The bed hangings were white muslin edged with lace, as were the curtains at the window. The pale blue velvet coverlet had been embroidered in white wildflowers. The furniture was golden oak and not so heavy as to overpower the room. The chair had a floral needlepoint cushion in shades of blue, pink, and white. On the table beside the bed was a safety candle, its dish filled with water. Two

Baxter prints brightened the wall. One was of a spaniel, the other a pastoral scene with a boy shepherd and a flock of sheep. Teresa was pleased with the room.

When all her clothes were put away and Hal had been sent to carry the empty trunks into the attic, Teresa left Salvatore unpacking the paints and canvases and went outside. The air was cool but pleasant; the breeze was scented with spring. As butterflies danced above the flowers, she again listened to the lilting birdsong she had heard on their arrival.

The cottage and its small garden had been designed to be picturesque, and its architect had done his job to perfection. As she walked down the paved path, she noticed the aroma of mint as her skirts brushed the plants growing along the walkway, and farther on, runners of thyme brought yet another fragrance.

The stream was fairly wide, but she judged it was probably not deep. Downstream she saw a series of artfully arranged stepping-stones at the water's edge. Willows arched protectively over the stream, their greens and golds reflecting in the water's surface. Teresa had the uncanny sensation of being in a living painting.

Hearing the sound of a horse, she turned to see Lord Kincaid ride up, dismount at the edge of the yard, and come toward her. This was her first view of him since the day in her father's studio when they had agreed to come here. He was more handsome than she remembered, and taller.

"Hello," he said when he was near her. "Welcome to Hawthorn Manor. I apologize for not being here to greet you upon your arrival."

"That's quite all right." She watched the sunlight spangle the russet highlights of his hair and lighten his eyes to leaf green. He wore a smoke-colored frock coat over dove-gray trousers that fit close to his muscled legs. He looked as casually elegant as royalty.

"Are you pleased with the cottage?"

"Very much so, but I am curious about something. Katie said no one has ever lived here."

"What she has said is true, but let me explain as I show you the grounds." He matched his steps to hers as they strolled along the bank of the stream. "The idea is for my guests to happen upon it as a surprise as they walk through the woods. It's a hermit's cottage."

"Without a hermit? I still don't see . . ."

"It's here to amuse the guests at Hawthorn. If the owner of an estate isn't fortunate enough to have authentic ruins or a picturesque cottage on the place, he has it built. It's quite fashionable."

"And the people for these interesting cottages? Are 'hermits' employed to occupy them for the amusement of guests?"

"Sometimes."

For a moment Teresa thought that he might have brought her and her father here just to inhabit his folly, but then realized that it was her guilt that precipitated such an absurd conclusion. It was she and her father who were the frauds. An uneasy prickle of fear crept up her neck, but she shook it off.

"You're frowning. Did I say something to upset you?" he asked.

"No, no. I was just concentrating. English is sometimes difficult for me to understand." This wasn't entirely true, but she had to give him some excuse.

He smiled. "After a while it will be easier for you. The way to learn a language is to use it regularly."

She nodded. The warmth of his smile had already put her more at ease. Getting back to the subject that most interested her, she asked, "Has your family lived here long?"

"Always. The construction of Hawthorn was begun in 1580 during the reign of Queen Elizabeth. Prior to that we lived in a castle that dated back to a Norman ancestor. You can see the ruins of it if you ride beyond this arm of the woods."

"If you have a genuine ruin, why build this cottage?"

"The castle is too far from the manor house to make a pleasant walk. It was, however, the inspiration for the

Benchleys of Smythfield to erect their folly. There is a bit of rivalry between us, though the reason for it is long forgotten. We have a Norman ruin, so the Benchleys had to have a Roman one."

"You have a rivalry to produce the best folly?"

"It's not just that, but our families have been in competition with one another for generations. My father and the father of the present viscount, Lord Ashford Benchley, vied for the same seat in Parliament. Our grandfathers courted the same girl—mine won her, incidentally. It's an amicable rivalry on the part of Ashford and myself, but I understand it was a blood feud at one time."

"I see."

As they retraced their steps in silence, Teresa considered how pleasant it was to be in the company of a man without her father looking over her shoulder. Seldom had she had such an opportunity, and never with one so handsome as this. When the breeze was right, she could smell his clean, masculine scent. Surreptitiously she glanced at him and noted the sureness of his stride. Not only was he impeccably attired, even to the high gloss on his boots, but the way he walked reflected the confidence he seemed to exude.

"Is your father receiving yet?" Brandon Kincaid asked when they reached the yard. "I wouldn't want to disturb him if he is resting from the trip."

"No, no. Papa is in the studio."

Kincaid gazed down at her, his clear green eyes free of any guile. "I'm glad you came, Miss Verdi. I hope you'll be happy here."

Teresa searched his face before she said, "I hope so too. At the moment, I feel very far from home."

He smiled and nodded. "I can see how our quiet countryside must seem alien to you after the excitement of Venice. I hope homesickness isn't too much of a problem." He found he was paying particular attention to the soft glow of her rounded cheek and the way the sunlight cast lacy shadows beneath her long eyelashes.

Her hair shone with bluish highlights, and her eyes, which intimately stared directly into his, were as enchanting as fairy dust. All at once he had an almost irresistible urge to kiss her.

His head lowered toward hers, and she swayed slightly toward him. But before their lips met, he straightened abruptly, and a muscle tightened in his jaw. What was he doing? He could never let himself think of Teresa Verdi in a romantic vein. He wasn't free to encourage her, and he was too honorable to lead her on. When he stepped back, she blinked in confusion. Evidently she had felt the same urge to kiss him.

"If you'll excuse me," he said. "I'll go speak with your father."

"Of course," she replied. Then added, "Once he begins work, he will allow no one in his studio, but now I think he will not mind."

He left her standing in the shade of the willow trees, a puzzled look on her face. Brandon silently chided himself for allowing his feelings such free rein. He had known when he first saw her in the art gallery in Venice that she was not a woman he could deal with lightly. When he reached the studio door, he looked back to her and added, "I've planned a reception for you and your father on Saturday night. I hope that will be convenient?"

Wordlessly Teresa nodded her approval. Brandon gave her another long look, then rapped briskly on the door. When Salvatore opened it, Brandon glanced back, but Teresa was gone.

If Teresa expected the reception to be a small one, she was greatly mistaken. A horse and gig had been put at their disposal, and they had chosen to avail themselves of it so they would not have to walk back home after dark. By the time they arrived, Hawthorn was glowing with lights in every window, and numerous broughams, and landaus victorias were parked out front.

Teresa wore a gold velvet dress with a full skirt. A

beautiful shawl of white chantilly lace, threaded with seed pearls, attached to the front of the dress with pearl buttons and draped almost to her elbows. She wore fashionable white silk mittens that left her fingers bare. Her hair was coiled in two large buns, one over each ear, with red silk flowers nestled in the dark tresses. When she saw the other guests, Teresa was glad she had taken so much care in dressing.

All of London's best society were present. She might know none of their names or faces, but she could discern wealth in any country. Diamonds, emeralds, and rubies flashed from the women's fingers and from around their necks. Luxurious gold fringe graced their shawls and bodices, and white *organdie canezou* of incredible delicacy jacketed many of the matronly bosoms. The men, as well, were elegantly dressed in blue and black frock coats and embroidered or brocaded waistcoats.

Music from beyond the foyer blended with the cultured rise and fall of voices and the click of glasses upon silver trays. An army of crimson-liveried servants milled about the throng with offerings of food and drink. Teresa held to her father's arm and tried to refrain from bolting.

Fitch, the butler they had met the day they moved in, escorted them down the length of the ornate marbled entry to the ballroom. The enormous room seemed filled with people, from the doorway where they stood to the far end, where the musicians were seated beside a forest of potted plants.

Fitch lifted his head and majestically intoned, "Signorina Teresa Verdi and Signor Salvatore Verdi."

The sea of faces turned to the guests of honor, and Teresa had to fight hard to overcome her panic. Her father seemed to have turned to stone by her side. For the first time Teresa grasped the enormity of their deception. They were not merely here to paint pictures in the seclusion of the quiet countryside. They were being presented as though they were royalty. After this night, hundreds of people would know them.

Brandon saw them and smiled as he left the group of people with whom he had been speaking. The crowd in front of Teresa and her father parted to let him in. Teresa's heart pounded almost audibly. Had she thought him handsome? He was a god! His black coat was set off with a dark blue waistcoat shot with silver, and his black trousers hugged his legs. He wore a lingerie-silk cravat that was expertly tied, and a heavy gold watch chain with a fob embossed with his coat of arms.

Ceremoniously he offered his arm to Teresa and bowed to Salvatore. "I'm glad you're here. Everyone is clamoring to see the paintings."

Teresa's stiff lips managed a smile. What if someone here was familiar with her father's real style and decried these paintings as frauds? She had no choice but to let Brandon lead her down the length of the ballroom to the small stage where the paintings he had bought were veiled with silk draperies.

With a look of pride and satisfaction, Brandon stepped onto the stage and went to the first painting. "This is the moment you've all waited for, my friends," he said to the throng who crowded about. With a flourish he unveiled the first, the scene of the ladies sun-bleaching their hair on the *altana*.

An appreciative murmur swept through the room. Teresa edged closer to Salvatore. Here in the English ballroom the painting seemed exotic, though in Venice such a scene was quite common.

"The Fisherman's Catch," Brandon announced as he went to the next easel. He pulled away the cloth to show the glistening fish and the dripping net knotted in the fisherman's rough hands. Again the crowd made a purring sound of approval.

One by one Brandon showed the paintings. Each was enthusiastically received. Gesturing toward Salvatore, Brandon said, "I give you the master, Salvatore Verdi."

Applause rang out and Teresa looked around nervously. Men and women crowded near, all trying to speak to her father at once. To Teresa's surprise, Salvatore blushed as modestly as if he had indeed painted the canvases, and he accepted their accolades as his due.

Teresa was proud for her father and glad that, at last, he was getting recognition for his work, even though the finishing touches that made it all possible were her own. As she stood by his side, she accepted the praise for herself as well, even though no one but her father knew she was deserving. However, when she was gently nudged away so more people could meet her father and shake his hand, she experienced a deep disappointment that she hadn't expected. At her father's side, Brandon Kincaid was making introductions as effortlessly as if he were close friends with everyone in the huge room. As Teresa looked on, she allowed herself one more moment of regret that she would never stand where her father stood. Then she realized the emotion she felt was selfish vanity and dismissed it.

The musicians started another song, and when Teresa turned to watch them, she found herself looking up at a tall man who bore a remarkable resemblance to Brandon. The man bowed from the waist and said to her, "Good evening, Signorina Verdi. I'm Mitchell Kincaid. May I have the honor of this dance?"

Teresa glanced back at Brandon Kincaid. This seemed to be an evening filled with disappointments. The night before, Teresa had dreamed that the Viscount of Hawthorn had asked her for the first dance, and only minutes before, on their way to the manor house, she had naively thought he might. But that was a silly notion, for Lord Kincaid had neither spoken to her nor sought out her company since the day of their arrival, and now he was much too busy with her father to pay attention to her. As she placed her hand in Mitchell's, she said, "I'd be honored."

Mitchell was an accomplished dancer, and as she circled the floor under his lead, she looked to see whether her father had noticed she was dancing—not that she needed his approval, but more from habit.

Salvatore was engaged in an animated discussion with several men, but Brandon was no longer with him. She didn't see him anywhere. After three dances in a row, Teresa and Mitchell left the floor for a rest.

"Brandon never told me the artist Verdi's daughter was also a work of art."

Teresa glanced up in surprise. In her sheltered life, she had received few personal compliments, only praise for her art. With her cheeks glowing, she managed to say, "Thank you."

Mitchell led their conversation to a variety of subjects of a general nature. Teresa enjoyed his company, but couldn't refrain from comparing him with Brandon. He was easily as handsome, but she much preferred Brandon's lighter hair, and Brandon's green eyes seemed to sparkle more than Mitchell's gray ones. Had she seen Mitchell first, it might have been he who stole her heart instead of his brother. But what was she thinking? Stolen her heart? Why, Brandon Kincaid had barely spoken to her. How could she be feeling such things for him? Quickly she passed off as a fantasy the recollection that he had almost kissed her. Why would he have wanted to? Another glance around the room showed her that he wasn't even there.

Following yet another dance with Mitchell, she found herself at the far end of the ballroom. "May I get you some punch?" he asked.

"No, thank you." She wasn't about to let him abandon her in this sea of foreign faces. Besides, she hoped the more time she spent with Mitchell, the less she would think about Brandon.

As she struggled to follow the innuendos and shades of meaning of Mitchell's conversation, another man joined them. Mitchell said to Teresa, "May I present Colin Kincaid, our youngest brother. Colin, Signorina Verdi."

The man, who appeared to be perhaps in his mid-twenties, bowed, his green eyes sparkling beneath light brown hair. "Has Mitchell been boring you with his medicine talk?"

"Why, no," Teresa stammered. She hadn't noticed that he was ill. She would have guessed him to be in excellent health.

"Then you are both fortunate and rare. Most of us avoid him completely." Colin winked at his brother, and she was surprised to see Mitchell grin.

"Don't let him fill you with lies," Mitchell said good-naturedly. "Colin is only jealous because I'm studying to be a doctor, and he has no idea what to do with himself."

Teresa was relieved—not only that she had misunderstood him but also that she had not embarrassed herself by asking about his health.

"Nonsense," Colin objected. "I plan to be a professional scoundrel." When Teresa looked confused, he added, "With Brandon being the lord of the manor and Mitchell setting out to cure the world of its ills, somebody had to be the black sheep, and I'm the only one left."

"Besides," added Mitchell, "the role fits him perfectly."

Noting the curious look on Teresa's face, Colin explained, "The black sheep is the one in the family who tends to discredit all the rest. My greatest fault, they say, is that I speak what's on my mind without considering the consequences." As the music began again, Colin bowed to her and asked, "May I? If we're separated in this crush, I may never locate you again."

After a nod from Mitchell, Teresa put her hand in Colin's, and he led her in to the dance. His steps were livelier than Mitchell's, though less precise, but nonetheless he was a marvelous dancer. As he whirled her about the floor, she found she couldn't help put wonder what it would be like to circle the room in Brandon's arms.

As if her thoughts had caused Brandon to materialize, he swept by, but with a beautiful blond woman in his embrace. The expression on their faces made Teresa lose the beat, and her steps faltered.

"I beg your pardon," Colin said with automatic politeness.

"No, it wasn't your fault. I merely stumbled." Her eyes followed Brandon as he swirled past, his gaze only for the woman in his arms.

Colin followed Teresa's glance. "That's Lady Barbara Weatherly, Brandon's fiancée," he offered in explanation. "They make a handsome couple, don't they?"

"Fiancée!" she blurted out. This time her feet ended up beneath his, and he stumbled too. "I'm so sorry, Lord Kincaid."

"No, no. I'm not a lord, only an honorable. And please call me Colin."

As Brandon and his fiancée passed close by again, Teresa heard Brandon murmur something to the lady that caused her to laugh aloud. Feeling almost unable to breathe, Teresa said, "Could we step outside for air? I feel rather faint."

Colin led her off the floor and into the velvety night. After the closeness of the ballroom, the night air was quite cool. Colin glanced at her sideways as if he were quite aware of her thoughts. "My brother is a handsome man," he said.

"Mitchell? Yes, he is."

"I meant Brandon."

"All of you are handsome." She felt dull, as if she were coming down with some illness, although she had been quite well before she saw Brandon with his fiancée.

"I gather Brandon didn't tell you he was going to be married."

Teresa shot him a reproving glance. "It's none of my business at all." Then less tartly she asked, "Is it a love match?"

"I suppose. Brandon doesn't confide in me as Mitchell does. He's always kept matters to himself."

"Have they been promised for long?"

"Yes, for ages. At least that's the way Barbara puts it. She came out into society a little over a year ago, and became engaged to Brandon soon afterward."

"I see." Teresa wasn't familiar with British customs, but she assumed that made Lady Barbara younger than herself. Once more she was unpleasantly reminded of her encroaching spinsterhood. "I hope they will be happy together."

"Barbara will be. She's getting Hawthorn, a title, and a generous dowry. Brandon will be too, unless he has to carry on a conversation with her. I won't say Barbara is dull, but she lacks a cutting wit."

"No wonder you're the black sheep of the family. You certainly speak freely."

"That's the privilege of being incorrigible," he said with a telling grin. "Incidentally, neither Mitchell nor I have a lady, though Mitchell's love for his studies almost qualifies as one."

Despite the heaviness around her heart, Teresa smiled. Why did she always want the unattainable? Even though both Mitchell and Colin were obviously interested in her, and she found them both attractive, it was Brandon who stirred the depths of her soul. This perverseness of her nature might never let her rest so long as she allowed herself to be the victim of her feelings.

"Brandon says—"

"Let us not talk of him," Teresa interrupted, deciding to take charge of her circumstances, "but rather of you." She rested her hand lightly on Colin's forearm and beamed him a smile.

Colin leaned closer, and as he gently kissed her cheek, she inhaled the spicy scent of his cologne and sighed. As he put his arm around her waist to kiss her properly, Teresa closed her eyes and hoped that this would help her forget the deep-seated yearning that had come to trouble her so.

Suddenly a hand on Colin's shoulder drew him back just as his lips brushed hers. When Teresa opened her eyes, she found Brandon's angry green eyes staring at her.

"Well, little brother. You don't waste much time, do you?"

Although Colin couldn't have missed the sparks in his brother's eyes, he nonchalantly shrugged and grinned at him. "I was just telling Teresa how I was the black sheep of the family."

" 'Teresa'?" Brandon asked pointedly. "Don't you mean 'Signorina Verdi'?"

Teresa sprang to Colin's defense. "I gave him permission to use my name." This wasn't entirely true, but she had not objected, because she preferred the less formal use of her given name. Besides, the rules of British society were not her rules.

"I see." Although Brandon's words were spoken unemotionally, his expression was accusatory.

"No, you don't see," Colin put in, his voice firm, though not threatening. "I was kissing her, not the other way around."

Teresa couldn't believe the men were getting into an argument over who kissed whom. If she had broken another of the Britishers' precious social conventions, what did it matter? All this tension and confusion were making her head pound. Interrupting them, she said, "I have a headache. Will you find Papa and ask him to drive me home?"

Brandon glanced back at the ballroom. "I can't ask your father to leave his evening of glory. I'll drive you."

"No, I will," Colin said as he watched Teresa for her reaction.

"You have done quite enough," Brandon said in obvious dismissal. "Signorina Verdi is in my charge, and I will see her home."

After a moment Colin shrugged. "Whatever you say."

Brandon led Teresa around the end of the building to the waiting carriages. Although she knew his hand was on her elbow only as a formal courtesy, she felt the contact with every atom of her being. She could also tell he was unaccountably upset. After all, it had only been a kiss, and both of them were of age and unencumbered. It couldn't be jealousy, because Brandon was engaged.

He helped her into the gig and went around to step into the other side. The narrow seat made it impossible for his thigh and hip not to touch hers. She wondered if he cared.

"You shouldn't take Colin seriously," he said, abruptly breaking the silence between them as they drove out of the courtyard. "He's as frivolous as they come."

"I wasn't taking him seriously," she responded. "I was kissing him. In my country this isn't considered a crime."

"You aren't in your country."

"Then kissing is a crime here?" she asked, being deliberately argumentative. "How awkward."

"It's not a crime." His voice in the darkness sounded unnecessarily harsh. "It's just not done. At least not until a couple are promised."

"Then it must be remarkably difficult to reach that state."

"We manage."

A dagger of jealousy twisted in her middle. "Does that mean your fiancée allowed you no kisses before you proposed?"

"How do you know about Barbara?"

"I saw the two of you dancing and Colin told me about your engagement. She's quite pretty." That was an understatement. The woman was beautiful and had blond hair Teresa would have died for.

"Yes, she is."

His answer piqued her further. Without thinking, she added, "For a blond."

He scowled at her and urged the horse to a brisk trot. The moon-washed driving lane stretched like a silver ribbon before them, gilded in the light cast by the buggy lamp. "I take it you are unattached?"

"Completely," she replied with cool arrogance.

"By your own choice?"

"Naturally!" she snapped. She had no intention of telling him that her father had guarded her so closely when she came of age that most of her prospects had been reluctant to confront him, and now were gone.

Brandon was quiet for a moment. "I didn't mean for that to sound insulting."

She stared straight ahead at the horse's rounded rump and arched neck.

When she didn't answer, Brandon reined the horse to a stop. Without the sound of buggy and hooves, the night silence wrapped around them. Brandon turned toward her. "Please accept my apology. I don't want hard feelings between us."

Teresa remained silent. She was all too aware of his masculine virility to dare speech. Her verbal sparring with him had done nothing to defuse her growing desire for him.

"Teresa?"

Had he intended for his use of her given name to sound as if it were a caress? She turned her face toward him.

"Forgive me," he said in a strained voice. "I meant 'Signorina Verdi.' "

"If you wish, you may call me Teresa."

He was quiet for several seconds. "I suppose we could call each other by our given names. After all, you live on my estate, and your father and I will have a close relationship. I will be almost like . . . an uncle to you."

"No, you won't," she said in a way that could only be construed as an endearment, then wished she hadn't. She had no right to let him know how she felt.

Brandon stared at her in the faint light from the coach lamp without speaking. Teresa wanted to tell him to drive on, but the words wouldn't come. When she looked away from him, he cleared his throat and said, "I have to get you home."

He slapped the reins on the horse's hindquarters, and the gig rolled forward. Teresa straightened in her seat and stared ahead. Although her experience with men had been very limited, she knew this was the best thing for them both—even if it wasn't what she felt in her heart.

All too soon the gig reached the cottage. The lamps Katie had left on to light them home gave the cottage a welcoming, homey feel. Teresa suddenly wished with all her heart that she and Brandon were a couple returning home after an evening with friends. The intimacy of the thought was disconcerting.

He handed her down and walked her silently to the door. "I hope your headache subsides soon," he said with stiff politeness.

"What? Oh, my headache. I'm sure it will." She had almost forgotten her excuse. "You will tell Papa where I am, won't you? I don't want him to be worried."

"Of course."

He hesitated as if he were reluctant to leave. Teresa gazed up into his troubled eyes and wished she had the right to step into his embrace.

"Good night," he said at last, then turned and walked hurriedly away.

"Good night," she murmured. For a tremulous moment she had thought he was about to kiss her.

As he drove away, Teresa let herself into the cottage. Of the three Kincaid brothers, she had no doubt as to which one she wanted. With a sigh she shook her head and told Katie good night before going to her room. As always, she wanted the impossible.

3

Teresa sat on the neatly clipped lawn outside their cottage several yards away from her father. She was sketching a delicate arrangement of flowers beneath a fernlike branch of a weeping willow, while Salvatore filled the upper part of a canvas with the piles of clouds that mounded in the western sky. Of the two subjects, the tumultuous clouds were by far the more interesting to Teresa, and her fingers itched to paint them alongside her father, but to do so would be risky. Thus she contented herself by memorizing the subtle shadings of purple-blue and pewter while her hands drew the clump of daisies. Later, in the privacy of the studio, she would capture the clouds on a canvas of her own.

Voices punctuated with rippling feminine laughter wafted over the grasses, breaking Teresa's concentration. A group of men and women were walking toward them. "We have company, Papa."

Salvatore glanced up and frowned. He hated to be disturbed when he was painting, and the distant storm clouds were too transient to wait until the group left. "Get rid of them."

Her eyes found the tall figure she sought. "I can hardly tell Brandon to leave us alone. He's our patron and this is his estate."

"*Brandon?*"

"He gave me permission to use his first name," she said. "I could hardly refuse."

50

"I will refuse for you. He is 'Lord Kincaid' to both of us." Salvatore glowered as the group neared.

The blond woman at Kincaid's side exclaimed, "Oh, Brandon, how lovely! It's so much more picturesque with people here!"

Teresa frowned. She hadn't noticed Lady Barbara was with him.

"I must say," said a younger looking man with ginger-brown hair, "you've done me one better this time."

Brandon went directly to Teresa and their eyes met. For a moment she felt as if they were alone in the muted shade. Then he said, "Please forgive our intrusion. We were out for a walk before the storm breaks, and Lady Barbara wanted to pass by the cottage."

Turning to the ginger-haired man, Brandon said, "This is Lord Ashford Benchley, from Smythfield, the adjoining estate, and these are Lady Barbara Weatherly, Lady Cecilia Perth, and Lady Rochelle Watson."

Teresa nodded. "Lord Benchley, ladies."

"Ashford, this is Teresa Verdi and this is her father, Salvatore Verdi."

The rather insipid man bowed slightly and strolled over to look past Salvatore's shoulder at the canvas. "Not bad. You've a fine start there."

From Salvatore's arched eyebrow, Teresa knew the man had raised her father's artistic ire with his poor choice of words, and it was a struggle for her to refrain from smiling at the thought that if the man pushed his luck he might find himself wearing home the colors on Salvatore's palette.

"Come here, Brandon. Look at this," Ashford said.

Brandon went to stand beside him. The three women, led by Barbara, came to Teresa. For a minute Teresa's eyes met Barbara's, and she was surprised at the veiled animosity she found there.

"This isn't bad," Barbara said condescendingly as she looked at the drawing in Teresa's hand. "Have you been sketching long?"

"All my life." Her father wasn't the only sensitive

artist in the family. Refusing to say more, she went back to drawing the flowers.

Barbara smiled at her two friends. "Isn't this quaint? I'm so glad Brandon added to the folly in this way."

"Only Brandon would think of putting an artist in a folly," agreed the dark-haired one, as if Teresa were as deaf as the willow tree.

"I told him it would be a great success," Barbara said softly. Her words reached Teresa's ears, but not Brandon's.

Teresa's fingers faltered. "What do you mean by that?"

Barbara looked mildly surprised, as if she hadn't expected Teresa to speak to her. "Surely you know what a folly is?"

Teresa nodded.

"Brandon and Ashford have the nicest estates anywhere around here. Each works hard trying to outdo the other. By bringing you and your father here to live in the cottage, Brandon has topped Ashford quite neatly."

"We aren't here merely for show, Lady Barbara. This isn't a menagerie."

"Goodness. I never suggested it was."

"My father is an accomplished artist, and he and Lord Kincaid have a business arrangement."

Barbara laughed softly and winked at her friends. "Of course they do. But you must allow that you *are* picturesque. The darling little cottage and your bright blue dress and amusing accent."

"It's simply too perfect," Lady Rochelle agreed. "I wish my father would hire someone to live in our garden."

Anger flushed Teresa's cheeks, and with only a few bold strokes on the sketchpad she had turned the peaceful willow to a branch lashed by a storm.

"There! You've quite ruined it," Barbara admonished in her honeyed voice. "We haven't upset you, have we?"

Teresa turned to a fresh sheet of paper. She would gain nothing by letting the women goad her.

Brandon came back and took the sketchbook from her. "May I see?"

She nodded curtly. How could she have been so foolish as to think he had cared for her, even a bit, the night of her father's reception? She was no more to him than a butterfly to adorn his garden.

"This is quite good," he said. "Especially the way you have the willow tossing in the wind."

"I think it's rather overdone," Barbara said as she put her hand possessively on his arm. "It's almost frightening."

"Nonsense," he laughed. "Frightening?"

"You know how I detest storms." Barbara glanced at the bruised sky. "Speaking of storms, shouldn't we be on our way?" Nervously she wet her lips.

Teresa, who loved storms, stared at her in puzzlement. Barbara was as pink and white as sugar candy and seemed almost as delicate. Even her voice was pale and wispy, as if she were afraid of being too noticeable. Teresa thought it was a pity the woman was so waspish underneath that fragile exterior.

Brandon patted his fiancée's hand. "I'll see that you are back inside Hawthorn long before the storm breaks. You're perfectly safe. Don't worry."

"I feel safe beside you," Barbara said as she demurely lowered her eyelashes.

Teresa grimaced. The woman had no more substance than a meringue.

Brandon went back to look at Salvatore's painting as the others clustered around Teresa to watch her begin a sketch of a poppy and a butterfly. To Salvatore, Brandon commented, "Your daughter is also talented." When Salvatore glanced up sharply, Brandon added, "For a woman. I'd like to see some of her other sketches someday."

"Perhaps someday," Salvatore evaded. "My Teresa is modest and seldom shows anyone her efforts."

"Modesty is an admirable virtue."

Salvatore rested his hand on his leg, the paintbrush poised away from the canvas. "Lord Kincaid, I feel that as a father I must speak to you, but because of our unique relationship, I don't know how to begin." Salvatore looked over at his daughter to be sure she could not overhear their conversation.

"Say what you please. We speak freely here."

"My Teresa is my pearl of great price, my most prized possession. Her mother died giving her birth, may she rest in peace, and since that day, my daughter has been the most important person in my life."

"I can understand that." Brandon looked over at Teresa for a long moment, watching her concentrate on her sketch. "She's a very special woman."

"She has also lived a sheltered life. Always she has been surrounded and protected by her family. She doesn't know what it is not to trust someone. Nor has she had much experience with suitors. As I have said, she is my perfect rose and has always been shielded from life."

"Signor Verdi, are you saying one of my brothers has done something to—"

"No, no. I said nothing of your brothers. I only wanted you to know. Teresa has so little artifice and no social skills at all when it comes to flirting or puffing herself up as some women will. She is too outspoken and trusting for her own good, perhaps."

"What are you saying?"

"I'm asking you, as one honorable man to another, to help me shield her. Had her mother lived, bless her, she would have taught Teresa to be as other women, but I am a man, and she grew up in a household of men. How can I tell her to be less direct, less honest? How can I say to her, for instance, that it is improper for her to ride home alone with a man in the dark, even if he is our patron?"

"I see." Brandon glanced from Teresa to her father. "I can assure you nothing at all happened. I gave her a ride home because, as I told you when I returned, she had a headache and I didn't want to disturb you. I meant nothing improper by it."

"I understand, Lord Kincaid." Salvatore made a gesture of nonchalance. "I am a man and I know you were being honorable. My Teresa, however, may read more into a ride home than, say, the lovely ladies over there."

"Perhaps I should tell you that Lady Barbara Weatherly is my fiancée. We're to be married within a few months."

Salvatore smiled. "Congratulations, Lord Kincaid. That's good news indeed."

"So you see, you have nothing to fear from me in the way of improper advances. As for my brothers, I will see to it that they know of your daughter's naiveté."

"Then you will help me protect her? I thank you," Salvatore said smoothly.

"Her honor is safe at Hawthorn." Brandon bowed. "If you'll excuse us, we should be going before the storm breaks."

Salvatore nodded as he resumed his hasty brush strokes on the canvas.

Brandon was uncomfortably aware that the older man not only had put him in his place but also had warned him away from his daughter! As if Brandon had designs on her at all! He looked at Barbara, who was standing so daintily behind Teresa. True, Teresa had a much more vivid, sensual beauty. But Barbara was betrothed to him. He had no right at all to think of another woman in that way!

As he approached the ladies, Brandon was drawn to notice how snugly Teresa's blue dress fit the narrow span of her waist. He remembered how sweet her breath had been in the night when she had swayed toward him and how her eyes held mysterious golden lights. Hastily he stepped to Barbara's side and said, "Let's go."

Teresa wondered why his tone was so harsh, but she wasn't sorry to see them leave. If either Lady Barbara

or Lord Ashford had made one more ridiculous statement about painting, she was certain she would have
told them both that they knew less than the rawest
novice.

All the same, her eyes followed Brandon as he and
Barbara went down the curving path past the cottage.
Angrily she snapped her eyes back to her sketchbook.
Barbara had said Brandon considered them to be no
more than colorful additions to his folly! She could
hardly wait to confront him with that! She hadn't come
all the way from Venice to be gawked at!

"Let's go in," Salvatore said as the first rumble of
thunder sounded in the distance. "The rain is coming."

"I hope they all get caught in it! Papa, did you know
Brandon brought us here to be *picturesque?*" She said
the word as if it were poison.

"*Lord Kincaid,*" he corrected, "is paying us handsomely.
For this price I can be picturesque."

Teresa snapped her sketchbook closed as she scram-
bled to her feet and grabbed up her stool. "I can't be.
We have our pride, Papa."

"Have you so soon forgotten how we were in Venice?
No students, no commissioned paintings. Artists are
forgotten in these days. All is railroads and new streets
and new gadgets to do this or that. We can live here
comfortably and not have to worry whether we will
have to sell our palazzo for want of money. We have no
noisy renters over our heads, no shrieking children in
our patio." He closed the lid of his portable paint box
with more force than was necessary, causing a loud
pop. "We can accept being picturesque."

Teresa looked down the slope to see Brandon and
his visitors entering the back gardens of Hawthorn.
"I'm not so sure I can, Papa." Her heart ached at the
sight of Lady Barbara's tiny hand resting so possessively on Brandon's forearm.

She looked down at her own hands. Hers were strong,
the palms square. Artists painted delicate hands with
tapering fingers, but rarely were their own hands of

such a nature. As if Brandon might see them, she hid them in the folds of her skirt. She could never hope to be as delicate and as sweet as Lady Barbara.

The following week Brandon was gone to York on business, and Teresa was surprised to discover how empty the estate seemed. Brandon had developed a habit of dropping by every couple of days to check on her father's work and ask about his needs, and she missed seeing him. Even Salvatore, who claimed to dislike the visits, remarked on Brandon's absence.

Colin, on the other hand, came by more frequently than before. Teresa began to wonder if he were merely passing by so often or whether he was going out of his way in order to see her.

"Hawthorn is dull with Brandon in Yorkshire," Colin complained. "Mitchell is so busy with his preparations to leave for Germany that he's no company at all. You'd think no one had ever studied to be a doctor before, from all the fuss he's making. He'll only be gone for a year, you know. By this time next year, he'll be finished with his schooling."

"Why, Colin," Teresa teased, "I believe you're jealous."

"Nonsense," he scoffed without meeting her eye. "I could be a doctor if I wanted to be. No one is stopping me."

Teresa looked up from the bouquet of flowers she was cutting. "What do you want to do with your life?"

Colin shrugged. "I don't know that I'll do anything in particular. It's not as if I have to earn a living, you know. My estates may not bring in ten thousand pounds a year as Brandon's do, and I may be the youngest son, but I do have a comfortable living."

"Ten thousand pounds a year?" Teresa had had no idea Brandon was so wealthy. "You shouldn't go about telling people that."

"You can bet Lady Barbara knows it, and to the last farthing at that. I've always felt she would have refused him if it weren't for his wealth."

Teresa turned back to the flowers and snipped a purple blossom to add to the array of pink, yellow, and white. "All the same, Brandon might not appreciate your telling how much money he has."

"Conventions! Do you realize how much we are all hemmed in by conventions? Take me, for instance. There isn't a single profession I would like to lay my hand to, and that disturbs everyone beyond all bounds. Now, why is that? Why can't I do as I please and let the world go hang?"

"Is that what you really want?" Teresa asked with a smile. She had learned that Colin frequently said things he didn't necessarily mean, to see what reaction he would get. "Don't you want a wife and family, and a respectable position?"

"Why must it all go together like a cup and saucer or bread and butter? Perhaps I would be happier married to a woman who could also flaunt propriety."

"I've heard there is a Gypsy caravan at Harrow On The Hill. Perhaps you could find a bride among them."

"Maybe I should," he said, flashing her his quick grin. "That would set Brandon back on his heels, wouldn't it!"

"Quite probably." She snipped a pale pink flower and turned the bouquet about to see if it was full enough.

"Lady Barbara isn't good for him, you know."

"I don't think he shares your opinion."

"Before they became engaged, Brandon was much more interesting. Now he's as staid as Mitchell. She's been the ruin of him."

Teresa didn't answer. Thinking of Brandon in conjunction with his fiancée was painful. "He must not agree, or he would break off with her."

"Perhaps. Brandon has a sense of honor that's out of proportion with reason, however. Even if he regretted his proposal, I doubt he would dishonor Lady Barbara by breaking it."

Teresa pretended to occupy herself with her flowers

in hopes that Colin would continue talking about Brandon.

At that moment Colin caught her hand and drew her around to face him. "Let's go into London."

"What? Why would we do that?"

"Because it's a lovely day and we've never done it before." When she looked doubtful, he added, "Ask your father if he will come too."

"I suppose I could ask." Her eyes lit at the prospect of seeing the city. Although she loved the seclusion of the cottage, she sometimes missed the noise and bustle of a crowd.

Salvatore was reluctant to leave his studio, but when Colin mentioned the possibility of his finding new subjects to paint, the older man agreed. Colin soon had them in the comfortable coach and on their way to London.

They entered the city on Oxford Street and turned left onto Regent. On the right-hand side of the street was All Souls Church, which had been built by John Nash the year before Teresa was born. She thought it strange to see so many new buildings after the ancient ones of Venice, but she dutifully agreed with Colin that the church with its needle spire was lovely.

From Cavendish Square they went down Holles Street, and there Colin pointed out the house where Lord Byron had been born. Teresa had read his poetry, and was suitably impressed.

On Marylebone Road Colin signaled for the coachman to stop and they got out of the carriage. Teresa looked inquisitively at Colin. "Why are we here?"

"This is Madame Tussaud's waxworks."

"Oh? What sort of place is it?" she asked.

"You haven't heard of Madame Tussaud? Wait until you see inside." He paid their entrance fee and they stepped into a wonder world.

Teresa's mouth opened in amazement when she saw the first of the lifelike wax figures. Salvatore's eyes narrowed in artistic appreciation. "From such models, painting would be easy," he said as he examined the translucent colors in Queen Elizabeth's wax flesh. "Who is this Madame Tussaud?"

"She studied in France under her uncle, Philippe Creutz, who began his waxwork exhibit sometime in the 1770's. Madame Tussaud has been in London for a number of years now and is quite advanced in age. However, you can see she still has great skill."

"And she's a woman, Papa," Teresa couldn't refrain from pointing out.

"And these are waxen dolls. Not paintings," he countered.

"This is a self-portrait of Madame," Colin said as he indicated a wax figure. "She did it three years ago when she was eighty-one. Behind her are Henry VIII and all six of his wives."

"The poor women," Teresa murmured. "He must have been barbarous to live with."

"On the other hand," Colin said, "he may have had ample reason to divorce and behead them. At least in his own mind."

They strolled through the tableaux, admiring Mary of Scotland awaiting her execution and the sleeping form of Madame Dubarry. In the Chamber of Horrors, Teresa drew back at first; then her curiosity got the better of her. Marie-Antoinette and Louis XVI, along with Marat, Robespierre, and Fouquier-Tinville awaited the blade in lifelike poses. Nearby was one of the original guillotines used during the French Revolution.

"They look so real!" Teresa marveled. "Look at those features!"

"In a sense, they are," Colin said. "The faces are from death masks made by Madame immediately after their executions."

Teresa recoiled. "How terrible! You mean she actually . . ."

"She certainly did."

Even Salvatore looked a bit repulsed by the idea. "Art may be carried too far, perhaps."

"How else could we know exactly what they looked like? I think it's fascinating."

"So do I," Teresa agreed enthusiastically. When Salvatore rebuked Colin for bringing his daughter into a place that might disturb her sensibilities, she knew her trip to the waxworks was at an end. As they left, she whispered, "May we come back again? Without Papa?"

Colin grinned and winked at her as he handed her into the carriage.

They passed the Royal Academy of Music and turned north to Regent's Park. Nash had designed the landscaped park to be surrounded by terraces of elegant houses, though not all his buildings had been completed. From there they continued north to Primrose Hill.

Salvatore's eyes lit up at the view of London spread before them. "What a picture it will make," he exclaimed. "I'll frame it with that plane tree on one side and the sycamore on the other. Teresa, what do you think?"

"I like it, Papa, but shouldn't there be people in it?"

"Diana," he said decisively. "I will show the goddess Diana gazing down on the city as if she had come upon it by surprise. Think of the contrast between her Roman simplicity and this magnificent city with its trains streaming smoke and the Thames crowded with ships. Nothing like it has ever been done." To Colin he said, "Thank you for this inspiration. I will begin it tomorrow!"

Teresa smiled. She knew that whatever else they might see, Salvatore's mind would still be here. Already she could imagine him working out the perspectives and planning how to mix the various greens of the landscape with the rosy bricks of the buildings.

As they rode back down the hill, Salvatore was busy sketching the scene on the pad he always carried with him, and making notes that were legible only to him. Colin watched him with curiosity, but Teresa gazed out the window, surreptitiously memorizing the colors, distances, and cloud patterns in order to provide her part of the painting.

They rode south toward the Thames and then turned west on Millbank. After a time Colin pointed to the Houses of Parliament and across the street to an impressive Gothic structure. "Westminster Abbey," he said.

As they alighted from the carriage, Salvatore said, "Go, go. I must get this on paper."

Teresa and Colin walked toward the huge building. "This is old even by Venice's standards," Colin told her. "Legend has it that there was a church erected here by Sebert, who was king of the East Saxons in the early seventh century. Before that it was said that King Arthur held a tournament near here and Queen Guinevere went a-maying in the fields that were here then. Elaine the Fair is supposedly buried here."

"Is she really?"

"No one knows for sure, but who could prove that she isn't?"

They went into the hushed nave past the chapel dedicated to St. George. Teresa craned her neck as she admired the intricate stonework overhead. Ahead was a steepled and gilded organ loft and choir. At the far end she could see the buttress-shaped east end that sheltered the tombs of Elizabeth and her arch rival, Mary of Scotland, separated by their grandfather, Henry VII.

"It's breathtaking," Teresa murmured. "I could be in Venice, it's so beautiful!"

Above them the stained-glass windows of the prophets gave a mellowed light to the interior. Centuries of reverence lent a stillness, and it seemed to Teresa that she could almost smell the incense and hear the chants of Catholic priests of long ago.

"When Edward the Confessor built the monastery, London was miles away over fields and quite separate from this place, which was to be the seat of his government. The palace here was the royal family's primary home for the next five centuries."

The Purbeck marble floors and walls hollowed the
sounds made by their feet and voices, and the immense
volume of the space swallowed the sounds as soon as
they were made. Teresa felt her heart soar with the
grandeur, and she wished it were Brandon who was
showing her this and not Colin. At once she felt guilty,
because Colin was her friend and her thoughts were
unfair to him.

"You care a great deal for Brandon, don't you?"
Colin said as if he had read her mind.

Teresa avoided his gaze. "He is Papa's patron. Of
course I am grateful."

"I mean you care for him personally."

"I have no idea what you're talking about," she said
with cool reserve.

"Come now, I thought we were better friends than
that."

She saw a trace of pain on his handsome face. "I
don't know how to answer you."

"For days I've come to your cottage, hoping to see
you alone so we might talk." He gestured wryly at the
impressive abbey. "Now we are finally out of your father's sight and hearing and we're in a church." He
drew her into one of the columned aisles that flanked
the nave. "Stop a minute and talk to me. Have I any
chance with you or do you want only Brandon?"

Teresa looked away. "You shouldn't ask me that.
How can I reply to such a question?"

Colin took her chin gently in his fingers and drew
her face back. "I think you just did."

"I had no idea you wanted to be more than my
friend," she said. "Whenever we have talked you've
made a point of always saying you have no intention of
settling down. You said you wanted a Gypsy or a Lorelei or anything except an average, everyday sort of
woman."

"But you, Teresa, are neither average nor everyday."
His deep voice was sensuous and caressing, but it failed
to thrill her the way Brandon's did.

"Let me explain myself here, in this place where there are no lies," she said. "Always I have wanted what I couldn't have. I don't know why I'm that way, but I am. As a child I wanted to run the fastest and climb the highest, all the way to the stars. I'm still like that."

"I know. That's what I see in you. You're the Gypsy and the Lorelei I've been searching for."

"No, Colin," she said. "I wish I were. A woman would be blessed to have a man like you, but you aren't for me."

"Is it because you know you can have me?" He sighed as his eyes searched her face. "How appropriate. I at last find my will-o'-the-wisp and she vanishes. Brandon must be blind."

"He is in love with Lady Barbara. It's as simple as that."

"And if you had him, then what? Would you tire of him and go on to the next unattainable man?"

"No," she replied softly, taking no offense. "I'm not inconstant. If I had him—which I never will—I would be faithful to him with all my heart, forever."

A shadow of pain flickered in Colin's eyes, but he smiled. "I knew you were worthy the moment I saw you."

Teresa put her hand on his arm. "Colin, I wish I were different. I wish it were you that I long for."

He nodded. "So do I."

"Someday you'll find your Lorelei."

"Of course," he said with no conviction at all. "In the meantime I must get you home or we'll have to arrive after dark."

Teresa unhappily followed him back to the carriage. If only she had been more observant, she chided herself silently. If only she had somehow refused his suit more gently and with greater circumspection. Always she was given to such abominable bluntness!

Salvatore scarcely glanced up when they entered the carriage, and the ride home was painfully quiet. Teresa wished there were some way she could comfort Colin, but she was afraid any word she spoke would be taken as encouragement, and she didn't want to cause him further anguish.

When Colin dropped them at the cottage, Salvatore went directly to his studio while Teresa lingered by the stream beneath the willows. Dusk softened the colors, and small insects sang to the approaching night. It was a time for lovers and for spinning dreams, and she had neither.

At the sound of hoofbeats she looked up to see Brandon galloping toward her up the green. Her breath quickened at the sight of him and she unconsciously took a step forward.

He swung down from his horse and tied it to a branch before striding toward her. She saw that he was upset and her eyes widened. "Hello," she said when he gave her no greeting. "I didn't know you had returned."

"I came home this afternoon to find Colin gone and the cottage deserted." His voice touched a chord in her heart. "I wasn't sure where you had gone."

"Colin was kind enough to take me into London."

"So he said."

Teresa looked at him with interest. She could almost swear that it was jealousy that made his eyes so dark. A tiny smile lifted the corners of her mouth. "We had quite an enjoyable day."

"He told me as much."

Lowering her eyelashes as she had seen Barbara do, Teresa turned and strolled along the water's edge, her full skirts brushing the tender grasses. "Colin showed me Madame Tussaud's waxworks. They truly are a marvel, aren't they?"

"He said he even took you to the guillotine room! Colin knows better than to alarm a lady like that."

"I wasn't alarmed," she protested in surprise. Then she remembered that a lady should have been, and hastily amended, "At least not much." She made her voice soft and timid like Barbara's and glanced back to see what effect it had on Brandon.

"Why are you talking like that?" he demanded. "Did something happen that I don't know about?"

She widened her eyes innocently. "What do you mean?"

Brandon frowned. Colin had intimated that the day had been one of special closeness. He had hinted that Teresa had favored him with a kiss, though Colin was too much a gentleman to come right out and say so. Since Brandon had seen her kissing Colin at the reception, he hadn't doubted that was what Colin meant. All the way to the cottage he had told himself he was upset because Salvatore had enlisted his help in protecting Teresa and now his own brother was trying—and perhaps succeeding—in seducing her.

Teresa turned away again, and he had no choice but to follow her down the curving bank away from the cottage. "He also showed me Westminster Abbey. It's marvelous."

"Yes." His tone was brusque. "Teresa, what else happened?"

"Nothing," she said a bit too quickly. She wasn't about to reveal what she and Colin and talked about in the nave. She was, however, growing curious about what Colin had told Brandon to upset him so.

He looked as if he didn't believe her, and Teresa wasn't surprised, though she did feel guilty that she hadn't told him the whole truth.

Brandon turned as if he were about to leave, and she said quickly, "Papa enjoyed the outing too."

"He was with you?" Brandon paused and looked back over his shoulder.

"Of course."

At first he stared at her; then he began to smile. Teresa said, "Welcome home. We've missed you." She didn't see any reason to admit she had missed him much more than Salvatore had.

He acknowledged her words with a curt nod. "I missed you too. You and your father, that is." He strode toward his horse and mounted with fluid grace.

For a moment he gazed down at her, then repeated, "Yes, I did indeed miss you." Before she could reply, he reined his horse around and galloped back down the green to Hawthorn.

Teresa hid her smile behind her fingertips. Whatever Colin had told him, the effect was quite pleasant. She decided to continue to keep Brandon off balance for a bit and see what happened. As she returned to the cottage, she was humming.

4

Brandon enjoyed riding alone over his estate. Even as a child he had preferred to ride by himself through the woods and across the fields of Hawthorn or whichever of his family's holdings his parents were occupying at the moment. Unlike Mitchell, a serious, studious child who had preferred to be in his room, and Colin, who had been a hellion and was happy in crowds, Brandon loved his lands. Even as a youth he had known that as the eldest son he would someday inherit every acre, and he had accepted this as his due. All his people knew him, and by the time he became master of Hawthorn, his workers were accustomed to giving their loyalty to him.

Hawthorn comprised not only the house but hundreds of acres. Brandon knew every inch as thoroughly as a lover would know his mistress's body. The analogy was a sound one, for Brandon was fiercely protective of his land and the people who worked upon it. His other estates were well-tended and carefully husbanded, but Hawthorn he cherished.

He nudged his tall gray horse into a rocking canter that carried him over a field dotted blue and purple with speedwell and wild pansies. The pale pink blooms on the crab apples in the hedgerows scented the air with their delicate perfume. Brandon enjoyed spring. Good things had always happened to him in the spring of the year, and he had come to expect it, though Mitchell decried such a belief as superstitious.

Mitchell. He was going to miss him. Although Brandon would never admit it, he was as protective of his brothers as he was of his estates. Much as an elderly patriarch might have felt, Brandon was reluctant to see them getting out into the world. But with Mitchell, it was only for a year, and since he'd had his heart set on being a doctor—and had not wavered in his decision since boyhood—Germany was the best place for him to complete his education.

Colin, on the other hand, was an enigma. He had a quick wit and a glib tongue, but no ambition at all. Brandon had more than enough money to support the young man; it wasn't that. But he worried that Colin might never take life seriously. His dalliances were a good indication, Brandon thought as he rode. The lad showed no sign of wanting to settle down. In fact he had paid more attention to Teresa Verdi than he had to any of the gentry's daughters.

Brandon's dark brows gathered in a frown. Teresa was quite eligible and her family was certainly a good one, but he felt a responsibility toward her, especially since Salvatore had asked him to protect her. He wasn't at all sure the young woman could distinguish between a flirtation and a serious courtship. Perhaps Colin couldn't either. Brandon recalled the way Colin's eyes followed Teresa, and how he had hinted that she found him interesting. Not that Colin would harm her; there was no devilment of that sort in him, but Teresa was so untouched, so pure and yet so provocative. This was an explosive combination.

He slacked his horse's pace as they entered the park-like woods and headed downhill to a lowland where the shade lay glossy green upon the grasses. An unexpected flash of rose-red caught his eye. Ahead of him, Teresa was sitting in the low fork of a tree.

For a minute he doubted his eyes. What would she be doing out here alone? And in a tree?

She turned toward him and her eyes lit expectantly. She didn't seem at all perturbed that he had found her in such an unlikely place.

Brandon could scarcely ride on as if he hadn't seen her, and even if propriety had allowed it, his curiosity wouldn't have. He rode nearer and came to a halt, their eyes almost on a level.

"It's a lovely day, isn't it?" she said cheerfully, as if they had met under the most ordinary of circumstances.

"Yes, it is."

Her full, rose-hued dimity skirt billowed like a flower beneath the close-fitting bodice that accentuated her breasts. White lace at the wrists of the long sleeves matched that of the dress's high lace collar. But in sharp contrast to the decorum of her attire, Teresa's long black hair was loose, flowing in sumptuous waves that curled well below her waist.

Brandon swallowed hard to put his heart back in place. "How did you get up there?"

"I climbed, of course." She leaned back against the wizened chestnut tree, looking as comfortable as if she were in her father's parlor.

"But *why* are you up there?" Brandon couldn't recall seeing any girl old enough to wear petticoats try such a thing.

"To rest," she said as if that were obvious. "I didn't want the grass to stain my skirt, and this looked comfortable, so I climbed up." She patted the limb beneath her, which was larger around than she was. "Would you like to sit beside me?"

"No, thank you," Brandon said as he struggled to regain his composure. Glancing around, he added, "Where is your father?"

"In the studio, I suppose. He's working on a study of Diana viewing London."

"You're out here alone?" Brandon asked with a frown as he looked around again. "I don't see your horse."

"I walked. That's why I was tired."

"You shouldn't be out here without protection!"

"But I'm not. You're here."

He gave her an exasperated glare. "Does Signor Verdi allow you to run about like this?"

"When Papa is painting, the rest of the world disappears." Her laughter reminded him of the sound of musical bells. A breeze lifted her hair, draping it over her shoulder in a way that was both innocent and seductive. She lowered her lashes and peered through them. "Besides, no one tells me what to do."

This was a far cry from the shy and sheltered picture of innocence Salvatore had depicted. When Teresa swung her foot, exposing a trim ankle, Brandon felt a surge that had nothing to do with protectiveness. "You shouldn't walk out here alone. You might encounter a band of Gypsies or thieves."

Her eyes sparkled. "Are the Gypsies still about? Perhaps I'll have them tell my fortune."

"You're to stay well away from them!"

With a tilt of her head, her gleaming hair cascaded over her shoulder and pooled like black silk in her lap. "I wasn't aware that you had been appointed my guardian."

Brandon rode closer and kneed his horse next to the limb. "Get on behind me."

"Why? I know my way home. I walk this way often."

With her face framed by her loose hair, she looked as if she could be one of the Gypsies, or perhaps a wood sprite. And she was utterly desirable. "Signorina Verdi—"

"I thought you were going to call me Teresa."

"Put your . . ." He paused, wondering how to delicately refer to a lady's leg. To call it a limb sounded as if she were shrubbery, but to call it by any other name would be to imply she was less than a lady.

Gathering her skirt, Teresa put her foot over the horse's round rump and dropped astride behind the saddle. Brandon's eyes widened in surprise. "You aren't sitting pillion!"

"Of course not. I might fall off. I haven't ridden very often." She put her arms around him and the tips of her breasts brushed his back. Brandon felt the contact all the way to his soul. He was also painfully aware that he sat inches from her wide-spread legs. A fine sweat beaded his forehead.

"I love it here," Teresa said in her lightly accented voice. "All this space and trees and meadows. I never dreamed I would see a place I liked as well as my Venice, but I feel as if I truly belong here."

"Yes." He didn't trust himself to say more.

The wind shifted and Teresa's hair curled seductively over his arm. Tentatively Brandon touched it, and found it warm with sunshine and as soft as he had envisioned it would be. He stiffened. "In England, young ladies wear their hair confined."

"They do in Venice too," she agreed. "I think it's a silly custom. Why have hair at all if it has to be pinned in a knot close to your head all the time?"

He took a deep breath. "It's a treasure for your husband. A beauty saved only for him or . . ."

"Or a lover?" she suggested.

Brandon shifted uneasily in the saddle and dared not look back. "I was going to say your husband or your hairdresser."

"I have no hairdresser. Katie Banning is a fine maid, but she has no feel for arranging hair." She tossed her head so that her hair flowed like a mane. "Besides, I may never get married, and then it would be lost entirely. No one would see it but me. What do you really think, Brandon? Don't you like my hair free?"

He glanced back and saw the teasing light in her eyes. "What I like or don't like is of no consequence. We're talking about proprieties."

"Then you don't like my hair?"

"I never said that," he answered, tight-lipped. Every step of the horse brushed her breasts against him; he felt as if he were on fire.

"Then you do like my hair?" She leaned forward, pressing her breasts fully against his back, and he closed his eyes as he fought to maintain control.

"Oh, look! Stop for a minute." Even before the horse came to a stop, Teresa slid off and ran to a spectacularly blossoming crab apple. "How beautiful!" She ran her arms around the boughs and gathered the blossoms to her.

"You shouldn't jump off a horse like that," Brandon scolded. "You could get hurt."

"Don't go here, don't do that," she teased with a laugh. "Is there nothing a person *should* do in England?"

He dismounted and tied the horse to a limb of the tree. He didn't know how to answer her. She was so free and unfettered by convention. Among the masses of pink flowers, her rose dress blended as if she were more akin to them than to prosaic humanity.

Teresa looked back at him, her white teeth flashing and her cheeks glowing. "I wish I were a butterfly so I might visit all the flowers on Hawthorn and sleep among them at night." She moved around the branches so that he saw her through the clustered boughs.

"You're like the flowers," he heard himself say. "You remind me of birds' songs and starlight and rainbows."

The teasing light wavered in her eyes, and she gazed at him in surprise.

Brandon, caught up in the enchantment of the moment, circled to stand beside her. Hesitantly he lifted his hand and caressed the gleaming silk of her hair. From there it was but a mere movement of his hand, then he was cupping her cheek in his palms. Teresa's eyes searched his, and he found he was unable to form words. What he felt and what he hoped were much too fragile and delicate to be given to speech.

Slowly he bent his head, and as their lips touched, she parted hers as naturally as if they were lovers. Her breath was sweet in his mouth, and her skin as soft to his touch as an apricot. Brandon's arms circled her waist and drew her to him as his passion grew. Teresa swayed against him, molding her body to his as she held him tightly. This was no ladylike kiss, and Brandon was almost confused into thinking her expertise came from practice rather than from her sensuous nature. But there was a purity about the way she returned his kiss that negated experience on her part. This woman was simply one of the rare ones who was made for loving.

When he lifted his head, Brandon felt dizzy. Every muscle in his body was whipcord tight. Teresa gazed up at him, her eyes soft and misty, her lips dewy and still parted a bit, as if she wanted him to kiss her again.

Brandon's hands shook as he put one on each of her arms and held her away. Unconsciously she swayed, as if her natural place were in his arms.

"I'm sorry," he ground out. Not taking her into his embrace and kissing her until the world dissolved was the hardest thing he had ever had to do. A muscle ridged in his jaw with the effort as he said, "I shouldn't have done that."

He started to turn away, but Teresa caught his arm. "Yet another rule! Why would you apologize for what we both wanted to happen?"

"Because it was quite improper," he snapped. "You need not fear that I will ever do it again."

"Fear? How could I fear you or anything that could happen between us?" She pulled him around to face her. "You didn't force me to kiss you, Brandon."

Pain lay naked in his eyes as he said, "I know that. And I know nothing would ever happen between us without your consent. But, Teresa, I'm promised to Lady Barbara."

The name lay between them like a blight. Teresa drew back and let her hand drop to her side. Her eyes were veiled, but Brandon could see the hurt she was feeling. "It's not honorable," he continued, "to kiss one woman when I'm pledged to marry another."

"No," she agreed. "It isn't."

"I knew where this could lead. I should have stopped it. I should have been stronger."

"So many 'shoulds'!" she said angrily. "Do the men of England have no wants, no 'coulds'?"

He was silent for a moment, then replied, "We have many wants. However, there is always a matter of decorum. Of propriety. My kissing you was unforgivable."

"To whom?"

They stared at each other as the pink blossoms wafted

a spring-sweet air about them. Brandon moved as if he were about to gather her back into his embrace. Teresa's body leaned toward him eagerly. Again he pulled himself back, and with an iron will turned and untied his horse. He mounted, then kicked the stirrup free and held out his hand to her.

Teresa shook her head, her golden-brown eyes swimming in tears. "I prefer to walk."

Still he hesitated, though he knew they couldn't restrain themselves if she again mounted behind him. He nodded brusquely, turned his horse away, and kicked him into a canter.

Teresa watched him go as the knot of longing tightened in her middle. She had never dreamed a kiss could be like that—so gentle and loving, and at the same time with such a promise of passion. She ached for Brandon to hold her and kiss her again, and she felt a primeval urge to become his woman in every sense of the term. Even in her dreams she couldn't aspire to anything greater than to be loved by him.

Teresa let the tears flow unchecked as she started her walk toward home. She lifted her hands and twisted her heavy hair back into a chignon and fastened it in place with the pins from her pocket.

Brandon cared nothing for her, not really. She could see that now. He must not have even enjoyed the kiss that had seared her soul. If he had, surely he would have kissed her again.

Unwanted visions of Brandon holding the insipid Lady Barbara etched her mind. He wouldn't pull away from *those* soft arms and rosebud lips; of that she was certain. She scowled. Kissing Barbara must be as exciting as kissing the back of his own hand. With a shot of pain she recalled this was not an arranged marriage. Whatever Teresa thought about Barbara didn't matter; Brandon liked her well enough to want her as his wife. Teresa's tears flowed faster.

By the time she reached the green that sloped down to the cottage and past it to Hawthorn, her crying was finished, but she ached with sadness. She felt as if all her hopes were trapped in an iron box beneath her rib cage and would never be free again. He cared nothing for her. Nothing at all.

She glanced back, then looked again. Silhouetted on the rise of the hill was a tall man on a magnificent gray horse. She couldn't possibly mistake those broad shoulders and that proud carriage. Her steps slowed, and she paused to stare back at him over the sweeping meadow. For long moments they stood locked in wordless communion; then he nudged his horse into a gallop and thundered down the slope to Hawthorn.

Teresa was completely confused. He had rejected her and said he was sorry he had kissed her, yet he had watched her until she was safely home. Brandon Kincaid was an enigma that Teresa couldn't understand. Seeing him on the hill, as silent and protective as a knight, made her feel special. Again she thought that he might care more for her than he was willing to admit—more than he might even be aware of.

Brandon was still upset over the emotions Teresa had stirred in him as he rode to Barbara's house in London. Since the evening promised to be clear, he had taken the runabout and had given the coachman the night off. Brandon was in no mood for company, even that of his silent driver. If Barbara hadn't been expecting him to take her to Cecilia Perth's engagement party, he would have sent word he was indisposed.

Teresa had haunted him all afternoon. Not only the way her black hair flowed about her like a cape and the saucy golden light in her eyes, but most especially the way she had felt in his arms—at home there, as if they were two halves of a whole. The memory of her soft lips beneath his brought a low growl from his throat. He had to forget that! Above all, he had to be certain it never happened again. God, but she had been warm and sensual in his embrace! Brandon urged the horse into a quicker trot and fastened his gaze on the nearing buildings of London.

The Weatherlys' house was tall and narrow, and expensive. A stained-glass fanlight glowed above the front door and a gaslight lit the porch in welcome.

As usual Barbara wasn't ready and Brandon had to sit in the uncomfortably formal parlor and try to talk to her equally stiff parents. Lord Weatherly was a portly man with bristling salt-and-pepper side whiskers and piercing eyes that seemed disapproving of whatever they surveyed. Lady Weatherly was thin and mousy and often had a deprecatory smile pasted on her face, as if she were ready to apologize for everything.

Lord Weatherly, after the usual length of strained silence, began discussing politics, a subject in which Brandon had little interest. Although Barbara's parents were no more boring than usual, tonight Brandon felt as if he were seeing them with new eyes. He didn't like what he saw. They both fit perfectly in the frozen time of the parlor. Lord Weatherly's thick fingers looked too large for the teacup he held, and his bulk made the chair creak when he moved. His demeanor was that of a man who had paid for every article in the overcrowded house and who gloried in every minute detail of his ownership.

During a pause in her husband's tirade against Parliament, Lady Weatherly attempted to mention the weather.

"Of course it's still cool," her husband snapped. "It's not but April. What else would it be?"

"I'm not sure," she replied meekly. "I only thought it remarkable, since it was warmer on this day last year." To Brandon she explained, "I keep a diary. A poor thing, really—just my thoughts and observations. And I noted last year that it was unseasonably warm on this day."

"Unseasonably. That explains it." Lord Weatherly laughed with all his body except for his eyes. "If it was unseasonable, that means it was out of the usual run of things then, not now. Hah!" That seemed to settle the question once and for all, so Lady Weatherly gave her uncertain smile and was silent. Brandon wondered if he would ever feel close to Barbara's parents, and whether he really wanted to care for them at all.

When Barbara at last appeared, Brandon and her father stood. "I'm so sorry I'm late," she said lightly. "That foolish maid of mine was all thumbs."

"No trouble. We always enjoy a chance to talk with your young man," her father boomed.

Brandon tried not to frown. Lord Weatherly was the only man in the world who ever referred to him as if he were a callow youth. "We should be going. Lady Cecilia will be wondering where we are."

When they stepped out into the night, Barbara made a pouting grimace. "The runabout? You could have at least come in the brougham."

"I wanted to give James the night off. His wife hasn't been well."

"That's hardly reason to inconvenience us. My goodness, there are men all over London who would jump at the chance to be your coachman, if he feels his job is too great an imposition."

"He didn't ask for the night off. I told him I wouldn't need him." He handed Barbara up onto the cushioned leather seat, then climbed up beside her. "Besides, it's a nice night."

"The wind will muss my hair," she predicted.

Cecilia Perth and her parents lived only a few streets away. Although Barbara and Cecilia had been close friends most of their lives, Barbara had been very pleased when she herself was the first to become formally engaged. Now Cecilia had agreed to marry, and the small party was to honor that contract.

"I see Ashford Benchley's landau," Brandon said as they reached the house. "Who is that with him?" He looked more closely. "It looks like Rochelle Watson."

Barbara frowned. "I believe you're right. I didn't know they were seeing each other." Her lower lip protruded as if she weren't at all pleased, despite the fact that both Ashford and Rochelle were her friends.

Ashford and the blond woman beside him arrived

before Brandon and Barbara had alighted from the runabout. While Brandon tied the horse to the post, Barbara said to Rochelle, "I told Brandon he should have brought the brougham. My hair must be blown all over my head!"

"No, no," Rochelle said soothingly. "It's perfect."

"Yes, it looks lovely," Ashford said as his eyes met Barbara's.

His words seemed to reassure her, and she was smiling by the time Brandon joined them on the steps.

Cecilia was holding court in her mother's front parlor, playing the pianoforte while her fiancé, Edwin Sergeant, sang. They broke off in mid-note when their guests entered, and Cecilia blushed as if they had been caught in a moment of intimacy.

"Don't stop on our account," Barbara urged. "Play something else."

Cecilia allowed herself to be coaxed, and they all joined around the piano. Brandon had a good voice and enjoyed singing. First it was "After the Ball," then "The Last Rose of Summer," and by the time they launched into the "Grace Darling Song," Brandon was in full throat, his baritone voice filling the parlor, dominating the weaker and less accomplished singers.

Barbara put her hand on his arm and gave her head a small cautioning shake as he reached the stanza where Grace Darling saved the shipwrecked crew. At once he cut back on his unbridled exuberance. Barbara smiled at him as she would at a small child who had dutifully responded to her command, and tuned her warbling soprano to the others. Brandon felt as though he had been chastised, but he refused to show it.

As the women chose a new sheet of music and began to match their voices into the harmony, Brandon and the other two men withdrew to watch. Edwin was several years younger than Brandon and Ashford, and a bit of a dandy. His hair was slicked to a sheen with pomade, and he smelled strongly of bay rum as a result. And his cheeks were pale from the whitening powder of his Whitecastle shave. Brandon wondered what Cecilia could possibly see in him.

"They sound like birds in song, don't they now?" Edwin murmured beneath the strains of the melody.

"They do indeed," Ashford agreed. "Barbara's voice is as pure as an angel's."

"Come now," Edwin admonished in a playful manner. "You must boast on your own girl, mustn't he, Brandon? Rochelle's voice is quite sweet."

Brandon heard only bits and pieces of the exchange. He was thinking of Teresa, framed in the delicate pink blossoms of the crab-apple tree. She had looked as if she were born dancing, and he wondered if she could sing as well. If she could, he was willing to bet she had no vibrato like Barbara's, but rather a sure and true voice.

With the end of the song, Barbara declared herself too exhausted to sing another. Brandon noticed her cheeks did indeed seem unusually rosy. She avoided Ashford's eyes and came to stand close to Brandon. "Mercy, I nearly sang my heart out."

He smiled. "It was quite pretty."

Barbara caught Cecilia's hand and said, "I'm so happy you and Edwin have decided to make a couple. Have you found a house yet?"

"As a matter of fact, we have. Edwin's father is giving us a house on Mary le Clare. It's the one with the charming bow windows and the green-and-white awning."

"I know that house!" Barbara turned to Brandon. "Isn't that grand luck? The one next to it is also for sale. Let's buy it so Cecilia and I will be neighbors."

"We'll live at Hawthorn," Brandon protested with a laugh. "Not in London."

Barbara pouted prettily. "Surely you don't mean to stay in the country all the time. We never discussed such a thing."

"Hawthorn is barely out of town. You can be on Cecilia's doorstep in half an hour."

"That's not the same thing at all!"

"You may as well give in, old man," Edwin said with a grin. "I've found when a woman sets her head for something, there's no swaying her."

"Barbara's right," Ashford agreed. "No lady wants to be shut up in a country house when she could have London."

Brandon smiled politely, but his voice was firm. "We'll live at Hawthorn."

Barbara frowned and turned away abruptly. He could see she was angry, but he had no intention of changing his mind. Not about this.

Rochelle went to a large wicker basket on a side table and asked, "What are these things, Cecilia?"

Cecilia went to the basket and took out a bouquet of paper flowers to show them. "It's my month for the missionary basket. See? We have pen wipers shaped like dahlias, and felt books for sewing needles. Look at the adorable mittens Mrs. Barnes knitted. Aren't they sweet?"

Barbara took out an apron embroidered in flowers. "This is too pretty to use."

"Isn't it?" Cecilia agreed. "But those have sold terribly well. I asked Miss Hanson to sew up several more." She rummaged through and found a set of egg cozies. "I crocheted these myself."

Both Barbara and Rochelle exclaimed over the stitchwork as Cecilia tried to look modest. Barbara showed the set to Brandon and said, "I simply must have these. Look how precious they are!"

Brandon, who saw little to admire in a set of egg cozies, looked unconvinced.

Immediately Ashford dug into his pocket and brought out some coins. "Let me buy them for you, Barbara."

"Why, I couldn't possibly," she said with her blue eyes shining.

"Nonsense. It's for a good cause." Ashford handed Cecilia the money to add to the missionary fund.

Barbara looked as if he had given her diamonds. "Thank you, Ashford."

"Not at all." He smiled down at her as if he wished they had been diamonds.

Brandon watched the exchange in surprise. When had Barbara last smiled at him like that? These days she smiled so seldom when they were alone. She was more likely to reprove something he had done than to gaze up at him as if he were her hero.

As the conversation drifted to other subjects, he watched more closely. Barbara and Ashford almost always agreed or had their heads bent together over a game or a sheet of music. More than once their hands brushed or their eyes met and held. Brandon was surprised he had never noticed this attraction before. He was amazed that he felt no jealously at all.

When the party was over and he was driving Barbara home, he said, "Will Ashford and Rochelle become a couple, do you think?"

"That empty-headed little flirt? I doubt it!"

"I thought Rochelle was your friend."

"She is, but she shouldn't set her cap for a man like Ashford. If she has, she will be sadly disappointed, I'm afraid."

"Oh?" He wondered why he felt no anger. It was as if Barbara's opinion of Ashford didn't touch him at all.

They rode for a while in silence, each locked in private thoughts. Finally Barbara said, "I told Papa we will be married June sixth."

"You did? We never discussed that." He turned to stare at her.

"I know, but that seems like a good day to me. Cecilia and Edwin will be married the following week, and I ought to be the first down the aisle. After all, we've been engaged for ever so long."

Now he felt something. He felt trapped. "June is a bad month for me."

"What do you mean?"

"As you know, I've arranged several exhibits this summer for Signor Verdi. We will be busy most of June."

"You never mentioned that!"

"I must have. These exhibits aren't exactly a secret." He tried to laugh, but he felt cold inside. Marriage to Barbara no longer seemed appealing at all.

"Well, you'll just have to change them or let Signor Verdi do them alone."

"It doesn't work that way, and I can't change the schedule, because I've already sent out the letters to arrange the shows."

Barbara frowned. "You can't expect *me* to change the date. Papa will have told everyone by now."

"Why didn't you discuss this with me first?"

"How could I know you had planned all those ridiculous exhibits?"

Brandon reached out and took her gloved hand. "There's no harm done. Simply tell your father you made a mistake, or tell him I did. I don't care which."

"I won't!" She jerked her hand away and stared sullenly out of the buggy.

"Then you'll have to have the ceremony without me, because I'll be in New York on June sixth."

"That's not amusing!"

He reined in the horse and turned to her. Behind and in front of them the coach lights lit the area well, but inside the runabout it was dark. "What's happening with us, Barbara?"

"I have no idea what you mean," she replied haughtily.

"Yes, you do."

"You're changing," she blurted out. "I thought you'd be sweeter to me and give in to me. Papa said you would! I thought you'd be more like . . ."

"Like Ashford?"

She jerked her head away from his gaze. "At least Ashford is a gentleman."

"And I'm not?"

"Sometimes you frighten me."

"I do?" He was amazed at her words.

"Yes, you do. You move with such determination, and you sing so loud, and . . . and you kiss me . . . well, in a way that you shouldn't." He could tell by the tightness in her voice that she was blushing and upset.

He scowled. "We're engaged to be married. Of course I kiss you."

"But you do it with such—forgive me, Brandon, but you do it with such passion."

For a moment he could only stare at her. Then laughter began to well up inside him. He held it back as long as he could, but it bubbled out despite his efforts.

"You dare to laugh at me?" Barbara gasped.

"I'm sorry," he managed to say. "I know I shouldn't be laughing."

"No, you shouldn't! And you shouldn't kiss me like that either. It makes me feel . . . well, cheap."

His laughter quit abruptly. "Cheap?"

"Yes, cheap! If you kiss me like that now, what must you expect license to do once we're married?" She covered her lips with her gloved fingers and closed her eyes. "Forgive me for speaking so coarsely, but I had to say it."

Brandon gazed at her. "I had no idea you felt that way."

"What lady wouldn't? A lady has sensibilities, you know."

Brandon thought of Teresa kissing him with such abandon that afternoon. "A woman should enjoy it as much as a man."

"A woman, maybe; a lady, never!"

He sat back in hurt masculinity. "Are you saying you don't ever feel a need for my kisses or for my touch?"

"Brandon, I can scarcely credit that we're having such a low conversation!"

"Answer me!"

"No! Those things are a woman's duty, not her pleasure!"

Again he recalled Teresa's laughing eyes and flowing hair. He shook his head to chase away the image. "You're just upset. We won't discuss it further. At least not tonight."

"We won't discuss it at all," she said in a shocked voice. "Not at all!"

He signaled the horse to move along, but his thoughts were whirling. He knew they were discussing much more than kisses. If Barbara detested their few embraces, what would she be like in his marriage bed? He had assumed she was shy, and he had heard that a woman didn't enjoy lovemaking as much as a man, but he had felt certain that that information must be exaggerated. Certainly he had thought she would like it a little bit!

At her door Brandon paused, then bent to kiss her. As always, Barbara allowed him the kiss, but her lips stayed firmly shut and her hands remained on his arms. Feeling great frustration, Brandon pulled her close, crushing her breasts against his chest and trying to force passion to her lips. Barbara remained coolly pliable—and that was all.

When he released her, he saw the fear in her wide eyes. Dammit, he thought, he hadn't meant to frighten her!

Barbara fumbled with the doorknob and let herself into the house without even saying good night. Brandon stared for a minute at the closed door. Then he went back to the runabout and headed for home. He had a lot to think about, and none of it was pleasant.

5

Brandon looked down at the crisp note card he held in his hand, then up at Barbara. "I told you our wedding had to be postponed."

"I know you did, but I didn't think you meant it."

"Why would you assume that?"

"Well, you *did* kiss me on my doorstep when you took me home," she said in her defense. "Besides, Father had already arranged to have these invitations printed, and I didn't know how to tell him."

Brandon looked back at the note inviting the bearer to the wedding of Lady Barbara Weatherly and Lord Brandon Kincaid on the sixth of June. "I've already told you I will be in York on that day, and from there I'll be going to Scotland. None of these have been sent out, have they?"

"Not yet."

"Good. See that they aren't. I'll speak to your father myself."

Barbara began to pout. Pleading, she said, "I won't have you jilting me, and neither will Father. You can't shame me in front of all of London."

After considering her words for a moment, he said, "I find it remarkable that you speak of jilting and of convention, but not of love. Exactly how *do* you feel about me, Barbara?"

She turned away and ran her gloved hand along the back of the sofa as she walked to the wide span of windows. Looking out at the expanse of Hawthorn's lawns, she said, "I love you, of course."

"Do you? I almost never hear you say the words, and often it's only when I ask."

"For goodness' sake, Brandon," she said impatiently, though in carefully modulated tones. "One doesn't go about laying one's soul bare all the time, now, does one? Naturally I care for you."

"But do you care for me the way a woman should care for her husband?"

"I care for you as a *lady*," she corrected. "We discussed this the night of Cecilia's party. I see no reason to go into it again."

"If your father hadn't printed the invitations, and if no one knew that a date had been set, would you still be against postponing the wedding?"

After a brief pause she said, "Not at all." She sounded choked up and refused to look at him.

"Barbara, you know that once the vows are said and we are married, there's no turning back. Are you certain this is a step you're prepared to make?"

She squared her shoulders as if his words were a burden, but she made no reply.

Brandon frowned at her silence. Was it possible she was having as many doubts as he was? "Is there someone else?" he probed.

She whirled to face him, her eyes wide and frightened. "Certainly not! I'm appalled at the very idea! To think you would accuse me of . . . of . . ." She fluttered her eyelashes in a pitiful sort of way.

Her sudden defensiveness provoked even more concern. "I accused you of nothing at all." He paced the width of the library and looked across the room at her. She was beautiful in a pale, fragile sort of way, but she had no depth. He had never before noticed how lacking she was in spirit. Even when she was angry or upset, she had no inner fires that blazed brightly. Suddenly she reminded him of her dull, mousy mother.

Walking back to her, he said, "I'll give you the perfect excuse. You can say that you decided to put me aside. You jilted me. You'll be a heroine to all your friends."

"I'll be no such thing! They're all terribly fond of you. They would think me a fool to turn you down." She snapped her lips shut before she could say too much, then belatedly added, "Besides, I love you."

"That's right. I had forgotten." Brandon rubbed his chin as he considered his other alternatives. "Very well, then, I'll ride into town tonight and talk to your father. Perhaps when I postpone the wedding, he'll refuse to give you to me."

"No! Not tonight! That is," she stammered, "I . . . I have plans . . with Cecilia. We're going to trim bonnets tonight."

"Oh?" Something was definitely going on here; he was growing suspicious.

"Besides, I don't want to postpone it. I want to get married as soon as possible."

"Why?"

"Why not?" Barbara said with an attempt at lightness. "We've been engaged for so long, and Cecilia will be married in such a short time—and she's only been promised for a couple of months."

"Surely that's not your reason—to beat Cecilia to the altar!"

"Don't be ridiculous," she said as she turned her back on him.

Brandon stared at her back for a moment before he said, "Then you must speak to your father and explain to him that the wedding date has to be changed."

"One would think that if you loved me, you'd postpone the trip to York with this pet artist of yours," she said, her voice filled with contempt.

"And one would think the prospective bride would discuss the wedding date with the prospective groom before she printed the wedding invitations," he retaliated.

"There's no need to be rude to me!" Barbara flounced

across the room and paused at the door to say, "I'm shocked at you, Brandon."

He merely stared at her. She looked as if she were afraid of him, though he had scarcely raised his voice. What would she do if they had a real argument? In all the years he had known her, this was as close as they had ever come to one.

She tossed her head and left, pulling the door silently shut behind her. Brandon scowled. She didn't even slam doors when she was upset! Were all her emotions kept in a corked bottle? How was he to get out of this? He really didn't want people saying he'd jilted her. Barbara was as delicate as a camellia, and that concerned him. But on the other hand, he wasn't at all eager to forfeit his freedom just to protect her feelings. If only she weren't so damned fragile and sensitive!

He called for his horse, and within a few minutes he was riding across Hawthorn's fields, hoping to sort out his feelings.

Teresa had gotten up at dawn, dressed, and gone out to enjoy the day. May had brought wild berry blossoms and a profusion of oxeye daisies and red clover. Although she carried a sketchpad, she had no intention of drawing anything as insipid as a flower. She had sketches of flowers and fruit and trees enough to fill all her nightmares. Teresa was in search of a weightier subject, one that would be suitable for the large canvas she had stretched the night before.

Dew frosted the fresh grasses and moistened her shoes and the hem of her skirt, but she didn't mind. This was a beautiful day, and nothing would mar her spirits.

Feeling more adventuresome than usual, Teresa wandered farther than ever before, eventually into the forest on the back side of the parklands that surrounded Hawthorn Manor. Tall trees laced their leaves above her head, and in the filtered sunlight the celandines had opened their tender yellow petals, and pale green lords-and-ladies nodded in the breeze. Being in a particularly fanciful mood, Teresa wouldn't have been surprised to see one of the fairies Katie had assured her lived near here.

As she continued, the trees thinned, and soon Teresa came upon an open field. On the summit at the far side were the ruins of an ancient castle. Her eyes lit with wonder as she hurried toward it. A tall tower, now crumbling with age, stood in the center of what had once been the surrounding walls. Most of the walls and half the gatehouse lay strewn about the green like enormous building blocks.

She climbed a grassy ridge that had once been a protecting earthwork and picked her way among the rubble. Speedwell and ground ivy sprawled over the fallen stones, softening their craggy angles. Beyond the remains of the gatehouse was a paved courtyard, now clotted with creeping grass and weeds. Many of the tiny rooms that lined the wall were in ruin, but beyond the tower the great hall stood in abandoned splendor.

Cautiously Teresa opened the sagging door and looked inside. Although the walls had only narrow windows that could be easily defended in case of attack, the elements had removed the roof so that the entire room was now bathed in sunlight. Two huge fireplaces of blackened stone stood on either side, and at the far end of the hall was a stone dais where the lord of the castle had sat.

Her face was rapt with wonder as she walked the length of the hollow room. A field mouse scurried to safety, but she paid it no heed. In her mind's eye she saw brilliantly attired lords and ladies and their jostling retinue, age crowding upon age, all lost in the whispers of time.

At the end of the hall, a stone staircase rose partway up a turret before rubble checked its steps. The chambers it had led to were now a crumbled mass against the back wall. Teresa sat on the edge of the dais and opened her sketchbook. Under her quick fingers the castle again came to life, with knights making courtly bows to blushing maidens and the floor of the hall billowing with rushes that insulated their feet against the cold.

The morning passed swiftly, as Teresa was lost in her fantasies. When she heard steps in the courtyard she froze, almost expecting a knight to enter and demand her business there. When Brandon came through the door, she caught her breath. For a moment a trick of the light convinced her that he was, indeed, a knight.

"You!" he said. "For a moment I thought . . . Never mind. How did you find this place?"

"I came upon it by accident." She quickly closed her sketchbook and stood. Clasping the book to her breasts, she waited for him to cross the hall. "I came inside. I hope that was all right."

He looked puzzled. "I seem to come upon you in the oddest places. First in the fork of a tree and now in a ruined castle."

He didn't seem to be angry, only surprised to find her there, so she smiled. "To call it a ruin makes it sound so ugly." She looked about her and said, "I think it's magnificent."

"Then you weren't troubled by the Gray Lady, I gather," he said with a smile.

"The what?"

"Our family ghost. This is Bridestake. So named for an ancient gathering that seems to have been akin to a maypole dance, but has the celebration of a marriage. It has long been haunted by a certain mysterious Gray Lady. She supposedly comes down those stairs over there to frighten away those who don't belong in the castle."

"She must have accepted me," Teresa said with a smile, "because I've seen nothing of the kind."

Brandon looked at her for a moment as if he were considering her words. "On the other hand, perhaps when the roof disappeared, she did too."

Several feet separated them, but Teresa could feel his magnetism like a physical force. "Yes," she said. "I suppose that could be."

He stepped closer. "I'm rather surprised to find you here. Gray Lady or no Gray Lady, ruins are frightening to many people."

She gazed up into his green eyes. "I'm rarely frightened," she said, although his closeness made her heart pound, and she had to struggle to keep from bolting as the field mouse had. She knew, however, that it wasn't Brandon she feared, but herself.

Reaching out, he took hold of her sketchbook, his eyes never leaving hers. "May I see what you drew?"

"No!" She pulled the book from his grasp and held it to her breast.

"Come, now. I wouldn't have expected shyness from you."

She had no choice but to offer the book to him or appear even guiltier for having snatched it from him. With an inspiration she flipped the pages to one of a group of wildflowers she had done the day before.

"Ragged robins? In this setting? I find that rather odd. Especially since they grow in wet meadows, and Bridestake is high and dry." He turned the page and silently studied the accomplished sketch of the castle as it might have been.

When he made no comment, but continued to stare at it, Teresa took it back hastily and closed the book. She couldn't risk his knowing how accomplished she was.

"That's a sketch worthy of your father's genius," he said at last.

"You're exactly right. He drew it yesterday. I brought it here to compare it to the ruins," she explained hastily. "How clever of you to discern it was his."

"Who else could have done it?" Brandon said with a laugh.

Her eyes flashed resentfully, but she bit back her words.

"How odd that he did it in your sketchbook."

"You know how artists are. When the muse speaks, they draw on whatever is handy."

"You sound upset. Surly you don't mind him using your book."

"Of course not." She frowned up at him. Why were all men so convinced that a woman could do nothing more complicated than flowers and fruit?

"I like your sketch of the flowers. They're an unusual choice of subject. Most women would draw roses or dahlias or something more easily found. Certainly something more classically beautiful."

"I prefer wildflowers to the garden varieties."

"Yes," he said slowly. "You would."

Her eyes met his, and she couldn't look away. There was some emotion stirring in the gold-flecked depths that she couldn't quite name, but which made her feel warm all over. Suddenly, without thinking, she tiptoed up and kissed him.

Before he could respond, she jerked herself back, her eyes wide with shock at her own daring. He put his hands on her waist and tried to draw her to him, but she broke away and ran. Tears of embarrassment stung her eyes, and she couldn't bear to face him.

Brandon ran out to the rough courtyard and watched her as she fled down the green toward the woods, her full skirts billowing behind her. For a minute he considered riding after her, but checked the impulse. He knew exactly why she had run away, and he knew she needed to put distance between them. He needed distance himself.

What was it about her that turned his world upside down? She had none of the genteel reticence he usually found so attractive in ladies. In fact, she had little reticence at all. He couldn't even imagine Barbara kissing him of her own accord; and he was engaged to marry Barbara.

With a low curse he watched her disappear into the

woods. No, Barbara would never have kissed him like that.

Somehow he had to find a diplomatic way of extricating himself from his promise to Barbara, especially since Teresa had started cropping up even in his dreams, and in a manner no one could call platonic. She haunted him as surely as the Gray Lady had ever haunted Bridestake.

He rode in the opposite direction from the one Teresa had taken so he wouldn't run across her again. But even at that, he wasn't positive he wouldn't. The woman had an uncanny way of popping up in the least likely places.

As he rode, he tried to keep his mind off Teresa's soft lips and warm curves. The sketch—that was it. He would think of the sketch. It had been good. Almost a picture ready to be framed just as it was. He hoped Salvatore planned to put it on canvas. There was a strength to the lines and a character to the faces that had been missing in the painting of Diana viewing London from the hilltop. As a matter of fact, the execution of the picture was subtly different from anything he had seen Salvatore do. It was more like the product of a person schooled by the same master who had taught Salvatore. The shading of lines, proportions, the placement on the page—all were similar, but not exactly like the work Salvatore might produce. That, of course, was nonsense. No one but Salvatore could have done it. Clearly it had been the work of a master artist.

Brandon was so lost in his thoughts that before long he had crossed the boundary of Hawthorn and ridden onto Smythfield, Ashford's estate. As soon as he realized where he was, he abruptly reined his horse around, wanting to be alone.

But before Brandon could turn back the way he had come, he saw two riders cross the far side of the field. The distance obscured their identities, but he had no trouble recognizing Ashford's bay hunter. The white mare being ridden by a woman also looked quite familiar. Unless he was mistaken, it was the one he had given to Barbara on her last birthday.

The riders drew their horses to a stop and talked for a few moments before riding on. Neither showed any sign of noticing Brandon in the distance.

Brandon studied the completed painting of Diana over London, and marveled at the miracle that had occurred during the week. What had been a pedestrian work had suddenly blossomed into a masterpiece. Diana's skin glowed with life and her face held a mixture of surprise and mild regret, as if she preferred her woodlands to the infringing city. One of her rounded arms encircled a doe, poised for flight, as if startled by the viewer. The tall trees were tossed by a wind that heralded a storm. The painting was alive in every respect.

"It's magnificent!" Brandon exclaimed. "A masterpiece!"

Teresa's lips lifted in a small smile, and she turned away. Salvatore tried to appear appreciative as he responded, "Thank you—you are kind."

"No, I mean it. This is . . . alive!" Brandon turned to his protégé. "We must take this with us to York."

"If you say so." Salvatore gave his daughter an enigmatic look. "It will be dry by then."

"Good. When will you be ready to leave? I have rooms booked for us on June first in Birmingham. It's a bit out of our way, but there's an important gallery there. We can leave on the afternoon of May thirtieth and stay in an inn to break up our travel, or we may drive straight through on the thirty-first."

"I think we should break our journey, since Teresa isn't accustomed to travel."

Brandon's mouth dropped open. "I hadn't expected . . ."

Salvatore held up his square palm. "I must insist. I will never consent to leave her behind."

"But Katie and Hal are quite capable of seeing to her."

"No," Salvatore said firmly. "If I go, Teresa goes. She is my good-luck charm."

Teresa smiled. She knew exactly why her father insisted upon her presence. If he saw something he wanted to paint, it was necessary for her to see it as well. Even months later, her trained mind could recall the subtle shades and lights. He might still resent her finishing touches, but he knew now they were necessary.

"I can't agree to it. We will be staying at inns, and some of them aren't proper for a lady."

"I'm not afraid of rough talk," Teresa said. "In Venice there was little privacy, and I doubt I will hear anything I haven't heard before."

"Then there are the privations," Brandon persisted. "There's no room to take a maid with us."

"I'm quite capable of surviving without one." She met his eyes resolutely. "If Papa wants me to go, I'll go, and that's all there is to it."

"Signor Verdi, please reason with her. This is a business trip, not a pleasure junket."

"Where I go, Teresa goes," Salvatore repeated. "As I have said, she is my good-luck charm."

Teresa smiled at her father and put her arm about him. "Thank you, Papa."

Salvatore gave her a level look as if he wished he could indeed leave her behind, but he said, "Don't mention it, *cara mia*."

Teresa knew neither of them wanted her along. Her father's pride was still bruised, and her presence was a constant, if necessary, reminder of his weakness as a painter. Brandon evidently didn't care for her at all and wasn't looking forward to being in such close proximity to her for so many days. Since the day at the castle ruins when she had impulsively kissed him, he had hardly spoken to her. She wondered what his lady would say about her going with them. Probably nothing. Lady Barbara looked as if she had little to say about anything.

Brandon's brows knit. He knew when he was defeated. Salvatore's artistic temperament had to be pampered, and there was nothing to do but gracefully relent. He just wished there were some way to buffer his almost overwhelming physical attraction to Teresa. Each time he was around her, he found restraint more difficult than before.

Brandon changed the subject. To Salvatore he asked, "Have you started the canvas of the castle?"

"What castle?" Salvatore gave him a blank look.

"He means the ruins of Bridestake," Teresa said quickly. She grabbed her sketchbook and thumbed through it to the drawing of the lords and ladies. "Brandon saw it by accident one day." Her eyes met her father's.

Salvatore scowled as he looked at the sketch. For a long time he was silent. Then he said, "I have no plans to do this one on canvas." He shoved the book back at Teresa.

"Why not?" Brandon asked. "I think it shows remarkable promise."

"*I* am the artist," Salvatore thundered, glaring from Brandon to Teresa, who looked remarkably guilty. "*I* decide what I will paint and what I will not!" With a last reproving look at his daughter, he strode from the room.

Teresa appeared to have been chastened, as if she were somehow at fault. "I didn't mean to upset him," Brandon offered in condolence.

"It's nothing. An artist's disposition is very volatile." She glanced after her father and closed the sketchbook, though her hand stroked it longingly. "I, too, think it would have made a good painting."

"Good? It would have been great! Perhaps if I speak to him again, I—"

"No, no. I think it's best if you leave. He will work

through his anger, as always, with his paintbrushes, but he hates to paint with anyone around."

Their eyes met, and Brandon saw such unhappiness in her that he took a step toward her as if to comfort her. "He won't take his anger out on you, will he?"

"Papa? Never."

Reluctantly Brandon nodded and took his leave. Teresa waited until he was gone, then reopened her book to the drawing of Bridestake. He was right. It would have made an excellent painting, but with Salvatore so upset, she wasn't sure she should attempt it. Filled with regret, she closed the book again.

6

Teresa found the journey through the English countryside much less arduous than Brandon had implied. Not only was the Kincaid coach mounted on good springs and the seats well-padded, but they made frequent rest stops in the villages they passed through, to buy scones and cheese and milk. The inns where they stayed were clean, and catered to a far better clientele than he had suggested. And even though nothing was said about his misrepresentation, Teresa knew he must be feeling guilty, because most of the time he looked quite miserable.

The paintings Brandon and Salvatore had agreed to bring with them were enclosed in watertight crates, and even though they had been packed carefully, Salvatore insisted on rechecking the precious cargo each time they stopped. Late in the afternoon of the first day on the road, when it began to rain, Salvatore groaned as if it were a personal curse from God, and didn't relax until after his next inspection.

In Birmingham Salvatore Verdi was well received, and by the time they departed, Brandon had successfully negotiated a contract for two landscapes that Salvatore would paint after his return to Hawthorn.

As they continued on toward York, Salvatore occasionally asked that they stop so he could make sketches of subjects he wanted to paint. While he did so, Teresa made copious notes for herself in what she purported to be her travel journal. She jotted down quick descriptions of the types of trees she saw, what the people wore and did in their everyday lives, and above all, the colors of the buildings and countryside that she couldn't easily see again.

"Do you plan to become a novelist? You always have your nose buried in that notebook," Brandon asked as he approached her. Teresa was sitting on a mounting block at an inn, sketching furiously to catch the bustle of departing coaches.

She glanced up at him and held the book so that he couldn't see that she was drawing rather than writing. "Perhaps." This was the first time since they'd left London that Brandon had initiated a conversation with her, other than the routine exchange of amenities necessitated by their traveling together, and she wasn't sure she was pleased. She hadn't finished her sketch, and would be unable to do so as long as he was watching her. Besides, he had obviously been avoiding her as much as he could under the circumstances.

"I don't recommend it. Only men make it really big in the field of letters."

Not only had Brandon picked the wrong time, but the wrong subject as well. In a derisive tone she said, "Tell that to Miss Austen or Miss Radcliffe."

"Ah, yes, the formidable Miss Radcliffe. But surely you have to admit that these ladies are the exception and not the rule."

"I admit nothing of the kind."

"Not everyone has a *Pride and Prejudice* or a *Mysteries of Udolpho* in her."

"Perhaps not, but there are no limits to the numbers of prides and prejudices, as far as I can tell."

"What do you mean by that?"

She frowned up at him. "Why do men think that only other men have the heart and talent for greatness? A woman can have the same depth for art as can a man."

"Oh? Name one." His green eyes seemed to be laughing down at her.

Teresa snapped her mouth shut. She didn't want to be baited, and she didn't dare open her "journal" to prove him wrong.

"Aside from the two ladies we've already mentioned, I can think of no others," Brandon continued.

"Not in the field of writing, but what about art?" She knew she was treading on dangerous ground, but couldn't seem to stop. "What about Marie Vigée-Lebrun of France, Angelica Kauffmann of Germany, and Rosalba Carriera in my own Venice?"

"Portrait painters." He dismissed them with a wave of his hand. "They turned out pretty pastels suitable for the decoration of drawing rooms and salons, and a few oils, but name one true master who was a woman. One equal to Titian or Tintoretto. Hah! You can't do it because there are none. Why, even the word 'master' itself precludes a woman from the ranks."

Teresa stood abruptly. "I have no desire to talk to a pigheaded fool, so if you'll excuse me, I'll see what is keeping Papa!" She tried to storm past him, but he caught her arm.

"Pigheaded, am I? For speaking the truth?" He dropped his hand from her arm as if he couldn't stand to touch her. "Go ahead. Prove me wrong."

She glared at him, wishing she didn't still feel the heat on her arm where he had touched her. Days of such close proximity had frayed both their nerves until they were scarcely civil to each other. "Someday maybe I will prove you wrong!" she muttered.

"Give it a try, but don't talk to me of pastel portraits that haven't any more to recommend them than a like- ness to the sitter!"

"Why are you so angry at me?" she challenged. "I was sitting here minding my own business, and you came over and started an argument. Have you no more to do with your time than to torment me?"

He matched her glare for glare. "If you choose, I can send you home on the next coach headed south. You can easily be out of my company by merely saying the word."

"I wouldn't give you the satisfaction!" She turned on her heel and walked briskly into the inn.

Brandon drew a ragged breath and ran his hand through his dark hair. The woman was driving him mad! Never had anyone evoked such diverse emotions in him. One minute he was aching to touch her; the next minute he wanted to wring her neck. He had only intended to engage her in pleasant conversation when this all started. Brandon wasn't sure what had set her off so, but reflecting on the exchange, he decided that it was probably better that it had ended in an argument than a kiss. As miserable as he was, he didn't want things to be worse.

On the sixth day of June they opened the showing in York. The gallery was an exclusive one that catered to the royal family as well as to the nobility. Its curator, Calvert Fitzhubert, was an aesthetically pale man with long hands and more Irish blood than he would admit. It was because of his sharp eye for talent and keen business sense that he was able to have the best to offer his clients. When he saw the painting of Diana overlooking London and the one of the Venetian fisherman, his eyes widened and he began wringing his hands in anticipation.

"These are all you promised they would be, Lord Kincaid. All indeed."

"Naturally," Brandon said with casual self-assurance. "Have I ever led you astray?"

"Never. But with these you have indeed excelled." He turned to Salvatore and shook his hand vigorously. "Stupendous, Signor Verdi. Absolute genius!"

Teresa hung back somewhat. On the one hand, she glowed in the private knowledge that her work was so well appreciated, yet on the other, she felt a gnawing resentment of society's prejudice against women as master painters.

Fitzhubert smiled beatifically as the first customer came through the door. In half an hour the gallery was packed with curious onlookers as well as serious buyers. Teresa stayed on the sidelines and enviously watched her father accept all the compliments. She had thought that in time their ruse would grow easier to endure, but instead it was becoming harder.

Brandon saw her standing apart from the others and came to her side. "Your father is a great success, just as I expected."

"Papa has worked hard for this." It was true. Salvatore had painted every day since he was old enough to hold a brush correctly. Like his brother, Mario, he had been taught every trick of shading and perspective by his father. Just as Antonio Verdi had taught Teresa. However, at that moment Teresa wished the seeds of greatness had blossomed in Salvatore and that she had no higher ambition than to turn out a passable still life.

"I'm glad to see he is enjoying the fruits of his labor. Painting is a lonely profession."

"You have no idea how lonely it is," she murmured.

"I wish your father were a twin," Brandon said in high humor. "Think what a sensation it would create in the art world if there were two such talents!"

"He has a brother, but we haven't heard from Uncle Mario in years."

"Oh?" Brandon's eyes lit with interest.

"Uncle Mario is a good technician, but he's always been weak on composition. You would find he is no Salvatore Verdi."

"A pity," Brandon said, dismissing the man from his mind. "Good technicians are easy to find. Not everyone can make a painting live, however. That's the touch of a master."

"Yes," she said wryly. "I know."

That night in the inn, Teresa walked in the walled garden in moonlight. She was tired, but pleased by the way the paintings had been received. She knew some of Salvatore's subject matter was a drawback, though he would never be able to accept that. The picture of Diana, for instance. Why put a Roman goddess in England? The theme might be currently popular, but she wanted to paint pictures that were ageless. Like the sketch she had done of the busy yard at the inn or the one of knights and ladies at Bridestake. Or even more, the creation of the world and other subjects that the great masters of the past had used. She didn't dare do any of these, even under her father's name, for he would be appalled at her daring.

She was so busy with her thoughts that she didn't notice Brandon when she wandered into a trellised bower where he was sitting. When he moved in the deep shadows, she jumped. "I'm sorry to intrude on your privacy," she said hastily. "I had no idea you were here." She felt his eyes upon her in the silvery moonlight, but she couldn't see his face and had no way of knowing whether she should stay or go.

"You aren't intruding. Please stay. I have been wanting to apologize to you for our argument the other day. I want you to know I intended no offense." His voice was strained, and he sounded unhappy, as though he were greatly troubled.

"And I, too, apologize. I often say too much of what is on my mind, and my nerves are on edge. I suppose it's the excitement of the travel." She stepped nearer. "Is something wrong?"

"No, no. I was only buried in my thoughts."

"They must not have been pleasant ones."

He tilted his head and moonlight fell on the planes of his handsome face. "They weren't."

"Do you want to tell me about them? Sometimes it helps to talk to someone."

His lips tilted in a mirthless smile. "That may not hold true in this case."

"I know I often talk too much, but I can be a good listener. Please."

After a contemplative pause he said, "This is June sixth and I was wondering what I'm really doing here in York."

"Why, you're here for Papa's art debut, of course. What do you mean?"

"I was to have been married tonight." He consulted his gold pocket watch. "Fifteen minutes ago, to be exact."

"Oh." She felt a tremendous weight around her heart. "You must be missing Lady Barbara a great deal."

He was silent for a long time. "I suppose I must." His words were puzzling. Almost defensively he added, "She's perfect for me, you know. Her parents were all for the match. At least they were until I postponed the wedding. They aren't too pleased with me at the moment."

"Have you set a new date?" she asked with forced casualness.

"No."

Teresa stepped into the deeper shadows to stand beside him. Lacing her fingers through the trellis, she said, "Was Lady Barbara upset at the postponement?"

"Naturally. She has assured me that I have made her the laughingstock of London." She had not, however, mentioned a solitary ride with Ashford Benchley, and Brandon hadn't mentioned it to her either.

"You could have changed this tour to another date."

"Perhaps."

"I would have understood and so would Papa."

Again he was silent. Was Barbara with Ashford tonight? Brandon was angry at their underhandedness, but he still felt no jealousy at all. He wondered if it was because his feelings were too shallow. He had also never felt an overwhelming love for Barbara, or misery when they were apart. Maybe he was incapable of deep emotions where marriage was concerned.

"If someone called off my marriage to travel around England with an artist and his daughter, I'd be furious," Teresa was saying. "Was she furious?"

"Lady Barbara would never stoop to such a response," he protested. He felt Teresa draw back at the rebuff.

"You may not think it appropriate, but you can wager I would express it! What kind of a woman would simper and nod at having her wedding canceled?"

"She didn't simper and it isn't canceled! Just postponed."

"You needn't snap my head off."

"I'm sorry. You just seem to bring out the rough edge in me."

She moved away to the end of the trellis. "I guess Lady Barbara brings out only the smoothness."

"As a matter of fact, she does."

"How dull." Teresa gave him a cool smile and glided out into the moonlight.

He followed her and caught her beside the splashing fountain. "What we have isn't dull! Life isn't a carousel. What you think about her isn't important. It's only what I think about her that matters. We're perfectly matched!"

"Oh? Then why are you protesting so much? Why not let me think whatever I choose to think about her?"

"Lady Barbara is exactly that—a *lady*. Ladies don't climb trees and let their hair hang loose and explore ruins alone!"

"No? What do they do?"

"They sit at home and embroider silk and make things like egg cozies for charity baskets."

Teresa laughed. "Exactly what I said—they're dull!"

"It's not dull to make a man feel as if he's a king whenever he's near you. To be sweet and feminine and dainty!"

"I don't need any lessons in femininity," she retorted. "And I can tell you this—my man will feel like a king, but he will also know he has a queen right by his side."

"You don't know the first thing about being a lady!"

Her mouth fell open, and she almost stammered from the fury she felt. "I may not know how to sew a fine seam, and I may therefore not fit your qualifications for being a lady, but I can tell you that I know exactly how to be a woman!" Before he could hurt her further, she turned and ran, not stopping until she reached the sanctuary of her room.

Throwing herself on her bed, she muffled her sobs into her pillow. He had said she was no lady! And it was true. Never had she so keenly missed the softening influence of a mother. Old Catherina was a hardworking servant, and had had neither the time nor the expertise to teach Teresa the gentler arts. As for Salvatore and her grandfather, they had been so engrossed in painting that she had grown up before they knew the years had passed.

She held up her hands as tears coursed down her cheeks. Small, but square and capable, these weren't hands to inspire a sonnet. They were hands for stretching a canvas tight and for putting in tedious brush strokes by the hour. They were not the hands of a lady.

When the knock sounded on the door, she stiffened. "Teresa?" she heard Brandon say. "Teresa, answer me." She buried her face in the pillow and curled into a tight ball.

"Are you in there?" He sounded genuinely concerned. "Teresa, are you all right?" He tried the doorknob, and to her chagrin, she realized she had forgotten to lock it.

He stood in the doorway, his large frame filling the opening. "Teresa?"

She turned her head back to her pillow. "Go away," she commanded in a muffled voice.

He hesitated, then came in and shut the door. She could tell he was at a loss as to whether he should sit on the bed beside her or stand, and she took pleasure in his discomfort. Finally he sat next to her and pulled her up. Although Teresa struggled against his strength, he drew her implacably into his arms.

The rough linen of his frock coat was surprisingly comforting against her wet cheek, and she listened to the steady thud of his heart as he held her close to him. She still trembled, but her tears finally stopped as he held her and stroked her back and shoulders.

When she was composed, he said, "I'm sorry. What I said was unforgivable."

She nodded, not yet trusting her voice.

"Does that mean you won't forgive me?"

His tones were deep and mellow, and his voice touched chords in her aching heart. Why did he have to be kind to her now when she was so defenseless? "I forgive you," she murmured.

She felt his muscles relax a bit and realized her forgiveness had been important to him.

He rubbed his cheek against the top of her head and said, "I don't know what you do to me. When you're around, I say and do things I would never consider with anyone else. Even my brothers don't make me as angry as you do."

"I'm sorry you find me so disagreeable," she said stiffly.

"Not disagreeable, disturbing. You bring out qualities in me that I never knew existed."

Slowly she raised her face to look at him. He was so close, so desirable. His eyes were troubled and his features tormented, as if he wasn't at all sure what to do with her.

Brandon gazed down at her and felt a wave of tenderness. Her nose was pink from crying—he had never seen Barbara's do that despite the buckets of tears she had shed for one reason or another, but then Teresa's sobs had been more heartrending than anything Barbara had ever produced. Teresa's honey-brown eyes were still swimming in unshed tears, and she looked as miserable as any street urchin. Her lips were rosy and slightly parted, showing the tips of her white teeth. She was so beautiful, it took his breath away.

"Don't misunderstand me," he said with firm resolve. "Lady Barbara and I are still engaged. The wedding was postponed, not canceled."

"You've already said that."

"I just want to be perfectly sure that you do understand."

"If you love her, why are you holding me and why are you looking at me like that?"

Brandon quickly rose to his feet. She had the damnedest way of putting things! "I was worried about you. My words were rude and insensitive."

"Yes, they were. And they were true. I don't know how to be a fine lady. No one ever taught me."

He backed toward the door, belatedly realizing how it would look if anyone saw them alone here in her bedroom. Her reputation would be ruined in an instant.

"But, Brandon, I really *do* know about being a woman," she continued. "And if you loved Lady Barbara enough to marry her, you wouldn't be here in my room. You wouldn't even be in York." He stared at her across the room as though he knew she was right, but couldn't admit it.

"I've told you how things stand," he said. "The wedding will be rescheduled as soon as I return to Hawthorn." Checking to be sure he wasn't seen leaving her room, he let himself out into the corridor.

Teresa dried her eyes and squared her shoulders. He had told her, all right, but his words didn't mean a thing. No man who really loved one woman would have held and stroked another woman on what was to have been his wedding night. She just hoped he wouldn't marry Barbara before he came to see matters as clearly as she did.

From York they traveled north to the coal port of Newcastle, then north again to Edinburgh. The broad Yorkshire accent that was so difficult for Teresa and Salvatore to interpret gave way to the burr of the Scots. Teresa again began to doubt her proficiency with English amid the rolling R's and the unfamiliar Gaelic words.

Edinburgh, with its stone castle dominating the town from a craggy hill, fascinated Teresa. Old Town, with its maze of streets and jumble of shops, reminded her in some ways of Venice, with its throngs of jostling people. New Town, to the north of the road that connected Edinburgh Castle to Holyrood Palace, had been built during the previous century and was a masterpiece of town planning, with gardens and churches and expansive parks. As they drove down the shop-lined Princes Street, they passed the recently completed monument to Sir Walter Scott, and Teresa leaned out the carriage window so she could see the top.

They settled in an inn near the Firth of Forth, and Teresa was excited to find that her window overlooked the water. As soon as her trunks were safely in her room, she walked down for a better look at the lake. A cool breeze floated around her, first lifting her skirt into a bell shape, then collapsing it against her thigh. She breathed deeply of the sea air and strained to see down the firth and out toward the sea.

She heard familiar footsteps behind her, and was surprised to see Brandon approaching. Since that evening in York when she had cried in his arms, he had been distant; and because she thought he might be suffering guilt and she didn't want to complicate matters, she had decided to let him come to her. But avoiding him hadn't been easy. Often she thought of the comfort of his arms and longed to be there again, and in order to keep up her resolve, she would remind herself of the cutting remarks during their argument that night.

"Do you like the view?" he asked.

"Yes, I've missed seeing water." Her eyes continued to gaze out over the changing hues and the distant shore, though what she really wanted was to lose herself in the depths of his green eyes.

"Homesick?"

"At times."

He sighed as if he wished she were being less reserved with him, but she had to be firm. Silently she reminded herself of the sting she had felt over his past remarks. Not a lady, indeed. She had later deduced that her line of ancestors was probably longer and more aristocratic than her rival's.

She watched several seabirds dipping over the choppy water. This wasn't Venice, but the smell of water and the birds' cries were the same. "Do you suppose birds have accents?" she asked.

"I don't know." These were the first friendly words she had spoken to him in days, and he wasn't sure how to respond to them.

"They probably do."

"Some accents are quite pleasant on the ear," he observed.

"French?"

"I was thinking more of Italian."

She peered over at him, the sun striking golden lights in her eyes. Brandon gave her a friendly smile, and she looked away.

"When I was a child I used to mourn the fact that I had black hair and not gold," she said tentatively. "In Venice it's stylish to have titian-gold hair. There are little porches called *altane* built on the rooftops where women sit to bleach their hair. I tried it once, but my hair stayed the same color and my skin tanned brown."

He smiled at the idea of Teresa as a young girl trying to sun-wash her hair to gold. "I like dark hair. Women with vivid coloring can be striking."

He was so close that the aroma of his cologne filled her nostrils. She shouldn't let him do this to her, she reminded herself. When he was next to her, she ached for his strong arms to enfold her, but those arms belonged to another. It wasn't fair. "What about ladies?" she asked in a stinging retort. "Should they be blond and have faded blue eyes?"

"Her eyes aren't faded blue," he snapped, "and you said you forgave me for that."

"I did. But I haven't forgotten it." She strolled along the rocky shore and watched the wavelets kiss the stones.

"Colin told me about the ships that used to travel from here to London and on to Europe and even beyond that," she said carelessly. "Colin said he rode one once. Not a frigate like we came on, but a warship. I wonder if we'll see one."

"Colin ran away and stowed below decks. When the captain found him, he sent him home by the first boat. Colin was twelve at the time."

Teresa smiled. "He must have been a very handsome boy."

Brandon's eyes narrowed. What was this sudden interest in Colin?

"I miss him," she said. "I never noticed how often he came by to pass the time of day with me. Don't you miss him?"

"Not especially. How often *does* he go to your cottage?"

She only glanced at Brandon with a smile. "I also heard Lady Barbara say that you weren't as interested in being Papa's patron as you were in finding a picturesque artist to live in your folly. Is that true?"

"Why would she say such a thing? Of course it's not true!"

"I wonder. Colin said it wasn't so, but I have my doubts. Especially now that I've traveled some and see what store you Englishmen place on your gardens. Why, you could probably charge an admission for people to come and see us—especially on the days when Papa works outside." She noticed Brandon's frown and knew she had finally broken the shell of aloofness he had erected.

"That's not true and you know it! I haven't ever considered putting you on display!"

"No? Colin said Lord Benchley has hired a hermit to live in the ruins he built."

"Ashford goes to extremes that I wouldn't stoop to."

"I wonder what he pays the hermit and what the man's duties are. I mean, how can you be a hermit if you have people all around?"

"I have no idea." Brandon's words were clipped.

"I'll ask Colin."

All the comfort went out of the day for Brandon. Couldn't she talk about anything but his brother? Jealousy assaulted him. Abruptly he said, "When you finish your walk, have the carriage bring you to the gallery, if you care to see the exhibit. I have to be on my way to help set it up."

"I think I'll skip this exhibit," she said as she gazed out toward the sea. "I'd like to be alone with my thoughts."

Brandon darkly wondered what thoughts those were and how largely Colin figured in them. As he strode away, he couldn't help but think what a cad he was to be jealous of this woman's affection for his brother. He had no claim on her. He couldn't have because he was promised to marry Barbara. He had hoped that Barbara would free him from his duty by leaving him for Ashford. Then he would have license to court Teresa. Now, for the first time, it occurred to him that Teresa might not be available. The thought was almost too much to bear.

After Edinburgh they headed north to Dundee, the last of their stops. After the exhibit they took a day to visit Perth and see Ruthven Castle with its ancient twin towers.

"It's called Maiden's Leap," Brandon told Teresa and Salvatore. "The legend is that one of the former earl's daughters had a lover in that tower. She was visiting him one day when she heard her father coming up the steps. To keep from being caught, she jumped from that window across to the other one." He pointed up the sheer walls to the narrow openings.

"She must have been quite desperate," Teresa observed.

"Or she knew she well deserved the wrath of her father for being alone in a bedchamber with a man," Salvatore said, then gave Brandon a level look.

Brandon frowned. Salvatore hadn't seen him coming out of Teresa's room in York. Surely she wouldn't have told him they were in there alone. He glanced back and found her father's eyes still upon him. Teresa's lips were turned up in a smile as she gazed up at the windswept windows, but he couldn't decipher her thoughts.

The day before they were to start home, Teresa insisted she must see the cliffs that lined the road to Montrose, even if she had to go alone. Salvatore was too tired to go with her, but Brandon volunteered to accompany her on the expedition, and he chose his words in such a way that Salvatore could hardly object without offending him. For days Brandon had tried to find time alone with Teresa, but her father had been constantly by her side. Salvatore stayed at the inn to rest up for the long journey home, while Brandon and Teresa hired horses and rode out of town.

A fierce storm was blowing offshore when they arrived, though the weather wasn't threatening on the cliffs. Huge waves roared in from the North Sea, hurling themselves at the rocky barriers. In order not to frighten the horses, Brandon tied them to a bush several yards from the edge, and together he and Teresa walked nearer the precipice. Below them, the sea churned and foamed over blackened rocks, its growl never fading.

"Isn't this glorious!" Teresa said as the wind whipped color into her cheeks. "Look at those waves!"

"Aren't you frightened?" he asked in some surprise. "Those waves are taller than the buildings in London!"

"They can't reach us here." Impulsively she loosened her hair and let it flow on the wind as the gale pressed her skirts tight against her body.

"You look like a pagan paying homage to King Neptune," he said.

"Don't tell Papa," she said with a laugh, "or he'll have me posing for a canvas."

He watched the wind rippling through her ebony hair, and the excitement that sparkled in her eyes. "Even Salvatore Verdi couldn't do justice to this."

She looked at him, her eyes darkening to the shade of raw honey. He had never seen anyone look so completely irresistible. She was part of the storm, wild and untamed, and one with the tempestuous sea and awesome cliffs. Passion leapt in Brandon, and he stepped nearer without realizing he had done so. "Teresa," he whispered, knowing the wind snatched the words away before she could hear him.

She swayed nearer, and he found his hands nearly spanning the slenderness of her waist. He couldn't remember reaching out for her; it was as if she were where she belonged.

Together they melted into a kiss, neither waiting for the other's compliance. Her lips were moist and warm beneath his and tasted tangy with sea salt. Her hair lashed about them, now caressing, now stinging as the wind tossed it. Brandon laced his fingers in her hair and held her face so he could gaze deeply into her eyes. Dark within them blazed the fire of her desire, and something else he dared not name. He didn't know the same love was mirrored in his own eyes.

Again his lips covered hers in a fierce kiss that demanded more. She opened her mouth and met his tongue with her own. The desire he had for her thundered through him, and he kissed her with an intensity he would never have unleashed in more civilized surroundings.

Teresa's arms encircled him and her hands stroked over the hard muscles of his back. A tiny moan escaped her, but he knew it was born of passion and not fear. The sound went through him like a searing flame.

His hand cupped her breast as he continued to kiss her. Her nipple was hard beneath the fabric, and he discovered she used neither lacings nor ruffles to accentuate her figure. This inflamed him all the more. Beneath the thin layer of cotton and the sheer fabric of her chemise, Teresa's body was soft and warm, with womanly curves that cried out to be enjoyed. There was no doubt that she wanted him; her kisses proved her desire.

"Teresa," he said again, his lips barely a breath away from hers.

"*Caro mio,*" she replied, the wind tearing at her words. "*Amore mio.*"

Brandon knew only enough Italian to conduct his business, though he did understand her to say "my love." But was that only an endearment, or was she saying she loved him? And did he love her? What about Barbara? Anguish ripped through him. He forced himself to push her away so that the gale could find its way between them.

"I can't take you like this!" he ground out, his face etched with longing. "Dammit, I can't!"

She stared at him, her hands gripping his arms as if to keep her balance.

"I can't make love to you when I'm promised to someone else!" The words were as bitter as gall in his mouth, but he had to say them. "Even if I were free, I couldn't lay you on the hillside as if you were a shepherdess! Not you!"

"Why not?" Her voice was as strained as his.

"Because I . . . care about you!" he said loudly against the rising wind. "You aren't some light-o'-love to be taken carelessly. You're . . ." He didn't know how to explain any further, not without expressing feelings he was only now beginning to admit to himself.

"Then you don't want me?" she asked, her eyes etched with pain.

"Yes!" He pulled her back into his embrace and held her tightly. "God, yes, I want you! Heaven help me—I do want you!"

They stood together against the wind, afraid to go further and unable to go back to what they had been. The storm whirled and gusted about them, but together they held firm.

7

"Papa, I don't want to go."

"Nonsense, *carina mia*. This is a party. All young people love parties." Salvatore smiled beneficently at his daughter. "Ever since we returned from the trip, you've been so moody. The party will do you good."

"I'm not going." Teresa crossed her arms stubbornly and tossed a frown in his direction. "I would rather be alone than with those silly women—like Lady Barbara."

"You may as well get to know her. When she marries Lord Kincaid, you'll see her nearly every day, and I understand the wedding date will be set quite soon."

"When did you hear that?"

"Hal told me when he was helping me crate the paintings to ship back to the gallery in York."

"What does Hal Lunn know? He's only a footboy."

"Perhaps so, but he is a cousin of Fitch, who is butler at Hawthorn, and Fitch is certainly informed as to his master's plans."

Teresa turned away. Could it be true? All the way home from that storm-tossed cliff in Scotland, Brandon had been quiet and withdrawn. He had hardly spoken to her even in the close confines of the coach. In the two days since they arrived home, he had avoided her completely.

"Master Colin is coming to call for you at eight," Salvatore said in a cajoling tone. "You aren't becoming too attached to him, are you? He's a nice-enough young man, but he's only an escort, remember."

Teresa sighed. She was tired of her father's constant reminders that she had to keep safely aloof. She was tempted to accept Colin's proposal just to show Brandon she wasn't waiting for any crumb of affection he might toss her. But she couldn't do that. She liked Colin far too much to use him so cruelly. If only her hair were blond and her form as dainty as Barbara's, maybe Brandon would take her more seriously. "I wish I were prettier," she said.

"Prettier? But you are beautiful!" Salvatore went to her and put his arm across her shoulders. "You are my pearl, my flower. My treasure. Who has said you aren't pretty?"

She sighed. "I was comparing myself with Lady Barbara and I find myself lacking in many ways."

"Nonsense. When she is older, Lady Barbara will look like a scrawny chicken. But you, now, you will only grow more beautiful with maturity."

"Oh, Papa." She laughed in spite of herself.

"It's true. I may not have my father's skills, but I have his eyes. I know beauty when I see it. Has Master Colin been paying you compliments?" he probed.

"I'm not interested in Colin. Not that way."

"Good girl. But you're going to the party. I insist upon it. You're young and you should have some fun. You never see any young ladies here. You should make some friends."

She knew there was no point in arguing, but she didn't bother to hide her frown. Salvatore was right in saying she must go. To offend their patron would be foolish at this point in their career. Too much hinged on Brandon's help in making Salvatore's art known to the world.

After dinner Teresa dressed in her pink taffeta dress with the satin ribbon stripes. The white lace collar met around the rose-hued petals of a silk flower, and a group of three more roses nestled at her waist. She brushed her hair into ebony coils and pinned another flower in the middle. On her hand she slipped a pearl-and-garnet ring that had belonged to her mother. Except for the expression in her eyes, the looking glass told her she was quite presentable.

Teresa sat on the edge of her bed and clasped her hands in her lap. How was she supposed to endure an evening of seeing Brandon and Barbara? She sat there miserably until she heard the rumble of Colin's buggy out front.

Brandon frowned at himself in the cheval glass. He wasn't looking forward to this evening. Colin had planned the party as a surprise, and naturally he had invited Barbara. Brandon adjusted his frock coat and ran his hand over his hair. What was he going to say to her? " 'Excuse me, but we've made a mistake'? 'You're in love with Ashford, and I'm in love with Teresa'?" Brandon knew what would happen if he said such a thing, and above all else, he disliked unpleasant scenes.

Perhaps Barbara would confess her feelings for Ashford of her own volition, he thought hopefully. Then he could be properly rejected and go on from there. But no, he thought more logically, Barbara would never tell him she cared for someone else. He knew her too well to hope for that. Unless Ashford was cad enough to actually propose marriage to her while she was still officially engaged to Brandon, she would be afraid to chance losing them both. Barbara had no intention of ending up as a spinster. Not even if it meant marrying a man she didn't love.

The small marble clock on the mantel in his sitting room struck eight, and he walked across the bedroom to the door. His guests would arrive soon. The time had come to act as if he were enjoying himself. Brandon had never been especially fond of pretending to be happy when he wasn't, but he had been parlor-trained from his earliest childhood. He doubted that even Barbara would see through his veneer of good manners.

As he had expected, Barbara and Rochelle Watson, accompanied by Rochelle's new beau, Charles Laibrook, were the first to arrive. Barbara came demurely through the door and handed her lace shawl to Fitch as nonchalantly as if she were already mistress of the house. When they went into the hall, Barbara took the liberty of rearranging the table that the housekeeper, Mrs. Dennison, had spent several hours preparing. Brandon refrained from comment.

The next coach brought a number of Colin's friends, a mixture of aristocracy and artists that Brandon found irritating. Colin's choice of friends usually ran to the eclectic, but Brandon welcomed them to Hawthorn just as he would have had their clothes been less extreme and their words not so liberally sprinkled with slang. This was, after all, Colin's party.

Colin arrived next with Teresa, and as she walked into the room, Brandon felt as if his world were set atilt. She wore a pink dress with a shiny ribbon in the same color, and her hair was piled into feminine loops and twists. He could see her nervously glancing about the room, and he wondered if she felt shy in the crush of strangers. Brandon automatically took a step toward her.

Barbara, feeling him move away from her side, put out her hand and caught his arm without pausing in her discourse with Rochelle.

Brandon said, "Excuse me, I hear more guests arriving."

She looked across the room, and narrowed her eyes when she saw Teresa. "Colin is here now. He can greet them. Besides, I want you to hear this."

Brandon could hardly pull away without appearing impolite, so he pretended to listen to her account of Cecilia's wedding. As if Teresa were a magnet, Brandon's eyes returned to her. When she looked in his direction, their eyes met, and he was unable to look away. He recalled the softness of her lips from their kiss on the cliff in Scotland, and his arms felt achingly empty.

With a pretty pout, Barbara said, "Brandon, aren't you listening to me?"

"What?" Guiltily he looked down at his fiancée.

"I said Cecilia had six bridesmaids, all dressed in the strangest shade of yellow. So I plan to have eight and have them wear pale blue. What do you think?"

"Barbara, I have to speak with you." He couldn't let this go on any longer. Not when every fiber of his soul was so aware of Teresa.

"In a minute," she said offhandedly. "Won't you get me a glass of punch? I feel light-headed."

He had no choice but to comply. By the time he returned, Teresa had slipped into the crowd. Barbara took the glass, sipped it daintily, and put it down. Brandon watched her dispassionately. What had he found in her that had seemed remarkable enough to inspire a marriage proposal? True, she was pretty, but she had no more substance than a shadow. Although her words were disguised as wit, she was shredding her best friend's marriage, wedding dress, and future house.

Brandon's eyes roamed the crowd in search of Teresa, and because of her distinctive pink dress, she was easy to find. She was speaking animatedly to Colin. His brother bent his head to catch her words, then laughed spontaneously. Brandon felt envy gnawing in his middle.

As another guest arrived amid a flurry of greetings, Brandon heard Barbara's voice falter, then continue with her deprecating comments on Cecilia's wedding. Brandon looked to see who had distracted her, and realized it was Ashford Benchley. He had come alone, and was threading his way toward them through the crowd. Brandon's eyes narrowed when he noticed the look of anticipation on Barbara's face.

"Hello, Ashford," she said in her sweetest voice. "I was wondering if you were going to come tonight."

"Would I miss a party at Hawthorn?" Ashford shook

hands with Brandon and Charles and nodded to Rochelle. "Colin throws quite a bash, doesn't he?"

"It's one of his most obvious talents," Brandon remarked dryly.

"He still has no idea about his future?" Charles asked with all the assurance of a man whose future was already cut out for him.

"Colin?" Barbara asked with a tinkling laugh. "Mercy, no. I expect he will end up living on our hearth, a male version of a spinster."

Brandon frowned. "That's unlikely. Barbara, I must speak with you. Will you walk with me in the garden?"

"In a minute. I don't want to leave just yet." When her wide blue eyes met Ashford's, she glanced down demurely.

Brandon's lips tightened. He didn't mind giving his claim up to Ashford, but he didn't like having them make sheep's eyes in front of him.

"Who is that with Colin?" Charles asked. "I've never seen her at any of our parties."

"That's just Teresa Verdi," Barbara said with mild contempt. "She's the daughter of Brandon's pet painter."

Brandon's face darkened. "Signor Verdi is hardly a 'pet.' He's probably the most accomplished artist in England."

"He's a foreigner. From Venice," Barbara explained to Charles. "I suppose that accounts for the odd dress his daughter is wearing."

"It does look foreign," Rochelle said in agreement. "Look at the shape of her collar. And no one is wearing roses this season."

"I think she looks quite nice," Charles said. "Don't you think she's pretty, Ashford?"

"With skin that swarthy?" Barbara exclaimed. "She looks like a red Indian!"

Brandon couldn't hold his tongue any longer. "I think she's beautiful. As for the color of her skin, she's no darker than most brunettes." He was noticing how Barbara's skin tended toward the pink side when she was upset. It was quite pink now. "If you'll excuse me, I'm going to greet her."

He knew Barbara was glaring at his back, but he made his way to Teresa nonetheless.

She was laughing at one of Colin's jokes, and her breath caught in her throat when she found Brandon beside her. Although he was only slightly taller than Colin, his presence was overwhelming. Brandon seemed to dominate whatever room he was in, and Teresa was surprised he had come so near without her noting his every movement.

"Your party is a success, Colin," he said in the deep, mellow tones that seemed to enfold her soul.

"How good of you to come all the way across the room to tell me," Colin said, glancing from his brother to Teresa.

"Good evening," Brandon said formally to her.

She inclined her head slightly, not trusting herself to speak. Across the room Barbara glared at her, then said something in a whisper to Rochelle Watson. They both giggled. Teresa indignantly turned her attention back to the men beside her. "Colin was telling me the story about the goat and the tennis court."

"Actually," Colin said, "I was about to ask Teresa if she would like to walk out to the courts and see them for herself. I don't think she believed my story at all."

"Then she shows rare insight." Brandon looked down at her in a way that caused her heart to thud. "I'm not occupied at the moment. I could show her the courts."

"And leave Lady Barbara unattended?" Colin pretended to be shocked. "Her father would call you out for such an offense. I'll show them to Teresa."

"You, on the other hand, can't leave your own party," Brandon countered. "All your guests haven't arrived."

"I suppose I'll have to see the courts another time," Teresa said quickly. "Besides, I've seen them in the daylight, you know."

"They look entirely different at night," Colin protested.

"One tennis court looks pretty much like another," Brandon snapped.

Teresa glanced at him in surprise. He actually sounded jealous! She turned to Colin with a smile that would have melted marble. "However, I would love to see the conservatory. That's close enough for you to notice the arrival of any latecomers." She lowered her eyelashes as she had seen Barbara do.

Colin chuckled softly. "The conservatory it is. Brandon, if you'll excuse us? I think Lady Barbara is about to send an envoy after you." He offered Teresa his arm, and she took it with a smile.

As they left the hall and went past the screens passage, Colin said, "Well played!"

She glanced sharply at him. "I don't know what you're talking about."

"Yes, you do." He led her into the corridor past the morning room and writing room, and into the billiard room, which opened into the conservatory.

Teresa walked across the brick-paved room and touched a trailing orchid. She was direct by nature, and it went against her grain to use subterfuge.

"My brother can be both blind and stubborn," Colin said as he joined her. "In my opinion you are a better choice by far than Lady Barbara."

"Excuse me? My English is not good."

He laughed again. "You understand me perfectly. Brandon's greatest failing is that he really cares what people think. He was the only one of us to accept our parents' teaching about propriety and social obligations. If you ask me, he wants to break off his engagement to Barbara and is afraid to do so."

"Brandon? Afraid? I don't think so."

"I don't mean he's afraid for himself, but he worries about what such a thing would do to Barbara. There aren't that many eligible men in our circle of friends, and he wouldn't want to ruin her life."

"He would rather ruin his own?"

"That could seem preferable to Brandon. Now, me,

I'm entirely undisciplined. If I wanted one woman and was engaged to another, I would sit them down and explain to them how matters stood."

"Both of them at once?" Teresa had to smile. "There would be a battle royal!"

"Probably, and I would marry the survivor."

"Colin, be serious," she said with a laugh. "You'd do no such thing."

He shrugged. "The point is, Brandon wouldn't. Therefore an alternative would be for you to marry me."

She studied him quickly. Although he was still smiling, she knew he was serious. "You know I can't. I told you that in London."

"I know, but some ladies are taught that it's proper to refuse the first three proposals. I figure you won't give me your true answer until I ask at least once more." His eyes searched hers. "Am I right?"

"No, Colin," she said gently. She put her hand on his arm and said, "I'm not playing with your affections. I would never do that."

"Then you really do love Brandon?"

She turned away. "I never said that."

Colin pulled her back around to face him. "You don't have to say the words when I can see it in your face. When you look at him, it's as if you glow from the inside out."

"Colin, don't care for me. I'm not noble like Brandon. I don't care if Lady Barbara is a spinster or not, or whether I shock all of England by my actions. You deserve much better."

"Do I? Someone like Lady Barbara, perhaps?"

"No. Someone who believes your stories about goats and tennis courts. Someone who can spin stories of her own to amuse you. Someone who loves you."

He gazed down at her with sadness in his eyes. "I had hoped you would be that one."

"I wish I were. I truly do."

He put his arms around her and held her close. "Brandon is a fool, and I think I'll tell him so."

"You'll do nothing of the kind!"

"It might help."

"It could drive him away forever!"

Inside, Brandon had waited as patiently as he could, but when Colin and Teresa didn't quickly return from the conservatory, he went to look for them. He arrived in time to see Colin take Teresa in his arms, hold her close, then bend his head and say something so quietly Brandon couldn't hear. Pain tore through him. How could she kiss him with such wild abandon, then embrace his brother? "Excuse me," he said coldly.

Teresa jumped away from Colin, and Brandon was glad to see she at least looked uncomfortable. "Colin, you have guests arriving."

Colin smiled at Teresa. "Greet them for me, brother. I haven't finished showing Teresa the conservatory."

"They are your guests, not mine. I'll show her the flowers."

Colin and Teresa exchanged an enigmatic look and Colin said, "If you'll excuse me, Teresa, I have duties."

Brandon frowned after him. The young whelp didn't seem to have any compunction at all about leaving her with him, and he had obviously been about to kiss her. To Teresa he said, "I seem to be forever interrupting you and my brother at an awkward moment. May I assume you've set your cap for Colin?"

"You may not assume anything of the kind."

"I see. It was just to be a kiss between friends." His voice was strained and all his muscles tense.

"I wasn't kissing him. And if I were, it would be none of your business!"

"I see."

"Stop saying that!"

"What would you have me say? 'Choose one of us or the other'? 'Kiss one or the other, but not both'?"

"I wasn't aware I had a choice!" she snapped back. "And I wasn't kissing him!"

Brandon stepped nearer and glared down at her. "How many others have you kissed?"

Her mouth dropped open in shock. "What do you mean by that?"

He knew he was going too far, but he felt a primeval surge carry him forward. "I've held you and kissed you and I know all too well how much you enjoy it!"

"What's wrong with that?"

"It's not proper! Do you think Lady Barbara enjoys kissing like that? Or any other of the ladies in there? No! A lady is a lady!"

She stepped back as if he had slapped her. "And you," she said, "are a fool!" Before he could stop her, she opened the glass door and ran out into the night.

"Teresa!" he called out as he ran after her. "Teresa, come back here." After the bright light of the conservatory, he couldn't see her at all. "Teresa!" he bellowed out into the night.

Cursing himself, he ran across the lawn, but she was nowhere to be seen. Glaring about in the darkness, he wondered what had possessed him. How could he have said those hurtful things to her? True, Barbara would never kiss him the way Teresa did, but he *liked* the way Teresa kissed him. He enjoyed her responses to his embraces much more than he ever had Barbara's. It wasn't her fault if he felt guilty. Teresa wasn't responsible for his frustrations over Barbara.

"Brandon?"

He recognized Barbara's voice and reluctantly turned to face her. She was standing in the door of the conservatory. "Yes?"

"What are you doing out there? Colin said you were in the conservatory."

Leave it to Colin to tell her that, Brandon thought angrily. She came out to meet him, her steps mincing and dainty. She looked for all the world like a china doll on wheels.

"I have to speak with you," he said. This was a good time to get the unpleasantness over.

"We can't talk now. There's a party going on inside

and everyone is asking for you. Come and see the adorable puppy Mary Bennett brought Colin."

"Another dog. What luck," Brandon growled as he looked again into the darkness for Teresa's pink dress. "Colin has a veritable zoo as it is now."

"Don't be such an old bear," Barbara said in a little-girl voice. "Come see the puppy before Fitch takes it away."

He sighed in defeat. This didn't seem to be the time to confront Barbara with her feelings for Ashford or his for Teresa. At the moment he wasn't sure of anything at all. He only knew he still hurt from having seen Teresa in Colin's arms. Forcing himself, he followed Barbara back inside.

When they were gone, Teresa stood up and pushed her way out of the concealing bushes. All her anger had turned cold and knotted inside her like a stone. He hated her, or at least he didn't care about her, despite what he had said in Scotland. What was she supposed to have done when he kissed her on the cliff? Stand there like a stick? She didn't know much about flirting or the ways to attract a gentleman, but she knew what was supposed to happen between a man and a woman. There had been a kitchen maid in the Verdi palazzo who had told her all she needed to know about love-making. Even without the kitchen maid's graphic instructions, Teresa had known how to kiss Brandon. It wasn't fair for him to expect her to curb her instincts.

She stood in the shadows and watched Brandon through the window. In contrast to his gruff words, he held the fuzzy puppy gently and scratched its ears in a way all dogs liked. Barbara hovered by his side, looking up at him as if he were her own private possession—which he seemed to be. Teresa felt hot tears run down her cheeks. Brandon would certainly never have reason to scold *Barbara* for not being a lady. She acted as if any strong emotion at all would send her into a swoon.

Teresa turned and walked into the night. She wasn't afraid to go home alone, and she had no fear at all of losing her way. In her mind she came to Hawthorn frequently, though in her fantasies Brandon was always by her side.

Though there was only a half-moon, she had no trouble finding the footpath. The June night was warm and clear, so she took her time walking up the sloping green. She had to forget Brandon. There was no choice. Especially after the way he had spoken to her tonight. Once he might imply she was no lady and be forgiven, but not twice. Teresa had as much pride as he did, and her morals were just as firm. If he ever dared to kiss her again, she would upbraid him so strongly he would crawl away in shame.

Teresa wondered if she could ever really convince herself of that.

Brandon felt miserable all that night. Like most people who habitually bury their feelings, once he had begun to voice them, he said too much. Worse, he hadn't even spoken the truth.

Colin had given him no explanation for the embrace he had interrupted, nor had he asked for one. Colin had been upset when Teresa didn't return to the party, but had been unable to go searching for her. When Hal Lunn came to say she was safely home, Colin seemed content to leave it at that. Brandon couldn't understand his brother at all. If he were courting Teresa, he would have gone after her, guests or no guests.

By the end of the evening Brandon was even doubting whether Barbara was infatuated with Ashford. They seemed to be avoiding each other. Brandon had to admit he couldn't understand the way Barbara's mind worked, any more than he could Teresa's.

He sat out the night until dawn, trying to figure out the twistings of his life. Teresa must not care for him, or she wouldn't have been in Colin's arms. Barbara, on the other hand, had hung on Brandon's arm all the rest of the evening, and Ashford had left the party quite early. Surely if they were really attracted to each other, she would have paid Ashford more attention. After what he had seen in the conservatory, Brandon was glad he hadn't been rash in calling off his engagement with Barbara. There was no need to hurt her if she didn't care for Ashford and if Teresa wanted Colin.

A marriage of convenience. Brandon thought of the familiar term and wondered if such liaisons were really convenient for those involved. Barbara certainly was a comfortable match: their parents had been close friends, she would be a beautiful hostess for Hawthorn, and she was familiar to him. But shouldn't there be more? What about the nights when she would lie unmoving in his arms—and he no longer expected her to do anything else. And shouldn't a man and a woman be able to talk about something other than the weather and how their days had been? Barbara hadn't the slightest interest in art, and he couldn't care less about the newest fashions in bonnets.

By midmorning Brandon had to admit he needed to see Teresa. He had to find out whether or not she cared for Colin. If she did, well, he would try to convince Colin to marry her. He wanted Teresa to be happy. But with Colin? Brandon's face was stony as he rode to the cottage.

Teresa had been painting since early that morning. As always, she found surcease for her problems in laying paint on canvas. She was working on the scene she had sketched of the inn yard. Because Salvatore was working outside, she had the studio to herself. Her quick fingers blocked out the scene in a sienna wash; then she corrected her lines with umber. She laid the painting out in shades of brown so the final pigments would carry a gold glow like sunshine.

Going to a sunny window, she tested a tray of linseed oil and found it had thickened to the proper degree. She poured it into a bottle, then added the same amount of clear varnish and a bit of Venice turpentine to cut it. Antonio had worked out the exact proportions years before, and she had never found a better recipe for the medium.

The paint powders were kept in clay pots with cork stoppers, each labeled in clear letters. Carefully she measured out the shades of brown and white, then added the medium to it to make paint of the proper consistency. Starting with the darkest umbers, she began painting.

Time passed quickly when she worked, but her thoughts kept returning to the day she had made the sketch. Traveling with Brandon in such close proximity had been so bittersweet. She treasured the memories of how he smiled, and the little gestures he made without thinking, and the way he sat or stood or walked. But, she chided herself, she had to stop thinking about him with such longing, for he would never be hers.

At the knock on the door, she paused. Not many people came to the studio; it almost had to be Brandon. If she didn't answer, however, he might look through the window and see her at work. Hastily she got up and pulled off her paint smock.

She opened the door, and as she had expected, Brandon stood on the low stone step. For a long moment they stared at each other.

"Is your father here?" he asked at last.

"No. He's sketching at the ruins."

When she didn't invite him in, he asked, "May I come in and see the sketches he did of my hunter?"

"No, Papa doesn't like people in his studio when he isn't here. You know how artists are."

"But you're in there."

"I'm the exception."

"Then will you walk with me for a while? Perhaps he will return."

She wanted to refuse, but the offer was too tempting. "I suppose I could take a short walk."

They followed the stream beneath the willows; the silence between them was awkward. Teresa felt an uncharacteristic urge to sit down and cry. He was so right for her and so wrong for Barbara! Couldn't he see that?

"I wanted to apologize to you for what I said last night," he said stiffly. "It was inexcusable of me."

"Then why should I forgive you?"

He looked at her as if he hadn't expected her to say that. "It's just an expression. Of course you should forgive me."

"Last night wasn't the first time you said such a thing to me. If you don't mean it, why do you continue to say it? If you do mean it, I have no reason to forgive you." She glanced up at him. "Which is it?"

A rumble came from deep in his throat. "I didn't mean what I said. I was angry at finding you in Colin's arms, and I lashed out at you."

"Why?" She stopped walking and stared at him. "Why would that make you so angry?"

"Because it's not proper!"

"Is that another foolish English rule? In Venice we are not so straitlaced."

"You aren't in Venice, and even if you were, I doubt it's considered proper for a woman to kiss any man who tries to kiss her."

"I wasn't kissing Colin, and I don't kiss every man I see!"

"Don't get angry all over again!"

"I'm not! I never stopped being angry the first time!"

Again they walked, each wondering how to breach the chasm between them. At last Brandon said, "The reason I came here this morning was to ask your father to paint a canvas for my bedroom."

"What?" She hadn't expected him to change the subject so abruptly.

"I'd like a reclining nude, about the size of the Diana picture. Will you tell him?"

"Tell him yourself."

"In view of the animosity between us, I think that I should avoid contact with you. If you won't give him my message, I'll send a boy up with a note after your father returns."

"I'll give him the message." She turned on her heel and walked briskly away.

Brandon frowned after her. He had offered his apology, and she had refused to accept it. That should tell him where he stood with Teresa Verdi.

Perversely, he wanted to run after her, but he made himself stand his ground, then started off at a right angle to the path she had taken. He wouldn't run after her! Especially not when she was so clearly rejecting him.

He was better off without her. That was obvious. With Teresa out of the way, he would fall back in love with Barbara and settle down into an orderly life.

Brandon felt as if he had lost something irreplaceable.

8

"Nobody tells Salvatore Verdi what to paint!" he yelled at the top of his voice.

Teresa's rose too as she said, "He wasn't giving you an order, Papa, he was commissioning a painting!"

" 'Will you please' and 'if you would be so good' —these are words for a commission. Not 'I want'!"

"Perhaps it is done differently here in England. He is our patron. You can't refuse him."

"Can't I? Can't I? I refuse! There! I've done it!" He thrust out his chin at her, and they glared at each other.

"It's just a nude, Papa," she said cajolingly. "One small nude. No bigger than the Diana painting."

"No bigger than that? The Diana is four feet long! What does he want? Life-size?"

"I can't talk to you!" She gestured with her palms up in frustration. "What does it matter if you paint a nude next or a landscape?"

"It matters to me. First, my daughter must finish my paintings. Now my patron must tell me what to paint. It is too much!"

Teresa glanced at the door that led to the rest of the cottage. Fortunately they were speaking in Italian so Katie and Hal couldn't understand their words. "All right, Papa. Calm yourself. I will send Hal to tell him you said no."

"You can't send a servant on an errand to refuse such an important man."

"Then you go."

"No! Salvatore Verdi does not run errands. Not even to Lord Kincaid. *You* will go."

"Not me!"

"Why not you? You were the one to agree to this foolishness. You will be the one to get me out of it."

"No! I won't do it!"

"Why not?"

Teresa frowned. She could scarcely tell her father that she was in love with Brandon but he was scorning her. "You are the artist. You tell him."

"No!"

"Papa, I think you're being unreasonable."

"At my age I don't need anyone to tell me what is reasonable."

"Very well!" She whirled about and flounced to the door. "I will tell him. I will say Salvatore Verdi is too pigheaded to accept a commission from his patron!"

"Your mother would roll in her grave if she could hear you!" he roared after her.

Teresa's anger hadn't entirely cooled by the time she reached Hawthorn. Fitch let her into the morning room and she paced in irritation. A nude wasn't much to ask. As patron, Brandon certainly had a right to suggest subject matter. Besides, everyone painted nudes. Diana wore only a wisp of gauze, and it was almost transparent. Her father's pride had always been too great.

Brandon came to the door, but paused. Teresa wondered if Fitch had told him who was in the parlor. He looked as if he would like to leave again. "This is a rare surprise," he said dryly. "To what do I owe this honor?"

"I talked to Papa about the painting you wanted," she began.

"Of course. The painting. I should have told you, I expect to pay for it."

"You do?"

"Of course. As I said, I want it for my room here at Hawthorn." He named a sum that was more than generous.

Teresa's eyes widened. "For that one painting?"

"Of course. Not only is his work worth it, but it will set a precedent for his other sales. Will he agree to it?"

She thought quickly. "Yes. Yes, he will agree." She felt only a small pang of conscience. Surely for so much money her father could swallow his pride. Catherina had written recently that the palazzo's roof was in need of repair. She couldn't afford to turn down that much money.

"Good." Brandon gazed at her with his unsettling green eyes. In a softer voice he said, "I wish we could call a truce."

"I don't know what you mean."

"Yes, you do."

Teresa studied his face. How could she love him and still feel so angry toward him? No one else in all the world could make her emotions reach such peaks and such depths. "I suppose we could try."

"Let me begin by apologizing again for the things I said to you at Colin's party. I truly didn't mean them."

"I accept your apology," she said warily. "And I *wasn't* kissing him."

He frowned as if he still didn't believe her, but he said, "Accepted."

"And I apologize to you for the things I thought about you," she added. "About your being foolish and thickheaded."

"I accept that as well." A muscle ridged in his jaw.

"And I apologize for the things I thought about Lady Barbara, about how cold and unloving and manipulative she seems to be. Do you forgive me?"

"Yes!" His lips tightened and his eyes were darkening in anger. He forced himself to smile. "And I apologize for thinking you flirted with me in order to get Colin's attention, and that you used me most disgracefully."

Her lips parted in surprise. "You thought that?"

"What else was I to think?"

"You might have thought just the opposite. Colin and I are only friends. I've told him that's all we can ever be."

Brandon studied her eyes for any trace of lies. "I know Colin. I think he really cares for you."

"I don't love him, and I told him so."

Brandon stroked his chin thoughtfully. "You've given me a great deal to mull over. It seems I really do owe you an apology."

"You seem to be inordinately fond of making them."

He turned away. "I must remind you that I am engaged to be married."

"I know that."

"Only the lowest sort of man would encourage one woman when he has spoken for another."

Teresa stared at him. What was he trying to tell her? At times her English still wasn't up to the subtleties of the complicated language.

"I don't think I should say any more." Although he kept his back turned, she could see his muscles were tight beneath his coat.

He was telling her that she had no hope—she felt foolish not to have seen it earlier. She wished with all her heart that she could take back her words and let him continue to think she was interested in Colin. Unable to face him, she silently left the room.

"But I can say this," Brandon continued, not realizing she was gone. "If Lady Barbara will allow me, I intend to cancel our wedding plans."

Colin heard Brandon's voice and looked in the door. Finding his brother alone, he came in and watched Brandon with great curiosity.

"I'll talk to Lady Barbara within the week. Then I'll be free to speak to you about our future."

"I had no idea you felt that way," Colin said with a laugh.

Brandon spun about and looked around. "Where did she go? What are you doing here?" He looked back at the window to see Teresa starting up the hill toward the cottage.

Colin stood beside him and also watched her. "So that's who the speech was for. I can tell you, brother, you'll need more than calm speeches to win that one."

"What do you mean by that?"

"I mean Teresa will need to be wooed by more than words, or she will never be won."

Brandon glared at him. "When I need your help, little brother, I'll ask for it."

Colin laughed again. "Suit yourself, big brother. And if you fail, I'll be here to pick up the pieces. I wouldn't mind at all being second choice—as long as I win in the end."

Brandon sighed heavily as he turned away. "I'm not her first choice. Every time I see her, we argue."

"Every time?" Colin asked innocently.

Recalling the kisses he and Teresa had shared, Brandon didn't answer.

"Neither you nor Mitchell has ever understood women," Colin observed.

"And you think you do?"

"Brother, I know I do." With a maddening grin Colin sauntered out of the room.

"Teresa! Listen to this!" Salvatore gave the messenger a coin and hurried into the parlor as he waved a sheet of paper in his hand. "It's from Mario."

"Uncle Mario? How did he know where we were?"

"It says Saberio Valore told him. You'll never guess where Mario is!"

"Where?" she asked with trepidation.

"In London!"

"London! Why is he there?"

"He has taken the position of art director for a private school. Maidenhode, it's called."

"Maiden? Is it a school for girls?"

"No, boys. Who can understand English? Anyway, Mario has moved to rooms on Ramsden and will be out to see us tomorrow."

"Tomorrow?" She thought of the paintings scattered about the house and studio. "Won't Uncle Mario be able to tell your style has changed?"

"What if he does? Often artists change their style."

"But, Papa . . ."

"Quit worrying. He will never suspect you had a hand in the paintings. You're a woman."

Teresa frowned. "Fortunately my female sex hasn't impaired my ability to paint," she said. She was getting tired of her father's constant reminders.

"Yes, it is fortunate," he agreed, missing her point altogether. "You must put away the inn scene you're painting. The style is much too distinctively yours, and the subject is inappropriate for a woman."

"I suppose you want me to start one of violets instead?" She knew he was right. The inn scene was much too full of vibrant action, with stamping horses and a bawdy barmaid and a group of mischievous boys. But she still disliked having him tell her so.

"Violets would be good."

She sighed and turned away. When his mind was occupied, Salvatore couldn't hear irony. "Violets it will be. Large purple ones," she added, "tossed in a storm and flattened by rain."

"No storm," he said absently. "No rain."

She shook her head. Her father also wasn't overburdened by a sense of humor.

The following day at precisely two o'clock, Mario Verdi arrived. As he embraced her father, Teresa noted their strong family resemblance. Both had black hair liberally shot with gray, impressive mustaches, and brown eyes. Both were medium in height and tending toward the heavy side, and were loudly jovial. Neither seemed to remember they had not parted on the best of terms.

"And this is little Teresa?" Mario exclaimed. "She is a woman! And every bit as beautiful as your Eva Maria, may she rest in peace."

"Lucky for her she took after her mama and not her papa, eh?" Salvatore gazed with pride at Teresa.

"Very lucky," Mario laughed. "What would such a beautiful woman do with a mustache?"

Teresa laughed, but she kept her distance. She had

never liked her father's only brother. Not that he had ever said or done anything to her, but she had never trusted him. When her grandfather died, Mario had taken charge of the family finances, and as a result, she and her father had become penniless. Salvatore had always maintained it was due to a run of bad luck, but Teresa noticed Mario's own luck had been good. So good he was able to study in Paris.

They sat in the parlor, and Teresa listened to Salvatore and Mario catching up on the time since they had last seen each other, often both talking at once or veering off onto some irrelevant subject or nearly forgotten memory.

Mario looked over at Teresa and said, "You must be bored with hearing two old men reminisce about things that couldn't interest you."

"Not at all, and neither of you is old."

"Old?" Salvatore said with a booming laugh. "Never! I'm but in my prime. Now, Mario, *he* is old!" Again they laughed.

"Teresa, do you still paint?" Mario asked in a condescending manner. "Remember, Salvatore, how she was forever climbing in Papa's lap and watching every brush stroke he made? For a girl, she wasn't bad. Not bad at all."

"Yes," she said quietly. "I still paint."

"Flowers," Salvatore said quickly. "She paints flowers and still lifes."

"I'm especially proficient at assorted fruit." Her words dripped with sarcasm. Salvatore avoided her eyes.

"Well, show me your studio," Mario said as he leapt to his feet. "All this talk, and I have yet to see a canvas. For shame, Salvatore."

Teresa followed them back to the studio and sat on the window seat as the brothers went to the Diana canvas. Mario's smile wavered and he glanced at Salvatore. "You did this?"

"Can you no longer read?" Salvatore asked. "Here is my signature."

Mario backed away from the canvas and studied it solemnly. "Your Diana is alive. I swear I can see the wind passing through her veil. And those clouds! I can smell the rain approaching!"

Salvatore beamed. "Praise from you is like hearing praise from Papa. You were always the best technician."

"No longer true. You have always had a talent for composition, but what is composition without life? You have learned to breathe life into your canvases! Show me another!"

Salvatore took out the one of the Chioggia fisherman. Mario drew his breath in sharply. "A masterpiece! I can see a universe in each droplet of water. How did you do it?"

Teresa watched impassively as her father shrugged. Unreasonable resentment sparked in her eyes. She knew he had to take the credit for her work, but did he have to revel in it so? She almost thought he was starting to believe the paintings were entirely his own.

"Look, Mario," Salvatore said, "here is a painting of violets Teresa started yesterday."

"Very nice." Mario scarcely glanced at the small canvas. "Show me more of your work, Salvatore."

As Salvatore pulled out the canvas of ladies bleaching their hair in the sun, Teresa rose. "I must see to supper. Will you excuse me?"

"Yes, yes." Salvatore seemed eager to get her out of the room.

Teresa tried not to mind, but she was resentful. Would no one ever give her the recognition she deserved? At once she felt guilty. After all, this ruse had been her idea—she had even insisted upon it.

Mario looked from canvas to canvas. He found it incredible that Salvatore had learned to produce such work. Of the two, Mario had always shown more promise. True, his own composition was weak, but that could be copied from someone else's, and he had always excelled in technique. Mario could paint anything he could see. "I would never have thought of placing a goddess on a hill overlooking London," he said. "That is so like you. Or this one of the fisherman. To see it from this angle, one would have to be in the water rather than on a boat."

Salvatore shrugged. "It just came to me."

"But the way you painted the skin, the water, the scales of the fish. You have surpassed our teacher!"

"Papa? Never!" Salvatore frowned as if the idea were impossible, but he looked closely at the painted surface. "You're mistaken, Mario. No one could paint better than Papa."

Mario didn't argue the point, but he knew it was true. Somehow his dolt of a brother had stumbled into true genius. "Could I come over and paint with you? It would be like old times."

Salvatore hesitated only the barest second. "Of course, of course. As you say. It will be like old times. The Verdi brothers together in a studio. If only Papa could see it."

"Yes. If only he could." Mario put Teresa's picture of violets aside and put the fisherman on the easel. Sitting on the window seat, he stared at the painting, memorizing each line, every shading. As were all artists, he was trained to carry thousands of details in his head. Whatever Mario could see, he could paint.

As Teresa passed the studio, she stopped and pressed her ear to the door. She could again hear two voices. Every day for two weeks, Mario had come out to the cottage. Every day she had been forced to leave her easel and pretend not to mind. Salvatore's work was also suffering, because he was afraid to do much painting in front of Mario, lest he give himself away. To catch up on lost time, Teresa had started painting at night, often until the wee hours, transforming her father's finished works into masterpieces, and she was tired of the routine.

Teresa breezed in, hoping that her presence in the studio would be disruptive enough for her uncle to decide to take his leave, for he was even more sensitive than her father was about distractions. She began bustling about the room, making as much noise as she could without betraying her intent.

"Must you clean brushes now?" Mario finally asked.

"I'm afraid I must. You know how forgetful Papa is and how expensive brushes are. Why, some of these are already hardening."

"She takes good care of me," Salvatore said.

"She will make someone a good wife," Mario commented.

Teresa clicked the brushes even louder against the jar of turpentine.

"I am in no rush to lose Teresa," Salvatore said as he put the finishing touches to a pastel sketch of a pair of stag hounds. "If she were to marry, who would take care of me?"

Teresa's hands stilled. She had never thought of that. If she married, how could she work on Salvatore's paintings? And without her touch his canvases would be worthless. The color drained from her face. She was trapped in a web of her own weaving. She set the jar down too hard, misjudging the height of the table as a chilling wave of anxiety swept over her. As she wiped up the spilled turpentine and laid the brushes to drain on a cloth, she looked from the corner of her eye to see whether she was being watched. Her father and uncle seemed not to have noticed. Even if a miracle made Brandon fall in love with her, she couldn't marry him without admitting the deception she and her father were perpetrating. And that would expose her father, and Brandon himself, to public humiliation. Teresa had rationalized to herself that those who bought a Salvatore Verdi painting were getting true value for their money, and that it was she who was suffering for not receiving credit. But she knew that she and her father were technically guilty of defrauding Brandon. And if this deception were to become public knowledge, Brandon might be accused of being an accomplice. Even if it didn't become a legal problem for him, it would destroy his reputation in the art world. Hastily she left the studio.

"Teresa seemed upset," Mario observed.

"She is getting older every day, and girls worry about such things."

"Has she no suitor?" Mario asked in surprise. "With her beauty?"

"You know how Teresa is. Her interests lie in the paint box."

"That shouldn't preclude her wanting to marry. Most husbands would be glad for wives who could paint little pictures to decorate their homes. She has a bit of talent."

"Teresa has more than a bit," Salvatore said. "Quite a lot more."

"Spoken like a doting father." Mario glanced at the violets on the small canvas. "She must not have painting in her blood as we do, for she hasn't touched this canvas since I first saw it."

"She has been busy."

"You should encourage her to marry. It's not natural for a girl not to have her own family."

"That's easy for you to say when you have no daughter. I can truthfully say I don't know what I would do without her." Salvatore looked over at the drying canvas of Brandon's gray hunter. Teresa had worked her magic upon it the night before, and now the horse looked as though it might plunge off the canvas at any moment. "No, I couldn't do without her."

Mario finished laying a deep purple on a bank of stormy clouds over a Roman temple. Stepping back, he viewed it critically. The clouds were a study in excellence, each rolling thunderhead rising in perfect relation to the next. But should the temple have been put in the exact center of the canvas? he wondered. His sense of proportion said yes. The temple was perfectly symmetrical, with columns as straight and as exact in their placement as human fingers could make them. His depth and proportion were textbook-accurate, but the painting lay flat upon the canvas, as stilted as any composition could be. He turned it to the wall to dry. Salvatore would honor his privacy.

Crossing the room, Mario looked over Salvatore's shoulder. "You're sketching again? I thought you were painting."

"The drawing must be exactly right."

"I've heard Papa say so many times. As for me, I want to get right onto the canvas."

Salvatore refrained from pointing out that brevity of planning always showed. "I make dozens of sketches before I ever stretch the canvas. Once I begin, I always know how the composition will be laid out. I have no surprises waiting to trap me."

"So much sketching is tedious. You have half a dozen rearing horses there, and I don't see a hair's difference in any of them."

"Don't you?" Salvatore asked in surprise.

Mario shrugged. "Sketch forever if you like. In my opinion, painting is the thing." He walked across the room to the painting of the fisherman and sat down to study it again.

"You're wearing the paint off from looking at it," Salvatore teased. "Every day you stare and stare. Don't you know the painting by now?"

"Can one look too often at greatness?" Mario stood and stretched his muscles. "Tell Teresa I won't stay for dinner. I have to give a private lesson tonight."

"How are your pupils? Are there any with promise?"

"No, they all have hands of clay and brains to match. You can't let a boy reach ten or twelve years having never touched a sketchbook and expect him to be able to do anything with it. Some of these boys don't seem able to grasp even the simplest rules of color, let alone composition."

Salvatore nodded, but didn't point out that Mario had never showed much skill in composition either.

"So I have them copy from other paintings or do still lifes that I arrange for them."

"Is that a good idea? It works in theory, but shouldn't they also do originals?"

"For these boys it doesn't matter. When they leave Maidenhode, they will never pick up a brush again." He glanced once more at the painting of the fisherman. "I must be going or I'll be late. A living is a living."

All the way to London, Mario thought of the picture, reconstructing the way the drops of water slid down the net to splash into the ocean, the seamed brown face of the fisherman that showed his inner strength.

Mario left his horse at the livery on Ramsden, then walked the remaining blocks of the narrow street to his building and let himself in. As he ascended the steep wooden stairs that loomed before him in deep shadows, he held tightly to the rail. Inside the rooms he had rented, he was met by the pungent odor of oils and turpentine, but these scents were so familiar he didn't notice them. He tossed his coat onto the threadbare couch before going to the large canvas that dominated the tiny room.

Standing back, he studied the fisherman as he rolled up his sleeves. The face was the right color, but it looked like paint, not skin. No intelligence sparked the man's eyes, though Mario had copied their color with exact precision. He picked up his brush and began to work on the drops of water that clung to the net.

Teresa painted long into the night, until her arms ached and her shoulders burned from being in the same position for so long. She no longer waited until her father's paintings were complete before she started working on them. To put in that certain sparkle as the layers of paint grew was much easier and had a better result. Between working on her father's canvases, she painted her inn-yard scene. It was good and she knew it. Not being chained to dull subjects had freed some of the restraints on her talent. The horses' hides were flecked with sweat, and mud dappled the side of the carriage. The driver's nose was red, as if he were fond of strong toddies, and the barmaid was giving him a look that suggested she was free for the night. Salvatore had been upset at the realism of the scene, but Teresa didn't care. This canvas would never be seen by anyone but the two of them, and for once she was going to paint what she wanted to paint.

Carefully she placed the canvas into a drying rack so Mario wouldn't see it by chance, then crossed the studio and looked at the canvas her uncle was finishing. The temple was in the exact center from side to side, and the horizon was the prescribed two-thirds of the way up from the bottom. As a result, the painting seemed to be more a lesson in colorful mathematics than an object of art. Even the storm clouds, which were painted as realistically as the eye could see them, were frozen in the constrictions of perfect proportion.

Teresa shook her head as she replaced the canvas. If the underlying composition was no good, all the talent in the world couldn't save it.

She put away her brushes and cleaned the paint from her hands before removing her smock. She noticed the canvas of violets she had begun and made a mental note to work on it while Mario was there the next day. Otherwise he might get suspicious.

Stepping out into the night, Teresa breathed in the fresh air. She had to paint with the windows covered so no one could see her, and the studio often became uncomfortably close.

Far below she saw a light in one of the upper windows of Hawthorn. Could it be in Brandon's room? No, she decided, it was too near the eaves and must be a servant's room. Perhaps one who was sick or unable to sleep. Perhaps it was a couple making love.

The idea brought a longing. Would she ever make love with Brandon? Her entire body ached for him. Since the day she realized she could never marry without betraying her father as an artist, she had had an overwhelming urge to go to Brandon. What demons of

perversity lurked within her, she wondered, that would
send her plunging into the thing she must avoid? Perhaps each act of suppression had its opposing act of
release. She could never stand on the edge of a precipice without picturing herself leaping over and falling,
falling. This longing to run to Brandon was just such
an urge. And like the leap into space, it was to be
firmly squelched.

Did people really make love with the lights on? she
found herself wondering. The kitchen maid at the palazzo had not mentioned the finer details.

The small light went out, leaving Hawthorn in darkness. No, Teresa thought, they probably didn't. The
artist in her rebelled. She would like to see Brandon in
all his natural glory.

Suddenly she became aware of what she was thinking, and she pulled herself up straighter. If her father
was upset at her painting a bawdy barmaid, what would
he make of her thoughts of Brandon's naked body?
Resolutely she went inside and closed the door.

9

Brandon knocked at the door of the Weatherlys' town house, mentally rehearsing his speech. After several sleepless nights he had come to the conclusion that he would have to be the one to break his engagement to Barbara, and that the sooner he did it, the better it would be for all concerned.

He was admitted by their butler and was asked to wait in the parlor. He had always hated unpleasant scenes, and this promised to be a bad one. He wasn't surprised when Lord Weatherly instead of Barbara came into the room.

"Hello, my boy," Lord Weatherly boomed as if Brandon were barely out of short pants. "We haven't seen you in a week or more."

"I've been rather busy. Is Barbara coming down?"

"In time, in time. I know how young love is. So impatient."

Brandon wondered how Lord Weatherly would take the news. He had the right to challenge Brandon to a duel if he were so inclined. From what he knew of Lord Weatherly, that was a distinct possibility.

When Barbara finally made her appearance, she looked prettily flustered. "I'm so glad you came tonight. Mother and I were just trying to decided whether to order blue silk curtains or red velvet for the front parlor."

"What front parlor?"

"Ours, silly."

"Hawthorn doesn't need new curtains."

"There now, Barbara, you've spoiled the surprise," her father admonished. "That's my wedding gift to you—a town house next door to her friend Cecilia."

Brandon frowned. "Barbara and I have already discussed it, and I prefer to live at Hawthorn."

"Nonsense, my boy. You can't fasten your wife up in a country house at her age. Stay in London, where there are things to do. You have plenty of time to gather moss in the country when you're as old as I am." He laughed and his belly jiggled.

"Barbara, I must speak with you about something very important," Brandon said.

"But the selection of my draperies *is* very important," she objected. "The blue ones have silver fringe and a lovely weave. The red ones are a claret shade and have gold fringe."

Lord Weatherly shook his head and laughed again as he said, "Female prattle. Never could understand it myself. Well, I'll leave you two lovebirds alone to plan your nest." Chuckling at his wit, he left the room.

"Now, Brandon, don't be mean about this. I don't want to live in that old country house. The one Father is buying us is just perfect—and it has two more bedrooms than Cecilia's, *and* a bay window."

"Barbara, you can't make decisions like that without consulting me!"

"But I *am* consulting you. Which do you prefer, red or blue? I think the blue, since I've ordered blue chintz for the chairs."

"You've already ordered the furniture?" He felt a cold sweat forming on his brow.

"I couldn't wait until the last minute, you know. I ordered mahogany rather than oak because Mother says that is the newest style, and they are to be made up in the Hepplewhite design, only with extra turnings and some carved work on the arms. And the gifts have started to arrive. We got a lovely set of parian hunting dogs. They will be just right for the mantel."

Brandon knew he was in trouble. "Come sit down. We really must talk."

"For goodness' sake, you look so serious! I don't want to be serious tonight. It gives me a headache."

"I don't understand why someone would send us a wedding gift when we haven't even set a date."

"I suppose it's not *really* a wedding gift. It's from my Aunt Amelia. But she chose it because she knew we were about to marry. And that reminds me. We simply have to set a date. Everyone is beginning to wonder about us."

"I don't think we should set the date," he said carefully. "I've been thinking quite a bit lately, and—"

"Not set the date? Brandon, you can't be serious!"

"Try to stay calm. I believe it's best if we—"

"Not set the date!" She jumped to her feet. "I can't wait forever, you know!"

"I'm not asking you to. In fact, I've come to the conclusion—"

"What are you trying to say, Brandon!" Her voice rose hysterically. "Why shouldn't we set the date?"

"Dammit, if you'd quit interrupting me, I could tell you!" he burst out.

Barbara's white hands flew to her face and her blue eyes popped open wide. Drawing in a gasping breath, she swooned toward him.

Brandon caught her and was in the act of easing her down to the couch when both her parents rushed in.

"What's happened?" Lord Weatherly demanded. "What have you done to her?"

"My baby!" Lady Weatherly shrieked. "She's dead!"

"She isn't dead." Brandon awkwardly stuffed a pillow under Barbara's head. "I think she fainted."

Lord Weatherly went to the sideboard in the adjoining room and poured brandy into a snifter. To the butler he said, "Run next door and get Dr. Halsey. Hurry!"

Brandon felt for her pulse as her father put the glass to her lips. The pulse was strong and steady. Brandon stood up and frowned down at her.

"Must you give her strong spirits, dear?" her mother asked nervously.

Barbara took a larger sip than was prudent, and sat up coughing.

"Got to bring her about," Lord Weatherly said grimly. "It's not good to just leave her lying around." To Brandon he said, "What caused this, sir!"

"I was trying to tell her that I don't think we should—"

Barbara moaned loudly and dropped back onto the pillow, her listless hand trailing gracefully to the floor. Lady Weatherly gave a small shriek and clapped her handkerchief over her mouth.

"What's keeping that doctor?" Lord Weatherly shouted.

At that minute the butler returned with Dr. Halsey in tow. "What's going on here?" the doctor asked in his most professional manner. "Lady Barbara has fainted, has she?"

"So it seems," Brandon said mildly.

Dr. Halsey pulled up a chair and took hold of Barbara's limp wrist as he consulted his heavy gold pocket watch. He made a noncommittal grunt, then peered at her through the spectacles he had perched on the end of his nose. "What brought this on?"

"All I know, Doctor, is I heard Lord Kincaid using strong language," Lady Weatherly said in a scandalized voice.

The doctor shot Brandon a reproachful look, and Brandon frowned back. He refused to justify his words, nor did he believe a mere "damn" was enough to send anyone into a real faint.

Barbara's eyelids fluttered, and she put the back of her hand to her forehead. "Where am I?" she asked weakly. "What has happened to me?"

"Just lie still," the doctor said. "How do you feel now?"

"Weak. So very weak." Her voice was a mere breath.

"I expected as much." Dr. Halsey stood and rummaged in his black bag for a small bottle of medicine. "Give her a spoonful of this twice a day until it's gone, Lady Weatherly. It will strengthen her blood. As for you, young man, I would urge you to use more prudence in dealing with a lady of Lady Barbara's delicacy. She is of a temperament inclined to melancholia, and I can't stress too strongly how dangerous that can be! Why, I've seen healthy young ladies become invalids and waste away with the female humors. Dangerous. Very dangerous indeed."

Lady Weatherly stifled a sob, and Barbara moaned again.

"I assure you, I did nothing to—"

"Well, you must have done something," Lord Weatherly snapped. "She wasn't swooning before I left you two alone, and her mother and I both heard you curse."

"What I said could hardly be called cursing, and it certainly wasn't enough to make her faint!"

"I'm a better judge of my daughter's sensitivities than you obviously are, and if I had known you were the sort to use rough language, I would have never given you permission to call!" Lord Weatherly stepped menacingly toward Brandon.

Brandon refused to give way, as he met the older man glare for glare. "Then I think it best that you call off the marriage, because I refuse to curb my every word!"

"By God, I may do just that!"

"Do it! I accept your justification!"

"No," Barbara moaned weakly. "No. Mother, help me!"

"Please," Lady Weatherly said with tremulous voice. "Won't you gentlemen please restrain yourselves?"

Lord Weatherly's face was red and a vein was distended in his temple, but he said, "Very well. I've been hasty. I admit it."

"Father, please don't break my heart," Barbara pleaded as if she were using her last breath.

"I'd never do such a thing. There now. You see? We're shaking hands." He shoved his beefy hand toward Brandon, who had no choice but to shake it.

"What this young lady needs is peaceful rest," the doctor announced. "It's too soon to know if this is the onset of true melancholia, but we can't be too careful. I'll be back to check on her in an hour or so and again tomorrow." He scowled at Brandon as he added, "In the meantime, keep her calm and away from unsettling influences. It could mean her life."

"Thank you, Doctor," Lady Weatherly murmured. "What luck that you live next door."

"Yes, that is fortunate."

Brandon frowned at Lord Weatherly. "Does that mean you aren't revoking your permission for us to marry?"

Barbara gasped.

"Not a bit of it. If my daughter wants you, that's good enough for me." His features were scrunched so deeply into a frown that he resembled a large bull dog.

"I really think you should reconsider," Brandon said hopefully. "I am what I am. If Barbara is this delicate . . ."

"That nerve tonic will set her up nicely," Dr. Halsey said. "I make it myself, and it never fails in complaints of this sort. Why, I have some patients who order it regularly, just as a preventative."

"There, you heard the doctor," Lord Weatherly said as he patted Barbara's limp hand. "She will rally."

"Come," the doctor said as he slapped Brandon on the shoulder. "You can walk out with me."

Brandon was glad for the chance to be alone with the doctor. When they were outside, he said, "Tell me, Dr. Halsey. Is her constitution really so delicate?"

"I'm afraid so. All women are like that," the doctor said as he removed his spectacles to clean them. "It's those blasted female humors. They pile up in an unmarried woman and cause all kinds of troubles. Why, most all my women with this complaint are maiden ladies. Once they are properly married with a house of their own to tend and children to look after, they come right around. No, the best thing for Lady Barbara is for her to marry, and as soon as possible."

"If she's that delicate, it seems that the responsibility of marriage and children would be the last thing she needs."

"It doesn't work that way. No, sir. I've treated melancholia for years, and I know what I'm talking about. But you must curb your tongue around the frail sex. Why, you could have sent her into a decline from which she might never have recovered."

"I see." Brandon wasn't at all convinced, but he knew it was useless to argue. He nodded farewell to the doctor and mounted his horse. He should have known it was too much to hope for to have her father break the engagement or for the doctor to advise against her marrying. With a sigh he turned his horse toward home. He had to call off the wedding before Barbara bought any more furniture.

"Papa, you aren't being at all reasonable," Teresa said again. "He is willing to pay a great deal for this painting!"

"I don't care if it's a king's ransom. A man has his pride."

"But our palazzo needs a new roof."

"Saberio Valore has been known to exaggerate. That roof has been perfectly sound all my life and my Papa's before me. It will last a few more years."

"But our tenants won't pay their rent if the roof comes down on their heads!"

"Then we will get other tenants. Some who know that when it rains there are sometimes small leaks."

"What can it possibly matter if you do this one nude?"

"Am I a cartoonist to hire out my brain? My hands? Am I not Salvatore Verdi, a great artist? Did anyone tell Tintoretto what to paint? Bellini? Titian?"

"I don't know, Papa, but probably."

"I think not! An artist must paint with his heart, not his head."

"Even when his own patron has made the request? He has housed us and fed us and is making the name of Verdi even greater than Grandpapa did."

"No Verdi will ever be greater than my papa," Salvatore denied staunchly.

Teresa bit back her protest. Would her father be so adamant on this point if the paintings were entirely his own? At once she felt guilty at the thought. "Very well. It will be as you say. Even though I disagree."

Salvatore nodded. "Good. Now, run along and do whatever you had planned for the afternoon. I must get back to my paints."

Teresa, who had also planned to paint, nodded. She knew he didn't want her around now. "I'll go for a walk."

"Whatever, whatever." Already his mind was on the canvas.

She went outside and inhaled deeply of the fresh air. Lately she and her father always seemed to argue, and he seldom wanted her to be in the studio when he was painting. This made it difficult for her to do the work she needed to do, but he was adamant that he never see her touch one of his canvases. She wondered if he was becoming eccentric. Perhaps the strain of this deception was too great.

As she walked out of the garden, she saw Mario ride up and enter the studio. Why, she wondered, did Salvatore let his brother have free access when he wouldn't let her?

She went through the picket gate and closed it behind her. Honeysuckle entwined the arched trellis overhead, and honeybees hummed in the golden blossoms. On the sloping green lay clouds of brilliant crimson poppies interspersed with drifts of mayweed and fragile heartsease. She walked into the carefully groomed woods, where pink stalks of foxglove and carpets of ivy softened the tree trunks.

Ahead she saw Colin and almost changed her course, but she felt the need to talk to someone who wouldn't snap her head off.

"Good morning," he called when she drew near. "I see you and your father have company. The man passed me in the field."

"Yes, that's my Uncle Mario. He and Papa like to paint together."

"Oh? I always imagined artists to be solitary by nature."

"Most are."

As they ambled along together, he asked, "Is something wrong? I don't mean to intrude upon your thoughts, but you look as though something is troubling you."

"No, no. It's nothing." She paused a minute before casually asking, "How is Brandon?"

Colin chuckled. "He's as hard to live with as a bear. I don't know what happened the last time he went in to see Lady Barbara, but he was home early and has been in a temper ever since."

"I wonder why."

"He doesn't confide in me. He thinks I'm too frivolous and a ne'er-do-well."

"Aren't you?" she asked with a teasing smile.

"Of course. That's part of my charm."

"And you're so humble."

"If you ask me, however, I think he's trying to break it off with Lady Barbara and she's resisting."

"How can she do that? Surely an engagement isn't that binding."

"It is in principle."

"What woman would want to marry a man against his will? Where is her pride?"

"If I know Brandon, he's behaving in such a circumspect manner that Lady Barbara hasn't figured out yet what he really wants."

"Why not? All he has to do is tell her he doesn't want to marry her. Brandon is no coward."

"No, not at all, but he's a gentleman to the marrow of

his bones. He'll try everything he can think of to get her to be the one to break the engagement so she won't lose face."

"That seems rather chancy to me."

"Yes, but not everyone is as direct as you are."

"Do you really think he doesn't want to marry her?"

"All I know is that he rarely mentions her, seldom goes to see her, and spends an inordinate amount of time staring up the green toward your cottage."

"But every time I talk to him we either argue or he tells me he is going to marry her."

"Brandon is quite a complicated man. We have an old song here in England that goes:

It's gude to be merry and wise,
It's gude to be honest and true;
It's gude to be off with the old love,
Before you are on with the new.

"Perhaps Brandon is taking it to heart and is reluctant to speak to you about his feelings as long as he is bound to Lady Barbara."

"I only wish I knew for sure." Teresa had not given up hoping that she could find some way out of her dilemma. She loved her father, and she loved Brandon. But she would not have a problem to solve if Brandon followed through with his marriage to Lady Barbara.

"Is that all that's bothering you?"

"No, there is also Uncle Mario. Colin, I can't quite decide what it is, but I feel terribly uneasy around him. We have never been close, but since he moved to London, I feel as though there is something . . . well, sinister about him."

"Sinister? You haven't been reading Mrs. Radcliffe, have you?"

"I'm serious. He seems so intense, as if nothing misses his notice. I don't know. It sounds foolish when I say it aloud, but it's as if he is after something."

"Such as?"

She shook her head. "I'm being foolish. What could we possibly have that he would want? After all, he's my uncle, my father's only brother. Of course he wants to visit us."

"You just have an overactive imagination," Colin said with confidence.

"You aren't the first person to notice that," she said wryly.

Mario had watched every stroke Salvatore put on the canvas. For weeks he had ridden all the way out from London to study each nuance of his brother's art. He had seen dozens upon dozens of sketches and watched Salvatore assemble them painstakingly into a finished composition. He had learned the formula Salvatore used for his medium and where he bought his paint powders, but as closely as he had watched, he couldn't quite understand how the canvases seemed to bloom overnight.

Each day when he returned to his rented rooms, Mario worked on the other, secret paintings. He had a duplicate of the fisherman, the women on the roof, the Diana, and the gray hunter. Technically they were perfect. Artistically they were lacking.

By the middle of July Mario decided he had learned all he was likely to learn from his brother and had applied it to several of his own compositions. In addition to the Roman temple, he had a painting of a grove of trees, a country house in the symmetrical Palladian style, and a château and formal garden in the French style. With great excitement he made an appointment with his brother's patron, Lord Kincaid.

Brandon arrived at the house and looked around uncertainly. If this proved to be the home of a respectable artist, he would be surprised. Nevertheless, he knocked on the door. On his third knock a slatternly woman in a torn dress came to the door and demanded to know what he wanted.

"I'm looking for Signor Mario Verdi."

She balanced her grimy baby on one of her broad hips and jerked her thumb toward the steps. "He's up yonder. Up one flight, door on the right."

Brandon started up the dimly lit steps as he heard her say to someone in her room, "It's just some bloke looking for that schoolteacher." Brandon paused, then continued on. The man might not have Salvatore's class, but if he had his talent, this visit would be worth it.

He had barely rapped on the door when it was flung open. "Signor Verdi?" Brandon asked.

"Yes, yes. You must be Lord Kincaid. Come in, come in." Mario laughed self-consciously. "It's a far cry from my family's palazzo in Venice, but artists aren't choosy about where they live."

Brandon was relieved to see the strong family resemblance between this man and Salvatore. He had been concerned this might be a deception. "I have come to see your paintings, Signor Verdi. Where you live is of small consequence."

"Yes, yes. Of course." Mario rubbed his hands together in a washing motion. "Have a seat and I will unveil them."

Brandon noticed that the easels were indeed covered, and he stifled a sigh. Such pretension indicated a marked lack of professionalism. Nevertheless he sat on the rump-sprung couch and waited.

Mario went to the first easel and swept away the silk cloth as if he were a magician. Brandon made no comment. Moving uneasily, Mario uncovered the next.

When all were exposed to the critic's view, Brandon slowly stood. "Technically they're quite good," he hedged.

"Your lordship is kind." Mario beamed as if the praise were almost more than he could stand. "Then you would be interested in showing them?"

"I'm afraid you don't quite understand my role. I'm a critic. I don't own a gallery."

"Yes, I understand that, but a word from you will open the door of any gallery in England."

Brandon again studied the paintings. They were well-executed, but they weren't pleasing. The left and right sides of the French château were mirror images of each other. The same was true for the Palladian house. Even the grove of trees he had painted looked stiff, arranged in symmetrical rows. No amount of talent could compensate for the lack of imagination in the compositions.

"I can see you and Salvatore Verdi studied under the same master," Brandon said tactfully. "The way you handle light and shadow is quite similar."

"*Si.* We studied under our father, the great Antonio Verdi."

"So your brother told me. He was a great man, your father."

"*Grazie.* You are kind."

"However, I'm afraid I can't recommend your work."

"No? *Perchè?* Why not?" Mario stared at Brandon as if he were in shock. "Not recommend the work of Mario Verdi?"

"I'm sorry, Signor Verdi, but these aren't up to my standards, I'm afraid."

"How can you say that? It is my rooms! That's it! These miserable rooms don't show them in the best light. I should have brought them to you at your estate. I could do so tomorrow!"

"No, that won't be necessary. I've seen them, and I never let anything outside a painting itself color my judgment. I understand you're a schoolteacher?"

"I am art director at Maidenhode," Mario corrected.

"A fine school. It has a good reputation in London. Do you have a number of promising pupils?"

"My pupils are not in question."

Brandon smiled coolly. "I was merely trying to ease matters by making conversation."

"Then you really won't help me show my paintings?"

"Signor Verdi, that wouldn't be fair to either of us. Your skill as an artist is obvious, but your composition is too stilted."

"How can you say that? Each subject is precise to the minutest detail. I have even marked off the canvas with a ruler to get it just right!"

"Yes, that would explain it. I'm sorry, Signor Verdi, but I think you should stick to teaching art and reach acclaim through your students. If you're able to teach them your techniques, some of them may go far."

"Pah! They are all woodenheads. They don't care the first thing about art! When I was their age I had already completed the most rigorous instruction. None of them even knows how to shade a sphere properly!"

"Then I would say you have your work cut out for you."

"Is that your final word?" Mario drew himself up stiffly.

"I'm afraid so."

"Then I bid you farewell."

Brandon nodded. The man could also use some lessons in manners. "Good day. And good luck with your students." He let himself out.

Mario stared at the closed door, then snapped his head back to his paintings. Was the man mad? These were superior to anything Salvatore could do. He had even painted each brick in the château!

He removed his paintings from the easels and gingerly slipped them into the racks he had built along the back wall, as if they were too precious to be left out in the open. Then he put his copies on the easels. Once again he studied them. The fisherman was off-center, and the clouds in the Diana painting were piled up haphazardly. Why did this Lord Kincaid think that these were good and his own weren't?

There was only one explanation. Luck. Salvatore had always been blessed with more luck than anyone else Mario had ever known. Somehow that luck had convinced Lord Kincaid to give him a living and to be his patron.

In a burst of temper Mario grabbed up a brush and wrote "S. Verdi" on the right-hand corner where Salvatore signed all his work. Even the signature was perfect. Salvatore himself would have trouble discerning whether he or Mario had signed it. With grim determination Mario signed the others as well. He was as much entitled to luck as his brother.

Going to his table, he wrote a letter to a gallery owner he knew in Paris. He was sure the man would pay handsomely for a Salvatore Verdi now that the name was becoming so well-known. One by one he wrote to other galleries for each of the other copies. When he was done, he felt a keen sense of vindication. Now Salvatore would not be the only one to benefit from all those hours of study and practice they had been forced to endure.

10

Brandon sat astride his gray hunter as the horse threaded through London's busy streets. He nodded to a pair of bobbies who were strolling between carts of posies and polished apples, and tipped his hat to a lady who was examining the lace of another of the city's street vendors. To the south he could hear the sounds of demolition as the slums there were being razed to make way for the railroad lines. Every day more and more of the poor were made homeless by the strides of progress. Brandon deplored the plight of these people, but he could do nothing to alter it. Progress was necessary and the railways' cheapest route was through the slums. He was glad Mitchell was at medical school in Germany, unable to witness this newest degradation. Mitchell was such an idealist that he might take it upon himself to tackle the problem single-handed. Brandon reached into his vest pocket and tossed some coins to a group of ragged children standing on a street corner. They caught the coins and grinned their appreciation before turning and running down the street.

As Brandon watched them scurry away through the crowds, he was reminded of his preference for country life. The city was, of course, the ideal home for many people, and progress was necessary. But because he wasn't a part of everyday life here, he could see the effects of the changes more objectively. A new street, to be called New Oxford, was being hewn through the slum of St. Giles Holborn in order to relieve congestion on other thoroughfares. But the poor, having nowhere else to go, were being crowded into neighboring apartments, making the bad conditions there even worse. No, Brandon thought, Mitchell was better off ignorant of the changing situation here.

He turned his horse away to avoid riding into the east London slums. Even in daylight that was no place to ride alone. Brandon lost himself in thought as he rode. Barbara had to be told that he no longer wanted to marry her, despite her fragile nature. He recalled the disturbing scene at her parents' house, when she had ended up in a deathlike swoon. If only she weren't so delicate! He wasn't sure how he could give her such disturbing news without risk of permanently impairing her health. He wished he could ask Mitchell whether women were really that frail or if her father and the doctor had said all that for his benefit. But if women weren't so delicate, why did all of them so consistently act like they were? That is, except for Teresa Verdi. She was anything but frail. How could this be? Brandon had never been able to understand women; he doubted if anyone could. He shoved the thoughts of Teresa from his mind so he could concentrate on the odious task at hand.

Deciding that nothing would be gained by putting it off, Brandon nudged his horse in the direction of Barbara's house. Telling her next week or the week after would be no less difficult. Besides, the engagement needed to be broken before anything else was ordered for that town house.

Brandon had every expectation of finding Barbara still confined to her couch, and was surprised to see her riding down a side street not a block away from her home. He waved, but she didn't see him, so he reined his horse around to follow her. Because of the crowds on the street, he had to keep a decorous pace, and while he couldn't overtake her, he had her in plain sight. He could scarcely raise his voice to hail her as if they were inhabitants of Pudding Lane, so he continued to follow, knowing that she would eventually stop and he could speak to her then.

Barbara rode purposefully down the side street, then turned onto a smaller one. Brandon was now as much curious as he was concerned with overtaking her, especially when she turned into a private alley and dismounted at the back of a house.

Brandon stopped his horse at a distance and watched as she glanced from side to side, apparently not seeing him, then put her horse away in the small stable. He wasn't too surprised that she didn't recognize him, because he knew Barbara was quite shortsighted, and probably saw even his horse as no more than a gray blur. She let herself into the small yard with apparent familiarity. Coming the way they had, Brandon wasn't sure which street fronted the house. This might be the one Edwin and Cecilia had recently bought, but it was odd that she entered the back way even if it were. Brandon was about to ride forward and call out to her when Ashford Benchley, clad in his shirt sleeves, came out to meet her. She stepped lightly past him and into the house. The door closed.

Brandon could only stare. Unlike Barbara's, his eyesight was perfect, but he couldn't believe what he had seen. Still confused, he stopped a man passing with a wheelbarrow in the alleyway and asked him, "Who owns that house with the red shutters?"

"That be the Benchley house, sir."

Brandon thanked him. There was no mistake, then, no reasonable explanation—except for the obvious.

Slowly he dismounted and led his horse down the alley to give Barbara time to come back out if her business there were innocent, though there was no excuse at all for her coming to the back door by way of the alley or for Ashford to open the door while in his shirt sleeves.

When several minutes had passed, Brandon tied his horse to the fence and let himself into the yard. He was angry that they were deceiving him in such a blatant manner and that Barbara would come so eagerly to Ashford when she had always begrudged every kiss to him. Her persistent reluctance for physical contact between them left him unconvinced by this evidence of her betrayal.

With only one sure way to find out, he knocked on the door. In his haste to let Barbara in, Ashford had not properly fastened the latch and the well-oiled door swung open. Barbara and Ashford were locked in an embrace, her bodice loosened and his hand kneading her breast. That she was allowing Ashford to do this amazed Brandon more than anything else.

The door tapped back against the wall, and the lovers leapt apart. Ashford's face paled and his mouth dropped open; Barbara tried frantically to refasten her dress. Brandon smiled as he came into the room, but it never reached his eyes. "Hello, Barbara, Ashford. I hope you don't mind my interrupting."

"Now, see here," Ashford blustered in an effort to calm Brandon, "it's not what it must seem."

Brandon glowered at him. "Give me credit for a reasonable degree of intelligence," he said.

"What are you doing here?" Barbara demanded.

"It seems we could all ask that question. I was on my way to your house when I saw you riding away and followed you."

"Followed me! That's despicable!"

Brandon chuckled in a menacing way. "Before you get too righteous, I should tell you that you've mismatched the buttons on your dress." He ignored her livid blush. "Ashford, I wish I could say I'm surprised, but I'm afraid 'shocked' is a better word. I had suspected there was something between the two of you, but I had no idea it had gone so far."

"It's not what—"

"This is your moment, man. Don't spoil it for her by sniveling. Stand up to me. Tell me I'm a cad. Call me out at sunrise."

Ashford looked as if he were about to be sick. "You're demanding a duel?"

Brandon shook his head in disgust. To Barbara he said, "Why weren't you honest with me? Why didn't you tell me you wanted Ashford instead?"

She glared at him as she fumbled with the tiny buttons on her bodice. "You would never have released me."

"No? Listen carefully. I release you."

At once her lower lip protruded in a pout. "Don't tease me, Brandon. I know you would fight to the death to keep me."

Ashford groped blindly for the table to support himself. "Death?"

"Tease you?" Brandon demanded. "Tease you? I hardly think this is a situation for something so light as teasing. Do you, Ashford?"

Ashford silently shook his head. All the color was gone from his face.

Brandon looked back at Barbara. "Why? Why didn't you tell me?"

"Because I'm afraid of you!" She rushed to Ashford as if for protection. He stumbled at the impact and stared at her as if he would like to push her away and deny it all. "I've always been afraid of you!" Barbara announced dramatically. "If you had known I loved another, who knows what you might have done!" She buried her face against Ashford's chest and managed a sob. "Oh, Ashford! Now I must never see you again!"

"Look, Brandon, I—"

"Buck up, man. You heard the lady. She prefers you to me." Brandon found he was almost enjoying this.

"Brandon, I never . . . that is, I . . ."

Barbara peered up at Brandon. "What will you do to us?" she asked tremulously.

"Not a thing. Each of you deserves the other. I can't think of a more fitting punishment. You're welcome to each other."

Her head shot up. "What! Aren't you going to call him out?"

"Not me. Ashford, you're getting exactly what you deserve."

"You don't mean that!" Barbara whirled to face Brandon. "You would never let me go!"

"Yes, I will. You know as well as I do that I was about to call it off the last time I saw you."

She threw the back of her hand to her forehead. "I'm going to faint!"

"You'd better catch her, Ashford. She's all yours now."

"The room is turning black!" Barbara called out. "Oh!"

Ashford wasn't quite as well-coordinated as Brandon, and she was almost to the floor before he broke her fall.

Brandon shook his head. "You'll have to work on that, Ashford. She does this quite often."

Barbara's eyes flew open, and she jumped to her feet, almost knocking Ashford down. "You can't break our engagement! I won't let you!"

"I'm afraid you have forfeited your say in the matter. Tell our friends whatever you please, but make it convincing to your parents because if your father calls me out, I'll tell him the truth."

"You'd never do that!"

"No? Try me." Brandon again gave them his chilling smile, followed by a formal nod. "Good day to you both. If our luck is good, we'll see little of each other in the future."

"I say, this is awfully decent of you," Ashford began.

Brandon stopped him with a glare. "Don't press your luck, Benchley." Turning on his heel, he left. By the time he reached his horse, the smile had reached his eyes.

Teresa brought her father a bowl of apples, but he waved her away. "Aren't you hungry, Papa? You haven't eaten since supper last night."

"No, I'm not." He scowled at the canvas and rubbed his eyes as if he were having trouble getting them to focus.

She put the apples on the table and chose one for herself. "I suppose Uncle Mario will be out soon." Her displeasure was evident in her tone.

"He's your uncle. Show him respect."

"He might as well be my ward, as often as he's out here! Katie sets his place at the table as often as she does yours."

"In my house there is always a place at the table for him." Salvatore made a few indecisive jabs at the canvas.

"Think of me, Papa. I have to stay up half the night to paint. Can't you ask him to come every other day? I'm getting very little sleep."

"Then go to bed. I, Salvatore, will be doing the painting. Am I not the master?"

Teresa chewed her apple as she studied him. All day he had made odd remarks like that, and she was beginning to get uneasy. "Are you feeling all right?"

"It's this heat. I can't breathe."

She took another bite and tilted her head to one side. "It's not as hot as it would be in Venice in July."

"Don't tell me if I'm hot or not! This studio is like an inferno!" His hand quivered slightly, and he drew a deep breath to steady it.

With a frown, Teresa went to him and put her hand to his cheek. "You have fever!"

"Nonsense. I never get sick."

"Maybe not, but you're sick now. Go to bed. When Uncle Mario comes, I'll send him away and finish up for you here."

"Finish up for me? Are you the teacher and I the pupil?" He glared at her unsteadily. "No one touches the canvas of Salvatore Verdi!"

"Papa?" She tried to take his arm, but he pushed her away.

She would have gone back to him, but Mario came through the door after the most perfunctory of knocks.

"Salvatore, Teresa, I have brought wine to celebrate the sale of one of my paintings." When he saw his brother's pale coloring, he stopped. "What is wrong here?"

"Help me, Uncle Mario. Papa is sick."

Mario took a step back. "Sick? With what?"

"How should I know? Help me get him to his room." Again she tried to take her father's arm, but this time he shoved her roughly.

Mario edged toward the door to leave, but Teresa caught his hand. "You have to help me. I can't do it alone." Going to the door that joined the studio to the house, she called out, "Hal? Hal! Come here."

Katie stuck her head around the door from the kitchen. "He's in the yard, Miss."

"Run and get him. Papa's sick."

Mario had no choice but to loop Salvatore's arm around his neck and help Teresa maneuver him the short distance to his bedroom.

"What can it be?" she asked in great concern as they eased Salvatore onto the bed. "It came on so quickly!"

Mario shook his head. "He had a fever like this once before, when he was a young man. We never knew what it was, exactly. Papa called it a brain fever."

When Hal came hurrying into the room, Teresa said, "Take the horse and ride for the doctor. Tell him my father is terribly ill and that he must come at once." Hal nodded and ran to do her bidding.

"Let's get him to bed," she said as Mario again started edging toward the door.

"The doctor can do that."

"Uncle Mario!"

"We don't know what he has. We might catch it from him!"

"Nonsense. We have to do what we can for him. Now, help me undress him."

Together they stripped Salvatore down to his trousers and Teresa turned her back as Mario finished getting him into a nightshirt. She was growing more and more worried because her father had stopped struggling and no longer seemed aware of them. When Mario eased him back on the pillow, Salvatore turned his head restlessly. His lips moved but no sounds came out.

"I've never seen anyone become sick so fast," she said in a low voice. "His skin feels as if he's on fire!"

"It's like the other time." Mario's eyes were wide, and he crossed himself hastily.

"What happened then? Was he sick long?"

"A week or two. I can't remember."

"What did the doctor do then?"

"The usual. Purgatives and bleeding. I have to go."

"He wouldn't leave you if you were sick!"

"He has you to take care of him, and the maid is here to help you."

"But if he tries to get out of bed, we can't stop him! He's too strong for us!" She glared at her uncle. "Why are you so afraid?"

"I hate illness! No, I can't stay!" He shrugged off her hand and backed out the door, his eyes wide with fright. "You don't know what you ask of me. I can't stay!"

"But . . ." She watched helplessly as her uncle turned and ran from the house. She had always known he was inordinately afraid of illness of any kind, but she had expected more from him under the circumstances. She turned back to her father. His eyes were barely open and glazed with fever, and his breath was coming in rasping gasps.

"We don't need Uncle Mario," she said in a shaky voice. "I'll take care of you, Papa." She wet a cloth from his water pitcher and sat beside him on the bed. When she touched the cool cloth to Salvatore's forehead, he yelled as if she had burned him and his flailing arms almost knocked her off the bed.

"Papa, don't!" She grabbed at his arms and tried

desperately to restrain him. Had this fever madness been expected by Mario? She held tightly to Salvatore's arm, and hoped she could prevent him from falling out of bed.

"What's going on here?" a deep voice said from behind her.

"Brandon!"

"Katie let me in. She said your father is sick." He hurried to his protégé's bedside and helped Teresa restrain him. "It's a good thing I stopped by on my way home from London. Your uncle was leaving with such haste, I became curious."

Teresa wiped Salvatore's face with a damp cloth as she defensively said, "Uncle Mario is afraid of illness. He always has been."

"I thought perhaps he was going for help. I'm appalled that he would leave you in this predicament!"

"I sent Hal for the doctor. I've never seen Papa like this! He has been acting strangely all day, but all at once he became delirious. What can be wrong with him?" The fear in Teresa's eyes blocked all of Brandon's thoughts of why he had come in the first place.

"I have no idea." As strong as Brandon was, he was struggling to hold Salvatore on the bed. "He has the strength of a madman!"

"Don't say that!" Her terrified eyes were on her father's face. She looked as though she thought her father might have gone crazy. He couldn't recall ever seeing anyone so frightened.

"I'm sorry. I'm sure that's not the problem. A doctor will be here soon, and he can tell us how to help your father."

"What if Hal can't find a doctor?"

"He's a sharp lad. He'll find one." Brandon wished he could hold Teresa in his arms and comfort her, but he couldn't release Salvatore. As they waited, Brandon offered words of encouragement to her, but nothing seemed to help.

Several minutes later, Katie crept into the room, and Brandon was relieved that he and Teresa were no longer alone. Conversation between them had stopped, but Brandon's desire to reach out to Teresa hadn't. Katie's presence removed the temptation. Brandon immediately put her to work holding Salvatore's thrashing legs. The maid looked as scared as Teresa, but she did as she was told.

After what seemed an eternity, Hal returned with the doctor from the nearest village. "I brought Dr. Chasen," he said as he took Katie's place at the foot of the bed. "I was afraid a London doctor wouldn't come."

"Probably wouldn't have," the doctor agreed. "Let me see the patient."

Teresa hastily got up and let the elderly doctor sit where she had been. He pushed open Salvatore's eyelid and looked at the fixed, glassy eye. "How long has he been like this?"

"About an hour. It started all at once," she answered.

The doctor pressed his ear to the man's heaving chest and listened intently.

"What is it, Doctor?" Brandon asked.

"Can't say yet. Does he have a rash?"

"No, sir," Teresa said.

The doctor unbuttoned the nightshirt and looked for himself. "No rash. Has he eaten any foul meat?"

"No, *sir!*" Katie said indignantly.

The doctor held Salvatore's head still and parted his lips, but his jaws were locked tight and he couldn't see into his throat. With the flat stick the doctor normally would have used to hold down a tongue, he pried Salvatore's teeth apart and peered down his throat. "Inflamed," he pronounced. He put a corner of the sheet between Salvatore's teeth to keep him from cracking one of them.

"Well?" Brandon demanded.

The doctor looked thoughtfully at his patient. "An interesting case. He shows some symptoms of lockjaw."

"Lockjaw!" Teresa gasped.

"But I believe what he has is brain fever. Cerebritis, to be exact."

Teresa's face was filled with fear as he looked to Brandon.

"Twist several sheets into ropes and restrain him with them," the doctor said to Hal. "I must bleed him at once."

"Is that necessary?" Teresa asked.

"It's of vital importance. If we don't relieve the stress on his brain tissues, he will lapse into a coma and die."

"Die?" she repeated numbly. Katie handed the doctor the sheets he had requested, and the doctor showed them how to wrap them around Salvatore so that he couldn't move.

"You may want to leave, miss," Dr. Chasen said as he took a knife from his bag.

"I won't leave him." Her eyes widened, however, as the doctor put Salvatore's foot over the washbasin and opened a vein in his ankle. Although she felt sick, she held her ground.

"I need ice," the doctor commanded.

"Hal, go down to Hawthorn and tell Mrs. Dennison to let you into the icehouse," Brandon said.

By the time the boy returned, the doctor had finished the bleeding and had put a bandage on Salvatore's ankle. Next he took a razor from his bag and began to examine Salvatore's head.

"What are you doing?" Teresa exclaimed.

"We must cool his brain, and the best way to do that is to shave his head. If you wish to remain in the room, don't cause any further commotion."

Teresa's lips tightened as she watched the doctor shave away her father's thick hair. "Papa has always worried about being bald. I'm glad he doesn't know what's happening now." When all of Salvatore's hair was on the floor, Dr. Chasen had Katie chip the block of ice into a waterproof bag along with some water and vinegar, and he packed it around Salvatore's skull.

"That should do it for now. I'll be back tomorrow to bleed him again. In the meantime, apply more cold packs just like this one whenever his head feels hot. He may have a few more convulsions this evening, but by tomorrow they should end. Then we'll start the purgative."

"Are you certain it's brain fever and not lockjaw?"

"Yes, the tetanic grin is absent and the back isn't bowing. I've seen cases where the entire rib cage has been suspended over the bed by the muscle spasm of lockjaw. No, it's brain fever."

Teresa escorted the doctor to the door, then came back to her father's bedside. "Uncle Mario said Papa has had this before," she said uncertainly, "but brain fever sounds so terrible."

"Dr. Chasen is a good doctor. He'll pull him through." Brandon tried to sound more positive than he felt. He wasn't so sure that bleeding and purgatives were the best thing to do to someone who was already so sick. "The convulsions have almost quit."

Teresa sent Hal and Katie back to their chores, and even though Brandon thought it would be improper for him to stay the night, as her father was in no condition to chaperone them, he didn't want to leave her. If Salvatore became worse, she would have only the two young servants to help her. Another look at her worried face affirmed his decision. "I'm going to stay and help you care for him."

Hope lit her eyes, but she said, "I could never ask you to do that. He may be like this for hours."

"Days would be more likely."

"Days!"

"One of our coachmen had brain fever a few years ago, and it was over a week before he showed any real signs of improvement."

"A week?" She stared down at her father's trembling form. "How can anyone survive being so sick for that long?"

Brandon shook his head. There was no need to worry her by telling her the coachmen had never been the same afterward. The world might be losing a great artist, even if Salvatore Verdi survived, but Teresa stood to lose much more. "It's the fever you have to worry about, as I understand it. The ice pack will help."

Together they worked to keep Salvatore's fever down and make him as comfortable as possible. As he had promised, Brandon stayed with her, going to Hawthorn only for a few hours at a time to sleep and to bathe. Because of the severity of Salvatore's illness and the emotional strain Teresa was suffering, Brandon had resolved to maintain a respectable distance from her and refrain from mentioning anything about his broken engagement to Barbara.

It was three days, not one, before the convulsions stopped; and even then, any significant movement or emotion from Salvatore triggered another round of spasms.

Finally, on the fifth day, Dr. Chasen declared the crisis was over and gave them permission to remove the last of the restraints. Not only was Teresa physically exhausted, but she felt emotionally drained as well. After the doctor was gone and Salvatore was asleep, Teresa suggested they step out into the garden for a breath of air. Brandon was glad that Salvatore was recovering, but regretted that he no longer had a valid excuse to spend time with Teresa. "I couldn't have made it through this week without you," Teresa said. "I can never thank you enough for what you've done."

"There's no need to thank me. If you need me again, send Hal to fetch me."

Brandon stroked a tendril of her hair back from her face. "You look so tired."

"I am."

"I'll stay until you get some sleep."

She shook her head. "I'll ask Katie to sit with him. She and Hal have been wonderful through all this.

Besides, you've hardly been to Hawthorn long enough to sleep and change clothes for days as it is. We can handle him now, unless he relapses." Avoiding his eyes, she said, "I'm sure you're looking forward to getting back to your own pursuits."

"I do have things to attend to, but I'll miss seeing you so often."

Without speaking, Teresa turned from him and headed down the path toward the stream. Large tears welled in her eyes and flowed down her cheeks, but she kept her head turned so Brandon couldn't see them.

Why was she walking away? Did she not want to know that he would miss being with her? Brandon followed her to the bank of the stream, where she stopped beneath a giant willow. Feeling frustrated that he didn't understand her, he said, "I guess I should leave so you can get some rest."

"I suppose."

When she still didn't turn, he pulled her around to face him and was surprised to see her tears. "You're crying?"

She tried to pull away. "Don't look at me. I feel so foolish."

"All women cry."

"*I* don't. At least not in front of anyone." She turned away again.

Brandon pulled her back into his arms and held her close. After a moment's hesitation she put her arms around him and returned his embrace. "Why are you crying?" he asked softly.

"Because you're so good to me." She couldn't admit the love she felt for him, nor the fantasy she had lived during the days of Salvatore's illness. It was as though they had been a married couple during those days, striving to combat a single enemy and relying on each other's strengths. She had seen Brandon tired and disheveled, but he had consistently shown only patience with Salvatore. Brandon had been unfailingly gentle even when he was helping Teresa restrain her father. "I have no right to be with you like this," she added.

"Teresa, the day I came here and found your father so sick, I had come to tell you something."

"About your wedding?" She tried to pull away, but he held her firmly.

"No, my engagement to Lady Barbara has been broken."

"It has? Why?" She jerked up her head to look at him.

He was too much a gentleman to give Teresa the details of finding Barbara and Ashford together. By now Barbara must have told her friends and family that the wedding was off. He wondered what reason she had given. "Why it happened doesn't matter."

She pulled back and turned away from him. Since he wouldn't tell her the reason, it must not have been because he preferred her to Barbara. "She must be very sad." Teresa knew she would be, if Brandon had broken an engagement to her.

"She says she is, but I rather doubt it," he said sharply. The reminder of Barbara's blatant infidelity left a bitter taste in his mouth, and triggered his own guilt that he had fallen in love with Teresa when he was promised to someone else. "Teresa . . ." he began.

"Yes?" She turned back toward him and held her hands clasped tightly together, as if she were suddenly nervous.

He noticed the pallor of her skin and the lines of exhaustion on her forehead. This wasn't the proper time to speak to her of love. "Never mind. You're too tired to stand here talking. Go inside and rest while your father is asleep."

"But . . ."

"Don't argue," he admonished gently. "I can see you're exhausted. I'll come back tomorrow to look in on him." She pretended to be strong, but he knew she must surely be as delicate as any lady, and he felt like a cad for keeping her from her rest. That she had not collapsed from worry and fatigue was a miracle. Barbara could scarcely weather a day's shopping, and Teresa had spent five days with little rest. Protectiveness surged in him. "Now that your father is out of danger, I'll send up a woman to nurse him so you can recover from your own ordeal."

"Thank you." She stared at him as if she wasn't sure she was hearing him correctly.

He reached out and touched her cheek in a tender caress, then hurried away before he gave in to the impulse to kiss her.

11

For the next few days Teresa divided her time between her father and the studio. The nurse Brandon had sent was capable and strong. Teresa knew she could trust the woman to keep Salvatore out of the studio and in bed.

Brandon came up often, and although he frequently looked as if he were about to say something of importance, he always stopped himself. Teresa was beginning to feel quite nervous about his curious behavior. At first she had thought he was going to declare tender feelings for her, but when he didn't, she started to worry that he might be thinking something entirely different. With Salvatore sick, the painting had stopped, and as their benefactor, Brandon might be considering an end to his patronage. After all, a painter who produced nothing was of little use. At one point she peevishly thought that they weren't even picturesque anymore, with her father's short-cropped hair and his body so gaunt from illness.

Adding to her concern that Brandon might be trying to find a tactful way to ask them to leave, Teresa received another letter from the Valores asking her to intercede with her father in the matter of the roof. According to the letter, half the tiles on the palazzo's roof were broken and rain poured in with each storm. One of their tenants had already moved and others were threatening to leave if something were not done immediately. The only solution seemed to be in the generous sum Brandon had offered her father for a painting of a nude. She might be able to convince her father this time, but she knew he wouldn't be able to paint for weeks, if even then. He was still so weak he could hardly walk.

The only option left was for her to do the painting. But that presented a problem. Had her father agreed to do the work, he would have hired a model from London or one of the nearby villages to pose for him, but Teresa couldn't possibly hire one. It would give away their secret for the model to see her doing the painting.

She sat at her dresser pondering this dilemma. She had never painted or even drawn a nude. When her father or grandfather or uncle had hired a woman to pose, Teresa had been barred from the studio because they thought the sight of a naked woman would be offensive to her sensibilities. Teresa had always thought this was ridiculous—her sensibilities never came into question at any other time—but she had humored them. Now she was sorry. If she had ever seen the proper skin tones and proportions, she could do a nude from memory.

As she gazed at her reflection in the mirror, an astounding notion came to her. She did have a model! She stood and critically surveyed her body. Her waist was slender and supple, her breasts and hips full. If she changed the color of her eyes and hair, couldn't she paint her own reflection from a mirror? For a moment she was confounded by her own daring. What if Brandon recognized her? But he couldn't, of course, because he would never see her undressed, and therefore would never know it was her body in the picture. As for her features, she could paint the nude as a harem girl with a veil so that only the eyes—blue ones—would show.

That night after supper, she saw Salvatore to bed and had Hal carry the large mirror from the parlor into the studio. He seemed curious when she had him hang it low on the wall, but he asked no questions. Nor did he ask why she wanted her fainting couch moved from the parlor to the studio. Hal was becoming accustomed to odd requests from his employers and put it all down to artistic temperament.

When Hal and Katie and the nurse went up to their attic rooms for the night, Teresa went to the studio. For a moment she again considered the advisability of what she was about to do, then jockeyed the day recliner into position in front of the mirror. Carefully she closed the shutters so that not even a crack of light would show, then locked both the outside door and the one between the studio and the rest of the house.

In view of what she was about to do, Teresa felt shy. The studio had never seemed so large and public before. Then she thought of her home in Venice and how damp and poor they would all be if Brandon sent them packing, and she began to unbutton her dress.

Although the night was warm and the studio a bit stuffy with all the windows covered, she shivered as she draped her dress over a chair. Her petticoat, bloomers, and chemise soon followed it. Lifting her arms, she took the pins from her hair and let it tumble down her back. Only then did she risk a glance in the mirror. With the studio about her instead of her bedroom, she seemed naked indeed. She knew women who swore they wore a loose chemise even when they bathed so as never to be totally undressed, yet here she stood as bare as the day she was born. But then she glanced at the painting of Diana, who wore only a sheer strip of gauze. If a Roman goddess could do it, so could she.

Teresa took one of the silk scarves she used for her still lifes and pinned it so that her nose and lower face were hidden. Then she draped a larger cloth over the couch and reclined upon it.

She soon found it wasn't as easy to arrange a model as she had expected. Her elbows and feet seemed to be at odds, and she discovered the human body wasn't

graceful in all its attitudes. Finally she lay on her side,
her opposite knee bent and her feet tucked slightly
behind her. Her eyes narrowed as the artist in her
finally overrode the woman. With a background of a
sheik's tent and voluminous cushions beneath her, this
pose would do nicely. She pulled a strand of hair over
her shoulder and let it curl over her breast so that one
of her nipples could be only glimpsed. Auburn—she
would paint her hair auburn.

Quickly she sketched the composition. It worked on
paper, she was glad to see. She went to a new canvas
and started blocking in the drawing. To paint with no
clothes on felt strange, but it was also rather exciting.
Teresa wondered if she were becoming a hoyden.

Because she didn't dare take too long on this picture
and risk getting caught in nothing but her imagination,
she worked all night. As dawn softened the night outside, she put the wet canvas on the top drying rack,
then slipped into her clothes. She was almost too tired
to get to her room and into a nightgown, but she made
it. She smiled wryly as she crawled into bed, fully covered from chin to ankle. Why should she sleep in a hot
gown, when she had spent the night painting her nu-
dity for Brandon? She hadn't thought of it like that
before, and she felt a stab of misgiving. Even married
women undressed in another room from their husbands, or in the dark, and here she was rendering such
a provocative picture for a man she wasn't even promised to. She could well imagine what Catherina would
say about that, not to mention her father. However,
necessity was a powerful motivation, and Salvatore had
had ample opportunity to paint the nude himself. She
would just have to hope he never discovered the painting. In no time she was asleep.

For days Salvatore hid his infirmity from Teresa. At
first he had thought the tremors were lingering traces
of the convulsions of the brain fever. When he had had
the disease as a youth, he had suffered similar side

effects, though they were of short duration. But this time when his strength returned and the trembling of his fingers remained, Salvatore began to be afraid.

He tried everything—long walks in the sunshine, healthy food, plenty of rest. He built up the strength in his fingers by squeezing a rubber ball every day, for hours on end. His grip became stronger than ever, but the day he tested the results by holding a liner brush to the canvas, its point trembled as if he were palsied with age. Even his father's hands had been steadier on his deathbed than Salvatore's were now. He threw the brush away from him and stalked out of the studio.

Gradually Teresa realized something was wrong. For weeks Salvatore had not liked for her to be around when he was sketching or painting, but since his illness, he no longer let her so much as see what he had done.

"Papa, how can I work on the canvases if you won't let me see them?" she finally demanded in exasperation.

"Why should you work on them?" he countered. "I am Salvatore Verdi. I work alone."

Teresa frowned. There were dozens of oddities about him these days. Small things, such as his calling her by her mother's name and occasionally referring to Antonio as if he were still alive. She had hoped this vagueness would disappear, but if anything, it had become more pronounced with time. "Don't you remember? I always work on your canvases."

He looked blank, then nodded. "Of course you do. How else will you learn from me? Papa and I have also worked together like that." He squeezed the rubber ball in quick movement, then flexed his hand as if to see if the strength were there.

Teresa had almost finished the nude, which she now kept hidden under her bed. The long nights of work, however, had made her irritable, and she was in no mood for her father's capricious behavior. "Show me your canvas, Papa. Are you working on the one of the hunting dogs?" She went to the racks and began searching for it. "Where is it? I can't seem to find it."

"I painted over it," he said calmly as he again studied his hand.

"You what? But it was almost finished!"

"I decided I didn't like the subject." He wasn't about to tell her he had inadvertently ruined it in an effort to work on it.

"You painted it out?" she repeated. "Surely you didn't!"

"Yes, I did. Don't speak to me so sharply. A lady never raises her voice. Your mother never does."

Teresa saw a canvas on the floor that was the exact size of the one he had been working on. When she picked it up and held it in the light, she saw the pattern of brush marks beneath the white surface. "You did!"

He gazed at her absently and began squeezing the rubber ball again.

Teresa rubbed her forehead where a dull headache was beginning. "Thank goodness Lord Kincaid never saw it. He need not ever know what happened."

"No artist shows every canvas," he said in his defense. "Some are merely for practice, and I viewed that one as such. So I painted it out to use the canvas again."

"Next time, consult me," she said testily. "I could have finished the canvas in a couple of days and sent it to York."

"Who?"

"Papa, stop playing with that ball and listen to me." She put a canvas of a Venetian carnival scene on the easel. "Work on this one. Lord Kincaid says he has a buyer in mind."

"Tomorrow, perhaps."

"No, today!"

He looked as if he were about to reprimand her, but thought better of it. "Very well. Today. Now, run along, Eva Maria. You know I don't like for anyone to watch me at work."

"I'm Teresa, Papa."

"Yes. Yes, of course you are. Now, run along *cara mia*."

Teresa sighed and did as she was told. As much as she resented being banished from the studio, it was worth it if her father would start working again.

Salvatore waited until Teresa was gone, then began methodically to measure out his powders. At times she looked so much like her mother that he had trouble telling them apart, and this seemed to disturb Teresa. His Eva Maria was a remarkably beautiful woman. She always had been. As Salvatore studied the canvas, he thought that perhaps he would paint Eva Maria as an "Isabella" behind the figures of the "Arlecchino" and his constant companion, "Tartaglia." He might even paint Teresa in a "Colombina" costume, though children rarely wore the costumes of the adults. Teresa was growing up. She would be a young lady soon.

Salvatore shook his head. What was he thinking of? Teresa was already a grown woman. For a moment he had forgotten

He mixed shades of red and blue for the Arlecchino's multicolored traditional costume, and black for his grinning leather mask. What a shame, Salvatore thought, that the great Venice carnivals were no more. He could remember hearing his father telling him about them, though Salvatore, of course, had been born after they had been ended by Napoleon's invasion of Venice just before the turn of the century. Through his father's vivid descriptions and stories, the carnivals were as much a part of his memories as if he had actually seen them for himself. Brighella, the comic valet; Pantalone, the finicky old man; Isabella, the most beautiful of women. He remembered his father's old costume of Pulcinella with the huge nose, and that of his mother with its hawk-beaked mask and trailing black robes. For six months of every year the carnival had ruled Venice with its constant gaiety and costumes that had been handed down for generations, and the calls of *"Buon giorno, Signor Maschera,"*—Good day, Mr. Mask—for even good friends pretended not to recognize each other behind their masks. Then when the carnival ended in

Lent, all of Venice's population moved inland to cooler summer homes near Padua or Treviso until October, when the carnival resumed again.

"Ah," Salvatore said to himself, "those were days to be alive."

"Salvatore? How are you?"

Salvatore turned sharply to see Mario standing just behind him. "How did you get in!" he demanded. "How long have you been there?"

"I thought you heard me enter. You said something about the carnival in Venice." Mario gave his brother a peculiar look.

Salvatore felt a cold sweat bead on his brow. Had he been vocalizing his reminiscences? What had the brain fever done to him? "I was but thinking aloud. I do that sometimes. Everyone does."

"Of course, of course." Mario went to the carnival scene. "An Arlecchino and a Tartaglia. What memories this brings back! It's the Piazza San Marco, isn't it?"

"It will be in time. I've barely started it." Salvatore wondered how he could get rid of Mario without directly telling him to leave. Teresa had told her father that Mario had run away when she needed his help. Family disloyalty could never be tolerated. And then there was the tremor of his hand. Mario would be certain to see it.

"I miss Venice. But who would not? To be a Venetian is to be ruined for anywhere else."

"Perhaps you should go back there. It would be good for one of us to look after the palazzo."

"The Valores will care for it as they always have. My work is here."

Salvatore glanced at him quickly. "Here? Oh, you mean in London."

"Naturally." Mario pulled up a chair and straddled it. "Go ahead and paint. I won't disturb you."

Slowly Salvatore picked up his brush. Mario had sounded exactly like their father when he said that. If Antonio were here, Salvatore knew his hand wouldn't tremble. "Have you seen Papa today?"

"What?"

"Nothing." He had almost made a mistake that time. His father was dead and had been for a long time. He knew that. He dabbed the brush in the paint and started to put it to the canvas. The more he tried to steady his hand, the more it trembled.

"What's wrong?" Mario asked.

"How can I paint with you staring at me like that?" Salvatore glared at his brother. "Why are you in here anyway? I didn't give you permission to come in here!"

"Since when does one brother need permission to visit another?"

"Is this not my house? Is this not my studio? First I must chase out Teresa, and now it's you!"

"Chase me out!" Mario's volatile temper flared. "No one chases out Mario Verdi!"

"I allow no one to come in here! How did you get in?" Cobwebs were thickening in his mind and the resultant fright made him more angry than Mario's presence. He couldn't let anyone see the tremor in his hands! "You are here to spy on me!"

"How dare you talk to me like that? What do I care what you paint!" Mario jumped up guiltily. How had Salvatore known his reason for coming today?

"Get out! Get out of my studio!"

"I merely came to see if you were recovering," Mario said in a huff. "I had hoped time had mended our differences, but I see you are as bad-tempered as ever!"

Salvatore stepped menacingly toward him. There was something in the back of his mind, some long-forgotten grievance. As it surfaced, he said, "You have always wanted whatever was mine. Even Eva Maria! You tried to turn her against me!"

"What? What are you saying?"

"You said she flirted with you. Not my Eva Maria, my jewel. She told me you tried to force your attentions on her."

"Why are we fighting about that again?" Mario blustered. "She's been dead more than twenty years."

With a roar of pain, Salvatore rushed at him and grabbed him about the neck. Mario struggled to free himself from the iron grip. With a wrenching twist he jerked free and backed away as he rubbed his neck. "You'll be sorry you did that, Salvatore! You'll be sorry!"

"Get out of my studio!" he shouted.

Mario turned and ran out the door, nearly colliding with Teresa.

"Papa?" she said fearfully. "What has happened?"

"Nothing!" He turned back to the canvas and drew steadying breaths. What had come over him? That incident with Mario and Eva Maria had happened so long ago—two years before Teresa was born. Although he had never been able to learn the whole truth of what had happened, surely after this long, it didn't matter! Why, there were days, he told himself, when he couldn't recall the color of Eva Marie's eyes, or how her voice had sounded. Other days it was as if she were in the next room. "It was nothing," he repeated shakily.

Teresa closed the door and looked back at him. She was becoming terribly concerned about her father. "Were you painting?"

"No."

She went to the canvas and saw he hadn't put so much as a brush stroke to it since she had been gone. But he had mixed a great deal of paint. "Papa, tell me what's wrong. I can't help you unless you tell me."

For a minute she thought Salvatore would refuse; then his broad shoulders slumped, and he looked ten years older. Silently he held out his hands.

Teresa stared at them. The tremor was clearly visible to her. Even a tremor much less severe than this would be enough to hamper painting. Taking his hands lovingly in her own, she said, "Is it because you argued with Uncle Mario?"

"No. No, it has been this way since my illness."

"Oh, Papa!" Tears pooled in her eyes. "Why didn't you tell me?"

"What could you do? What could anyone do? But I

couldn't let Mario see. He might tell someone, and everyone would soon know Salvatore Verdi can no longer paint."

"In time it will go away. Uncle Mario said you were sick with brain fever before, and you had no lasting effects."

"I was young then and in my prime. Now I'm old."

"No, you're not. Why, Grandpapa didn't reach his peak until he was older than you are. Youth doesn't aid an artist."

"Papa's hands were as steady as a boy's. No, I'm finished as a painter."

"Don't say that!" Teresa gripped his hands tightly as if she could give him some of her health. "This is only temporary. You know how sick you were! Why, you've barely begun to heal."

"Do you think so?" he asked with a glimmer of hope.

"I know so." She managed a confident smile. She had no idea at all if his hands would ever be steady again. "In the meantime, we must keep anyone from knowing. Especially Lord Kincaid."

"Yes. Yes, that's necessary. But how can we do that? He will expect pictures, and when I can't produce any . . ."

"I can paint them."

"You? But you never saw a carnival!"

"No, but I've heard Grandpapa talk about them just as you have, and I've seen pictures of them all my life. You will sit with me and describe the scene exactly as you see it. I will be your hands."

"It will never work. A woman as a master artist? Impossible."

She knew his vagueness was returning. Quickly she asked, "Do you have a better idea, Papa?"

"No."

"Then we will try it. After all, it will only be for a short time."

He met her eyes and said, "You know what this means, Teresa? If you are my hands, you can never leave me."

She faltered, but said, "I don't want to leave you,

Papa. I will be your hands for as long as you need me."
She knew she had relieved a deep worry when he
relaxed.

"Good. I have worried about that more than you will
ever know. Of course, you've never had a serious suitor,
but if you did, how could I give my permission for you
to marry? Without you to finish my paintings, there
would be no Salvatore Verdi."

His statement was even truer now than it had ever
been. Even if she went no further than Hawthorn, her
marriage would put an end to her father's painting.
She couldn't leave her husband's bed and paint all night
here in the studio and creep back at dawn smelling of
paint and turpentine. Nor could she paint pictures for
herself. Not unless she could be content with an endless
succession of flowers and fruit. Her marriage would
mean the end to her art, and painting had always been
the most important thing in her life. "Surely if a man
loved me he would allow me to paint."

Salvatore patted her cheek fondly. "Yes, he would.
Flowers and still lifes and perhaps a landscape. Would
that be enough for you?"

She thought of the inn-yard scene and the nude
and the ruins of Bridestake with its ghostly knights.
"No. It would never be enough."

"And your marriage would also mean the end of my
career. Together we can achieve greatness. Alone we
are nothing."

"I would always take care of you. You would be
welcome in my home."

"I have a home. When you are an artist, you have to
paint. It's a grand obsession."

"I know," she said softly.

"Why are we so sad?" he asked. "We are borrowing
trouble. No one has asked for your hand."

"No," Teresa agreed quietly.

"There! We are unhappy for nothing. Put on your
smock and I will describe the carnival as I see it in my
mind."

Reluctantly she obeyed. Brandon hadn't given her any reason to hope he might ask for her hand. If anything, the opposite was true. Knowing she couldn't marry him, however, triggered the rebellion in her spirit. More so than ever, she wanted to be his wife. "Why do I always want what I can't have?" she asked her father as she tied the smock behind her.

"It's a woman's perverseness. Your mother was the same way, may she rest in peace."

"Did she want to paint too?"

Salvatore paused, then said, "Perhaps. She never told me."

Teresa stood at the canvas and took up the brush. Salvatore lifted his hand to point out the composition as he had envisioned it. Suddenly the vagueness was back in his eyes. "What will we tell Lord Kincaid?"

"We will tell him nothing. You've never let people into your studio when you're working."

"But the shows! Someone will notice my hands and comment on them."

"I'll tell him that you have become a recluse for art's sake. It's not so far from the truth. You were almost a recluse in Venice, and he will remember that."

"Yes. Yes, tell him that. And if he comes to the cottage, you must see him alone. He has sharp eyes. He would notice my hands."

Teresa looked at her father pityingly. She was now the protector, and he the one to be sheltered. "Don't worry, Papa. When I was a child you took care of me, and now I will take care of you."

"But remember, *cara mia,* it's only temporary," he said sternly. "When my hands are steady again I will be the master once more."

"Yes, Papa," she said gently. "It's only for a while."

Salvatore drew up a chair and resumed his discussion of the carnivals as his father had described them. Teresa listened to the familiar stories as she put the bright colors on the canvas, her hand sure, her movements precise.

12

After long days of deliberation, Brandon decided the time was near for him to begin his official courtship of Teresa. Barbara had spread it about London that she had been the one to call off their marriage—a woman's prerogative, she had said. Brandon had no idea what reason she had given, nor did he care. His only interest at this point was in protecting Teresa from possible gossip by waiting a decent interval before paying her suit. If he had done so immediately after the breakup with Barbara, some would surely have concluded that Teresa was the cause. The waiting was the hard part.

The cottage up the green seemed to draw him like a lodestone. From Hawthorn's conservatory he could see the lights from the cottage at night, and during the day he caught occasional flashes of the rose or yellow or blue-hued skirts that Teresa liked to wear. Of late the conservatory had become his favorite room. His social position rather reminded him of that of a widow forced to mourn a husband she hadn't loved. His love for Barbara had been so pale compared with his feelings for Teresa, it didn't even seem to be the same emotion.

He wondered how to approach marriage to Teresa. With Barbara he had first spoken to Lord Weatherly and obtained his permission to court Barbara. By the time he actually proposed, it was a foregone conclusion that she would accept and that her parents wholeheartedly approved of the match. With Teresa, he was sure of nothing.

He had often visited the cottage since Salvatore's recovery, and each time he was hard-pressed not to sweep Teresa away despite her father's need and precarious health. When he was there, Brandon found he could scarcely speak to her without wanting to blurt out his love as if he were the greenest of youths. A proposal of marriage required diplomacy, tact. A man couldn't babble out his feelings as if he were a schoolboy. Lately, he was spacing his visits farther apart in an effort to cool his ardor, but it wasn't working.

Teresa, on the other hand, had seemed quite reserved toward him, especially in view of the hours they had spent together while nursing Salvatore out of danger. Brandon had expected her to be more open, not the opposite. Was she trying to dissuade him from asking for her hand? Whatever reason Barbara had given for their estrangement, it would have certainly put her in the best lights; perhaps Teresa had heard something derogatory from Colin, for his brother seemed to be at the cottage every time Brandon asked for him.

Brandon's eyes narrowed. Now that he thought about it, he hadn't seen Colin for several hours. He went into the writing room, where Fitch was polishing the silver inkstand. "Have you seen Colin this morning?"

"Yes, Lord Kincaid. He rode up the green just after lunch was cleared."

With a frown Brandon said, "Thank you." So he was back at the cottage, was he? He went to the stable and had the groom saddle his horse. As if he were going for a casual ride, Brandon loped across the green and circled into the woods from the far side.

At the cottage, Teresa's eyes followed the rider as she listened to Colin's witty tale of a party he had attended the evening before. "Where do you suppose he's going?" she asked when Colin was finished.

"Who?" Colin followed her gaze to see Brandon enter the bridle path that led through the woods. "I suppose he's out for a ride." He glanced at her. "Have you seen him lately?"

"Not for a couple of days. I guess he grew tired of coming here, since he was here so often when Papa was sick."

"I doubt that. Teresa, I know it's none of my business, but hasn't he spoken for you yet?"

"Of course not. I don't think he cares for me at all."

"That's not what I hear in London."

"What do you mean?"

"At the party last night, the gossip was that Barbara had called off the wedding because she had found him with someone else."

"What!"

Colin looked at her in surprise. "You mean it wasn't you? I thought . . ."

"How can you be my friend and think that?" Teresa was all the more shocked because in her fantasies, she and Brandon were lovers and she knew she would go to him if he gave her even the slightest encouragement. "Did Brandon say he was with me?"

"No, no. He wasn't at the party at all. This was the gossip that's going around. Your name wasn't mentioned, but I assumed it could be no one else."

Teresa's eyes flashed. So he had another woman, did he? After calling on her and helping her nurse her father and being so nice to her? He must be trying to add her to his stable of conquests! "I can promise you, it certainly wasn't me! It must have been some fast woman he knows in London."

Colin shook his head. "Brandon doesn't associate with women like that."

"Then he must have a mistress."

"Teresa!"

"Don't look so shocked. It happens." She felt short of breath, as if she had been punched in the stomach. "In Venice they are quite common and almost respectable. Almost."

"This isn't Venice, it's England. I'm surprised to hear you suggest such a thing."

"Oh, for goodness' sake, Colin. Don't act so prudish. You'll lose your hard-earned reputation as a rake. Someone might even think you're becoming respectable." She tapped the toe of her foot angrily. Of all the things she had expected from Brandon, she had never dreamed he was seeing another woman. A fiancée, a mistress—and herself! The man must know no bounds! And all the time she had thought he was such a gentleman. She wondered what Barbara had seen them doing. "They had better not dare link *my* name in his sordid affair!"

"No, no. As I said, you were never mentioned. I'm sure no one would ever consider that—" He caught Teresa's furious glare and bit off his words. "I didn't mean it that way."

"I'm sure I don't know what you mean," she said haughtily.

"Come now, Teresa. Don't quarrel with me. We're friends."

"Some friend, to tell me such a thing! And to believe I might have been involved!"

"I'm sure there was a misunderstanding. You know how gossip is. There might not be a kernel of truth in the version I heard."

"I find it unlikely that there isn't some truth there. Especially since he told me himself that the wedding was off."

"Yes, he told me that the day after it happened, but not what caused them to call it off. I'll ask him."

"You'll do no such thing." Then she added, "But if he should offer a reason, and if you happen this way, you might mention it in passing."

"Of course." He smiled at her and she smiled back.

Brandon rode out of the woods nearest the cottage in time to see them smiling at each other. The sight brought a chill to him. Teresa might prefer Colin. Certainly Colin was handsome, and only a couple of years older than she was. He had no title, but he was a wealthy man from the inheritance of an aunt's estate. He would be a fine catch for a woman who had neither land nor title of her own.

As he rode nearer, Teresa gave him a frosty look and turned and walked away. Colin waved as he followed Teresa down the woodland path. Brandon's worries increased. Colin might not have any scruples about wooing Teresa for his own. Hadn't he told Brandon over and over that anything was fair in the winning of love?

Brandon knew he couldn't afford to wait any longer. He tied his horse at the gate and went in search of Salvatore. He found the man seated on a marble bench beside the stream, gazing at one of the peacocks that had wandered up from Hawthorn's lawns.

"Good day, Signor Verdi," Brandon said almost brusquely. "It's a nice day."

"*Si*. Nice, but hot."

"I expected you to be in your studio on such a sunny day. Do you have any new canvases for me?" He wondered where Colin and Teresa had been going, and why she had given him such a cold look. Was she warning him away as a suitor?

"I have nothing to show you today. Perhaps next week. My illness . . ." Salvatore shrugged stoically. "My concentration returns but slowly."

"Yes, I understand." How could Colin be so crass as to court Teresa when he knew Brandon wanted her? He wished Colin were still a boy so he could thrash him for his impertinence. But what if Teresa preferred Colin? No, she couldn't. Not and have kissed him the way she had on the cliff in Scotland. "Actually I came to talk to you on a different matter."

"Oh?"

"As you may have heard, my engagement to Lady Barbara Weatherly has been broken."

"I've heard a mention of that."

"Hawthorn is a fine estate and my family is old and of good lineage." Salvatore continued to gaze at the peacock as if he were only half-listening. Brandon had found this speech much easier to deliver to Lord Weatherly. "Are you listening, Signor Verdi?"

"Yes, yes. You're speaking of your lineage. Have you ever noticed the sheen on a peacock's neck? It's a difficult color to reproduce. Difficult indeed."

Brandon impatiently glanced toward the bird. "I suppose it would be."

"I've seen some butterflies that same color," Salvatore mused. "Nothing else."

"Yes. Now, as I was saying, I have a generous income from my properties. You could say I'm quite wealthy."

Salvator wagged his finger in disapproval. " 'Pride goeth before a fall,' young man. Remember that."

"Signor Verdi, I'm trying to ask for your daughter's hand in marriage," he said in exasperation.

That got Salvatore's full attention. "What!"

Brandon straightened and drew a steadying breath. "I want your permission to call on your daughter with the intention of a possible marriage."

"Teresa? You want to marry Teresa?"

"Yes, sir. That's right. If she'll have me."

"You would take away my Teresa, my jewel?"

"I guess I spoke too abruptly, but this has been on my mind so much of late that I thought you must somehow know."

"Have you spoken to her about this?" Salvatore trembled with emotion and Brandon noticed his hand quiver.

"No, I haven't told her how I feel. I thought I should discuss it with you first." Brandon smiled. He knew Salvatore must be shaken with relief that his daughter was to be Lady Kincaid, a viscountess.

"Good! You must not breathe a word of this to her."

"What?" Brandon stared at him in confusion. "Are you saying you would not approve our marriage?" He had expected to have to win over Teresa, not her father. He thought all fathers were pleased to see their daughters sealed into good matches.

"Approve? I forbid it!" Salvatore jumped to his feet and glared at his benefactor.

"Is it her age? Surely she is old enough."

"*Si*. Old enough and then some."

"It can't be that you hope for a better match for her. In all due respect, she has no title, no fortune."

"She is the daughter of Salvatore Verdi!"

"I know, but that is hardly coin of the realm. I know you're a master painter, but . . ."

"A master," Salvatore repeated as if the words were painful. "Yes."

"You need not give me your answer at once. Think it over and I'm sure you'll—"

"I will not! No! My daughter will never wed!"

Brandon was appalled. "Never?"

"Never! She has told me so. For you to press your suit upon her would cause her much grief. No! You must never approach her with this idea."

"But, Signor Verdi, all women marry."

"Not my Teresa!"

"I can understand your wanting to keep her near you, but she would only be as far away as my house yonder. A few minutes' walk would have you by her side. She could visit you daily."

"No."

Brandon tried another tack. "You've been gravely ill, *signore*."

Salvatore gave him a guarded look. "I can still paint. I am still a master."

"Yes, yes, I don't doubt that, but what if you fall ill again? What if, God forbid, you die? Teresa should have a life and a family of her own."

"No!" Salvatore's eyes widened as if he had never considered the prospect that he might die.

"At least give me your permission to ask her!"

"I forbid it." Salvatore glared at his patron as if he wished he could tear him in two. "If you or anyone else tries to marry Teresa, we will leave here and go where you will never find us!"

Brandon stiffened. "I had not expected this from you."

"It's not just me," Salvatore said in a calmer tone. "It's Teresa as well. She has said she will never leave me."

"All daughters say that, I should imagine, at some time or another."

"She said it only a few days ago. And she meant it. Teresa knows she will never marry, and it is her choice."

A muscle tightened in Brandon's jaw. "I would have her tell me that herself."

"As her father, I forbid it. Surely a father's wishes are respected in England."

"Yes, of course. But most fathers are more considerate of the happiness and welfare of their daughters."

"How dare you suggest that I don't know what is best for my own daughter! I know my Teresa, and I know where she will be most happy. It is by my side, where she belongs. As for my dying, I would prefer for her to marry a Venetian, and she knows that. In Venice we are very proud. We keep to our own kind."

"I don't know how to reply to that."

"You are upset because I have refused you something, and you have likely not been refused many things in your life."

"Then may I assume no one else has spoken for her and been accepted?" Brandon asked stiffly.

"As I said, Teresa will marry no one. If you respect her wishes, you will never broach this subject again. Especially not to her." Salvatore turned and walked away toward his cottage.

Brandon could only stare after him. His suit had been rejected as firmly as if he were a beggar and Teresa a queen! None of this made any sense. Why would Teresa tell her father that she had no interest in ever marrying? He knew quite well that she was a passionate woman, and he had seen her speak kindly to the children of his servants, so it wasn't that she was lacking a woman's sensibilities. As he went back to his horse, Brandon wished he could ignore Salvatore's ad-

monitions, but he was an honorable man and couldn't
do so in good conscience.

Teresa stepped back to study the painting of the
nude harem girl. Although the body and shape of the
face and texture of the hair were hers, the auburn
tresses and blue eyes, along with the veil, made the
likeness to her unremarkable. No one would ever guess
she had modeled for it. The rich velvets of the sultan's
pillows and the heavy brocade draperies had been an inspiration, lending the painting the exotic appearance it
needed to further distract the viewer from any connec-
tion with her.

She signed her father's name to the canvas and cleaned
her brushes. At last the late nights were over and she
could go to bed at a decent hour. By the time she
painted most of the day under Salvatore's strict supervision, she was too tired to want to paint half the night.

Again she studied the canvas. Was it true enough to
Salvatore's style to fool Brandon's discerning eye? Did
that drapery flare exactly the way he would have painted
it? Was that fringe on the pillows in her style or his? She
shook her head in resignation. This was the best she
could do, and it was a fine painting. She felt sure that
Brandon would assume any minor discrepancies were
due to Salvatore's recent illness.

She returned the painting to its place at the top of
the rack and stretched her aching muscles. Bed would
feel good after the long hours she had put in that day.
She turned down the knob on the gaslight and left the
studio in darkness.

In her bedroom Teresa undressed as quietly as possible. Since his illness, Salvatore had become a light sleeper,
and she had no excuse for being up at that hour. Only
the distance between his bedroom and the studio had
prevented him from finding her painting the nude.

Would Brandon like it? She allowed herself to think
about him as she slipped off the last of her garments.
She hadn't seen him at all since the day Colin told her

about the gossip concerning his engagement. She frowned as she wondered if the nude would remind him of his mistress. What did she look like? Perhaps she had talon-shaped fingernails, calculating eyes, and a painted face, but she doubted Brandon would be interested in someone who looked the part of a harlot. He seemed to prefer the weak, whiny sort like Lady Barbara. But then, men didn't always bed and wed the same sort of woman. The kitchen maid at her palazzo had been quite adamant about that.

At any rate, he clearly wasn't interested in Teresa. She felt quite sorry for herself as she poured water from her pitcher into her wash bowl and soaped the smell of oils and turpentine from her skin. Brandon would never be happy with a weak woman, and Teresa knew it. She didn't think he would be happy with a wanton either, but she had never met one herself, so she wasn't positive. Fast women must have some redeeming qualities, she mused, or men wouldn't choose them for mistresses. She thought of the vague references she had heard of the courtesans of Venice and wondered what that quality might be.

Automatically she began to put on her nightgown, but rebelled. The night was hot and the air heavy with the threat of rain. To swathe herself in layers of linen when there was no one there to see her seemed silly. Teresa pulled back the covers and slipped into bed with only the sheet over her. Her nipples beaded and her eyes widened at the unexpected sensuality of lying naked in the bed.

As thoughts of Brandon crowded about her, an ache started deep within. Once more she relived each memory of his kisses, the spicy scent of his shaving soap, the warmth of his body, and the strength of his arms. Was his chest hairy like her father's? Once when she was a child she had seen her father with his shirt collar unbuttoned, then again recently while he was ill. She had difficulty picturing Brandon with a mat of hair that extended even over his shoulders.

Timidly she touched her breasts as she imagined him there beside her. Would his hands be as smooth as hers? Certainly they were larger. Although her breasts were full, his hands would probably cover them. Would he look at her?

She pushed back the sheet and looked down at her breasts. Were they too large? Too small? What if they weren't the proper shape? Teresa thought of the painting and groaned. What if she showed it to him, and he said the harem girl's breasts were ugly or her hips too wide or her hands too square?

She closed her eyes and threw her arm over her head. No she told herself firmly, she was being foolish. While she might never have seen a live nude, she had seen many paintings of nudes. But none of those had been her body. If the Valores hadn't written to her that the palazzo's tenants were leaving because of the bad roof, she would forget the whole thing and paint over the harem girl.

Again her thoughts returned to Brandon, and she wondered where in his room the picture of her would hang. Over his bed? Above her own bed she had replaced the Baxter print with one of her own paintings. Would he perhaps put it opposite the bed where he could lie there and look at it? Would he see past the shadings and brush strokes to the woman? And would he see her in his dreams?

Teresa sighed as she sat up in the bed. Did everyone have these plaguing thoughts and these urgent yet elusive yearnings of the body? She wished she had a mother, or better yet, an older sister in whom she could confide.

Quickly Teresa got up and pulled on her sturdy linen nightgown and buttoned it up to the neck. No wonder she had been taught not to remove her clothes even in her own bed. Her thoughts were hard enough to control when her body was fully clothed.

She shut her eyes and tried to go to sleep. She knew she would dream of Brandon. She almost always did.

*   *   *

Mario waited until the lights in Salvatore's studio had been out for an hour before making his move. He had been amazed that a man as sick as Salvatore had been able to work so late. When he was certain everyone must be asleep, he went to the studio's outside door. Thankful that his brother kept no dog, Mario reached into his pocket and took out the key Salvatore had given him when they were still painting together every day and had forgotten to take back.

He let himself in and paused, straining his eyes in the darkness to make out the location of each table, chair, and easel. Any noise at all might alert everyone that he was there. That would be disastrous. Moving as silently as fog, Mario located the gaslight and turned on the valve. Quickly he struck a match and lit it. Stealthily he examined each of the canvases on the rack. Most of them he had seen before. There was the carnival scene that he liked, but what market could there be for that in England? Still, he sketched it on the pad he had brought and made cryptic notes in the shorthand he had devised for quick descriptions. No eyes but his own would ever see them.

On the top rack toward the back, he found the painting of a nude. Mario's eyes widened, and his breath escaped in an appreciative sigh. Salvatore had outdone himself on this one. The harem girl's eyes were almond-shaped, seductively promising delights to come. Her hair looked as if a breeze had just passed through it, or perhaps the fingers of her lover. He could almost see the breath of life stir the shimmering veil and lift her proud breasts.

Where had Salvatore found such a magnificent model? All Mario could ever afford were prostitutes with old eyes and dull hair. Even bathed, the street women never looked like this! Mario shook his head. Salvatore had always had all the luck.

He put the canvas on an easel and when to work, his deft fingers shading in the lights and darks until he had a perfect copy in black and white on his pad. Next time, he decided, he would bring pastels. He made notes about the base colors and what pigments had been used to enrich the colors in the subtle ways so clear to artists and so unseen by the casual observer. These subtle shadings would mark the difference between a Verdi and a less accomplished hand. Mario no longer studied his brother's work to improve his own. He had come to counterfeit Salvatore's paintings, and the copy had to be exact.

Before dawn he let himself out and locked the door behind him. The studio was exactly as he had found it. Judging by the wetness of the paint, the nude would be there several more days. If he got his eldest pupil to watch over the younger ones, Mario could paint most of the day. After he had seen the painting a few more nights, he could render a perfect copy of it. He did wonder, though, why Salvatore always put the subjects slightly off center. If the harem girl had been more to the right, she would have been flawless. Such was Salvatore's luck that he could paint off center and still produce a masterpiece. Since Mario was convinced that only luck gave Salvatore a blossoming reputation and a wealthy patron, he had no compunction at all about copying his paintings. Why should mere luck stand in the way of Mario Verdi's success?

Two days later Teresa went to check on her harem girl. The paints were drying slowly because of the dampness of the recent afternoon rains. The umbers were dry to the touch, but predictably, the whites were not. For some reason, white was always the last to dry.

After putting it away, she resumed her work on the carnival scene. From Salvatore's remembrances and the other pictures she had seen, the canvas was coming alive. The Tartaglia's clumsy foolishness was apparent in his stance, and Pantalone appeared so finicky and prudish that he was the perfect target for Tartaglia and Arlecchino's sly tricks. The only figure Salvatore wasn't pleased with was the one of Eva Maria, but she was a background figure, and since Teresa had never seen her, she couldn't capture her mother's perfect likeness. Over the past few days Teresa had repainted the elegant lady so often that she had begun to wonder if Salvatore's memory of her was all that exact. After all, he hadn't seen her in more than twenty years.

Methodically Teresa mixed the medium and poured turpentine into the bottle where the brushes would be cleaned, then laid out a square of cloth cut from one of her discarded dresses for use as a paint rag. Glancing at the canvas in order to match the previous colors exactly, Teresa started to mix the paint while she waited for Salvatore to return from his walk. There were a few details of the painting she would have changed, but in general she was satisfied with it. Above all, it was important for her to keep to Salvatore's style and not lapse into her own.

Out of the corner of her eye Teresa noticed that a piece of pastel chalk had fallen on the floor under a small table. That in itself wasn't a surprising object to find in an artist's studio, but she was perplexed. She swept the studio every day herself, because Salvatore refused to let Katie past the door. The chalk hadn't been there before, and it had been more than a week since she had used her pastels. As for Salvatore, she was positive he no longer tried to sketch or draw, because whenever he did, he sank into melancholia for days afterward.

She studied the piece of chalk, but found nothing unusual about it. It was the same brand they always bought; only its location was odd.

Going to her shallow tray of pastels, she opened the lid and was about to drop it in place when she noticed the slot for that color was already filled.

With a frown she went to the box Salvatore used. It, too, was full.

A deep uneasiness crept over Teresa. How could that be? Pastel chalk didn't come from nowhere and place itself under a table. She put it in the next slot and closed the box. Hesitantly she went to the outside door and turned the knob. As she had expected, it was securely locked.

Shaking her head, she put the thought out of her mind. There were many things in life that were a mystery, and this was just one of them. Again she started mixing the paint she would use that day.

13

Teresa waited impatiently for her father to leave for his daily walk. The harem girl had been dry for two days, and she was anxious to deliver it before she completely lost her nerve.

"I think I'll walk over to Bridestake today," Salvatore said as he finished his lunch. "The last time I was there, I thought it would make a good painting."

"I agree. It would be perfect. I already made a sketch, do you remember?"

"The one of the knights and ladies? Yes. I had in mind using the ruins as the focal point of a landscape. One with threatening clouds and sweeping pastures."

"That would be good too, but the one I sketched is unusual. Don't you think so?"

"It is indeed. But I am the master, and for my paintings I decide the subjects." He reached over and patted her cheek.

Teresa lowered her eyes. This was another of his bad days, when he seemed to forget that he wasn't the sole painter in the cottage. "Whatever you say, Papa."

"If Mario comes by, tell him where I am."

"Uncle Mario hasn't been here since your argument."

Salvatore looked confused, then nodded. "I said *if*."

"Yes, Papa."

He stood and ran his fingers through his still-short gray hair in the manner he had done so often to straighten it when it was longer. "Tell Catherina I would like *nero de seppie* for dinner and a bottle of Soave."

"Katie may be able to get the wine, but I doubt we have any squid in the keeping room."

Salvatore looked around the room as if he were surprised to see it rather than the palazzo. "Tell her to cook anything. Whatever pleases you." He turned hurriedly and left the room.

Teresa gazed after him. Even if marriage wouldn't mean giving up her art and possibly exposing herself and her father as frauds, she wasn't sure her father could manage without her. He was becoming more and more reclusive, and his bad days occurred with increasing regularity. Anything—a change of weather, a bad dream, a turn of phrase—could throw him into confusion. At times Teresa was quite sure he thought she was Eva Maria or even his own mother, who had died long before Teresa was born. Occasionally he even called her Catherina.

When Katie came in to clear away the dishes, Teresa went to the studio. She took down the nude and studied it one more time. She had put it in a frame that was elaborately carved and gilded. The sultry eyes and voluptuous body seemed more seductive each time she saw it, and worst of all, it looked more and more like her. Only the color of the hair and eyes kept it from being her mirror image. However, she didn't dare risk having a model in from London to pose while she repainted it.

Before she could change her mind, Teresa wrapped the painting in brown paper and tied it with string. It was large and heavy, but she didn't want to trust it to Hal for delivery. He might see it unwrapped and mention it to her father. So, for that matter, might Brandon. She decided she would handle that problem when it occurred.

Buttercups and marquerites dotted the green slope down to Hawthorn. Dog roses bloomed in the hedgerows, echoing their showier, more dignified cousins in

Hawthorn's rose gardens. The sun baked down on Teresa's shoulders as she carried the package down the green.

As if he had been watching for her, Brandon came to meet her at the edge of the lawn. He took the heavy package effortlessly. "What have we here?"

"It's the nude you asked Papa to paint." She flexed her arms to relax her strained muscles.

"Hal could have carried it for you, or I could have sent up a man."

"I wanted to deliver it myself." His green eyes held a question in their depths, and a veiled emotion she couldn't read.

"You have been avoiding me lately," he said.

"Have I? I thought it was the other way around."

With a puzzled look he said, "Come in out of the heat. This is the hottest August I can remember."

"It's not as bad as the summers in Venice. It's so hot and humid there during the summer, everyone who can afford it goes inland, preferably to the mountains."

"Did you?"

"Not recently. After my grandfather died our family had little money. There was some mismanagement of funds," she explained, thinking briefly of her Uncle Mario. "Artists rarely have a head for finances."

He held the door for her as they entered through the conservatory. Although the windows were open, the sun beaming through the glass walls left the room uncomfortably warm. Brandon ushered her down the corridor to the morning room. The thick walls and shade from the chestnut outside the window made this room quite pleasant. Teresa breathed deeply of the flower-scented breezes that perfumed the lovely old house. "It's so beautiful here."

"In England, you mean?"

"Yes. In England." She had really meant Hawthorn, but decided that sounded too forward.

"I thought you told me once that you could never be happy away from Venice."

She smiled. "I would always have to go back from time to time, but I could be happy here."

Brandon weighed Teresa's last words as he unwrapped the package. Perhaps Salvatore hadn't been entirely correct in his assessment of what his daughter did or didn't want. He might also have been wrong about her decision not to marry. "Is there a young man waiting for you in Venice?"

"No."

Only that; no explanation. Brandon's brows knit in his effort to understand her.

He pulled away the paper and stared at the painting for a long moment before propping it on a sofa and backing several feet away to study it.

Teresa stood stiffly, her hands tightly clasped. Finally she said, "Don't you like it? It's called *The Harem Girl.*"

"Not like it? It's a masterpiece! If your father can paint like this, why does he paint landscapes and horses?"

"Papa chooses his own subjects. He pointed that out to me only this morning."

Brandon stepped closer and studied the surface of the canvas. "There's something odd here."

"What?" She stepped forward anxiously. "Odd?"

"These feathered brush strokes. See? Your father usually makes bolder strokes."

"A bold touch there would make her skin seem less pliant," Teresa automatically objected.

"I know, and that's what makes this the work of a genius! The entire style is subtly different."

"It is?" Teresa asked in concern.

"Look at the expression in her eyes. She seems to be thinking of her lover. Every line of her body expresses desire for him."

Teresa's eyes widened. Maybe it had been a mistake to think of Brandon while she posed in the mirror. "It does?"

The art critic and connoisseur within Brandon was speaking. "Verdi never before put such sensuality into his work. You know, it reminds me of something, but I can't quite think what, or who, it could be."

She recalled the lusty barmaid in her picture of the inn yard. Brandon had seen the sketch. He had also seen the one she made at Bridestake, in which she had depicted the lady looking at her knight with adoration on her face. "It reminds me of nothing, and if you're wise, you won't mention that to Papa. One artist detests being compared with another."

"Of course. I'd never do that." He picked up the painting. "We must hang it at once. Come along."

When Brandon left the morning room and headed for the formal staircase, Teresa faltered. Propriety told her that guests, female ones at least, never left the formal floor. But when he turned and looked back at her, she found herself hurrying after him.

The stairs were broad and the wide banister was made of carved white marble. The garnet-and-gold carpeting on the steps was held in place on each step by gleaming brass rods. They climbed past the massive crystal chandelier that had been modernized with gaslights where candles had been.

At the top of the stairs Teresa found herself in an open area, somewhat akin to the foyer downstairs. Through the windows opposite the stairs was a loggia similar to the open-air porches of their palazzo, only much larger. To her right was a private chapel with stained-glass windows that glowed like precious jewels.

Brandon turned to the left and crossed the marble-floored reception area. Teresa tried not to stare at the sumptuous tapestries that decorated the paneled walls, nor at the life-size marble statues of Greek and Roman gods alongside each window. She had expected the upper floors to be less elaborate than the formal rooms downstairs.

Brandon opened a door on the far side and led her into a sitting room that had a magnificent view of Hawthorn's lawns beyond its stone balcony. The furniture here was masculine by design and looked quite comfortable. The wing-back chairs were covered in navy chintz and the curtains were deep garnet. An Oriental carpet cushioned her feet. Instead of a fringed mantel covering such as a woman might have chosen, the white marble fireplace was topped with an assortment of large natural crystals. A chair was on each side of the fireplace and a bear rug was in front of it, creating a cozy setting. The room exuded luxury and comfort.

He looked about the room for the perfect setting for the painting, then stepped into the adjoining bedroom. "Yes! This is the spot for it," he called back to her.

Teresa went to the door and looked in. She had never seen such a room. It was small and cozy against the chill of English winters, but it was also luxuriously masculine. Brandon's bed was made entirely of walnut, its spiraled corner posts, each as big around as Teresa's waist, supporting an embroidered canopy that almost touched the tall ceiling. The mounded feather mattress was so high, a needlepoint step stool was necessary for even Brandon to scale its heights. The counterpane was done in a blue velvet that matched the curtains at the window, and had been embroidered with the Kincaid family crest. The pile of pillows stacked against the headboard reminded Teresa of the sultan's pillows in her painting. The room was masculine but not overpowering, comfortable but seductive.

She almost blushed at the line her thoughts were taking. Brandon obviously thought nothing of bringing her here, so it must be all right.

"What do you think?" He had removed a landscape and hung *The Harem Girl* in its place.

She went to the foot of the bed and looked at the picture. "The left side should be lower."

He straightened the frame and stepped back. "That's just the place for it."

"I had thought you might have an Oriental nook. They're quite popular now, according to Colin."

"You seem to see quite a bit of Colin."

"We're friends."

"So he says. No, I have no Oriental nook. I think they are pretentious." He studied the painting again. "She appears almost able to breathe. Who is she?"

Teresa jerked her head around to face Brandon, and her eyes widened. "Who is she?" she parroted. Fortunately, Brandon was staring at the painting and hadn't seen her startled movements.

"The model. Is she a woman from London?"

"No. He used a local woman. I don't know her name."

"He must have given her far more grace than nature did, or I would have noticed her. Colin certainly would," he added.

Teresa was reminded of the gossip that Brandon had a mistress in London. "If you keep your eyes open, perhaps you will see her," she said with a tinge of sarcasm.

"I'm not interested in the model, only the painting." He shook his head. "You know, there *is* something familiar about her face."

Hastily Teresa turned away and walked over to a side table on which were several glass balls in various sizes, along with more of the prisms of natural crystal. "These are beautiful," she said to draw his attention.

Brandon looked over at her. She seemed to fit into his room as naturally as she did into his dreams. If she were ill-at-ease about being here, it didn't show. He went to her side and picked up a crystal obelisk as long as his hand. "They form this way by nature. I've collected them since I was a boy. Most of them come from America. In candlelight they shimmer like ice." He handed her the crystal.

"It feels warm," she said in surprise.

"You feel that too? Not everyone notices. No," he said when she started to hand it back. "You keep it. I want you to have it." He closed her fingers over the crystal.

Teresa gazed up at him as if she thought there might be an ulterior motive for his generosity. Brandon lifted a pale green glass ball. "These are called witch balls.

They say Gypsies and witches can read fortunes in them."

"Can they?"

"I have no idea. I don't know any Gypsies or witches. I collect them because of their beauty."

"They are indeed beautiful." She touched a brass stand that held a clear one with a spray of bubbles embedded in its center. "You know I shouldn't be here," she said bluntly, not meeting his eyes.

"I suppose I was wrong to ask you here, but I wanted your opinion on the hanging of the painting."

"Did you?" She looked as if she didn't believe him.

"Yes," he said softly. "I really did. Your opinions are important to me."

"And what about other people's opinions of me? A lady never enters a gentleman's bedroom and remains a lady."

"No one is around. The servants are having a celebration in their own hall in honor of the marriage between my valet and the parlormaid. You may leave at any time. No one will guess you were here." He paused before he added, "As for your being a lady, you could never be anything else."

"That's not what you said that night in the conservatory."

"I was a fool. I had seen you with Colin, and I was jealous."

"You were jealous over me?" she asked with a smile. He didn't answer, as he seemed intent on examining a pale purple crystal. "There's talk that you keep a mistress in London," she said boldly.

His head snapped up. "What? I have no mistress!"

"I've heard that's why your wedding was called off. That Lady Barbara caught the two of you together."

He scowled. So that was the story Barbara was telling! "She exaggerates. There is no mistress. I broke the engagement because I realized I no longer loved her. I suppose this is her way of saving face."

"It's a rather cruel one. Especially since I often walk

toward the Benchley estate and have seen Lady Barbara and Lord Benchley together."

"You have?"

"On several occasions."

Brandon went to a cabinet and took out a carafe of Madeira. Like the other carafes on the shelf, it had a witch ball for a stopper. He poured the wine into a claret-hued Bristol glass and handed it to Teresa before pouring one for himself.

"First you bring me to your bedroom, then you ply me with drink," she said wryly. 'What am I to infer from that?"

"You might assume we are about to drink a toast to your father's great talent." He looked at *The Harem Girl* and lifted his glass. "To the master's touch."

Teresa glowed with pride as she lifted her glass in salute, then put it to her lips. The wine flowed through her like seductive fire. "To the master's touch," she repeated, thinking of Hawthorn's master and not the painting. This was so much like one of her favorite fantasies. "I should leave."

"Yes," he agreed. "You probably should."

Their eyes met and Teresa knew he didn't want her to go. Her pulse quickened as she saw his eyes darken to the hue of fir needles. Everything in her upbringing told her to run from the room and get as far away from his temptation as possible. Instead, she stood there as if she were rooted to the floor.

Brandon put his glass down on the dresser and came to her. "You're right. You should go," he repeated softly.

"I know."

He took her glass and set it aside. "I've never shown my crystals to any other woman," he said. "Nor have I ever given one to anyone else. I want you to know that so you'll understand how special you are to me."

She nodded, unable to speak. He was so near she could feel the warmth radiating from his body, just as she had felt the crystal's warmth. "You're special to me too."

She had to break away or throw herself into his arms. With a great effort she went to the window and pushed aside the lace drapery. "It's raining again." Sheets of silver rain veiled the rolling grounds and hid the cottage from view. In the distance she heard the low rumble of thunder.

Brandon came to her and stood behind her, his hands on her arms. "It's as if we're alone here. No servants, no one to disturb us."

"Yes. As if we're shut off from the world and all its rules."

Slowly Brandon turned her in his arms and gazed down at her. "You're so beautiful, Teresa. Your eyes glow like warm honey. And your hair—such magnificent hair. I see it in my dreams as you wore it on the cliff in Scotland and beneath the blossoming crab-apple tree, loose and flowing. The truth is that I brought you here because I wanted to see how you would look in my room."

"But the servants . . ."

"They really are at a wedding celebration and will be for hours."

"I should go," she whispered.

"I know."

Teresa's eyes were as tormented as his, and she knew she couldn't leave him. What she was doing was wrong, and she knew it. What she was contemplating was a sin in anybody's opinion, but she knew she wasn't going to leave. "I won't go unless you tell me to leave."

Brandon tensed. "You know you should."

"Yes, I know. Are you telling me to go?"

"No," he said hoarsely. "I can't do that."

Teresa tiptoed up and drew his face down to hers. She had longed—no, ached—for his kiss for too long. If what she was doing was wrong, then nothing was right. She opened her lips beneath his and melted toward him as he swept her into his embrace, exploring the warmth of her mouth with his tongue. She put her arms around him and murmured at the sensation of kissing the man she loved with all her heart.

"Teresa," he said in a tight voice, "I'm not made of iron. For God's sake, go!"

"Is that what you want?"

"No, dammit!" He paused as if he expected her to shrink away. "No," he repeated in a strained voice.

"Then I won't."

Again Brandon's lips closed over hers, and when his tongue tasted the soft inner velvet of her lips, she met his with her own. He kissed her passionately, but with a bridled force that brought only pleasure. Teresa stroked his back and shoulders and sides, reveling in the taut strength she found there.

Her head whirled from his kisses. When he lifted her into his arms and carried her to the bed, she felt as if this was as natural as the rain that pattered against the windowpane. Gently he laid her on the cloud of a bed and gazed down at her. "Are you certain?"

She nodded, her eyes dreamy with love. He left her only long enough to lock the outer door, then sat beside her on the bed. He seemed almost afraid to touch her, so Teresa made the first move. After she pulled the pins from her hair, her tresses unfurled into loose waves across the pillow.

Almost reverently Brandon curled a silken tendril around his hand and let the ends coil about his fingers. Her hair was as soft as he had remembered. His eyes again met hers. "Teresa, you can still leave. I'll not think any the less of you."

"What will you think of me if I stay?"

He couldn't tell her of his love, and he was honor-bound not to speak to her of marriage. But he was a man in love and the object of his affection lay here in his bed with her hair loose and her body curved about his own. "I could never think less of you. If you stay, I will please you in every way that I can." Was he wrong about her innocence? He couldn't believe a virgin would behave this way. And if she wasn't a virgin, what would it matter if they made love? Once he had had her, maybe he could rid himself of his obsession with her.

Slowly he began releasing the pearl buttons that fastened her dress. She lay perfectly still and watched his face. Inch by inch the creamy skin of her chest was exposed, then the frothy lace of her chemise. He opened the buttons to below her waist and ran his hand across her shoulders. "Your skin is as velvety as it looks."

Teresa smiled at him; she couldn't speak for the emotions that were overwhelming her. His hand was large and warm and his thumb lazily caressed her as if he were in no rush to be done with her. She let him lift her to a sitting position and their eyes met. Gently she kissed him, and this time he groaned as if barely able to contain his passion.

He brushed the dress from her shoulders, and Teresa untied her petticoats so that the clothing pooled about her hips. Brandon reached down and removed her shoes and let them drop to the floor before he rolled down her white cotton stockings. As he stroked his hand up her leg, Teresa felt an urgency to be as close to him as possible.

She pulled off his coat, and he tossed it toward the chair as she unfastened his shirt buttons. He reached behind her to open his cuffs as he kissed the warm hollow of her neck and ran his tongue over the shell of her ear. When she parted his shirt, Teresa sighed with pleasure. He wasn't furred like her father, but had a sprinkling of soft hairs that curled over her fingers. Beneath his warm skin she could feel his hard muscles and the steady thud of his heart. She wouldn't have left now even if he demanded it.

"You feel so good," she sighed.

"You aren't afraid of me?"

"Never. I could never fear you."

He smiled. So she wasn't a virgin after all. Everyone knew virgins were exceedingly shy, even on their wedding nights and with their lawful husbands. He felt a twinge of disappointment that she wasn't as pure as he had thought her, and he felt a dig of jealousy at whoever had enjoyed her charms. But in a way he was relieved, because now he could love her and not compromise her. In time, when Salvatore was more reasonable, he could marry her.

Brandon stood and removed the rest of his clothes as Teresa knelt on the bed and watched. When he dropped his smallclothes to the floor, her eyes widened and her lips parted, almost as if she had never seen an erect man before.

She pushed her dress and petticoats away and gazed up into his eyes, her eyes as wide and vulnerable as a doe's. A deep tenderness washed over him as thunder growled outside the window. Brandon slowly untied the satin ribbon that gathered the neck of her chemise. The garment loosened beneath his fingers and slipped lower to drape low on her breasts, then fell to her waist. Brandon swallowed against his excitement as he looked at her. She made no modest motions to cover herself, but instead let him look at her full breasts. They were beautifully shaped and proud, with coral rosettes. Her nipples pouted for his touch, and when he covered her breast with the palm of his hand, the nipple beaded tighter. Teresa closed her eyes and let her head roll back as if she was enjoying this as much as he was.

Brandon bent and took the other nipple in his mouth and sucked gently. Teresa murmured and laced her fingers through his hair as if she wanted to give him more of herself. As he rolled his tongue over her nipple, he untied the waist of her bloomers and ran his hand over the curve of her hip. He felt as if he would burst from wanting her, but he forced himself to take his time. This first day of their loving must be special for her as well as for him. Never had he wanted to please anyone as much as he wanted to please Teresa.

She lay back on the mound of pillows and drew his lips to hers as he swept her chemise and bloomers down her legs and away. Desire for him flooded through her, and she hoped he wouldn't notice how terribly inexperienced she was. She wanted to give him so much pleasure that he would love her as much as she loved him, but she wasn't sure what would please him. She ran her hands over the muscles of his back and down his sides. He was so strong! She hadn't expected him to be built like an Adonis.

As his hand stroked her breast, she arched to give him greater access to her. Slowly, tantalizingly, he toyed with her nipple, rolling it between his thumb and forefinger, urging her to yet more passion.

She opened her eyes to meet his, and he smiled at her. "I like that," she sighed.

He looked a bit surprised, and she wondered if people were supposed to talk when they made love. His hand glided down her abdomen to the curls between her thighs. Her legs parted by instinct, and he smiled again as his hand moved to the inside of her thighs, then began to caress her most secret spot. "Do you like this too?" he asked as his hand moved against her in a way that sent fire through her veins.

"Yes," she breathed in ecstasy, "oh, yes." She knew she was wet there and getting wetter with each probe of his fingers, but he didn't seem to mind.

When he knelt between her legs, she had a moment of worry. The kitchen maid had assured her that this would hurt like the fires of hell. Teresa wasn't so sure she believed in hell, but it sounded quite unpleasant.

Brandon began to ease into her slowly, and her eyes widened at the unexpected sensation. She felt so full of him, yet it was so good! When he reached the barrier of her maidenhead, he paused and looked down at her as if he were confused.

To make it easier for him, Teresa pushed her hips upward. She felt a brief stinging sensation, and she held herself still, afraid to move.

"Teresa," he murmured. "Teresa, why didn't you tell me?"

Tell him what? He must know she had never been with a man before. Was she supposed to say something?

With a low moan he began to move within her. All at once the stinging stopped, and a warm glow took its place. She found herself moving in rhythm with him. When he murmured love words in her ear, she replied with words of her own—half-Italian, half-English, in a melodious mixture of loving.

All at once an urgency started to build deep inside her. She moved more deliberately, allowing the sensation to grow and take over all her senses. She could no longer hear the whisper of rain; only she and Brandon comprised the universe. He thrust deeper into her, and slipped his hand under her to maneuver her hips. When he did, the bubble of ecstasy burst and pleasure rained all through her.

She cried out with the intensity of her enjoyment, never knowing that she did. The steady contractions of her fulfillment triggered his own, and Brandon pulled her tightly to him as completion swept over him.

For a long time she lay in his arms, not daring to move for fear he might withdraw from her. She wanted to stay like this as long as possible, to be his woman forever.

"Teresa, why didn't you tell me I was your first?" he said at last.

"Because I thought you would send me away. Besides, I assumed you knew."

He held her close, cuddling her head on his shoulder as protectiveness overwhelmed him. She had given him her most precious treasure—her maidenhood. And he had not only taken it, but had assumed she was no virgin. He felt like a cad. Worse, he had ruined Teresa.

Closing his eyes against the bittersweet pain, he drew her even closer. "My Teresa," he said into the cloud of her hair. "My darling Teresa." His voice was strained.

"Have I done wrong in giving myself to you?" she asked in concern

"No. No, you did no wrong." He pulled back from

her and gazed down into her worried face. If anyone
had done wrong, it was he. Although he could do
nothing to replace what he had taken, he could at least
remove himself as a temptation. "I have to leave tomorrow. I'll be gone for several weeks."

"Gone?" She propped herself up on her elbow to
look at him. "Where are you going?"

Improvising, he said, "To Germany. There is a matter
at Mitchell's school that needs my attention." Lying had
always been hard for him, and this was especially difficult. By the time he returned, she might have realized
her error and learned to despise him. That would help
him refrain from making her his mistress. Teresa deserved so much more than that! Yet he couldn't marry
her and still keep his word to her father. If he stayed
and they became lovers, Teresa would become preg-
nant, and while that would convince Salvatore to let
them wed, it would shame Teresa. No, he couldn't consider such a course.

"Germany?" she said in a quiet voice. "That's so far
away."

"Yes. Yes, it is." He gazed across the room at the
seductive *Harem Girl*. For some reason she seemed even
more familiar than she had before.

Teresa sat up. She was keenly aware that he had said
no words of love to her, nor had he intimated that he
felt any. He hadn't even said he wanted to make love
with her again. Embarrassment colored her cheeks as
she slid off the bed and quickly dressed. He had only
used her for his own pleasure! She wanted to hurl
hurtful accusations at him, but her throat felt swollen
shut and she knew any words at all would bring a
torrent of tears. He didn't love her. Somehow she had
thought he would, if they made love. She had been so
naive! He had even said he was leaving for Germany
right away, as if nothing at all had passed between
them. She couldn't face him or meet his eyes.

Not bothering to pin up her hair, she ran from the
room.

Brandon leapt out of bed. "Teresa? Teresa, come back here!" He started to chase after her, but he was wearing no clothes. Cursing roundly, he ran back to his bedroom and started to dress hurriedly. Before he could work his arms into his shirt, he heard the front door slam with a reverberation that echoed throughout the house. In moments he saw Teresa racing up the hill, her hair streaming in the rain.

Brandon stopped dressing. Wasn't this what he had wanted? He didn't know what had upset her, unless she had suddenly realized what he had done to her. Most likely she would never speak to him again, and it was no more than he deserved.

He picked up the hairpins she had left on the side table and closed them into the palm of his hand. After several minutes he went to his dresser and laid them in the velvet-lined box that held his cuff buttons and cravat pins. Teresa was better off without him.

14

Brandon soon discovered that putting distance between himself and Teresa did him more harm than good. During the waking hours of his trip, he constantly worried whether she was all right, and whether she hated him for leaving her so soon on the heels of their having made love. Then at night he dreamed of lying next to her soft flesh. In no time at all Brandon convinced himself that he was more wrong for leaving than he would have been for staying. With marvelously clear hindsight he realized he should have swept her away to the altar and let Salvatore be as displeased as he might choose to be.

"Mitchell, what would you think of a man who loves a woman, but has been put upon his honor not to propose to her, yet makes love to her, then leaves town?"

"The man is a fool and a rounder and should be shot." Mitchell held his glass of brandy up to the firelight and studied its color.

Brandon nodded glumly. "I think so too. But he loves her, remember. That's why he asked for her hand and why he made love to her."

"He must not love her too dearly, or he wouldn't have given his word not to marry her."

"There were extenuating circumstances—at least that's what I hear."

"Then he should never have made love to her and then run away."

"He didn't run away. Not at all. He thought the distance might ease matters between himself and the lady."

Mitchell studied his brother. "You seem to know this man quite well. Who is he?"

"You don't know him. I've only met him myself recently."

"Well, if you ask me, he should either marry her or leave her alone. Anything else is insupportable."

"What if her reputation would be sullied if he married her?" Brandon asked, thinking about the rumor Barbara had started about him having a mistress.

"If he's that disreputable, I'm amazed she would consider marrying him."

Brandon could hardly explain that the fault lay in a lie started by a jilted lover. Mitchell might guess he was talking about himself. He looked around Mitchell's small sitting room in search of a new subject. "How's school?" he asked lamely.

Mitchell leaned forward eagerly. "I love studying medicine. Every day I wake up full of fire. It's hard work, but I can't get enough of it."

"That's good."

"Do you know what I've decided to do? I've decided to come back to London and set up my practice."

"That's what I expected you to say. It's about time someone gave old Dr. Halsey a run for his money."

"No, no. Not that part of town. I plan to go to St. Giles rookery."

"St. Giles! In God's name, why!"

"Because doctors are needed there."

"Am I paying for you to become a doctor so you can live in a slum? You can do that with no education at all!"

Mitchell merely smiled. "In the first place, you aren't paying for my education, and in the second, a doctor should go where he's needed."

Brandon frowned at his brother. He was in fact paying for Mitchell's education, but had kept it a secret. As the second son, Mitchell had inherited none of the Kincaid fortune, but had an inheritance from their mother's parents. Brandon paid for his schooling in order to keep Mitchell's small inheritance intact for when he started his practice and began his family. "St. Giles?" he repeated glumly.

"You don't know what it's like there. Have you ever ridden through the slums?"

"No."

"I have, and it's a sight to tear at your heart."

"That's no reason to *live* there. Work for social reforms, petition Parliament, complain to Queen Victoria, but don't move there."

"Brandon, there are families that live in only one room, sometimes for generations. Butchers toss offal into the streets at Smithfield. Bodies wash out of shallow graves at Bermondsey. Cholera and Whitechapel are almost synonyms. How can I, as a doctor, treat only patients in Regent's Park or Islington when there are children living in the streets in the dead of winter? Thousands of small children are being killed each year because their parents don't know any better than to feed them gin to stop their crying."

Brandon was quiet for a minute. "I guess of all of us, you will be the noble one."

"I'm not doing it to be noble."

"I know. That's what makes it noble. Very well. Go to the slums and cure the poor. As you say, the need is great. You always were one to collect people, just as Colin can't pass a stray cat or dog. Do you recall, when you were eight or nine, bringing home the orphan girl you found living in a ditch?"

"Yes. Mother nearly had apoplexy."

"She got over it. I saw that girl just the other day. She has a family over toward Reading and keeps a respectable house. If it hadn't been for you, she might have died or turned to prostitution."

"A lot of them do."

Brandon nodded. "You're right. The news just surprised me." After a pause he added, "I hope Colin develops an ambition someday."

Mitchell chuckled. "All Colin needs is the love of a good woman." Mitchell sipped his brandy and stretched his feet out to the fire. The school was located in the Bavarian Alps south of Munich, and even though August had barely given way to September, the nights at the higher altitudes were quite cool. "I rather thought he was taking a fancy to the Verdi girl."

"Teresa?" Brandon asked as casually as he could. "What made you think that?"

"He said so."

Brandon frowned and took a large sip of brandy.

"On the other hand, I thought you might be giving her the eye too."

"She's a beautiful woman."

"So I noticed. Don't look at me like that. I have no intention of marrying. My medical practice will be wife enough for me."

"That's just as well, considering where you expect to live. I can't imagine any woman of our acquaintance being eager to move to St. Giles."

Mitchell laughed. "Neither can I. Nor would I be likely to fall in love with a girl of the slums. No matter. I prefer a solitary life."

"Since you brought up the Verdis," Brandon said, "I should mention that Salvatore was quite ill with brain fever after you left. He survived but has become a recluse. Oddly enough, his talent was unharmed—actually he shows greater ability than he had before his illness."

"Strange, isn't it, how the brain works? It's a fascinating subject." Mitchell offered Brandon more to drink, but Brandon shook his head. "I saw a painting of his just the other day. I meant to tell you about it, but it slipped my mind."

"Oh? One of his earlier works, I assume?"

"No, as a matter of fact, it was one you exhibited at the party you had for him. The one of the ladies sunning on the rooftop."

"That's impossible," Brandon said with a smile. Mitchell had never had an eye for paintings.

"I'm quite sure it's the same one. I remember the unusual red dress."

"Red dress?" Brandon's eyes narrowed. The dress was indeed distinctive. "Where did you see this painting?"

"It's in the house of the college's art instructor. I saw it when I was there for a party a few weeks ago."

Brandon put down his glass. "No, you must be mistaken. The picture was sold to a museum in Paris with the understanding that it would be on exhibit there for a year before being resold."

"Perhaps they lied to you."

"I know the curator well; he's a man of principle."

"He may be, but few people put as much stock in principles as you do."

Brandon stood up and reached for his McFarlon coat. "I must see this painting."

"Now? It's cold outside," Mitchell protested.

"Come now, if you can't handle a night as cold as this, you'll never survive in the slums." He tossed Mitchell's coat to him.

The town where the college was located was nestled in a high, narrow valley. At the upper end stood the school and the houses of those connected with it. Below was the ancient town that had been on the mountain long before anyone ever considered the need for a college. The animosity between Town and Gown was as sharp as a wintry wind.

The art instructor lived in a two-story house that seemed to be clinging to the mountainside. Mitchell drew his collar up against the wind and knocked at the door. "I don't know him well at all, Brandon. This is an imposition. And it's too late to be calling."

"He's in the field of art. He'll understand."

The door was opened by a housekeeper who spoke

no English. Mitchell explained in German that they wanted to see the master of the house, and they were shown into the cozy living quarters to wait while she went in search of her employer.

The painting Brandon had come to see was prominently displayed over the fireplace mantel. His brows drew together as he crossed the room to examine the signature. It was clearly signed "S. Verdi" with the familiar flourish he had seen on the other Verdi canvases. Then he looked around the room. While it was spotlessly clean, the furniture was old and slouched from use, though the chairs and sofa backs were adorned with doilies to protect the fabric from men's hair dressings. The bric-a-brac on the side tables was tasteful but inexpensive—a small statue of the *Greek Slave,* a bell jar containing stuffed birds and a dried-flower arrangement, and a papier-maché inkstand in black lacquer with a gold design of stylized flowers. Beside a brass-bound Bible on another table was a group of "fairings" such as could be bought at any country fair, along with a good piece of parian in the shape of a Grecian urn. The room was not the sort Brandon would have expected of a man who could afford to buy a Salvatore Verdi painting.

Footsteps from the hallway heralded the approach of the room's owner, and Brandon turned to meet the man whom Mitchell introduced. Gustave Reinhardt was an aging man with an impressive gray mustache and white hair longer than was common. He had the abstract demeanor of one who sees in colors and textures rather than in concretes. His clothing, like his parlor, was tidy but had seen better days. Brandon was becoming quite suspicious.

"Herr Reinhardt," Mitchell said, "my brother was interested in the painting above the mantel there. He knows Salvatore Verdi and had to see it. I apologize for imposing on you."

"*Nein, nein.* It is an honor," Reinhardt said in heavily accented English. "You, too, have a Verdi?"

"You might say I have Verdi himself," Brandon said with a smile. "I'm his patron."

"How fortunate for you. He is making quite a name for himself."

"Indeed he is. Tell me, Herr Reinhardt, how did you come by this painting?"

"I bought it from a man who owns a gallery in Worms."

"Could I have his name and address, please?"

Reinhardt made a hopeless gesture. "Alas. I do not know it. I was there on holiday and merely happened in off the street." He touched the gold frame gently. "It was indeed my lucky day, was it not?"

"Yes. Yes, it was indeed." Brandon was trying to think which gallery owners he knew in Worms that might also know the curator of the museum in Paris.

As soon as was possible, Brandon made their farewells and he and Mitchell stepped back into the night. "I don't know what to make of it," Brandon said over the howling wind. "It's a Verdi, but how could it be here? He must have used all his savings to buy it. Herr Reinhardt isn't a wealthy man."

"No, he isn't. Are you sure Verdi did the painting?"

"Of course I am. The signature is right there on the canvas. I didn't examine it minutely, but it has to be authentic. The question is, why would the museum curator in Paris not keep our bargain? He understood it was important for Signor Verdi to have the exposure, and of course it was beneficial for the museum."

When they reached Mitchell's lodgings, Brandon shrugged off his coat and took down his traveling cases.

"You're leaving?" Mitchell protested. "I thought you were staying several more days."

"I have to look into this. I won't be able to rest until I know why Monsieur Le Blanc sold that painting. What he did was highly unethical." He didn't want to admit that he was even more anxious to get home and see

Teresa. Now that he was determined to leave, the miles between them seemed torturously long.

Early the next morning, Mitchell smiled at his older brother as he watched him continue packing. "All this fervor over a painting that you don't even own? You amaze me, Brandon. I would expect such a hasty departure if a woman were involved, but not a painting. At least I would if it were anyone but you."

"What do you mean by that?" Brandon demanded as he paused.

"You've always struck me as a cooler person. Lady Barbara would chill an icicle, yet you chose to ask for her hand."

"I assure you, I'm not quite as detached as you seem to think. Hand me those socks."

"You say you're not, but look how you're packing. Everything neatly in its place. If I were in a hurry, I'd throw it all in every which way. But then, I'd only get in such a rush if I were going back to a woman."

"I'm neat by nature," Brandon said testily. "And as a matter of fact, there *is* a woman I'm returning to."

"Oh? Not another Lady Barbara, I hope."

"I thought you liked Barbara."

"If you had married her, I would have welcomed her into the family, but I doubted you'd ever be happy with her. I can't imagine her in a nursery or raising a houseful of noisy children. Whom *are* you returning to?"

"I'd rather not tell you her name until I ask her to marry me and she accepts."

"Why not?"

"Hand me those ties and collars. You ask too many questions."

"Then it's someone I know." Mitchell sat on the side of the bed and watched his brother. "I confess I'm quite curious."

"I can assure you, she is nothing at all like Barbara."

"Then why are you here in Germany? Why aren't you home courting her?"

"Mitchell, as amazing as it seems to you and Colin, there are people who think with their heads first and not their hearts. I thought it best to leave for a while so matters would cool down a bit."

"There! You see? I said you were a cool one!"

Brandon gave him an exasperated look.

Mitchell scooped up the rest of Brandon's belongings and dumped them unceremoniously in the bag. "Brandon, if you care for her, run to her. Don't make asinine excuses about paintings being sold and don't pack as if you were laying out a surgical tray. Just throw your things together and hurry back to her. Look, women in love don't put logic before emotions. If she has any passions in her at all, she probably thinks you don't care anything about her or you would be there with her trying to win her hand."

Brandon recalled his fevered lovemaking with Teresa, and how he had poured out his love in giving her pleasure. "She must know."

"Did you tell her you love her?"

"Not in so many words, but I made it plain."

Mitchell shook his head. "Not good enough. Women have to *hear* it. And they have to hear it more than once."

Brandon frowned. Barbara had actively disliked protestations of love and certainly any gestures of physical affection. At least she had disliked those things from him. "I'm not so sure you're right about that."

"You can't measure all women by Lady Barbara's yardstick. Don't look at me like that, I know that's what you were thinking."

"I wasn't aware that mind-reading was part of the curriculum here."

"For once, listen to me. Get back to her as quickly as you can and tell her you love her, if you do, and act as any normal man in love would."

Brandon studied his brother's earnest face. "What makes you so sure that this is the way to win her? I should think a show of prudence—"

"Hang prudence. Colin isn't the only Kincaid who's been around the block. I was in love once, but I knew I had years of schooling ahead before I could start a home of my own, so I said nothing to her."

"I never knew that. What happened?"

"She married someone else. If I had told her how I felt, she might have waited for me."

"Do you still love her?"

Mitchell nodded. "I'll never forget her."

Brandon shut the bag and lifted it and the traveling trunk off the bed. "I'm sorry your love didn't work out for you, but I'm not convinced that a man should blurt out all his feelings. Women are sensitive, delicate creatures. A sudden shock—"

"Nonsense. In my experience a woman can take at least as much strain as a man. I think it's a myth about their delicacy, or they could never go through so much in birthings."

"But surely a lady—"

"Ladies also have babies and survive."

Brandon hadn't thought of it that way. Barbara had fainted at the least upset. Now that he thought of it, that last time she had done so had seemed a trifle theatrical. He thought of Teresa's firm body and strong sensibilities. He had never seen her swoon or even act as though she might. When they had made love she had been as passionate as he was, and she had been undeniably a virgin. When he took her maidenhead, she had neither screamed nor fainted as he had been led to believe all ladies did. Brandon was beginning to think both his younger brothers were far more knowledgeable than he was about the opposite sex.

He stopped long enough to shake Mitchell's hand and clap him on the shoulder. "Study hard, Mitchell, and come save London as soon as possible. She needs a man like you, and we miss you at Hawthorn."

The brothers hugged awkwardly. "Take my advice, Brandon. Don't lose your woman as I did mine."

"I won't," Brandon said firmly. "I won't lose her."

Stepping out into the still-cool morning air, Brandon was filled with resolve. He loved Teresa, dammit, and he had been a raw fool to let her father hoodwink him into not asking her to marry him. If Teresa didn't want to marry him, she could say so herself. Maybe Salvatore preferred for her not to marry or to have only an Italian for a husband after his death, but in the end, the decision had to be made between Teresa and himself.

"A fool," he muttered as he stepped into the coach that would take him to the railroad terminal in Munich. "A raw fool!"

After waiting several hours, Brandon boarded the train and was on his way to Paris, but the train seemed to be moving at a snail's pace. Sitting in a seat next to a window, he mentally urged the engine to greater speed, but his efforts were to no avail as the train stopped at first one village, then another, all along the way. Silently he begrudged every passenger that took up precious seconds in departing or boarding. How could he have been so stupid as to leave Teresa when he knew he loved her and wanted her for his wife? Especially after making love to her. She might think he didn't care for her at all! He considered telegraphing ahead to tell her he was coming, but he couldn't figure a tactful way to word such a message.

All he could think of was Teresa's soft lips and how she had murmured with pleasure while they made love. Her silvery laughter seemed to echo beneath the click of the train's wheels. He compared her with all the female travelers about him and found them all to be singularly lacking.

As the train roared through another tunnel, he was glad the passengers had left their windows closed so the soot and smoke would not fill the car, making it hard to breathe until they were again in the open. Brandon had never cared much for train travel, though it was more convenient than a coach and team. Now he wished for a genie's carpet to whisk him out of the flying sparks and rocking car and take him straight to Teresa's side.

How was he to ask the question? He knew it was important for a woman to receive a proposal that she could confide to her friends. But Teresa had no close friends, except for Colin. Colin! Brandon had almost forgotten about him! He had left Teresa in Colin's domain, and by now she might be promised to him! Brandon subconsciously emitted a low growl that drew the attention of a ribbon-bedecked matron in the next seat. She reproached him with a look over the top of her spectacles, and he responded with a humorless smile. She went back to her endless knitting.

What would he do if he returned to Hawthorn to find Teresa engaged to Colin? Why, she might even have eloped with him, since Brandon had ruined her and seemingly abandoned her! Now that he thought about it, he could claim to have done no less. And he had always prided himself on being a gentleman above all else!

Moonlight, he thought. If Teresa were still free, he should propose by moonlight. Unfortunately, September was too late for roses, so the rose garden was out of the question. A pity. Moonlight and roses might sway her to say yes on the romance of the moment. If she didn't love him as much as he loved her—and Brandon doubted that was possible—he could win her love once she was his bride. He racked his brain for a romantic place to propose. Hawthorn was undeniably beautiful, but it had so few romantic nooks! Perhaps in the ruins of Bridestake? No, he decided, proposing in a ruin might augur against him. Besides, unless England was warmer than Germany had been, she would be blue with cold before he ever got the words out.

At last the train reached Paris, and before doing anything else, Brandon bought his ticket to Calais, where he would cross the channel. The three-hour wait worked out perfectly so that he could visit the Le Blanc Museum and ask the curator why he had sold the Verdi painting.

He took a hackney to the museum. After consulting his pocket watch, he climbed the steps of the elegant building. As soon as the double doors closed behind him, the noise of the street was shut away. Here, in the hushed presence of art, was a world Brandon knew and understood.

He made his way through the large museum, taking a familiar path through the rooms that were devoid of anything but paintings and a few judiciously chosen sculptures. There were no children here, no laughter, no life. Just the two-dimensional portrayal of life as the artists had chosen to depict it. Brandon frowned. When and why had he let his love of art shape his own life into an airless museum? An existence where Barbara would have blended as smoothly as a pastel rendering. It had taken a woman like Teresa to breathe fire and life into him. He hoped his fire hadn't come too late.

On his way to the curator's office in the rear, he passed the room where he had last seen the Verdi painting, glanced in, and almost tripped. There it hung in all its exquisite beauty, the unusual red dress, the sunbathing ladies, and all, just as it should be.

Brandon stared at it a long moment, then approached it slowly. This wasn't possible! He had just left this painting in a mountain town in Germany, yet here it was in Paris. He felt as if his senses were reeling. This was a possibility he had certainly never considered. There were two of them!

He studied the canvas, moving from side to side as he examined Salvatore's distinctive brush strokes, the transparency of the glaze, the subtle shadings. Herr Reinhardt's parlor hadn't been as well-lit as was this museum, but Brandon had been equally sure that the painting had been by Verdi. Someone might copy a subject or a style, but the glazing and brush strokes were secrets handed down by masters to students and couldn't be copied so exactly. He wished now he had studied Reinhardt's painting more carefully.

Only one explanation seemed plausible: Salvatore must have painted two and sold one himself. Anger began to grow inside Brandon. He had been more than fair with the man. Not only did he provide a home and a living for Salvatore and his daughter, but he gave the man a generous portion of each sale. Under the circumstances, Brandon could have been far less generous and still have been considered lenient as a patron. He knew some patrons who never let their artists see a farthing of profit since their needs were being met under their patronage.

That brought to light an even uglier suspicion. Salvatore must have known Brandon would eventually find out he was being duped. What better hold could he have over his patron than to let the man ravish his unwed daughter?

Brandon knotted his hands into fists. All those protestations Salvatore had made about Teresa preferring not to marry! Naturally he would want to pique Brandon's interest in the woman, but not give her to him for a wife. But could a father be such a fiend as to use his own daughter in such a scheme? Brandon knew the answer. He had seen mothers selling their own daughters to sailors on London's docks to buy a measure of gin. To amass a fortune, Salvatore might be able to sacrifice Teresa's virginity.

A red haze seemed to float in front of Brandon's eyes as he glared at the painting. Had Teresa been privy to this? He didn't want to believe it, but she had certainly come to him willingly for a virgin! Nor had she asked him not to go to Germany. Instead, she had pulled on her clothes and run out of the room. Now that he thought about it, that was a rather peculiar reaction.

His thoughts were dark and tormented as he left the museum and walked all the way back to the rail station.

Thank God he had not already thrown his heart at her feet and proposed! He had to think about this and see just how Salvatore was managing to market the duplicate paintings—for there must be more than one. A thief wouldn't stop after one successful robbery, and neither would Salvatore.

If only the man weren't such a pure master of his art, Brandon would send him packing at once.

And if only he weren't, even now, still so much in love with Verdi's daughter.

15

When Brandon arrived at Hawthorn at midmorning, he found his butler in a state of turmoil. "I can't get them to see reason, Lord Kincaid. I've talked to both Signor Verdi and his daughter until I'm all undone, but they refuse to go to the palace."

Brandon again read the formal court summons and frowned at Queen Victoria's coat of arms embossed at the top of the card. "Did you explain that this is a command appearance? One doesn't tell the queen he won't be received by her."

"Yes, my lord. Of course I told them, but they were both adamant."

"For what reason? It says here the queen is interested in commissioning Signor Verdi to paint a portrait of her children!"

"Signor Verdi says he isn't a British subject and isn't compelled by British protocol. Signorina Verdi said her father is a recluse and refuses to travel farther than his garden gate."

"Preposterous!"

"My sentiments exactly, my lord."

"Where's Colin?"

"He's gone to the races in Ireland. He left the day before this card arrived."

"Damn!" Brandon looked back at the square of heavy paper. "Signor Verdi is supposed to be at court this very afternoon!"

"Yes, my lord. In three hours, to be exact," Fitch said as he checked the pendulum clock beneath the stairs.

Brandon muttered a few choice curses under his breath. "Get my horse. I'll go talk to Signor Verdi and try to reason with him."

In minutes Brandon was pounding on the cottage door. Teresa answered it herself, and by the fire in her eyes he knew she had expected to find Fitch on her doorstep. At once her face softened and her eyes searched his as if hoping for something.

"Where is your father?" Brandon demanded. He ached to pull her into his arms, but a royal summons had to take precedence over his emotions.

A veil seemed to drop behind her eyes. "If you're here about the summons, he won't go."

"Dammit, he *has* to go!" He clamped his mouth shut. All he needed was to alarm her into a fainting spell! "Let me talk to him," he said more gently.

From behind her he heard Salvatore call out that he was to go away. Then Brandon heard an outburst of rapid-fire Italian that was spoken too quickly for him to follow. Teresa answered Salvatore in an equally rapid manner. Both father and daughter were clearly upset. "You see?" she said in exasperation. "He won't go."

"Let me in. I'll reason with him."

"No, I can't do that." She knew her father's tremors were more pronounced when he was upset, and now he was shaking all over, as if he were in a chill. If Brandon saw him, he would clearly deduce that Salvatore was incapable of painting at all. "This has upset Papa to the point that I fear for his health."

"But he has to go to the queen!"

"No."

"Teresa," he implored, "he went abroad in Venice. He has gone to London. We went all the way to Scotland. Now, why can't he go to Buckingham Palace? His career would be assured if he were a court artist."

"I know," she said miserably. "But since his terrible illness, he has stayed at home, as you well know. He doesn't want to see anyone."

"But it's the queen!"

"What would you have me do?" she stormed, unable to stand anymore. "Turn him over my knee like a small boy? Scold him if he doesn't do what's best for him? He is my Papa! Besides," she added with a proud tilt of her head, "he is Salvatore Verdi, and all artists have quirks."

"Insulting a queen is not a quirk!'

She shrugged. "Your queen must find another painter, I suppose. Papa won't go." She wanted to throw herself into his arms and tell him how much she had missed him, but he was as remote as any stranger. She had planned to tell him that she loved him, but he was making it quite clear that he was here only on business. Tears burned her eyes, so she said coldly, "If you will excuse me, I must go."

"Teresa, it's a royal summons! Your father could become the foremost artist in Europe if he pleases the queen!"

She knew all too well what they were throwing away, but she also knew Salvatore's hands trembled visibly every day now. He couldn't possibly be seen. "Papa says his art must stand on its own."

There was another furious outburst of Italian from down the hall and Teresa said, "I must go. All this excitement is bad for him." She hastily shut the door.

Brandon glared at the door and considered banging on it again, but refrained. Fitch had obviously tried for days to get them to comply, and Brandon had no time to waste in argument. He rode back to the manor house and called for a bath. One didn't refuse a royal summons by messenger.

In an hour's time he had bathed away the dust of travel and dressed in his best day clothes. He rode to London, and on presenting the queen's card, was admitted to Buckingham Palace and finally shown into the queen's audience chamber. Although Brandon had been there on several occasions, he had never come to deliver an unpleasant message. He was too nervous to sit down.

The door opened and a short woman flanked by two ladies-in-waiting came into the room. The attendants remained by the door, and the plump woman stepped several feet into the room. Brandon went to her and bowed, "Your royal highness."

"Lord Kincaid." Her blue eyes darted about the room. "I'm surprised to find you here alone. Where is Signor Verdi?"

"He was unable to come, your majesty."

"Oh? Ill, I presume. I hope it's nothing serious."

"No, not ill exactly. The truth is, Signor Verdi is a recluse."

"He is? How odd. I heard he had been seen in a number of galleries."

"Yes, but that was before last summer. He had brain fever and nearly died. Since then, he never ventures farther afield than the boundaries of my estate, and rarely farther than his own garden."

"Extraordinary!"

Brandon was always surprised at Queen Victoria's stature. She was scarcely taller than a girl, though she was as plump as a partridge. If it weren't for her regal bearing, he thought she would look more like a housewife than a queen. "Signor Verdi sends his deepest apologies and begs that you understand."

"I am trying." Victoria crossed the room, her petticoats rustling beneath her taffeta skirt. "He shows a remarkable talent. We had hoped to have him do a group portrait of our children."

"He was honored by the request."

"It was more in the nature of a command."

Brandon shifted uneasily. A housewife? No, this woman was every inch a queen. "Yes, your majesty, but if he is unable to leave his cottage, I don't see how that would be possible."

She fingered a lacy handkerchief as she thought. "We could perhaps send the children to him."

"Send them to his studio?" Brandon brightened in relief. "Yes, that would work!"

"The prince consort and I could accompany them at times and watch him work."

Brandon's smile faded. "Please understand, Your Majesty, but Signor Verdi allows no one to watch him paint. Only his daughter is allowed in the studio."

Victoria looked unconvinced. "We don't send our children places where we can't go ourselves."

"Yes, yes, I understand that. Surely in this case Signor Verdi would make an exception."

Victoria's plain round face broke into a smile. "I thought so. Tell Signor Verdi that the royal children will arrive tomorrow promptly at four. They will sit for one hour each day, then leave. In a week we will ride out with them to see how the painting is progressing."

"Yes, Your Majesty. I'll tell him." Brandon bowed and was glad to leave the presence of his queen. All the way back to Hawthorn he congratulated himself on his stroke of luck.

"They can't come here!" Teresa gasped.

"I know it's a singular honor," Brandon replied confidently, "but it's true. The queen herself said so. Of course, I'm sure it will be only the three older children, since Prince Alfred is barely a month old and still with a nurse."

"Don't talk to me of nurses!" Teresa paced to the conservatory window and looked up the slope toward the cottage. She could see Salvatore in the garden, wandering among the bare trees and looking now and then at a shrub or bench. "No one can come to the studio. Papa has forbidden it."

"That's unreasonable in this case," he argued. "Obviously he had a girl to model for *The Harem Girl*. Tell him to think of the prince and princesses as models."

She bit back her denial. Of course Brandon must be allowed to think her father had painted *The Harem Girl* and that he had used a model in the ordinary way. "Papa doesn't do children."

"These aren't children. They are the *royal* children.

We were fortunate that the queen respects his desire for seclusion, or his career would be as good as ended. Just as royal approval can further a career, it can also kill one."

Teresa rubbed at a dull headache that was starting in her forehead as she tried to think. The children were no real problem. Princess Victoria, the eldest, was not quite four years old. The problem was with the attendants. "How many will accompany them?"

"I didn't ask. I suppose no more than three."

"No, it's impossible. With six people in the studio, Papa won't be able to concentrate at all."

"I think he should be the one to say where he can concentrate. He's a grown man, after all." Brandon hesitated, then added, "The queen and Prince Albert won't be here too frequently."

"The queen! And Prince Albert!"

"Naturally she wants to see how the painting is coming along."

"Papa will never agree to any of this!"

Brandon strode to her. "Your father and I have an agreement," he said through clenched teeth. "I have kept my part of it, but he has repaid me with duplicity and rebellion!"

Teresa turned pale. Had he found out she had painted *The Harem Girl?* "What do you mean?"

"Never mind." Brandon had decided not to confront Salvatore with the duplicate painting in Germany until he could determine whether Salvatore had copied other paintings or just that one. So far Brandon had been unable to get into the studio to look for others in progress. A new doubt entered his mind. Was Teresa against doing the royal portrait because she knew there would be no market for a duplicate canvas? He detested himself for wondering, but none of this made sense.

Firmly he said, "The children arrive tomorrow, and that's all there is to it. The queen's command of my protégé is a command to me. I will not be humiliated.

Either the portrait is painted, or Signor Verdi can consider my patronage at an end."

Teresa stared up at him. She didn't know what to say. She wanted to fling his patronage in his face, but that would be artistic suicide. Besides, if they had to leave the cottage, she would never see Brandon again, and she couldn't bear that. "You'd do that to us?" she asked in a choked voice.

"If I had to." His voice was as tight as hers, and pain was bright in his eyes.

Teresa could see only her own misery. "I see. After all, business is business."

"That's right."

She looked up at him and their eyes held. Long seconds passed but neither looked away. She knew she was too weak where Brandon was concerned. The sound of his voice, the scent of his cologne, the powerful charisma of his presence overwhelmed her. She should ask him to leave so she could deliver his message to her father. Instead she stood there gazing up at him.

"Teresa," he beseeched, "I don't want there to be hard words between us."

"Did you miss me at all?" she heard herself asking as she had vowed not to do.

"Miss you? Yes. I missed you."

Such simple words, but when he said them, Teresa felt them touch the strings of her heart and set her emotions thrumming. "I missed you too."

Brandon reached up and touched a curly tendril that had escaped her sleek coil of hair. "I've thought of you night and day. You must hate me for leaving you the way I did."

"I could never hate you." But she refrained from saying she loved him. Not until he gave her some reason to think he felt the same way. Brandon was a quiet and introspective person, and for her to blurt out her feelings might send him into retreat. After all, the woman he had first chosen to marry would never have said just anything that happened to be in her mind. Teresa told herself she must learn an equal restraint.

Her eyes lowered to Brandon's lips. They were gently curved but showed strength of character. This was no soft mouth, but neither was it a cruel one. She still recalled all too well how those lips felt on hers and how delightful it had been to feel them moving over the curves of her body.

All at once she was in his arms. The kiss they shared was so natural, she wasn't sure which of them initiated it. His arms held her with controlled passion as he drank hungrily from her lips. His tongue found hers and stroked it as she met his passion with ardor of her own.

"Teresa, you should leave at once," he managed to say as he held her close, his strong hands stroking her back and hips. "You should run up the slope and leave me."

"No," she whispered. She drew his head back down to her lips. In her heart she knew he was right, but she couldn't go from him. Her love for him sang in her veins and made her skin hot with desire. Besides, they were already lovers. "Love me," she murmured, her lips grazing his.

Brandon gazed down at her, his green eyes bright with emotion. "You ask me to love you? Do you understand what you're saying?"

"What do I have to hold back from you now? I've already given myself to you."

"Do you regret it?" A muscle clenched in his jaw in anticipation that she might say yes.

"No. I don't often regret anything I do."

He looked disturbed, as if this puzzled him, so Teresa smiled to put him at ease. "Do you regret it?"

"Yes. You were an innocent and I ravished you. You have every right to hate me."

"You didn't ravish me. I was willing." She ran her hands over the smooth weave of his coat. "Do your servants often come in here?"

"Not at this time of day."

"Then they shouldn't be too suspicious of a locked door." She went to the door and turned the key.

Brandon watched her in amazement. "What do you think you're doing?"

Teresa went to him and put her arms around his neck. "I'm seducing you."

"You can't do that!"

"I think I can." With a teasing smile she began to unbutton his shirt. When he stood there looking stunned, she nuzzled the warm skin of his neck and ran the tip of her tongue down the wedge of skin she had bared.

"Teresa, I know you don't realize how you're tempting me. An innocent lady like you—"

"Innocent? Not anymore."

"Is that it? Are you trying to torment me for my indiscretion? I offer you my deepest apology, though I know that will be of no comfort to you." His words spilled over one another as he strained to retain his composure. "I had no idea you were a virgin. Not when you came to me so willingly. I thought . . ."

Teresa finished unbuttoning his shirt and pulled it off along with his coat. Her eyes were laughing as she started to removed her own clothes.

"God, Teresa, don't do this if you don't mean it," he warned harshly.

She stepped out of her dress and petticoats, then untied the ribbon of her chemise. The filmy garment fell away, exposing her breasts and slender waist. Her skin was pearly white in the sunlight that filtered through the banks of leaves. She loosened her hair and it cascaded like nightfall over her back and down to curl about her hips. "I'm not merely tempting you, Brandon. I'm giving myself to you."

He swallowed as he let his eyes drink in her beauty. His memory had not failed him. She was more beautiful than any Lorelei his fantasies had ever conjured. And she was giving herself to him. Desire for her swept him up and drew her into his embrace. "Teresa, my Teresa," he murmured into the storm cloud of her hair. Words failed him. How could he express such love as he felt for her? Mere words seemed faint and colorless beside his passion. Instead of speaking them, he showed her with kisses and caresses that brought sighs of pleasure from her, and melting kisses.

He laid her down on the soft rug in the shadow of a bank of tall potted palms. No curious eyes could discover them there. It was as if they were in a forest glade filled with exotic plants. "Love me," he urged fervently. He couldn't bear it if she didn't love him. She had never once said that she did, and he willed her to tell him the words that he himself couldn't say. If she loved him—if she would only tell him so—he would propose on the spot and marry her before she could catch her breath.

Teresa ran her hands over the hard warmth of his body. She did love him. Indeed she loved him so much she was becoming a wanton for his sake. Yet he never spoke of love for her. She closed her eyes against the pain that thought evoked and kissed him with demanding passion to block out her fear that he didn't really love her. Her love for him was stronger than convention, stronger than her good judgment. She wanted to feel him holding her and delving deep inside her, even if his love were as transitory as lust.

Brandon's mouth found her nipple, and he tugged it with a gentle sucking motion. Laving it with his tongue and teasing it with his teeth, he gave her deep and exciting pleasure. He found Teresa's breasts were unusually sensitive, and he fondled her as he slipped inside the warm sheath of her body.

This time there was no barrier of innocence, and she sighed with pleasure as he claimed her. She was so warm and tight, he had to fight his natural impulses and hold back for her. Brandon was determined that she be as satisfied as he was with their lovemaking. He had learned the first time they made love that although Teresa looked and acted like a lady, she had the sexual proclivities of a wench. In Brandon's experience, this was an incredible paradox and nothing short of a miracle.

When he stroked deeply within her, drawing out all

the desire in her soul, Teresa murmured his name and matched her movements to his. Her eyes were mysterious pools of golden brown and her hair made a cape of jet beneath their bodies. Her nipples and lips were pouted full and pink from his kisses. She was the image of a love goddess, a pagan deity to be worshiped with his love as well as his body. Yet like a deity, she spoke no word of love for him, and the lack was a torment to Brandon.

As their passion increased, he rolled them over and let her sit astride his hips. Putting her hands on his chest, she rocked sensuously, drawing him deep inside her, then lifting her hips as if to pull away. Brandon groaned and covered both her breasts, entrapping curling wisps of her silken hair that swept over her shoulders. He toyed with her breasts, watching the ecstasy fill her face and enjoying the erotic movements of her hips.

All at once her rhythm changed, and her eyes closed. Teresa's head lifted and her back arched, pressing her breasts into his hands as hot spasms rippled through her. Brandon had wanted to give her more than one of these pleasures, but he couldn't suppress himself any longer. He felt his own release, hot and intense, and he cried out softly.

Teresa was in his arms, lying full length on his body, her face nestled against his chest and neck. She was light and warm and seemed to fit there so naturally that Brandon closed his eyes and sighed in contentment. Never had he been with anyone who made him feel like this. Protectively he smoothed her rumpled hair and ran the back of his hand over the petal softness of her cheek.

After several minutes Teresa reluctantly stirred. She didn't want to move, but she was afraid she might be too heavy on him, and Brandon wasn't on a soft bed, but on a brick floor covered by a rug. She moved away, but he drew her back into his embrace. They lay side by side, his leg curled over her hips and his shoulder cushioning her head.

They kissed and Teresa found his lips sweet and warm, the driving passion spent. He smiled, and she wondered if her own eyes were as dreamy as his. The gentle smile lingered on his lips and she kissed it again, enjoying the sweetness of his breath and the clean scent of his skin.

In the corridor beyond the door, Teresa heard the housekeeper giving an order to one of the young maids. Regretfully Teresa sat up and reached for her chemise. They might steal a few precious moments of heaven, but the worlds they lived in were still between them.

"Why are you dressing?" he asked as he sat up with a lithe movement. "The door is locked, and no one can see us here."

She shook her head and stepped into her petticoats. Once again she had let her heart overrule her common sense. He would think she was no more than a common tart at this rate! Why should he love her, when he could have her at his whim? This time she had even been the instigator! A rosy blush pinked her cheeks.

Brandon followed her lead and dressed hastily. He wasn't about to let her run away and leave him buck naked a second time.

She stood with her back to him as she buttoned her dress, her hair spilling over her shoulders. "Teresa?" he asked gently. "Why are you pulling away from me?"

"I have to get dressed," she said in a muffled voice. He would never love her now. Even the kitchen maid at her palazzo had been firm about that—men only fell in love with and married women who wouldn't let them have their way with them. Catherina had expressed this every time the subject of romance or marriage had been mentioned.

She looked past the forest of plants to the cottage on the slope, and she felt a chill of defeat. Whether Brandon ever loved her or not made no real difference. As long as her father made his living as an artist, as long as she had this burning compulsion to pour her heart out onto canvas, she couldn't marry.

Brandon came up behind her and stroked her hair. "You're so beautiful," he said lovingly. "So alive."

She gave him a sad smile. "We can never do this again, Brandon. I was wrong to tempt you like this, to make you hold me."

"You didn't exactly force me," he said with a chuckle as he bent to kiss her neck beneath the warm curtain of her hair.

"What you must think of me!" she murmured as she kept her gaze out the window. If she looked into his eyes, she might blurt out her love against all her restraint.

"Teresa," Brandon said as he turned her about so that she had to face him, "will you marry me?"

Incredulous hope leapt into her eyes. "Marry you?" she whispered.

"Your father no longer needs you. Katie and Hal take good care of him, and if he needs someone else, I'll hire a larger staff for him. Marry me, Teresa, and live here in Hawthorn as my wife."

Words failed her. Her lips moved, but no sound came out. Unwillingly she looked back at the cottage, then up at Brandon.

"He doesn't need you like I do," Brandon urged, his hands tight on her arms.

"Yes, he does," she heard herself saying over the crack of her breaking heart. "He does need me, Brandon. You'll never know how much."

Brandon stared down at her. "I'm asking you to marry me!"

She slowly shook her head. "I can never marry."

"What? Why not!"

Again she shook her head. "That's all I can say."

"There must be a reason! Are you already married or engaged? No! You've already said you're not. A vow of chastity, perhaps? No, I think that's hardly likely under the circumstances."

Teresa gave him a cool look.

"Is there insanity in your family? If so, we'll have no children. Mitchell or Colin can inherit Hawthorn."

"Don't be ridiculous."

"Then why in the name of God won't you marry me?" he thundered, momentarily forgetting the gentleness he believed to be the due of all women.

Teresa lifted her hands and began to coil her hair into a bun. She didn't meet his eyes. "I can't marry you, and I can't give you the reason why."

"You mean you won't!"

"No, I mean I can't." She replaced her pins and ran her fingers over her hair to be sure it was neatly in place. Only then did she meet his anguished stare. "I truly can't, Brandon, even though I desire above all else to be your wife."

"Yet you'll make love with me?" His expression was thunderous, but Teresa didn't shrink away.

After a painful pause she said, "I can be your lover, but not your wife."

"Dammit, I want you for my viscountess, not my mistress! Are you sure you understand what I'm saying to you?"

"I understand you. My English has improved greatly since I came here."

Silence strung tightly between them. Brandon had no idea what to say. He wasn't so vain as to think every woman in the world would leap at the chance to marry him, but he had ample reason to think Teresa would have him, even if only to recover her good name. He didn't know what to say. She had refused to give him a reason, and he was damned if he would grovel with declarations of love to try to coerce her. "Very well," he said stiffly. "I accept your rejection."

Teresa winced. When he spoke so dispassionately, so formally, she knew he was hiding deeper emotions. "I never meant to hurt you," she whispered.

"Hurt? Not I. As for your other, most delectable offer, I'll have to consider it."

She glared at him.

"You're surprised? I was prepared to offer marriage, not merely a dalliance." He smiled maddeningly. "I'm sure you could understand if the tables were reversed."

She lifted her chin to keep it from quivering. How dare he throw her offer of love back at her? "Perhaps I should make it easy for you and withdraw my suggestion."

"No, no, let it stand. I need to think on this. I admit to being perplexed as to why a woman would reject becoming the Viscountess of Hawthorn, and not hesitate to become my leman. If you disliked me, I could see your hesitancy to marry me, but that would certainly preclude your becoming my lover as well. Tell me, Teresa, what will you gain by this?"

"You don't understand at all!"

"You're right. I don't."

She turned her back to him. "I was wrong to give myself to you."

"Hah! Now I sense it coming. You shouldn't have, but you did, and now only gold will set it right?"

"What?" she gasped as she wheeled back around to face him. "Maybe as much gold as, say, a duplicate painting from your father would bring?" He was too angry to see the confusion in her eyes.

"What are you talking about? Speak more slowly."

"I thought you said you had mastered English. That you could understand all I said a minute ago."

"I did then; I don't now! What's this about a painting?" Cold dread gripped her. He must have somehow found out she was the painter and not her father!

"Never mind," Brandon said coldly. "I'll get to the bottom of all this with your father. In the meantime, expect the royal children tomorrow."

She felt as if his eyes were slicing into her soul, but she didn't dare ask any questions. If he suspected what was going on in the studio but had no proof, she and her father would have to be extremely careful. Not trusting herself to speak, she left the conservatory.

Brandon ached as she left. Why did they argue so often? He didn't know anyone who spent so much time agonizing over the woman he loved. Women, especially those in love, were sweet and pliable and obliging— weren't they? He couldn't recall a single exception. But then Teresa had never said she loved him, only that she would be his mistress. Was she afraid he was about to find out that Salvatore was defrauding him by making duplicate paintings? Brandon wanted her so badly, but not like that. He wanted her as his wife, and let her father chase the moon if he liked.

He wished he had never seen the duplicate of the *Ladies on the Altana*. He almost wished he had never heard of Salvatore Verdi at all, but then he wouldn't know Teresa.

Sweet Teresa, he thought as he climbed the broad stairs to his bedroom. She was gentleness and fire, and filled with such innocent seduction. Surely no other woman in the world was so right for him as was Teresa. He closed the door to his sitting room so no maids would disturb him, then went into the bedroom.

He could still see her lying there on his billowing feather bed, her eyes promising love such as he had never known before, her lips dewy from his kisses.

Brandon's eyes raised and his heart skipped as he found himself gazing at an exact replica of that guileless surrender. He stepped nearer the painting. The harem girl curled in sweet seductiveness, her almond eyes holding the exact suggestion that Teresa's had held. The gauzy veil hid her mouth, but the luscious body was there to prove its model. Brandon knew the exact texture of those breasts. He knew the warmth and pliability of that skin and the feel of those slender arms when they were entwined about him. The harem girl's hair might be dark red and her eyes might be blue, but dammit, that was a portrait of Teresa!

His eyes fixed on the Verdi signature, and shocked anger engulfed him. Teresa had posed—like this—for her father! A gasp escaped from him, and he had to steady himself against the foot of the bed. Teresa? And Salvatore had seen her naked and with that seductive promise in her eyes?

For a minute Brandon felt physically ill. With a great effort he steadied himself. It couldn't be. Teresa wouldn't pose nude for anyone, least of all her own father! No, now that he looked at it, the color of the hair and the eyes . . . No, it had to be someone else.

But there was that unmistakable curve of breast and the familiar swell of her hip, the proportions of her slender legs. Brandon was stunned. If it wasn't Teresa, it had to be her exact double.

·Teresa was innocent of any wrongdoing. Brandon was positive of that. Her only fault was that she was too loyal to the father whom she loved. If he had wanted her to pose, he would have convinced her that there was nothing wrong or immoral in her being the model. Poor innocent! Brandon trembled in his effort to control himself. No wonder she had been so nervous when he was examining the painting! All his anger at her was dissolved by compassion.

He had to watch Salvatore quite carefully in the future. If he had even the slightest hint that what he suspected was true, Brandon would sweep Teresa away for her own safety. He wondered if this secret shame was the reason Teresa felt she couldn't marry him, but would agree to be his mistress. That seemed logical. Love for her flooded over him. Teresa needed him to watch over her, and he was determined to do exactly that.

16

"Papa, what else could I say? It's the *queen*."

"She is not our queen. We belong to Venice."

"We live in England, and besides, she is our patron's queen."

"*My* patron," Salvatore corrected.

Teresa sighed. This was one of his bad days, when he couldn't recall who actually painted the pictures. "Nevertheless, a queen is a queen, and she deserves our respect. Not to mention the glory that would come to you with the designation of royal artist." She coaxed him with her smile. "And they are very small children. Only three of them."

"Three?"

"Lord Kincaid says the baby is unlikely to come so far from the palace in such cool weather." She put her arm around Salvatore's shoulders and leaned over his chair. "You know how you like children, Papa, and I hear they are quite pretty."

"All children are pretty," he acceded. "I suppose I could paint them."

"Of course you can."

He rubbed a hand over his eyes, then held it out in front of him as if surprised to discover its tremor. "*How* can I paint them? No, Eva Maria, I cannot."

"Teresa," she corrected automatically. "I think I know a way, Papa. You set up your canvas and arrange them just the way you want them. I'll stand behind you and watch. You know my memory is accurate. After they leave, I'll paint what I remember."

"Pretend to paint them?" he asked in a puzzled voice. "Someone will know."

"No, they won't, because I'll be there to make certain none of the attendants looks at the canvas."

"We must use two canvases. The one you paint and the one I seem to paint. No one would believe it if I never apply paint to canvas."

"You're right," she said with relief. "That's just what we'll do."

He got heavily to his feet. "I will go stretch the canvases." He frowned at his large square hands. "At least they have lost none of their strength."

Teresa took his hand and kissed it as a mother would a child's. "Don't worry, Papa. It will be all right."

He shook his head remorsefully. "I hope you're not wrong. It would kill my father if it ever became known what we are doing."

Teresa watched him go, a great sadness in her heart. She never knew if he would be logical in his thinking or not. At least the brain damage from his fever had not left him violent or too senile to hide his disability.

She went to the parlor and began to read the mail that had come. There was a letter in Catherina Valore's cramped handwriting with news from Venice. Saberio had been ill but was recovering, and the roof had been mended, thanks to the money Teresa had sent. There was great unrest over the detested Austrians, but no one was willing to lead a rebellion. The youngest granddaughter of the Valore family had married and was already expecting a baby.

Teresa was in no mood to hear about marital happiness. She had tossed and turned all night in regret that she couldn't marry Brandon. In the small hours of the morning she had decided to throw her art to the winds and marry him in spite of everything. By dawn, however, she had come to her senses. If she gave up her art for him, she would someday regret it. She might even blame Brandon for making such a decision necessary. Then there was her father to think of. Brandon would have to be told that he could no longer paint because of his illness, and that would destroy what pride he had left. No, she couldn't throw away all her years of study and her father's pride. To face the rest of her life without her beloved art would be like going blind or deaf.

She opened the other letter and read the signature of Carmelo Di Palma, the owner of the gallery in Venice. Quickly she scanned the first sentences, expecting the letter to be one of praise for her father's work, which it was, but it was not what she thought. The Di Palma Gallery had recently purchased a painting of a reclining nude that the owner felt surpassed anything Salvatore had done in the past. Di Palma said it was better than old Antonio's and likened it to the old Venetian masters'. He also raved about the exotic flavor of having the nude appear as a harem girl.

Teresa crumpled the paper in her fist. Brandon had sold *The Harem Girl*! How had he done it so quickly, and why? He had said he wanted it for his private collection! She recalled the long hours of painting and the fear she would be caught by Salvatore or one of the servants. Then she remembered that it was a painting of her own body that was hanging in a public gallery, and she groaned aloud.

"Katie," she called out, "if Papa asks for me, tell him I've gone for a walk."

As the maid nodded, Teresa took her blue wool cape from the hall tree. She would get to the bottom of this!

Summer had quickly given way to the chill of September, and the wind, which held an early bite of frost, swirled her cape about her as she stepped outside. How could he have done it? she wondered as she drew the cape warmly about her. The painting was his, of course, to dispose of as he pleased, but they were lovers. Couldn't he detect a resemblance between her and *The Harem Girl*? If so, wouldn't a lover keep the painting for remembrance? And how had he found a buyer for it in Venice in this length of time? He had said he had gone to visit Mitchell in Germany.

The grasses were damp from the rains the night before, so Teresa took the route of the riding path, which circled the green by the side of the woods and ended at the entry to Hawthorn. She hurried up the steps and waited impatiently for Fitch to answer her knock. "I must see Lord Kincaid at once."

Fitch, who was still displeased with the Verdis' lack of appreciation for Queen Victoria, said crisply, "I'll see if the master can be disturbed."

Teresa was led to the morning room, where she paced until Brandon came.

"If you've come to tell me again that your father won't paint the royal children," he said, "you're wasting your time."

"Bother the royal children," she said. It was a phrase she had learned from Katie, but judging by the way Brandon's eyes widened on hearing it, Teresa wondered whether she had misunderstood its meaning. But that wasn't why she was here. "I want to know why you sold *The Harem Girl*!" she demanded.

"What?"

"You told me how much you wanted a nude to hang here at Hawthorn, and you seemed pleased with it at the time. Why did you get rid of it?"

"Calm down. I don't know what you're talking about."

"No? Read this!" She thrust the crumpled paper at him and snatched away her hand before their fingers could meet. "Let's hear you explain that!"

As he read and reread the Italian to be sure he understood, she resumed her pacing. "To sell a painting is one thing," she said, lapsing into her native tongue, "but to sell that one is unforgivable!"

"Speak English or speak more slowly. I can't understand you."

"Pah!" she said unreasonably. "I learned your language, why can't you learn mine?"

Brandon finished rereading the letter and frowned. "How did the picture get to Venice?" he said almost to himself.

"How should I know? Why did you sent it to Di Palma?" She had visions of hordes of people gawking at the painting of her naked body.

"I didn't send it to anyone."

"I don't believe you. Signor Di Palma knows the painting. He even describes it!"

"Come with me." Brandon strode from the room, and when she didn't follow him, he caught her wrist and pulled her after him.

"Turn me loose!" Fitch gave them an appraising eye as Brandon led her up the staircase. "You can't drag me up to your room like this!"

He didn't argue the point, nor did he release her. She had no choice but to follow him across the wide vestibule, through his sitting room, and into his bedroom.

"There!" he said as he turned her to face the wall and the picture. "I didn't sell it to anyone."

Relief flooded over her, but it was quickly followed by confusion. "It's still here!"

"Of course."

He gave her an enigmatic look. "It holds a certain . . . interest for me." He looked from her to the canvas. "Something about the eyes and the curve of the breast."

She averted her eyes. Did he suspect who the model was? "What about the letter, then? How do you explain that?"

Brandon frowned and again read the letter. "I can't explain it. Isn't this the gallery where I met you in Venice?"

"Yes. Signor Di Palma is quite familiar with Papa's work. He would know a Verdi painting if he saw one."

"Would he?" He thought of the painting in Paris and its duplicate in Germany. Why would Teresa show him proof of her father's underhanded dealing? Didn't that prove she was innocent of any part of the scheme? "Does your father know about this letter?"

"No!" She could hardly tell him that Salvatore didn't even know the painting existed. "When I read it I came straight to you."

"Teresa, I don't know how to say this to you, but I have reason to believe your father is selling duplicates of his better paintings."

"What? That's impossible!" She drew herself up to her full height. "A Verdi would never do anything to stain his honor."

Brandon frowned. He knew of one Verdi who had suggested she become a mistress rather than a wife, and who had evidently posed nude for her own father. "I'm not as convinced of the Verdi honor as you seem to be."

She glared at him as he continued. "You see, this isn't the only Verdi painting that seems to have shown up inexplicably. There's another one in Germany. The one of the women on the rooftop." He watched to see if she looked surprised.

"The one of the woman in the red dress? It must have been sold. Didn't the gallery owner send you word?"

"That's just it. The painting is still hanging in the gallery in Paris. I saw it myself."

"Then the other one must be a mistake."

"No, I saw it also."

"How can that be?"

"In view of his recent success, your father may have decided to repaint his best paintings and sell them on his own."

"No, that's impossible. Papa would never do that. Even if he would, why paint the same picture twice when he could do a new one with no more effort? No, that's foolish."

"Still, it has been done before. As a result, the original becomes valueless and the artist loses his reputation."

"Naturally, but that hasn't happened here."

"You seem rather certain."

"I'm positive. Even if Papa would do something so despicable—and he wouldn't—he couldn't do it without my knowing about it."

"Surely you aren't in the studio every minute of the day." Disbelief was evident in his voice.

"No, but I am in there more than you might think. When a painting is in progress, it must be stored in the drying racks or left on an easel. A painting the size of *The Harem Girl* or *The Ladies on the Altana* couldn't be hidden under a dresser or behind a chair. I get canvases out of that rack every day. If there were a new one there, I would certainly see it. Besides, Papa just wouldn't!"

Both of them stared at the harem girl as if she could tell them the answer to the puzzle. At last Teresa said, "Di Palma must be mistaken. There is no other explanation."

"Perhaps." Brandon didn't sound convinced. "But I saw the other one myself, and it was identical, even to the glazing and shadings."

A suspicion was budding to life in Teresa. "You're sure of that?"

"Teresa, art is my life. I spend hours studying and comparing paintings. Of course I'm certain."

"Could one have been the work of, say, a man who had studied under the same master, who had seen and copied the original painting?"

Brandon's eyes searched her face. "I suppose that would be possible, but it's rare to find two students whose style is so similar."

"Rare, but not impossible. I know of someone who could do this."

"Who?"

"My Uncle Mario."

"Mario Verdi? I've seen his work. He lacks the compositional skill."

"If he were copying Papa's paintings, he wouldn't need to do composition. Uncle Mario has an unusual ability to reproduce anything he sees." She knew it was possible, because she had the same talent. "I'm positive he could do it."

"Your uncle? I find that difficult to believe."

She looked back at *The Harem Girl*. How could Mario have seen it, when even her own father hadn't? *The Ladies on the Altana* was understandable. Mario had spent hours studying it. But *The Harem Girl*? He hadn't been inside the house after Teresa started painting it. In fact, she hadn't seen her uncle for weeks. Now that she thought about it, that seemed odd too. "I would believe anything of Uncle Mario. I just can't understand how he could have seen this one to copy it. He and Papa argued, and he no longer visits us."

"Does he have a key to the studio?"

"No. No, Papa would never have given him a key. You know how Papa is about his studio."

"Yet he lets you in?"

"I can assure you *I* never painted a duplicate picture!"

"No, no," Brandon said with a laugh. "I didn't mean that you had."

Teresa scowled. Did he have to be so adamant that she couldn't have? She didn't dare challenge him, however. "All the same, I would consider the other paintings forgeries and not duplications."

" 'Forgery' is an ugly word."

"I can swear to you on anything you choose to name that my father's hand never painted the picture you saw in Germany or the one in Venice."

He paused, then said, "You're really that certain?"

"I swear it on my own mother's grave."

Brandon glanced again at *The Harem Girl*. "I'll leave for Venice at once."

"You always seem to leave the country whenever we make love," she observed dryly. "I'm not too surprised."

"I have to see the painting to know if it's a forgery.

And I don't leave the country every time we make love!"

"No? I'm coming with you."

"You'll do no such thing."

"Yes, I will. I can tell if it's a forgery more easily than you can." She knew Mario would be more adept at imitating Salvatore's brush strokes than her own, because Antonio had taught them identically, whereas she, as a girl, had had a less stringent apprenticeship. Mario might have made errors that would point out her own hand in the original. She needed to go to protect herself as well as her father.

"I'm an expert," Brandon explained patiently. "I can tell a Verdi when I see one."

"Can you?" she asked with some amusement. "Are you so sure?"

"Of course." He leaned closer to the painting on the wall. "Look how the mottling in the background—"

"I believe you," she said quickly. It wouldn't do for him to examine her painting so minutely. "But I'm still coming with you."

"Your father will never allow you to travel with me alone, and he has to stay to paint the royal children."

She hadn't thought of that. "We'll take Katie along as a chaperon. If you give me three days, I can go." In that length of time, if she painted quickly, she could block out the picture, do the undercoating, and leave it to dry until she could return.

"I don't want to wait that long. I plan to leave at once."

"Then it will be on your conscience that Katie and I are traveling alone, because I'm going to Venice in three days."

"I forbid you to do that!"

"You have no right to forbid me to do anything! You are neither my husband nor my father, and as far as I know, you haven't even decided to be my lover!"

"My decision on that seems to be unnecessary, since

we are, in fact, lovers already," he said. "And I'm amazed how casually you mention it!"

"What would you have me do? Faint and flutter like Lady Barbara? I already know we're lovers! Why pretend otherwise?"

He glared at her. "I never know what to expect out of you. You act like a lady, you look like a lady, but you think like a trollop!"

"A trollop!" She reacted before she thought, and her palm slapped his cheek. At once she was appalled at her action.

Brandon stonily stared at her. Slowly he rubbed the red mark on his cheek. "I deserved that, and I apologize."

"I'm . . . sorry," she stammered. "I've never in my life struck anyone! But no one else ever called me a name like that. How can you ask me to marry you and then call me a trollop?"

He surprised her by smiling. "The combination of trollop and lady isn't altogether undesirable."

Stoically she said, "I'll be ready to go in three days. Don't leave without me."

By the time she returned to the cottage, a light rain was falling, and the leaves were soggy under her feet. She shook the raindrops from her cape and hung it on the hall tree. "Papa?" When he didn't answer, she went down the corridor to the studio. "Papa, I have some bad news for you."

"It's not my father, is it?" he asked, then caught his error. "No, of course not. Sit down, *cara mia*. What is it?"

She went to the small hearth and warmed her hands before she sat on one of the straight-backed chairs. "I have reason to believe Uncle Mario has forged at least one of your paintings."

"Mario? No, he is in Milan."

"No, Papa, remember? He moved to London. He's been here, to the studio."

"Yes, that's right. For a moment I forgot."

Teresa leaned forward and put her hand on her father's. "Papa, please try to remember. Did you ever give Uncle Mario a key to the studio?"

Salvatore looked confused, but he said, "No. I would never do that."

"I thought not."

Salvatore said, "He has painted a forgery, you say? Mario?"

"It must have been Uncle Mario. Lord Kincaid saw a copy in Germany of *The Ladies on the Altana*."

"And he's just now mentioning it?"

"I don't know why he didn't ask us about it as soon as he returned. However, now there seems to be another duplicate of one of your paintings in Venice."

"Another?"

"At the Di Palma Gallery." She hoped he wouldn't ask which painting. "Lord Kincaid is leaving for Venice in three days and I am going with him. So is Katie, as chaperon," she added hastily. "I'll arrange to have food sent up from Hawthorn for you and Hal."

"You can't travel to Venice without me. What would your mother say?"

"Katie will do just fine," she argued. "You can't go because you have to be here to paint the royal portrait."

"Yes, the children. I almost forgot." Salvatore looked down at the canvas he was stretching onto the wooden frame. "I can't go." He gave her a worried look. "But neither can you. How can I paint if you aren't here?"

"I've already thought of that. We'll say the attendants must bring the children every day for three days. That will give me time to put on the first undercoat. It has to dry before the canvas can be worked, and you'll say it isn't dry until I return. Can you do that?"

"Of course," he said with a smile. "It's only the truth."

"I won't be gone any longer than I have to be," she promised, "and Hal will take good care of you."

"Don't worry about me. I'll spend the time sketching and blocking out a painting I have in mind about the cats of Venice." His smile broadened. "Do you remember the cats, *bambina*?"

She laughed. "Yes, Papa. I remember." In Venice it was considered unlucky to kill a cat, and that to do so would shorten the killer's own life. As a result, Venice was full of cats of all colors and sizes. "I would like to do a painting of the cats."

"By the time you have returned I will have it composed."

Teresa nodded. She wished she could feel as confident of the future as her father did.

17

For the most part Mario hated his pupils. Few of them had the least shadow of talent and none of them had any interest in art. He had actually heard them refer to his class as an easy subject to be got through with a minimum of effort. Mario had been appalled. Art—easy? Why, he and Salvatore and their father and grandfather had devoted their entire lives to learning art, and of them all, only Salvatore, and possibly Antonio, had learned enough to claim the status of master. Mario still didn't see how Salvatore had done it.

Over the weeks he had become bold in his efforts to copy Salvatore's work. Once he had brazenly stolen one of Salvatore's canvases overnight to study it in the light of his own studio. He doubted Salvatore even missed it. The painting had been the one of the nude harem girl, and because Salvatore had used brush strokes that were slightly different, he wanted more time with it. Also Salvatore had used a new method of giving luminescence to the skin. Mario had had to work hard, to duplicate the work of art. The effort had been worth it, however. He had sold it to Carmelo Di Palma's gallery in Venice. To send it to a city where he and Salvatore were so well known was a risk, but he had known Di Palma would give him a generous price. Besides, Mario didn't dare sell his forgeries in Britain.

He was barely able to sit through his classes at

Maidenhode. Discipline was a problem as usual, but Mario no longer minded. He merely pretended to be blind and deaf to his students' antics. They were there to while away an hour, and so was he. More and more he appreciated Antonio's quiet, ordered lessons with boys who were apprenticed from youngest childhood because they had shown a true talent and love of art.

He peered over the top of his sketchbook as the Mills boy threw a wad of paper at the Siler boy. Mario's eyes dropped back to the sketch he was making of a Roman pavilion. Let them throw their paper away. Their fathers could afford to buy them reams of it.

"Please, sir," a boy said to get the teacher's attention. Mario reluctantly looked up.

"How's this, sir?"

Mario studied the lopsided building on the boy's sketchpad. The lad was a churl, a talentless lump. "Very good. Your best effort yet." The boy beamed at the hollow praise.

Mario went back to his own drawing. There was no reason to correct the boy's lines or tell him the mysteries of perspective and proportion. Once he was out of school, the lad would do nothing more thought-provoking than to plan a shoot or tell a gardener to establish a garden.

When the last bell of the day rang, Mario got up from his desk with as much relief as any of his students. He had survived another day; the evening was his.

He went back to his rooms at Ramsden and crept silently up the stairs. He hadn't paid his rent in two months, and he knew the landlady was watching for him. Not that Mario didn't have the money, for Di Palma had paid handsomely for the nude. But Mario hated to pay for such a dismal lodging, and he thought if he saved his money until he was evicted, he could afford a nicer place. Unfortunately he had never had much luck in keeping money, and a surprising amount of it was already spent on ale and paints and a certain French red wine he had developed a taste for.

When he was safely inside and the door locked against his landlady, Mario went to his paintings. The neighboring building kept out the sunlight for the most part, but he could see well enough. These were jewels, he knew, and he could dispose of them for almost the same price as gems. The more Salvatore's reputation grew, the more Mario could demand for his forgeries.

He surrounded himself with paintings and gazed at them as he ate his supper of cold ham and cheese washed down with a bottle of the red wine. He was like a miser, surrounded by his gold yet wanting more.

As soon as the sun began to set, Mario put on his heavy cape and went around to the beggarly stable where he kept his old mare. The horse wasn't pretty, nor was she gaited, but she was reliable, and that's all Mario cared about. With her dark brown coat and his black cape, the horse and rider were almost invisible as soon as they left the lights of London.

He reached Salvatore's cottage in time to see his brother moving about the rooms extinguishing the gaslights and the oil lamps. Salvatore was up late. Mario wondered what had changed his routine. The delay was inconvenient. Mario shivered in the cold night as he waited for Salvatore to fall asleep. In the manor house down the green the lights were out except for those in the servants' quarters in the attic. That routine was also different. Mario didn't care what had caused the change, he just wanted to do what he had come to do and get back to his fire.

After a while he dismounted and tied the mare to a bush. Creeping nearer the house, he listened for any noises that would mean Salvatore was awake, but the house was silent. He took the key from his pocket and let himself into the studio.

Striking a match, Mario lit the hissing gas lamps, and looked nervously at the inner door. When he heard no one coming to investigate, he went confidently to the easels.

Two paintings were sitting out as if Salvatore had been comparing them just before he went to bed. Oddly enough, both were of the same subject, a group of three children. One painting was well under way in tones of sepia and umber. It was skillfully done, and although the canvas was barely covered, the children looked lively. The other was equally well-designed, but the lines wavered and the figures were stiff. Had Salvatore taken in an apprentice? If so, why on earth would he start the boy on portraits?

Mario shook his head. Salvatore would never be the teacher their father had been. As shaky as those lines were, the boy must not be accustomed to drawing, let alone painting. Salvatore was asking for trouble to jump him into oils and portraits so soon. But that was Salvatore's problem, not his.

He turned his back on the two paintings. Whoever the subjects were, they were no good to Mario. No one would want a copy of someone else's children.

He rummaged through the racks. There were several paintings he had already copied, and a number of flowers and still lifes Teresa had painted. He discounted all those. There was a new canvas of an inn scene, but he didn't care for it at all. Neither had Salvatore, evidently, because it was pushed to the back of the rack. Mario studied it and shook his head. The composition was filled with action: horses stamping in the traces and small boys running about and a saucy wench making eyes at the coach driver, who looked as if he were about to accept her invitation. Mario felt tired just from looking at it. He preferred much more orderly canvases, where everything was in its correct place. With disgust he went to the next canvas.

All at once he froze. Far back in the house he had heard something. Yes, there it was again! A footstep!

He quickly put out the light and hurried soundlessly across the darkened room. Just as he let himself out the door, Salvatore opened the inner door. "Papa? Is it you?" Salvatore asked. The question sent a shiver up Mario's back.

Salvatore looked around the large room, then went back into the main part of the house. Mario sat motionless in the shadows. Was Salvatore insane? Brain fever could do that. Did that explain the new brush technique in the nude? As quietly as he could, Mario slipped back to where he had tied his mare. With Salvatore awake, he couldn't return to the studio. He wondered if he could somehow use his brother's disability. Perhaps this mental abberration explained how Salvatore had suddenly become so talented. Mario had heard of madness creating genius in some rare cases. He had to think about this new development.

Venice shimmered like a jewel in the blue-gray of the Adriatic. Teresa leaned forward on the rail expectantly. Katie was scurrying about checking baggage and exclaiming over the sights, but Brandon had eyes only for Teresa. The cold, misty air brought pink to her cheeks, and her skin looked dewy and fresh. Her caramel eyes sparkled with the excitement of seeing her beloved Venice.

Brandon had never seen such a lovely woman. She was so full of life she almost crackled with energy, yet she held herself with composure. Droplets of water beaded on her hair beneath the brim of her garnet bonnet and clung to the saucy ostrich plume that curled around the crown of the hat. Her deep blue cloak was edged in white fur and reached almost to the hem of her wine-red dress. Most of the men on deck had glanced at her appreciatively and a few were staring frankly. Brandon wasn't accustomed to the Italian male's unabashed perusal of beauty. He stepped protectively closer to her.

Teresa took one hand from her white fur muff and put it on his arm. "Look! There's the dome of Santa Maria della Salute! Look at the *zattere*," she added,

pointing to a fleet of rafts moored to the north side of
the Giudecca Canal. "Oh, Brandon! I'm home!"

Brandon wasn't quite as thrilled as she had hoped.
He was afraid she might refuse to return with him.
During the entire trip, she had talked only of Venice
and how she loved her native city.

When they docked Teresa led Brandon ashore and
tiptoed to search through the crowd. "Saberio! Saberio!"
She waved until a tall, thin man with white hair saw
her.

Brandon nodded to the man he recognized as the
one who had admitted him into the Verdis' house on
his previous visit. Brandon assumed the man must be
something of a butler, but Teresa obviously expected
them to shake hands, so Brandon did.

"Katie Banning, this is Saberio. He will take you to
the palazzo along with the luggage. Just show him
which ones to load into the cart." She took Brandon's
arm. "We'll go by way of the canal."

She hired a gondolier and soon the slim black boat
glided out onto the water. As they entered the Grand
Canal the gondolier broke out into song, pausing in his
chorus to call out a warning to another gondolier who
was coming too close.

Teresa drew a deep breath of the salty, faintly fishy
air. She was home! Until she saw Venice, she hadn't
allowed herself to think how homesick she had been.
Now she wondered how she had ever been able to leave
it.

In a few minutes they reached the dock of the Verdi
palazzo. Teresa looked up at the ancient stones and
carvings of her ancestral home and her lips curved in a
smile at this homecoming. She was so eager to show her
world to Brandon. They went up the moss-slick steps
and Catherina threw open the door to welcome them.
In a torrent of fluent Italian, Teresa greeted the old
woman and was enclosed in a plump embrace that
smelled of cinnamon and apples and ham.

Teresa introduced Catherina and Brandon, and was

glad to see the approval in the old woman's smiling eyes. She thought of Catherina almost as a grandmother, and her opinions were important to Teresa. "Have you aired the best bedroom for Lord Kincaid?" Teresa asked.

"Of course. Do you think I have forgotten how to have guests? Come in, come in. The air is too damp out here."

She took them into the marble vestibule and shut the door. She automatically bent to pick up a bucket of burning coals as she chattered with Teresa in their native tongue. The palazzo was chilling cold, even though winter had not yet arrived. Brandon quickly discovered it was because none of the rooms had fireplaces.

The street door opened and Saberio, along with Katie and the luggage, came into the palazzo. Catherina gave the brazier of coals to Brandon and went to help her husband and the maid bring in and sort out the luggage.

"Why aren't there any fireplaces?" Brandon whispered.

"They take up too much room. We take a bucket of coals with us, so we'll be warm wherever we go. You can't do that with a fireplace."

He followed her up the wooden steps to the next floor. "We added these when we had to rent out the upper floors," she explained. "The main staircase is outside in the courtyard, of course. It is marble and much prettier than this one."

"Outside?"

"No one would use space inside for something as large as a stairway. Not if they have a courtyard."

They went down a narrow hall, and Teresa opened a door. "You'll stay in here."

Brandon looked around in appreciation. The room had once been one of great distinction, and the windowsills and doorway were carved of milky marble. Impressive paintings by Antonio Verdi hung on the oak-paneled walls, and the floor was tiled in a mosaic pattern and topped with a thick Oriental rug. He was glad to see there was a fireplace beside the large bed.

"This was my grandfather's room," she said as she gazed about the chamber. "Before that it was one of the state rooms. That's the good part about renting the upper floors—we got the prettiest rooms for our use. I was told a queen once slept in my room, but no one was ever quite sure who she was or which country she ruled. Perhaps it's just a legend. Venice has many of them."

Saberio came in with Brandon's luggage and Teresa left him in order to freshen up in her own room, which was across the hall. So much had happened to her since she was last in that room. She had fallen in love, and had become a woman. To her surprise, the room seemed smaller than it had before, yet she had been gone only a few months.

Saberio had already deposited her luggage in the room and Katie was opening trunks and unpacking. "Catherina will show you where you'll sleep, Katie. Also, I want you to get some of her recipes while we're here. It will please Papa to have foods he has always known."

"Yes, Miss."

Teresa went down the stairs and into the studio. The air here was dank and musty with the smells of oils and turpentine. She felt sad to see the room in disuse. Before, the studio had been the hub of the house. She went to a large window and looked out onto the canal. The gentle wavelets still slapped the stone foundations and docks, the gulls still circled and dipped for food, but she saw it with different eyes now. Venice was still her home, and she loved every lichen-encrusted stone, but she had another home as well, in the misty green countryside at Hawthorn. Perhaps, she thought, this was what love really was—knowing her true home was with the man she had chosen above all others.

"Teresa? Am I intruding?"

She turned with a smile to see Brandon. "Of course not. I was just looking at Venice, and really seeing her for the first time in my life. We never see our homes until we have something to compare them with."

Again he wondered if she would return to England with him. Hawthorn would be damned lonely without Teresa. "Are you rested enough to go to the gallery?"

"Yes. If the painting really is a copy of *The Harem Girl*, I want it out of the public eye as soon as possible."

He could see why that would be true if he was right about the model.

They exited the building onto the street, which was barely wide enough for a vendor's cart. Brandon was amazed at its narrowness and stretched his arms to see whether he could touch the buildings on both sides at once.

"There are others much closer together than this," she said with amusement at the wonder in his eyes.

The Di Palma Gallery opened onto the broad square of San Marco and Brandon was glad for the open space. He had felt claustrophobic in the narrow streets. Every time he had been to Di Palma's before, he had come from the other direction, where the streets were wider. The sounds of Venice were different from those of London, for there was no rattle and clank of traffic. The only sounds were those of voices talking and some even singing, and of an occasional cart being pushed along the street. Drifts of pigeons rose and fell to avoid the feet of passersby, and cats seemed to be everywhere. The mist that hovered in the air made the scene as soft and hazy as a watercolor on gauze.

"Would you like some hot cocoa to warm you?" he asked, gesturing toward a café.

"Not in there. That's Quadri's. Only Austrians go there. We'll go to Florian's later."

They went into the gallery and were met by Di Palma, his wrinkles arranged into a toothy grin. "Good day, Signorina Verdi, Lord Kincaid. Such an honor you do me."

Teresa gave him a level look. She remembered all too well how he had snubbed her the last time she had been in the gallery.

"I hear you have a nude painted by Salvatore Verdi?" Brandon said.

"*Si.* Surely you've not come so far to see it?"

"Where is it?" Teresa asked.

"Here, near the window, where all can admire it but sunlight can't mar it." Di Palma made a grand gesture toward a large canvas.

As Teresa and Brandon viewed it, she blushed brightly. In her studio she hadn't realized just how bare she would look in the light of day, nor how seductive the painting would seem. She refused to meet Brandon's eyes.

Brandon moved the canvas to catch the brush strokes in the light, and frowned. "These aren't quite like Signor Verdi's strokes. See how the background is mottled?"

"No, no," Di Palma said, making a bobbing motion in his effort to please his wealthy customer. "I assure you this is a Verdi. Ask the young lady. She will know her father's work."

Reluctantly Teresa leaned nearer. The technique was remarkably accurate, but her eye saw minute details only the artist could detect. Besides, she *knew* the person who painted it had made no copies. "It's a good forgery, but it's not one of Papa's."

Di Palma's face fell. "Not Salvatore's? This cannot be!"

"Where did you get this painting?" Brandon demanded.

"Why, I . . . I . . ." Di Palma was reluctant to name his source as Mario Verdi because Mario had been adamant that his name be kept out of it. Mario also knew Di Palma sold the paintings in his gallery for much more than he reported to the artists. Angering Mario could mean the end of his gallery and his livelihood, if Mario told his artist friends the truth. "From a stranger," he feebly offered.

"You buy paintings without checking on the source?" Teresa was suspicious.

"I thought he was reliable. He was recommended

highly, and I could see it was a masterpiece." Di Palma squinted at the painted face. "Look at the clarity of those colors, the depth! No, you must be mistaken. It's a Verdi."

"No, it isn't. Should we call in the authorities?" Teresa bluffed.

"No, no! That's not necessary!" Di Palma frowned at the painting. "If it's not a Verdi, who did it?"

"It's a copy," Brandon explained. "I have the original in my private collection."

"Signor Di Palma, have you talked with my Uncle Mario lately?" Teresa asked bluntly.

Di Palma paled. "Mario? No, no. Not in years."

Brandon didn't look convinced. "Signorina Verdi thinks her uncle may be involved in this."

"Mario? No! I've known Mario since we were boys together!" Di Palma looked as if he might faint.

"I think we should call in the authorities when we return to England," Brandon said. "Perhaps the other one is also a fake."

"I know the painting you have is a real Verdi," Teresa said with conviction. "This one is false. I would know the difference anywhere."

Brandon nodded doubtfully. He knew his had to be a Verdi, since he was almost positive Teresa was the model, but the technique was different from Verdi's earlier works.

"At least take it out of the window," Teresa said as she glanced at the busy square.

"I can't just store it in my back room," Di Palma objected. "I paid a good price of it!"

"How much for it now?" Brandon asked. When Di Palma named a figure, Brandon's eyes narrowed. "You have that much invested in it?"

"*Sì.* It's a masterpiece."

He knew the man's price was too high, but he had no choice but to pay it. Not only could he not afford to have forgeries sold under his protégé's name, but he didn't like seeing Teresa's curvaceous body displayed to all of St. Mark's Square. Reluctantly he gave Di Palma the sum he had asked.

As Di Palma wrapped the painting, Brandon said, "I strongly advise you not to purchase other pictures from the source who sold you this one. If I hear of another forgery being passed through this store, I'll have no hesitation in having you arrested."

Di Palma nodded miserably.

Brandon paid to have the painting delivered to the Verdi palazzo, and he and Teresa went out into the square. The mist was lifting and a weak sun was trying to penetrate the heavy clouds. "Now that our business has been taken care of, will you show me Venice?" Brandon asked. "I've been here only for business reasons and never had time to see it properly."

She smiled her agreement and led him toward the Rialto Bridge. "To really see Venice would take a lifetime. I'll show you what I can, and we'll come back another time and see the rest."

He wondered if she meant she would consider marrying him after all, but he was reluctant to ruin the day by asking and possibly being refused again. He still couldn't understand her firmness toward not marrying him.

The almost-three-hundred-year-old Rialto Bridge spanned the Grand Canal about halfway down its length. A double row of shops lined its sides, and the merchants had a bright display of goods to tempt the passersby. Jewelry, perfume, shoes, and trinkets were hawked from doorways and peddlers' carts.

"Years ago a decent woman wouldn't have come here," Teresa told him. "This was a brothel area and was frequented by courtesans in bright-colored dresses who carried yellow handkerchiefs to mark their trade."

"I'm surprised a lady would know about that." He was even more surprised that one would admit it.

With a shrug Teresa said, "Our courtesans weren't entirely without respect, though the common prostitutes were. During the Renaissance, it is said that there were more courtesans in Venice than in any other European city."

"Was that during the carnival years?"

"No, the carnival came later, though I suspect the courtesans were still here."

They walked through the fish and vegetable markets that had stood by the bridge and its predecessors since the eleventh century.

Brandon, who was accustomed to London's great age, was more impressed by the art he saw everywhere. Each building had a carved marble arch or a statue of some hero or god, or at least a decorative molding around the door or windows. "It's like living in a museum," he marveled.

"I suppose it is. I always took it for granted before. In Venice we love our art. See the stone slabs beside the windows on that building? They are used as shutters to protect the glass from storms, and as a barricade from the days when pirates were a threat."

"Stone shutters?"

"Wood burns too easily, and with the houses so close, that's always a problem. Iron rusts in our humidity. Of course we have to use iron chains to keep the buildings from leaning. Venice is built on an island of sand."

Because of the limited space, the owners of the cramped buildings had expanded over the streets to form tunnels that Teresa called *sottoporteghi*. Most of the larger houses had small walled gardens that contained the ancient wells, the outside staircases, and the back walls of the protruding chimneys. Although livestock were no longer allowed to roam free in the streets, the mass of people that jostled about made travel equally difficult.

"This building was once a *ridotto*, a gambling hall," Teresa said. "*Ridotti* were made legal in 1630 and were quite popular during the carnival days. Nobles could gamble here unmasked. They were discreet about their clientele, though no one openly admitted to being a gambler. In the less frequented parts of town there were *casini*, which had no living quarters as the *ridotti* did, and were meant only for parties. They were profitable as well. Venetians love to gamble."

"And you? Do you love gambling?"

She gave him an enigmatic smile. "In my way I'm the biggest gambler of them all."

"What do you mean by that?"

She only smiled. "See that bas-relief on the wall? Papa told me about it when I was a little girl. The couple nearest the gate are the husband and wife. The man standing just behind her is her *sigisbeo*. They were men paid to escort the wives when the husbands were away from home."

"The husbands allowed that?" Brandon asked in surprise.

"Often the *sigisbeo* was even named in the marriage contract."

"Then they weren't the wives' lovers?"

"Sometimes they were, I imagine. Marrying for love became popular only in the last century, you know."

"I don't understand your people. What about conventions? Morals?"

"We have our morals and conventions. Just because they aren't British ones doesn't mean they are any less important or that they don't exist." She frowned up at him. "If you ask me, it's ridiculous to put pantaloons on the legs of your English tables!"

"It's a new fad. I doubt it will last. And the table legs at Hawthorn are quite bare. Come to think of it, how do you know about the table pantaloons?"

"Colin told me. Come down this way." She led him down a *calle* so narrow his shoulders almost touched each side of the alley. The walls were so tall above them that the street was untouched by the rain.

At the end of the *calle* was a tiny church that looked more ancient than any of the surrounding buildings. "This is St. Sagredo dei Rio. The Grand Canal is behind it. Saint Sagredo is one of Venice's local saints. Come inside."

He hesitated but followed her in. When she touched her fingers to the bowl of holy water and crossed herself, he said, "You're Catholic?"

"Of course." She gazed up at him in surprise. "Aren't you?"

"No, I'm not. I never see you going to confession or Mass."

"You don't see a great number of things that I do or don't do."

The tiny church had only a few pews that were worn slick from years of use. "In here," Teresa said as she guided him to a side room.

The small room was lined with shelves of bell jars. In each was a wax head, and the brass inscription gave the name of each saint depicted. The heads were so lifelike that Brandon was startled. On closer inspection he saw the remarkable appearance was heightened by the use of human hair. The beards and mustaches seemed to sprout naturally from the wax skin, and the eyelashes almost appeared to quiver. "They're so real!"

She nodded happily. "One of my cousins made them. He wanted to be a sculptor, but he only liked to make heads and he preferred wax to marble. When he died, his widow gave his collection to the church, where they have been displayed ever since."

"Are all the men in your family artists? I'm quite impressed."

"No, we have one cousin, Giuseppe, who likes to write music. He's from a distant branch of the family, and I've rarely seen him."

"I can't get over how alive they look," Brandon said as he peered closely at the head of Saint Magno.

"It's the hair. My cousin said that was the hardest part—to find different hair for each one and attach it so that it seemed to grow from the skin." She lowered her voice to a whisper. "I think he got most of it from cadavers at the medical school or from unclaimed bodies at the morgue."

Brandon straightened hastily. "Very interesting."

"I think so," she said with some amusement.

As they left the church, Brandon said, "Is your religion the obstacle to our marriage?"

"No, Brandon. Catholics are allowed to marry."

"But I'm not Catholic."

"That could be worked out. No, I cannot marry for another reason."

"Why won't you tell me what it is?"

"Because I can't."

"But why?" he asked in exasperation. "If I knew what the problem was, maybe I could solve it."

She shook her head sadly. "Not this problem. There is no solution, and I'll never marry." Since returning to Venice, where art was a way of life, her resolve was strengthened. She would be happy as Brandon's wife, but she would never be whole without her art.

They took a sleek gondola north and out of the canal and disembarked at another church. "Venice is full of churches," she explained. "Most of our greatest masterpieces are hung in them. This is the Madonna dell'Orto, Tintoretto's parish church. He and his family are buried near the high altar."

Tintoretto's *Last Judgment* seemed to rumble with anger and violent energy. Brandon stared up at it and marveled at the unleashed power on the large canvas. To the artist there appeared to have been no gap between the familiar and the miraculous, and his tempestuous painting blurred the borders of reality for those who gazed upon it.

"Magnificent!" Brandon murmured.

Beside the altar hung Tintoretto's *Worship of the Golden Calf. Presentation of the Virgin* hung over the sacristy door. As always, Teresa felt her spirit soar in the presence of such greatness. Tintoretto's ethereal lights and shadows commanded an involvement and not merely a viewing. Every time she saw one of his paintings, she imagined she could feel a bit of what Tintoretto must have when he created them.

Teresa's face was rapt as she said, "To a true artist

the canvas is a siren call. Tintoretto could no more have put aside his art than he could his heartbeat."

"No. No, of course not. To suggest such a thing would be close to blasphemy."

She looked quickly at Brandon. "You can see that?"

"Certainly I can. A man with a soul like this couldn't give up painting."

"Women also have souls," she said carefully, "and they, too, must be fed."

"Of course they do. But a soul such as this?" Brandon gestured at the *Presentation of the Virgin.* "This is the soul of a master, not of a tender and gentle woman."

"All women's souls are not tender and gentle. Some have as much fire as any man!"

Brandon wasn't listening. "Look at the way the light falls on the Virgin! Never have I seen such a painting! Do you feel it, Teresa? The passion, the power?"

"I feel it," she snapped. He didn't understand. No man did.

"I see much of the same power in your father's work. Not the scope of subject, of course, but in the way the paints are handled."

"You do?"

"I've trained myself to recognize greatness when I see it," he said with great confidence.

"Have you now?" She turned away so he wouldn't see her smile. So he saw greatness in the Verdi canvases, did he? This was praise enough. No matter that he couldn't recognize the artist, if he could see the talent. It was safer that way.

At the end of the day they returned to the palazzo and a hot meal of *prosciutto* and *risi e bisi*, followed by *zuppa inglese*, which was a trifle and not a soup as its name implied.

After the meal was finished, Teresa and Brandon sat in the wide chamber with a brazier of coals at their feet.

"It's cold outside," Brandon remarked when she seemed unlikely to talk.

"You should see it when the *bora* winds blow. We don't have much snow, but it's miserably cold."

Again the silence stretched between them. Teresa raised her wide eyes to meet his. Seeing him here in her palazzo made it even more difficult for her to retain her resolve not to marry him. Was her art more important than her love? She had felt that it was when she was in the presence of her city's masterpieces, but here in the homey comfort of her *piano nobile* she wasn't so sure. She loved him and he loved her. Wouldn't he understand about her art?

"Brandon, what would you say about a woman who paints as a master artist?"

He shook his head. "Impossible. A woman would lack the fire of a Tintoretto, say."

"There already is a Tintoretto. What if she had an equal fire, but a less explosive one?"

"I can't believe any woman would be capable of such drive." He was full and comfortable from his meal, and not opposed to a light discussion of art. "Women are gentle creatures. They have no ambition such as a man has."

"No? Who told you that?" she demanded.

"I know it from observation. Have you ever heard of a woman being a master artist? Of course not."

"Perhaps that's because men are too thickheaded to allow them the freedom!"

"An interesting theory. No, women are more interested in running their homes and raising their children. To be great as an artist, she would have to pour hours of energy into painting."

"Is that how you see me? A person who would be happiest running your home and having your babies?"

He smiled hopefully at her. "Yes, and I think I could make you quite happy. You have only to say the word."

"You oaf!" Teresa leapt to her feet and threw the sofa pillow at him. "How dare you say that to me!"

Brandon caught the pillow by reflex and stared up at her. "What—"

"Don't you ever say that to me again!"

"What did I say? I didn't—"

"I have as much fire in my soul as you do," she stormed, "and I have a lot more to do with my life than see that your parlor is dusted!" She turned on her heel and ran from the room.

Brandon's mouth dropped open as he watched her go, wondering what he had said to upset her so.

Teresa threw herself into her room and across her bed. She couldn't stop the racking sobs that shook her. When Katie came to see whether she needed anything else that night, Teresa sent her away. She let herself cry until all her frustration was spent, then rolled onto her back.

What else had she expected? she chided herself. No man would encourage her to follow her art. Even her own father and grandfather, who had certainly been in a position to understand, had refused to encourage her. Even now when she was the sole Verdi artist, her father lived in constant worry that her name and not his would be connected with her paintings.

"It's so unfair," she whispered to her ceiling. "Why must I be suppressed just because I'm a woman?" There was no answer. Teresa suspected that had she had a mother to confide in, she still wouldn't have received an answer. Women were women and had their place in life, and none of them seemed to care that it was too small a place. Or did they? Teresa didn't know.

On the other hand, men also had a role to fulfill. They, too, had been taught from the cradle to think and react in certain ways. She couldn't blame Brandon for being what he was. Quite probably he had never questioned the roles men and women must play.

She got up and undressed, then slipped on her fine lawn nightgown. Neat rows of lace banded the neck and long sleeves, and it flowed about her like an angel's robe. She took down her hair and brushed it as she sat by her fireside. How odd, she mused, that the British had fireplaces in their communal rooms but froze in their bedrooms. Perhaps, she thought testily, it explained why English people were so reserved, and why Venice was known as a city of pleasure. It was all a matter of determining what was important.

She put down her brush and went to the door. The large palazzo was quiet for the night. Katie and the Valores were in their rooms off the downstairs kitchen at the far end of the house. Teresa looked across the hall at Brandon's closed door.

Was he angry with her? She knew he must be. Ladies weren't supposed to throw pillows at gentlemen, not even when they were sorely provoked. Lady Barbara would never do such a thing. Teresa was sure of that. And Brandon thought Lady Barbara was the final word in ladylike qualities. Teresa frowned jealously. Had Brandon been Lady Barbara's lover? He was a passionate man; surely he had bedded his own fiancée. That thought caused her much pain.

The hall was narrow, and she could be beside him in a matter of a few steps, but would her pride allow her? She wanted to apologize, and she knew he would never be so improper as to come to her room. Blast the British and their cold bedrooms that bred such reserve!

There was only one thing to do, so Teresa did it. She ran across the hall, her bare feet making no sound, and went into Brandon's room.

He was already in bed, and the only light in the room was from the flickering fire on the hearth. When she closed the door and leaned against it, he asked, "Teresa?"

Her hands and feet were cold, and she wondered whether she had done the wrong thing again. "I wanted to apologize."

Brandon sat up and the covers fell away to expose his bare chest. "Come here. The floor must be like ice."

Slowly she went to the large bed and stepped up on the brocaded bench to sit beside him. "I shouldn't have hit you with the pillow."

"Why did you?"

"At the time, it seemed the thing to do."

He gently touched her cheek. "I never meant to insult you. I don't even know how I did."

"You aren't really an oaf."

"I'm glad to hear that." He smiled and the firelight gilded the planes of his face. "Are you cold?"

"A little."

He drew back the covers and pulled her down to cuddle beside him. Her eyes widened. "Do all Englishmen sleep naked?"

"No. Most wear nightshirts. Do you mind?"

"I was just thinking this might be the first British custom that I really like."

He laughed softly. "You know you shouldn't be in here."

"I know." She ran her hand over his hard chest. "I'm glad you aren't as hairy as Papa."

"I wasn't thinking of your father." His large hand found her breast, and he toyed with it through the soft cloth.

"Neither was I." She laid her head on his pillow and smiled into his eyes. "You're a handsome man."

"Thank you. Do all your nightgowns have so many tiny buttons?"

She opened them for him and sighed with pleasure as he slipped his hand inside to stroke her warm breast. "Is this what it would be like to be your wife?"

"No, you wouldn't have on the gown in the first place."

"In an unheated bedroom? I'd freeze!"

"Not in my bed you wouldn't." He raised his head to kiss her gently, then more deeply.

"If I become your mistress, will you install a fireplace in your bedroom?"

"No, but I will if you become my wife."

"You make it tempting," she murmured as he brushed aside her gown to reveal her full breast. As he took her nipple in his mouth she laced her fingers in his thick hair.

"I intend to make it irresistible." He suckled gently as

his hand slid up her thigh to find the wet warmth of her womanhood.

Teresa sighed with pleasure as his lips and fingers gave her delights that left her throbbing for more. She ached to tell him she loved him, but she couldn't bring herself to say the words. Not until he confessed his love for her.

With great finesse Brandon stroked the small bud that triggered her deepest hungers. Teresa moved eagerly under his hand, knowing more was to come and that he would never leave her unsatisfied.

Brandon eased off her gown and let it drift to the floor. "This is how you should be," he said in a deep voice, filled with emotion. "Lying naked in my bed, warm from my kisses and with that light sparkling in your eyes, your hair spread over my pillow. This is how I see you in my dreams."

"You dream about me?" she whispered.

"Constantly. Day and night. You invade my every thought. I find myself wondering what you're doing at odd moments or what you would think about this or that. Marry me, Teresa. We belong together."

"I'll be your lover."

"What is the difference? Either way, you've given yourself to me."

"A mistress can come and go and have a life of her own."

"I've never known anyone as stubborn as you are!"

"That's probably true." She kissed him and ran the tip of her tongue over his lips. "You taste so good."

"So do you."

He came into her and loved her with all the passion he felt in his heart. Surely, he thought, when she saw how much he loved her, she would give up this foolish notion of being only his mistress.

She was responsive to his lovemaking, and when they reached their mutual culmination, she was reluctant to let him go. That pleased Brandon, for he enjoyed being sheathed in her body as the glow of afterlove melted through him.

"Marry me, Teresa."

"Don't ask me that."

"I wasn't asking, I was demanding it."

"You'll get further by asking me."

He sighed and cradled her head on his shoulder. "Go to sleep, darling. I'll wake you before dawn."

Teresa felt the endearment go through her like warm honey. "I wish I could marry you," she murmured. "I wish it with all my heart."

He didn't know how to respond, so he held her close and eventually she slept.

18

Brandon awoke before daybreak. At first he was aware only of a soft warmth curled against his side. He put his arm around her and buried his face in the fragrant cloud of her hair. As he breathed in, he grew more aware and his eyes opened.

Teresa's gentle breathing barely stirred her chest, and in her sleep she smiled as if her dreams were pleasant.

Brandon lay still, enjoying waking up with the woman he loved sleeping beside him. He knew mornings like this would be rare indeed. Lovingly he memorized the way her eyelashes made black lace on her cheeks and how the shell of her ear lay close to her head and how the hair grew from a peak on her forehead. When he was a boy he had thought it would be a simple matter to grow up, fall in love, and get married. Now that he was an adult, however, he saw it wasn't quite that simple. Loving Teresa was easy—it was possibly the easiest thing he had ever done—but marrying her was another matter entirely.

Again he racked his logic for some plausible reason she would not marry him, but he could think of nothing. He wondered if it could be that she simply didn't love him. That seemed unlikely in view of the fact that she was so willingly his lover. Could there be a shame in her past? She had come to him as a virgin.

Teresa sighed and rolled against him, putting her

arm over his chest. Sleepily she rubbed her cheek against his shoulder, then settled back into her dreams.

Out the window Brandon could see the pearl-gray light gathering. "Teresa?" he said softly. "Wake up, darling."

She buried her face in the hollow of his neck. Brandon kissed her forehead, her temple, and then her lips. She smiled and stretched without opening her eyes.

"Good morning," he said tenderly.

Her eyes opened, and in their depths he saw love shining. "Good morning."

"I didn't want to wake you, but I don't know how early the Valores and Katie will be up and about."

She looked at the window. "I should go to my own room," she said reluctantly. "I don't want to leave you."

He drew her into his embrace and held her close to him. "I don't want you to leave either. I want you to sleep with me every night and wake up beside me every morning for the rest of our lives."

"That would be heaven," she murmured as her hand stroked his side and chest.

"Let me give that to you."

Sadly she shook her head. "I can't."

"Why won't you?"

"I said can't, not won't."

"If you would just tell me why you won't marry me, I might be able to find some way around it."

She hesitated. Waking up beside him after an entire night, interspersed with kisses and lovemaking, tempted her to say yes. She would be happy with him. Although he had never once said he loved her, she thought he must. She was tempted to ask him and to tell him of her love, but that hardly seemed the way to refuse his proposal. "I have to go now. Katie will be up with my bathwater soon."

"You won't give me an answer, then?"

"I can't. Where is my gown?"

"On the floor there."

She slid out of his warm bed, and he raised on one

elbow to watch her as she slipped the voluminous gown over her head. Tossing her hair back, she fastened the row of tiny buttons. Then their eyes met, and she saw the naked yearning in his. "I don't want to hurt you, Brandon. If I could marry you, I would."

Before he could respond, she hurried from his room and across the hall to her own bedroom. Her feet were as cold as ice as she slipped into her cold sheets. Shivering, she fought the urge to run back to him. Further sleep was out of the question, and she was glad when she finally heard Katie's steps in the corridor.

For the next few days she continued serving as Brandon's tour guide. She could tell he loved Venice almost as much as she did. With his appreciation of art, he could hardly feel less for it.

Traveling by hired gondola—the Verdis had long ago stopped maintaining one of their own because of the cost—she took him to see the nearby islands such as San Lazzaro of the Armenians, which had once been a leper colony, and the Lido, with its marshes and Church of St. Nicolo, where Venice was annually married to the sea.

Heavy boats called *bragozzi* passed them in the morning and evening as the men went to fish the Adriatic. Their bright yellow, ocher, and red sails were like flowers of the ocean. The boats were emblazoned with colorful depictions of each owner's personal saint or of some ancient protective sign like the sun, moon, or stars. On each side of the stem post, large yellow eyes had been painted to frighten away sea monsters and other dangers of the sea and to help guide the boat back to Chioggia if the helmsman should fall asleep.

Brandon grew accustomed to the slow progress of the gondolas, to the cries of "*Sia de longo*" from the gondoliers as they approached other craft, and their singsong chatter as they mocked the archaic accents of the fishwives of Chioggia. He had never before seen the beauty of Venice, and he, too, was reluctant to leave.

Every night after the servants settled into their rooms, Teresa came to his bed. There they loved away the velvety dark hours to the flickering glow of firelight. Brandon was soon determined to install fireplaces in the bedrooms of Hawthorn, though he didn't tell Teresa. He wanted to surprise her, thinking for the moment that a warm, cozy bedroom might be an inducement for her to marry him. Although he knew he was grasping at straws, it was grasp or drown.

On their last full day in Venice, Teresa took him down the Grand Canal for one last view of the city. As they passed two identical palazzos she said, "Those belong to the Giustiniani family. At one time the family was almost extinct; only one son survived, and he was a monk. This was during the Crusades, when family was even more important than it is now, so the pope gave the son special dispensation to marry so the family name might continue."

"And he did?"

"Very much so. He and his wife had nine sons and three daughters."

"I gather he was in no rush to get back to the monastery," Brandon said with a laugh.

"Eventually he went back, and his wife entered a convent."

"Just how Catholic are you?" he asked. "Is this the reason you won't marry me?"

"As I said before, no."

"I could convert, you know."

"You would do that for me?"

"I'd do anything at all for you."

"That wouldn't be a very sincere conversion."

"It would be an extremely sincere marriage, however."

She smiled at him. "No." After a few minutes she called out to the gondolier and pointed to the bank. He guided his boat into the dock.

"Where are we?"

"This church is Santa Maria dei Miracoli," she said. "St. Mary of the Miracles."

The small church had a round vaulted roof with a group of circular windows and crosses beneath it. On each corner was the statue of a saint. Close beside it was a convent.

"Whose paintings are in here?" Brandon asked. "I thought we had seen every painting and sculpture in Venice."

"There are no paintings or sculptures of note in here." Brandon opened the door for her, and she went past him without a word and knelt at the altar rail.

Because Brandon was unfamiliar with her religion, he didn't know whether to follow her or not, so he waited at the door. After several minutes she rose and crossed herself as she curtsied. When she rejoined him, he raised his brows in an unspoken question.

"I'm in need of a miracle," she explained.

Brandon didn't ask what that miracle was, but he quickly sent up a silent prayer for one of his own. He didn't know whether Protestant prayers were proper in a Catholic church, but this was no time to stand on ceremony. He knew if he were ever to have Teresa for his wife, it would take a miracle.

Early the next morning the palazzo was in a bustle as they prepared to leave. Catherina quizzed Katie on the recipes Teresa had asked her to give the girl. Katie, like many people who could neither read nor write, had developed a keen memory, and she recited the recipes to Catherina without a single error as she helped Saberio load the handcart with luggage to take to the boat.

Brandon and Teresa sat on a window seat looking out at Venice's busy canal one last time. He wanted to put his arms around her, but he knew the servants' eyes were sharp and their tongues loose. He would do nothing to compromise her. "For a while, I was afraid you might not return to England with me."

She looked at him in surprise. "Not return? It never crossed my mind." She gazed back at the gray-green water. "I couldn't leave Papa there alone."

"Is that the only reason?"

"No. I would surely die if I never saw you again."

He caught his breath in expectation, but she continued to study the reflections in the water. "I hope you get your miracle," he said.

"So do I."

When they went out the canal door to board the waiting gondola, Teresa froze and stared at a passing boat.

"What is it?" Brandon asked. The only difference he noted was that the gondola that had caught her eye was more ornate than most, with a gilded statue of an angel on its prow. Behind it were several other ordinary gondolas, all moving at a majestic pace, but with an almost festive air.

"A funeral. They're on their way to the cemetery at San Michele."

"San Michele?"

"There is no longer any room to bury people in the churches," she explained. "Everyone is buried on San Michele." Her eyes followed the lead gondola. "It seems to be an ill omen—to see a funeral as our last sight in Venice. I feel a sense of foreboding."

"Nonsense," he said with a laugh. "It's just a coincidence." Leaning closer, he conspiratorially whispered, "I should think you might have felt more foreboding if the procession had been for the celebration of a birth, after the last few nights."

Her eyes flew open wide. "I never thought of that!"

"Maybe that will be our miracle. Then you'll have to marry me."

She was still staring at him as he handed her into the gondola.

Their next stop was Germany. Mitchell graciously offered to let them stay with him, but because his quarters were too small, Brandon got a room for Teresa and Katie in a nearby boardinghouse.

"I tried to get a separate room for Katie, but there isn't one to be had," Brandon said as he drew Teresa aside.

"That should keep us honest."

"You needn't sound so cheerful about it."

"You couldn't slip out of Mitchell's and past the desk without being seen. We may as well make the best of it."

"I see some English stoicism has rubbed off on you."

"Is that what it is? I thought I was merely becoming a pessimist."

"There's no such thing as a Venetian pessimist," he teased. "Are you afraid to stay here, with me at Mitchell's?"

"Of course not. Katie will guard me against dragons," she said with a laugh. "Will you be safe with me so far away?"

"Quite safe. I no longer have any interest in night life. Besides, Mitchell is much more staid than Colin. He's more intent on curing the world of all its ills."

"I'll miss sleeping with you," she whispered.

"If you look at me like that one more time, I'll haul you off to the magistrate or whoever it is here who performs marriage ceremonies, and you'll be a viscountess whether you want to be or not."

She smiled. "Go tell Mitchell we found a place. I'll freshen up and be ready to see you in an hour."

He looked reluctant. "I'll only be five doors down if you need me."

"I know. You showed me his place when we arrived, remember?"

"I don't want to leave you."

"When you look at me like that, I want to do something that would embarrass us both right here in the lobby," she said softly.

Brandon glanced around and found both Katie and the proprietor watching them. With resignation he smiled back at her. "I'll pick you up in an hour."

Teresa nodded and sent him on his way with a smile. After the glorious nights in his arms in Venice, she would indeed regret sharing her bed with only Katie. She hoped she didn't talk in her sleep, for if she did, Katie would have a lot to tell her friends at home.

As she followed the owner up the flight of stairs with Katie at her heels, she again considered the consequences of marrying Brandon. Her father would be furious; of that she had no doubt. Not for the first time, Teresa wished that she was just an ordinary woman with no more to worry about than whether or not her lover loved her.

The proprietor let them into their small room, and before leaving, he started a fire in the grate to dispel the chill.

Teresa admired the view from their small window. "Isn't it marvelous, Katie? All those mountains and valleys!"

"I don't mind the mountains, but I ain't lost nothing down those valleys, so there ain't no use in me looking down them."

"Are you afraid of heights?" Teresa asked.

"No, Miss. I'm afraid of falling into the depths. I could climb up all day long. I just couldn't come down again."

"I never realized that. Well, we won't be in Germany long." She looked back out the window, wishing they had no reason to be here. What her uncle was doing—and she was fairly certain he was the culprit—threatened to expose her and her father's secret. Pushing the thought from her mind, she remarked, "I've never seen such high mountains. They're so romantic."

"To my mind there's nothing so romantic as a walk out in the English gloaming on a Sunday."

"Do you have a beau?"

"Aye, that I do."

"Katie, you're full of surprises. Do I know him?"

"It's Allard Beck, the gardener at Hawthorn."

"I never realized! Do you plan to be married?"

"No, Miss. We can't afford it. Allard has an old mother and a sickly spinster sister to support. He can't take me on too. Especially since there would likely be babies."

Teresa looked over at her maid. "All these months, and I never realized you were in love."

"It's true, though. Me and Allard are trying to resolve ourselves. Maybe after his ma and sis are gone, we can have our turn. It's bad to love somebody and not be able to marry him, but there it is. Poor folks have to make do however they can." Her eyes widened as she remembered she was talking to her mistress. "Not that we are poor, Miss. Why, me and Allard figure ourselves lucky to have our positions. There are folks all over the country who wish they had good jobs like us."

"I understand, Katie. And you're right. It's a terrible thing not to be able to marry the man you love." She gazed at the snowy crevasses of the distant mountains. "Does he love you?"

"Oh, yes, Miss. Ever so much!"

"Then you will be married. I'll speak to Lord Kincaid about giving you more money."

"Do you think he will, Miss?"

"I have reason to think he will understand your plight."

"Thank you, Miss! To tell you the truth, I dreaded this trip because I would be away from Allard, but now it's turned out to be the best thing that's ever happened to me."

Teresa smiled but her eyes were sad. "I only wish all lovers' problems could be solved so easily."

In an hour Teresa was freshened and dressed in her bottle-green bombazine and matching hat with a curving cream-colored ostrich plume. Wrapping her dark cape around her, she left Katie to put away her things and straighten the room.

When she stepped into the lobby, Brandon rose to greet her. His eyes were admiring as he gazed down at her. "Not everyone can wear that shade of green. On you it's beautiful."

"Thank you."

"Are you satisfied with your room?"

"Yes, it's lovely. Brandon, I have a favor to ask of you."

"Anything. Would you like for me to get one of those mountains for you? It's yours for the asking. So is the moon."

"I had something more mobile in mind. It's Katie. She's in love and wants to get married, but he can't afford to have her."

"Whom does she have in mind?"

"Your gardener, Allard Beck."

"He's a good man. Allard's father and grandfather worked for my family. She could do worse."

"But he's the sole support of his family, I gather, and can't afford to marry. Could you help them?"

Brandon smiled down into her earnest eyes. "Of course. I'll even have an extra room built onto their cottage if you like."

"You know where he lives?"

"I know where all my people live and what their conditions are. That's part of being master of Hawthorn. The sister is a sad case. She's given to seizures, and I doubt she'll outlive the mother. It's so sad. She's a lovely girl."

"Can nothing be done for her?"

Brandon shook his head. "I've had Dr. Chasen look at her, but he can't do anything." Brandon smiled and added, "Perhaps Mitchell can work a miracle for her."

"I hope so."

As they stepped out into the blustering wind, Teresa pulled her cloak up close about her face. "Such a wind! I had hoped it would die down by now."

"I only hope the snows hold off until we can finish our business and leave."

The art instructor was expecting them, and his housekeeper had even put out a tray of coffee and slices of cake. Teresa was so distracted by the painting over his mantel that she wasn't sure she had made the appropriate response to Herr Reinhardt following Brandon's introduction.

"You see my Verdi," Reinhardt said with great pride. "I understand your father is the artist?"

"Papa painted an *altana* scene." She went closer. It was a good copy. A very good copy. But she knew the original dress had an undercoat of scarlet, not sienna as this one did. The scarlet had been one of those mistakes that turned out for the best, but the forger could not have known. "I'm afraid, however, that Papa didn't paint this one."

Reinhardt's smile vanished. "That cannot be!"

"Are you positive?" Brandon asked. "There's no mistake?"

"The color of the dress is off just slightly. No, I'm positive."

As tactfully as he could, Brandon said, "Sometimes an artist paints more than one copy. Could that be the case?"

"Impossible. Besides, Papa never does that. Only a student would do an exercise like that, never a master. There would be no need."

"Not a Verdi?" Reinhardt repeated.

Teresa pored over the canvas, studying it in minute detail, especially the signature. "Not a Salvatore Verdi. I think this was done by my Uncle Mario."

"Mario Verdi?" Reinhardt said. "I have never heard of Mario Verdi."

"No one else has either," Brandon told him. "Salvatore is the master artist. Not Mario."

"But this painting! Surely a master . . ."

"It's a copy, Herr Reinhardt," Teresa explained. "An excellent one, but a copy nevertheless. We found another in Venice."

"You're positive this Mario is the artist?" The German looked crushed. "I paid for a Salvatore! I paid handsomely for it!"

"I'm willing to buy it back from you," Brandon reassured him. "You'll not lose in the deal."

"It's not so simple. My friends, my colleagues, even my students! They all know I have bought a Verdi masterpiece. If they don't see it here, I'll have to admit I was taken in."

"This is an excellent forgery," Teresa said. "Anyone could have been fooled."

"I am not anyone. I am Gustave Reinhardt. My name

may mean nothing to you, but it is my name. If the college learns of this, my reputation will be damaged, perhaps beyond repair. I am the art instructor here, and head of my department!"

Brandon and Teresa exchanged a look. "Could we speak to each other alone?" Brandon asked.

"Certainly, certainly." Reinhardt stepped nearer the painting and stared at the intricate brush strokes.

Brandon and Teresa went across the room to the bay window. "Are you positive?" he asked again. "There can be no mistake?"

"Papa couldn't have painted that one. Besides, the signature has a flourish at the end that Papa never uses anymore. When Uncle Mario copied it, he must not have paid close attention to how the original was signed."

"I can't force him to sell it to us."

Teresa glanced back at the man. "Look at him. It hurts me to see how wounded he looks."

"When I first saw it, he was as proud of that painting as if it were a living child."

"We can't take it from him. Think of his professional standing among his peers. He's getting old and will retire soon. What if his pension were cut because it became known he had been fooled by a forgery?"

Brandon nodded. "What do you suggest?"

"I think we should leave it here. This is a relatively small town. Who is to talk about a painting in this isolated house?"

Brandon smiled. "I was thinking the same thing."

"Let's give him back his pride."

Teresa went to the worried old man and said, "Herr Reinhardt, Lord Kincaid and I can't agree that this is definitely a forgery. It may perhaps be exactly what you thought you were buying."

Reinhardt's wrinkled face cleared. "Exactly! It could be an authentic Verdi!"

"I do ask one favor," Brandon said. "If you ever decided to part with it, sell it only to me."

"I will never part with my Verdi. As the Bible says, it

is my 'pearl of great price.' I will, however, make with you an agreement. I'm an old man and my health isn't as good as it might be. I have no family. When I am gone, I will have my executor send you the painting. I only ask that I keep it these last few years."

With a broad smile Brandon put out his hand to seal their agreement. "Done! And may you enjoy it for many years to come."

Teresa felt almost tearful as she saw the old man's joy. She couldn't resist adding, "And I'm more and more positive that it may be a genuine Verdi." He nodded happily.

When they left, Brandon said, "That was kind of you."

"It *is* a Verdi. Just not a Salvatore."

"We should leave as soon as possible. If your uncle is forging paintings, he must be stopped quickly. Why would he do such a thing?"

"Uncle Mario has always been one to feather his own nest. I have reason to believe he spent Grandpapa's money rather than investing it as he was told. Papa thinks I exaggerate, though."

"Well, someone painted that copy. Is Mario talented enough to do it? His canvases I saw showed little talent."

"Uncle Mario can copy anything he has seen. I know he saw *The Ladies on the Altana*. What I can't understand is how he saw *The Harem Girl*."

"I suppose if he saw one, he saw the other as well," Brandon said with a shrug.

Teresa knew that was impossible, but she couldn't tell Brandon. She had been careful to hide it away from her father every night. Salvatore had been too sick at the time to go into the studio, and Mario supposedly had not been there since he and her father exchanged heated words. So how had Mario seen it, let alone seen it close enough to copy her subtly different brush strokes?

As they made their way toward Mitchell's lodgings, she felt quite uneasy.

19

By the time they left Germany, Teresa had proof that their hours of loving had had no consequence. She was surprised at how disappointed she felt after the first wave of relief. If she had been carrying the future heir to Hawthorn, she would have had no choice but to marry Brandon, and her painful quandary would have been ended.

When they returned to England, she threw herself into sketching and blocking out wild, tempestuous scenes of storms and twisted lightning bolts. The passion of the drawings alarmed Salvatore, who knew an artist presented whatever was in his soul, but the work helped Teresa cope with the turbulent emotions that Brandon had awakened in her during their stay in Venice.

Under her father's suspicious eye she found it harder and harder to meet Brandon, and when they were together they could rarely exchange more than a long-ing look or a brief clasp of hands.

Now that Teresa was home, Salvatore sent word to Queen Victoria that his canvas was dry, and the sittings with the royal children resumed. Teresa worked at her father's elbow, mixing his paint, cleaning his brushes, and always memorizing the subjects so she could later depict them on her own canvas. Because of the children's ages, the sittings were a series of short poses of one or another while the other two children played in the garden under the attendants' supervision. Salvatore was firm that they play outside and not in his studio, but one rainy day he relented and let the nursemaid read to them in one corner. This worked so well that from then on he had her read every time the children came, so that the one posing would be more patient and sit still for longer periods of time.

November arrived, and with it a series of rare warm days. The sun even deigned to shine, and Salvatore suggested that Teresa take advantage of the break in the weather by going for a walk.

She knew he was watching her from the window, so she didn't dare go down the path to Hawthorn. She missed Brandon with a physical longing as well as an emotional one, but she couldn't go to him, nor could he come to her. Since their return from the trip, Salvatore seemed to resent his patron's presence. Teresa didn't blame her father, for she knew he had reason to distrust them, but she wondered why Salvatore was so suspicious when he hadn't been before. She never thought that her own sketches might have alerted him to the fact that things were not as they had been.

As she stood there yearning to be with Brandon, an urge to go to the ruins of Bridestake came over her. With nothing else to do, she decided to follow her impulse.

As she looked at the ancient castle from atop a knoll, she noticed how the bare trees and yellowed grasses seemed more in the spirit of the crumbling ruins than had the green fields of summer. Teresa had less trouble imagining the elusive Gray Lady with the bleak backdrop of skeletal trees and gnarled, exposed trunks. The sky above was a washed-out blue, as if all the autumn rains had faded its color, but the air was warm. Draping her shawl across her arm, she picked her way down the rock slope for a closer inspection.

When she entered the open-roofed hall, she was again swept back into the ancient past. She could imagine the smell of a fire in the blackened hearth, and how the rushes on the stone floor must have felt springy underfoot. In her mind's eye she could see how the painted cloths and tapestries on the walls would shift and billow with the pressing wind from outside.

She heard a noise behind her and turned with a start. Brandon was standing in the tower staircase. For a moment the light tricked her into thinking she saw him wearing clothing of a bygone era, though his face was as dearly familiar as always. The instant he moved, the illusion was gone. "I had hoped you'd be here," he said.

"I didn't see your horse. You startled me."

"I came on foot. I've been here every day in hopes you would walk this way eventually."

She gazed across the hall at him. "You came all the way up here every day on the chance I might show up?"

"I know you're as fascinated with this place as I am. I couldn't send you a message and risk your father's intercepting it." He came out of the shadows and strolled over to her.

"He's watching me closely," she admitted. "Why do you suppose that is?"

"It could be that when you returned he saw you with new eyes and discovered not just his daughter but a young woman. Sometimes when we're around people every day, we don't see them as they really are."

"That could be." She had secretly been afraid Salvatore's suspicions were a mark of the further degeneration of his mind. Since her return, she, too, had seen him more clearly, and there had been a dozen things he said or did that had caused her great uneasiness. "He calls me by my mother's name almost all the time now," she said with a frown. "And he forgets that Grandpapa is dead."

Brandon was silent for a moment. "I had wondered if the fever had left him impaired in any way. Are you afraid of him?"

"Afraid of Papa? Of course not," she said with a laugh. "But it's unsettling. Young Hal is superstitious and is convinced Papa is seeing ghosts. Hal may give notice if Papa keeps it up."

"Footboys are easily replaced. What about Katie?"

"She's completely loyal. Since you cleared the way for her to marry her beau, she would walk through fire for either of us. When Papa asks if she's seen Mama or Grandpapa, Katie humors him."

"So he's sunk that far, has he?"

"It hasn't affected his art," she said quickly, realizing that she shouldn't have revealed any of this to him. It was just that Brandon had become so easy to talk with and confide in, she had momentarily forgotten to keep her guard up about her father's ability to paint.

"No, it hasn't. As a matter of fact, based on what you've just told me, I'm greatly surprised. If anything, his work is progressively better. The last canvas you showed me has such power that it seems to move and breathe."

Teresa smiled. "Thank you. I'll tell Papa you said so." She treasured all the compliments Brandon gave her work, and she knew they were genuine because he had no idea he was talking to their actual creator.

She and Brandon walked to a sunny spot where a drift of leaves softened the floor. He spread her shawl on the leaves and they sat down.

"I'm glad for these last few warm days," she said. "Katie tells me the winters can be quite fierce here."

"Not to someone such as you, who is accustomed to sea storms just beneath your windows. England gets more snow than Venice, but the winds won't be so cutting."

"Winter is a time for families to sit around the hearth. I no longer have much family left. Just Papa. I don't count Uncle Mario."

"The man I said I would speak with about your uncle has agreed to help us keep an eye on him, but he says we cannot accuse Mario of forgery without proof. We have to catch him making a sale."

"Can't you go look in his house? He must have canvases there."

"I have no right to look there, I'm afraid. Suspicion isn't justification enough. Besides, I'm not sure he could be convicted of copying one of the Verdi paintings for his own pleasure or instruction. You can be certain he would say he never intended to sell it if he were confronted."

She shook her head sadly. "I still can hardly believe he has done this. If Papa ever finds out, I don't know what he would do." She remembered the violent quarrels he and Mario had had over less important issues than this. "Papa must never know."

"I agree there's no reason to upset him unnecessarily. If Mario is arrested, Signor Verdi will have to know then because it will go to court. Until then there's no reason to tell him." His eyes studied her face lovingly. "I've missed you since we came home."

Teresa felt a warmth flood her cheeks. "I never know what you may say next."

"We have little time for courting in the usual way, and we have gone beyond the bounds already."

"Do you regret that?"

"Not for an instant. I only regret not having you for my wife."

She smiled at him, and he bent to kiss her warm cheek. "I wish I could be your wife. Nothing would please me more."

"Then marry me."

"Papa would never allow it. Since I returned, he watches me constantly. As I said, he often seems to think I'm my mother and is jealous of my even saying your name."

"You can't live that way. Besides, he told me that it was your own decision not to marry."

"When did he say that?" she asked in surprise.

"A long time ago, when I asked him for your hand."

Happiness sparkled in her eyes. "You never told me you did that."

"There was no reason to, since he flatly refused to let me court you."

"Yet you didn't give up?"

"I'll never give up until I make you my own."

"I'm already yours."

"Not the way I have in mind."

"Papa told you the truth. The decision not to marry was my own."

"Well, can't you change your mind? Other women do it all the time." He put his arms around her and laid her back on the shawl. "Marry me, dammit!"

"Such a pretty proposal," she said with a laugh.

"You frustrate me more than any woman alive," he growled. "I never used such language with a lady before you came along."

"I don't object to your language, but I'm refusing your proposal." Then wistfully she added, "Because I must."

"That doesn't make any sense!"

She put her arms around his neck. "We have so few moments together. Must we spend them in arguments?"

"No," he said softly. "I would rather spend them loving you." He closed his lips over hers.

As his hands caressed the curves of her body, Teresa felt her will weakening. What was art to compare with her love for him? She no longer wanted to choose her father over Brandon.

His kisses kindled fire in her veins, and she ran her hands under his coat to feel the warm strength of his muscles beneath his fine shirt. "Brandon," she whispered as the fever of love burned through her. "Love me, Brandon."

"I do love you, Teresa," he ground out as he kissed the tender spot in her throat. "I love you more than life itself!"

She drew back to look at him. "You do?"

He frowned. "Of course I do. Don't you know that?"

"You never said so."

"Teresa, I've shown you my love in every way I know how. I've asked you over and over again to marry me, I've made love to you all night long, I've done everything in my power to show you how much I love you."

"But you never said the words."

He stared at her. "I must have! No, I wouldn't have omitted a thing like that!"

"You never said it."

For a moment he thought about it, and he honestly couldn't recall having said the words. "I showed you by my actions. That's more important."

"A woman needs to hear the words, Brandon."

"I love you."

"I love you, Brandon."

A smile lit his face. "You never told me either."

"I couldn't tell you until you said the words to me first."

"Yet you could become my lover? I'll never understand you, Teresa."

"No, I doubt that you ever will. Just love me and let that be enough."

"It's not enough. Marry me, Teresa."

She hesitated. Brandon was a proud man, and he wouldn't wait forever for an answer. The idea of losing him made her feel almost sick. No matter how much she loved her father and needed her art, she loved and needed Brandon more. "Yes," she said simply.

"Yes, what?" he asked in surprise.

"Yes, I'll marry you."

"You will?" He stared down at her, filled with amazement.

Teresa nodded as happiness misted her eyes. "I love you, Brandon. I want to be your wife."

He didn't understand her sudden reversal, but he wasn't about to question it. "I'll make you happy, Teresa."

"I know you will. And you'll be happy too. I promise it."

"Teresa," he murmured. "My darling Teresa." This time when he kissed her it was with the tenderness of a love that would last forever.

She held to him and let her love flow out in kisses and touches and words that mingled her language with his. In their hearts the words were perfectly understandable.

"I want you," he whispered. "I know I shouldn't, but I do."

"What difference does it make if we have a roof over us or not? If your ancestors hadn't built Hawthorn, this would be your home."

"But out in the open like this . . ."

She laughed in delight. "At times you can be such a prude!"

He grinned because he knew it was true of him in the past. "You're fast changing all that."

She slipped off her pantalets and tossed them aside. Her laughing eyes dared him to shrug off his inhibitions as easily.

"Usually it's the man who teaches the woman to be lusty," he pretended to scold.

"If I waited for you to forget you're a gentleman, we would both have long white beards," she countered with a laugh.

"Am I as bad as all that?"

"You're as wonderful as all that."

They made love tenderly, not caring that they lay just out of view of the meadow and that there was no roof to shield them. Teresa reached her summit quickly, and though she tried to hold back to prolong her pleasure, Brandon's lovemaking was too persuasive.

As she floated in love's glow, he began to move within her again. Teresa's eyes widened as she felt her body respond eagerly. He smiled down at her and held her tenderly. "Once is not enough for a woman like you."

Teresa gave herself to him, and this time when she could hold back no longer, she felt him reach his own culmination. Time hung suspended as their souls entwined and floated in a gossamer of gold-and-pink rainbows.

After minutes of silence as their world slowly reformed around them, she happily murmured, "I never knew I could feel this way."

"Neither did I."

"But you've been in love before," she protested. "You must have felt this."

He chuckled and held her close. "I thought I was in love, but I was so wrong. What I feel for you is greater than anything I ever felt for anyone else."

She smiled smugly. "Good."

He looked down at her. "Do I detect a touch of jealousy there?"

"Perhaps a touch, but it's fast dying."

"I have to admit I was jealous too. Of you and Colin."

"Colin? He's just my friend."

"I have the feeling he would have liked to be more."

She gave him an innocent look. "Maybe."

"Then it's true?" He drew back with a frown.

"And then again, maybe it's not. A woman has a right to her secrets."

"I laid your jealousy to rest, and you've resurrected mine. That hardly seems fair!"

She laughed and rolled so that he was half-beneath her. "You have no reason for jealousy, *caro mio*. I'll be your own true love and never look at another man."

"I love you."

She kissed him gently. "I love you too."

After they dressed, Brandon said, "When should we set the date? I don't see any reason for a long engagement, do you?"

"Not too long, but I have to prepare Papa, and there is sewing that must be done."

"You won't need linens and all that. Hawthorn is packed with sheets and towels and everything else we'll need."

"I doubt it has a wedding dress in the closet, or a trousseau," she teased.

"I can't help being impatient. I'm afraid you'll back out and not marry me."

"I said I will, Brandon. Stop worrying."

He nodded, but he still felt uneasy. "Should we tell your father now?"

"I think it would be best if I do that alone."

"Are you sure? If there's any unpleasantness, I should be there."

"There will definitely be unpleasantness, as you call it. And you should not be there. I can handle Papa." She smiled with confidence.

"I saw you walking with Lord Kincaid," Salvatore said as soon as she entered the cottage. "It's not proper for you to walk out alone with him!"

"Papa, I have something to tell you. Brandon has asked me to marry him."

"*Lord Kincaid.* I hope you told him never to mention it again! The scoundrel!"

"I said yes."

Salvatore glared at her. "That's impossible!"

"No, it isn't, Papa. We love each other." She spoke in Italian so Katie and Hal couldn't understand them if they were to overhear the conversation.

"You can't marry him or anyone else, Eva Maria. I thought we had been through all that! You're mine and you'll remain mine!"

Teresa's eyes widened. "I'm Teresa. Your daughter."

Salvatore's expression became blank for a moment. "Yes. For a minute . . . Well, you can't marry him. What about me? What about Salvatore Verdi, the master artist?"

"You would still live here just as you do now. I will come up every day, and we will paint. Just as we always have."

"And when you have babies? What then? A wife has duties and obligations that you don't have. Your days will be full with running Hawthorn and being a wife and mother! Your art—*my* art—will be forgotten!"

"I could still paint, I think." She wondered from the way Salvatore had acted whether her mother had been quite as saintly and pure as Teresa had always assumed. "My art is part of me," she protested. "I won't put it aside."

"You'll be reduced to forever painting daisies and

fruit," he threatened direly. "You know how you'll dislike that!"

"A father should be happy to see his daughter marry the man she loves! Don't you want me to be happy, Papa?"

"*That* is why a woman can never be a master," he countered ferociously. "She puts her heart before her head. A master must put everything behind his art! You are no master, Teresa!"

She paled. "That was cruel, Papa."

"It's true and you know it! Would my papa have made his art fit into his life? No! It was the other way around, just as it was for me. Everything else was second place. Ask your mama—she's always harping that I pay her no attention!"

Teresa stared at him, speechless.

Salvatore frowned. "You cannot marry this man. I forbid it."

"I'm a grown woman. I can marry him if I want."

"Not and remain my daughter."

Her father's words knifed deeply into her heart, and silence hung thick in the room. Teresa felt tears clogging her throat and burning her eyes. Without a word she turned and ran from the room.

For hours she wrestled with her desires and her obligations. How could she turn her back forever on her father, when he had no one but her? She was not only his child but also his only means of support. True, he could return to the palazzo in Venice, but the tenants didn't supply enough income for him to live there, and she knew he would never accept money from her if it came from Brandon. If she married, it would mean the loss of all she had ever known. And without Salvatore as a shield she would indeed be reduced to a life of painting daisies and fruit.

When a concerned Katie came to call her to dinner, Teresa rolled onto her side and refused to come. Until she made her decision, she couldn't sit at the table with her father. If he took her from her love, she wasn't sure she could ever forgive him.

Not forgive Papa? All her life he had been both mother and father, as well as her daily companion, teacher, and mentor.

Teresa buried her face in the pillow and sobbed.

Later, after Salvatore and the servants had gone to their rooms, Teresa ventured out. The cottage was quiet, with only the soft ticking of the mantel clock. Teresa went to the kitchen and cut herself a slab of bread and cheese and poured a glass of Soave that she had brought from Venice. She sat at the wooden table and ate slowly, forcing the food past the knot in her throat. Afterward she felt a little better, but melancholia threatened to overwhelm her.

Not marry Brandon? The only man she had ever loved and the man whom she wanted with all her heart? Unthinkable!

She knew she couldn't sleep, so she went into the studio. The familiar smells of oil and turpentine were comforting to her. All her life she had turned to paint and canvas when her daily problems seemed insolvable.

She put on her old smock and placed the royal portrait on the easel. There was no point in lying in bed being miserable when she could be miserable in here and get something accomplished at the same time. She didn't even bother to close the shutters, but went straight to work.

Methodically she mixed the paint to the colors on her father's canvas. His strokes were faulty and his painting lifeless, but at each sitting he mixed the correct colors and put them on the canvas in a way to direct her brush in the actual painting.

Teresa sat on the straight chair and adjusted the easel to her comfort, then began to paint. Only the faint hiss of the gaslight, the soft sounds of bristles moving on canvas, and the punching sound of stippling being applied were to be heard. The door blocked out all the tiny sounds of the sleeping household and the noises from the night birds outside. Teresa was enclosed in her own world, and soon her senses shut out all but the canvas in front of her.

After several hours of work the portrait was finished. Teresa sat back and studied the youthful faces to be certain she had nothing else to add. Princess Victoria, or Vicky as she was called, protectively held her younger sister's hand as she showed her a toy tea cart. Princess Alice, called Fatima for some unknown reason, reached out one pudgy hand for a tiny teacup. Prince Albert, known as Bertie, looked on with a satisfied expression as if he already knew he would be king someday. The children were undeniably royal, yet they were also shown as healthy, active children. Teresa was satisfied.

She took the small brush she used for signatures and dabbed it in the blue she had used for the prince's eyes. Behind her she heard the sound of a door opening, and she paused. She was still in no mood to confront her father.

Hoping he would go away, she proceeded to sign his name in the lower-right corner. Then she methodically cleaned the palette and brush. Wondering why her father hadn't spoken, she glanced behind her and discovered not her father, but her Uncle Mario.

"So," he said smoothly as he strode to the center of the room. "It was you all along. You're the reason Salvatore has suddenly developed such talent." His eyes, so much like her father's but with none of Salvatore's affection, regarded her coldly. His lips smiled. "It was little Teresa all along."

"How did you get in here!" she gasped.

Mario held up a key. "It seems we both have our secrets."

"You have been coming here at night! Does Papa know about this?"

"Certainly not." He went to gaze at the finished portrait. "The royal brats. How delightful for your career —or should I say Salvatore's? I gather no one knows who really is painting the pictures these days?" He looked at Salvatore's poor efforts on the other canvas. "And this is the depth to which my dear brother has sunk. He's useless. Less than the most rank apprentice. If only Papa could see his fine favorite now."

"Leave this house at once," Teresa commanded through clenched teeth. She didn't dare awaken anyone. "If you don't, I'll call Papa," she warned, though she knew it was an empty threat.

"Go ahead. I'll ask him to paint a picture for me, and I'll exhibit it everywhere. Or maybe I'll take this one." He stepped closer to Salvatore's canvas.

With a quick motion Teresa grabbed her palette knife, made sharp from years of use, and slashed the canvas from top to bottom. "Take it," she challenged. "There is no signature, and no one will look twice at a ruined painting."

Mario laughed without humor. "You always did have a quick temper. That's the main thing you seem to have inherited from your mother."

Teresa glared at him. "Leave my mother out of this!" Attempting a desperate bluff she said, "This isn't what it seems. I'm not the artist, Papa is. That's my canvas I ruined."

"No, Teresa. I was watching you through the window before I came in. I was standing right behind you when you signed the canvas."

"I know something about you too, Uncle Mario," she snapped. "I know you've been forging Papa's paintings and selling them abroad."

"Have I been found out already?" he asked mildly.

"You admit it?"

He shrugged. "I had to make a living, didn't I? The paintings are mine. Only the compositions were your father's—or were they yours?"

"You're nothing but a forger!"

"So are you."

She frowned but had no rejoinder.

"I'm amazed that the high-and-mighty Lord Kincaid would sanction such a deception."

"Brandon doesn't—" She snapped her mouth shut, but it was too late.

"He doesn't know? Interesting! And it's 'Brandon,' is it? That's intriguing as well. In my knowledge of English etiquette, I've noticed a person must be on quite intimate terms with another to use his first name."

Teresa blushed painfully. "Get out of here!"

"Well, well! I seem to have hit upon another secret. Does Salvatore know what you're up to?"

"Of course he knows I paint. How else could I do it?"

"I meant does he know how ... close you and Lord Kincaid have become?"

"Lord Kincaid has asked me to marry him," she said coldly.

"Indeed! England's foremost art connoisseur to marry a forger. Fascinating!"

Teresa dared not say anything else for fear of making matters even worse. If Herr Reinhardt was worried about his small reputation, what could this do to Brandon's much greater one?

"I believe we can work out a compromise," Mario said thoughtfully. "I grow tired of painting and having to exactly match Salvatore's—that is, your—technique. Especially since yours is somewhat different from the one I was taught. I could be convinced to keep quiet for a sum of money."

"Impossible! Papa and I have little money. All our needs are supplied for us by our patron. What little money we get is sent to the Valores for their salaries and the upkeep of the palazzo."

"I don't care about that." Mario looked about the room. "If you have no money, I suppose I'll have to make other arrangements."

"What do you mean by that?"

"I want a painting."

Teresa glared at him. "There's a landscape in the front of the drying rack. Take it and get out!"

"Teresa, you've always been so temperamental." Mario went to the rack and greedily took out a landscape with the Verdi signature already in place. "Lovely. Just what I had in mind."

"Now, go and never come back here again!"

"You misunderstand me. I can't live forever on the sale of one painting. You're good, but you're not *that* good. No, I'll need canvases regularly."

"I refuse!"

"Very well. I'll ride down to Hawthorn in the morning and tell Lord Kincaid all I know."

She knew he would do exactly that. Panic rose as she tried to think of a way out. Awakening her father would do no good. In his present state, Salvatore was useless as a threat to Mario. "Lord Kincaid will never believe you."

"Yes, he will. From the lines on this canvas I'd guess Salvatore has a most noticeable tremor. If he does, Lord Kincaid has only to separate the two of you and see if any paintings are produced. You see, you have no choice."

"You're playing a dangerous game, Uncle Mario."

"On the contrary. It's no game at all. And since you have so much to lose—Salvatore's reputation and your marriage—I doubt you'll be anxious to see me get caught, for then I'd have to tell everything I know." He shrugged and smiled wickedly.

"I suppose I have no choice."

"None at all. I'll pick up the next painting in three weeks."

"Three! I'll have no time to work on anything else!"

"That's not my problem. I won't come here. It's too chancy. When the time comes, unstretch the canvas and roll it up. Do it carefully so it's not marred. The paint will still be pliant then and won't crack if you're careful. Then bring it at night to the White Swan."

"The White Swan? Do you mean that tavern at the edge of London? I can't go there alone at night!"

"Certainly you can. There are wenches in and out of there all night." As he spoke, Mario wrapped brown paper around the landscape to protect it. "Come at midnight, three weeks from tonight."

She couldn't answer. The White Swan looked disreputable enough in the daylight. At midnight it would be fearful indeed.

Mario went to the door and gave her another mirthless smile. "Don't disappoint me, Teresa. I would have no regrets in exposing you and Salvatore. And now that I have this," he added, gesturing to the landscape, "I can probably pin my forgeries on you as well. I'll go free and you'll both go to prison. _Ciao_, Teresa."

She stared after him and felt sick to her stomach. Never had she considered that something like this could happen. Her deception had seemed so harmless in Venice when Salvatore agreed to let her paint. Now they could be ruined!

She ached to run to Brandon's protecting arms, but she knew that was impossible now. As tears gathered in her eyes she realized Mario had also stolen her future happiness with Brandon. As his wife she would hurt him and his name too badly if her deceit ever became publicly known. It would be disastrous enough if she were only his protégée. She would have to break their engagement as soon as possible.

20

As soon as Teresa's eyes opened the next morning she remembered Mario's visit. Blackmail, the English called it—a mild word for the rage she felt. She rolled out of bed and dressed. A patter on her window told her the rains had returned, and she wasn't surprised. A sunny day would have been too much at odds with her dour mood. A sunny day would also have tempted her to meet Brandon at Bridestake, and she must never do that again. By the time she left her room, Teresa felt as if a black cloud had settled inside her.

Salvatore sat at the table reading a London paper while he ate breakfast. When she came into the room, he glanced at her, then resumed his reading, his face set in stubborn creases.

Teresa served her plate from the sideboard, English style, then took her usual place at the table. She didn't greet her father, because she wasn't sure what to say.

"Katie's cooking has improved after her visit to Venice," Salvatore said at last.

"Yes, it has." Teresa hadn't tasted any of the breakfast she was eating.

Her father drew his brows together in a deep frown and stared at her. "There's no need for you to be so perverse and willful. I love you, Teresa, and I have your best interests in mind."

She returned his steady gaze without speaking.

"If you marry, you will give up all you've worked so

hard for. All your life you've dreamed of being the first woman master. Foolish, I thought—but it has happened! Early this morning I went to the studio and closely examined the portrait of the royal prince and princesses. They are *alive, cara mia!* They seemed so lifelike, I thought they might move. You cannot throw away a talent like that! Not for a mere marriage."

Teresa sighed. There was no reason to tell him about Mario's visit. This was one of his lucid days, and they were too rare to spoil. Besides, there was no predicting what he might do to his brother to protect her. If he upset Mario, her uncle might go through with his threat to tell Brandon all he knew. If Brandon were to learn the whole truth, he would find it impossible to continue as their patron, and they would have to leave the cottage. This way she could at least live near him and see him occasionally.

"A talent like yours must be protected! You owe it to the world, not just to ourselves. What if Canaletto or Bellini had decided to marry and become a fishmonger or a vendor? Where would the world of art be?"

"You're probably right about that."

"In all of England there is not one master artist at this time. Oh, there's the Landseer fellow, but he paints deer and portraits. There is no VanDyke, no Da Vinci, no Rembrandt. None of the really great artists have been British! You could be the first!"

"I'm not British either, Papa."

"No, but you're the closest they have to one at this time. You will be their Bellini!"

"You aim high." She sipped Katie's weak coffee.

Salvatore, encouraged that she was no longer angry, put his hand over hers. "You can be great, Teresa! Truly great!"

She felt the tremble of his hand and saw the pain in his eyes. Salvatore was not well, and she realized he might be in worse health than she had thought. She couldn't desert him even if Mario had not made it impossible for her to marry Brandon. "You're right, Papa. The Verdi name can be great."

"Not just our name, but *you!*"

"No, Papa. The name of Salvatore Verdi can become great, not Teresa Verdi. As you have always said, a woman cannot be a master. There isn't even a word for what such a woman would be."

She put down the coffee cup because her own hand was shaking with suppressed emotion. "All my life has been lived to put me in the position I'm in now. I never regretted spending my childhood and youth behind an easel, because I loved art with all my heart. Now . . ." Her voice faltered. "I have given my heart elsewhere, but that doesn't change who and what I am." With a tremendous inner courage she said, "Any woman may fall in love, but how many may be a Bellini?"

"Wise words, Teresa. Your grandpapa would be proud. So would your mama."

Teresa rose in a hurry and squared her shoulders. She knew her bravery had its limits, and she needed to do what had to be done while she could. "I must go tell Brandon that I can't marry him."

"In the rain, Teresa? Wait awhile."

She shook her head with determination. "If I wait, I may not be able to do it."

For a fleeting moment she thought she saw regret cloud her father's face before he looked down to his paper, but it was mere sadness he was feeling, a necessary sadness.

"All great artists must make sacrifices," he said in a low voice. "Perhaps the greater the talent, the greater the sacrifice must be."

Casting an angry look at him, Teresa said, "Nonsense! My sacrifice was in spending hours of work each day when I might have been playing. Of giving up my youth to perfect a method of shading and a technique of glazing. Don't talk to me of sacrifices!"

His unhappy eyes lifted to meet hers. "It's the only way, *bambina.*"

"I know." On her way out, she wrapped herself in her woolen cape and pulled the hood over her head. This was the most difficult message she hoped she would ever have to deliver.

As the rain sliced down in silvery sheets and the distant thunder rolled over the hills, Teresa ran down the riding path, hoping the overhanging trees would provide some protection. The air was noticeably colder than the day before, and she worried that all this exposure to the elements might make her ill. But she couldn't let that happen; she couldn't afford to be sick because she had to paint that cursed canvas for Uncle Mario.

She cut across the yard and stood shivering on the porch until Fitch let her in. He failed to hide his displeasure at the puddle that dripped from her cape, and Teresa took that to mean Brandon had not yet announced their engagement to his staff. At least she could be thankful for that.

Brandon was in the morning room, and when she entered he strode to her as if he would take her in his arms. Teresa turned away and walked to the nearest window. "I must speak with you."

His eyes narrowed. "Oh?"

"I . . . I can't marry you." She forced the acrid words from her mouth and tried to swallow the vile taste they left behind.

During the long silence that followed, Teresa was afraid to turn around. When his voice sounded, immediately behind her, she jumped. "What sort of game are you playing with me, Teresa?"

"It's no game. Yesterday I followed my heart, but today I know I must refuse you." She prayed she could get through this without crying.

"That's not good enough. Did your father send you here with this message?"

"In a way."

"That does it!" Brandon strode toward the door. "I'm going to go up there and give him a piece of my mind!"

"No, no! You mustn't do that!" She ran to him and grabbed his arm. "Please, don't do that!"

"Why not? He's destroying both our lives. Doesn't he love you enough to want you to be happy?"

"Yes! Papa loves me very much. It's for my happiness that he is doing this. You and I would be happy at first." Her voice was wistful at the thought. Then with determination she added, "However, in the long run, it wouldn't work."

"Why in hell not?" he roared.

"I can't tell you, but it's true."

"What deep, dark secret could you possibly have that would make me fall out of love with you? Do you think my affections are so shallow that I would be no more constant than that?" His fury darkened his eyes; he looked as if he wished he could shake some sense into her.

"I was not raised to be a man's wife."

"What could you need to know? You manage your household; mine is not much different. Mrs. Dennison does all the hiring and sees after the staff. You wouldn't need to cook as much here as you do in the cottage, Bess Jackson does that. Jane Marek does all the sewing. What else do you lack? God knows you have the knowledge to be my lover!"

"A lover is all I can ever be to you. Nothing else."

A stony silence separated them. "If you will not be my wife, I'll not have you as a lover!"

"I expected you to say that." She turned away again, and feigned an interest in a paperweight of amethyst crystals on the side table. "I saw Uncle Mario, and he has agreed to stop copying Papa's paintings."

"Just like that? And you believed him?" His pain and frustration were evident in the harshness with which he spoke.

"I have every reason to believe him."

"Well, I don't! Has your father finished that landscape yet?"

Teresa paused to compose herself, then lied. "Papa had to paint over it. The perspective was wrong."

"He did what? Fitzhubert's Gallery in York has a buyer for a landscape such as that."

"Papa will paint another. It won't take him long." She would need to paint fast indeed to double her present output. "The portrait of the royal children is finished. As soon as it dries you may deliver it to Buckingham Palace."

"Signor Verdi won't come out of his self-imposed hermitage even for that?" Brandon's words were tinged with sarcasm.

"No, not even to deliver it to the queen herself. It's odd, isn't it? We came here to inhabit your hermit's cottage. At the time I was offended because I was afraid you brought us here merely to be picturesque for your London friends. Now you rarely have friends out, and Papa is in truth a hermit."

"That doesn't mean you have to be one too. Why the hell won't you marry me!"

"I should never have said that I would. It was wrong of me. I already knew I could marry no one."

"That doesn't make any sense at all!"

"Yes, it does. I just can't tell you the reason. If you knew all the particulars, you'd see why I have to refuse you."

"I would never see that."

"Nevertheless, you must accept it." She turned to face him, her eyes filled with anguish. "Can't you see it's as hard for me as it is for you?"

He took her in his arms despite her halfhearted protest. "Teresa, I love you. Don't take our future away from us." He embraced her tightly, as if his strength could vanquish this enemy. "If it's your father, it need not be forever. I've seen how his health has deteriorated since you came here. Forgive me for saying it, but he won't live forever."

Her sigh was as heavy as the weight on her heart. "Papa may be more ill than either of us knows." But that didn't alter the fact that she was now implicated in Mario's fraudulent scheme. If the truth ever became known, Brandon's reputation would be ruined, and if she were his wife, it would be even worse for him. "No! I can't expect to profit by Papa's death!" She jerked away from Brandon.

"I didn't mean it that way. I was only telling you that I will wait for you."

"No," she whispered. "You mustn't wait because even then I won't be able to marry you. It's your duty to marry and have an heir to carry on your name and be master of Hawthorn."

"One of my brothers can do it. Hawthorn can pass to a nephew—it's not tied to direct lineage, nor is my title."

"Brandon, I cannot marry you! Not ever!"

"You mean you will not!" His voice rose to match hers.

"Don't you know I would if I could? Don't torment me this way!"

"You're in torment?" he scoffed. "I see no evidence of it. Any woman may produce tears at will. That's no proof. Are you fainting? No! Are you weak in any way? No! Why you enjoy baiting me, I don't know, but it's obvious that you do. Now you even expect me to believe your Uncle Mario has blithely agreed to give up his lucrative career of forgery just because you asked him to do so!"

"He has! And for a good reason."

"But I'm not to know what that reason is either?"

"That's right!"

"Good-bye, Teresa. It's been a very interesting relationship."

"Where are you going?"

"To London. Not every woman I know is so ambivalent in her feelings toward me."

Her eyes snapped toward him, and she felt a sharp pain in her bosom. "You forget me rather easily for a man who professes to be in love!"

"I do love you. But I'm not a docile puppet to dance to your whims."

She took a step closer to him and glared up into his eyes. "I hope you enjoy your trek to London, my lord, and I hope you fall off your horse and break your neck!"

"Thank you, Teresa. At the moment I could wish you the same."

She bolted from the room, grabbed her wet cape from the hook in the foyer, and dashed out into the rain as she swirled it about her. She didn't really wish him ill—she loved him with all her heart and superstitiously hoped her hasty words wouldn't bring him misfortune. But damn him! How could he say such things to her? As she ran, tears streamed down her face at the idea of his rushing to the arms of some other woman.

She was still sobbing when she entered the cottage and ran to her room. Both Salvatore and Katie tried to coax her to unlock her door, but she refused. She wanted to be left alone in her sorrow.

Brandon rode straight to London in a driving rain, having left behind orders for his valet, Robert Flynn, to follow him immediately with enough clothing for a stay of several days. At his club he asked for the key to the room he kept reserved there. In minutes he had shed his wet clothes in favor of his dressing gown, and was seated with a pressed newspaper before a warm fire. He had always liked his club because it provided a purely masculine atmosphere of tweed-and-leather comfort. Tonight he was in great need of comfort.

He stared at the page for several minutes without reading a word, before admitting to himself that Teresa was no easier to forget than he had thought she would be. All he could see were the tears in her eyes. What could possibly prevent her from becoming his wife? He had explored every possibility, and nothing made any sense. It wasn't as if he had nothing to offer her or as if they weren't in love.

Love! Brandon had never known such a gentle word could hold such agony. Love was a capricious mistress that brought as much pain as delight. He wondered darkly why the poets bothered to write about it at all.

Within the hour Robert Flynn arrived with Brandon's bag and one of his own. Brandon nodded a greeting to his valet and the man went about the business of unpacking and seeing to Brandon's wet clothing. Robert always accompanied his master to the club and stayed in the room that adjoined Brandon's by way of the writing closet.

The rain continued for hours, and as the outside temperature dropped, the room followed suit. Without being asked, Robert added more coals to the fire and soon had the iron grate glowing again. Brandon would have preferred to remain in physical discomfort to match his disposition, but he could hardly insist that Robert be uncomfortable as well. Without Teresa, Brandon knew he would never be whole or entirely happy again, so what difference did it make if his feet were warm?

For the entirety of the next day, Brandon wallowed in misery; then anger began to surface as the sun was going down. Almost aloud, Brandon rationalized that if Teresa didn't love him enough to marry him, he should just let her go. He was in London, the most fascinating city in Britain. Why mope about his room like a lovesick swain when the town was full of eligible women? He had often told Colin that there were plenty of fish in the sea and a man had no reason to grieve if one got away.

Brandon dressed and sent Robert around to the Bennetts' residence with his card. Robert soon returned to say Miss Bennett was receiving. Brandon brushed his thick hair and put on his beaver hat. Miss Mary Bennett was a lovely young woman from a good family, and she was thoroughly English. She would soon help him forget Teresa Verdi.

Mary was waiting for him in her mother's fashionably cluttered parlor, her slender fingers busy gluing shells to a decorative box. She greeted him sweetly and had him sit beside her on the horsehair sofa.

"Very pretty," Brandon said as he watched her push the tiny pink shells into the mucilage.

She smiled and lowered her dark lashes over her pansy-blue eyes. He had never noticed her hair was the same color as Teresa's. "Thank you, Brandon. It's a cigar box for Father." She paused, then said, "I saw Lady Barbara the other day."

He looked blank for a moment. Barbara seemed to belong to some other life. "Oh?"

"I suppose I shouldn't mention it, but she was in the Benchley carriage with Ashford sitting beside her."

"Why shouldn't you mention it?"

"I wouldn't want to make you jealous." She shot him a glance to see if he was upset.

"I couldn't care less whom Lady Barbara rides with."

"She's put it about town that she let you down for Ashford."

A devilish grin spread over Brandon's face. He had had all the chivalry he could stand. "That's close enough to the truth."

"Then it isn't *entirely* true?" Her blue eyes sparkled mischievously. "I thought not."

He shrugged. He didn't want Barbara, and it shouldn't matter to him what reason she gave for their wedding being canceled. At least this reason was preferable to the one about his keeping a mistress. Against his will he noticed that Mary's perfume smelled a bit like the one Teresa used.

"Have you heard from Colin lately?" Mary asked with great casualness.

"No, he's in Ireland to buy a horse. You know Colin and his animals."

"Yes, I do. How is the puppy I gave him?"

"He's thriving. At the rate he's going, he'll be larger than Colin's new horse."

"Oh, dear. The vendor said he would stay small."

"Colin likes all sizes. It doesn't matter."

Mary selected another shell, and Brandon couldn't help but contrast her languid, ineffectual movements to Teresa's sure and precise ones. If Teresa cared to cover a box with seashells, he was sure she could have finished the entire project in the length of time it had taken Mary to arrange three of them—and it would probably have been prettier too.

"I wonder when he will be back."

"Who?" Brandon asked.

"Colin, of course." Again Mary's eyelashes lowered. "We had words before he left, you know. I had hoped that's why you had come here."

Brandon hid a groan. He had completely forgotten the reason Colin had headed for Ireland with such haste. He remembered now that Mary had set her cap for Colin and was pressing him to set a date. "Actually, I was only in town and thought I'd drop by to visit."

"Colin probably sent you to see how I'm doing," she said sadly. "You may tell him I cried."

Brandon leaned forward to peer at her eyes. "You aren't crying."

"Not at the moment, but I have been. I was disconsolate yesterday."

"It was a bad day for everyone," Brandon wryly observed.

"Yes. The rain and all. Tell me, Brandon, does Colin have a sweetheart in Ireland?"

"In Ireland? Knowing Colin, I wouldn't put it past . . . I mean, no, not that I know of." He was wondering how he had gotten himself into this, and more, how he could gracefully get himself out.

"I know Colin has a man's natural reluctance about settling down. I'd be surprised if he didn't. But honestly, Brandon, don't you think I could make him happy?"

"Well, I . . . that is, I think any man would be fortunate to win your hand, Mary."

"You do? Then you'll tell Colin? Oh, Brandon, I

don't know how to thank you." She blushed, but Brandon couldn't tell whether it was genuine or affected. "If all goes well, I hope you'll stand as godfather to our firstborn." She lowered her lashes and turned scarlet.

Brandon stared at her, completely at a loss for words. "Yes. Well. I have to go now. I have some other calls to make."

"Of course you do! How selfish of me to keep you like this. I just enjoy talking to Colin's family. How's Mitchell?"

"Fine, just fine. He plans to set up his practice here in London when he becomes a doctor."

"How marvelous! I'll go to him, and I'm sure all our other friends will also."

Brandon grinned at the idea of Mary Bennett in St. Giles rookery. "I'll tell Mitchell you said so."

Brandon was glad to escape from the Bennett house. Colin wasn't going to be happy about his visit—it looked too much as though it had been done with the intent of matchmaking. Brandon shook his head. Mary was a lovely girl, but she had the instincts of a spider, and Colin would be lucky to avoid her web.

Brandon had no plans to call on anyone else, but he was too restless to return immediately to his club. No place satisfied him for long without Teresa. He wished she were even a fraction as set on marrying as Mary was. If Mary were less possessive, he would feel sorry for her, because he knew Colin had no intention of marrying anyone.

He walked the streets of London, noticing neither where he went nor where he had been. After an hour he found himself in front of Maidenhode, the school for boys. Most of the students here were sons of wealthy tradesmen or of the lesser nobility who were too tight with their purse strings to send their sons to the more prestigious schools. It was also the school where Mario Verdi was the art instructor.

As he was about to retrace his steps, Brandon saw Mario come out of the alley that led to his lodgings and turn in the opposite direction. Under his arm he carried a large package that could only contain a painting.

Being careful to keep some distance between them, Brandon followed him. Mario walked with the assurance of a man who has nothing to fear. Brandon had no trouble at all in following him to the wharf. Mario boarded a ship called the *Maid of Kent,* was belowdecks for several minutes, then reappeared without the package.

Brandon waited behind a pile of crates for Mario to leave, then went to the shipping clerk's office. "The ship out there being loaded, the *Maid of Kent*—where's she bound?" he asked the man in charge.

"She's headed for America, my lord, but we have no staterooms. She's a cargo ship."

"I'm interested in her cargo. Do you have record of a painting by Salvatore Verdi that's to be shipped?"

The man consulted his list. "We don't have one down here, but that don't mean much. There are several crates that don't have the contents listed, or it could be in a seaman's room. Sometimes they sees to a fancy item like a picture and gets paid for their troubles. We closes our eyes to it usually. May I ask if it's important? The *Maid* is ready to pull out. She can't tarry long and still go out with the tide."

"No, don't hold her up. If you have no record of the painting, it might take hours to locate it." He thanked the man and walked back toward his club. Whatever Mario had said to Teresa, he had almost certainly lied. True, the painting could have been one of his own, but they were so lacking in imagination that Brandon doubted anyone would send across the Atlantic for one.

After three days of trying to be happy in London, Brandon gave it up as a lost cause and returned to Hawthorn. The first person he saw walking along the road was Teresa, and had she not seen him at the same time, he might have ridden into the woods to wait for her to pass. He wasn't so callous as to gallop past her, so he signaled for his valet to continue to the house, and he reined in.

A muscle tightened in his jaw as he fought the urge to sweep her into his embrace. "How are you?"

"I'm all right," she said. She appeared to be feeling as awkward as he was. "And you?"

"Quite well."

"Did you enjoy the ladies of London?"

He frowned. He had seen no woman at all but Mary Bennett. "That's hardly any concern of yours."

She was about to walk by, but he stopped her by saying, "I saw your Uncle Mario. He was putting a parcel on a ship bound for America. It was a rather curious parcel—shaped exactly like a painting."

She jerked around. "What are you saying!"

"If it wasn't a forgery, it looked damned suspicious."

"Perhaps I should remind you that Uncle Mario is also an artist. If you didn't see the painting, you can't possibly know whether it was a copy or one of his own." She knew all too well it must have been the landscape he had taken from her.

"A short time ago you were positive he was duplicating your father's work and you were as eager as I am to see it stopped."

"I told you he agreed never to do it again."

"How can you accept the word of a scoundrel like that!"

"Must I remind you he is my uncle? If I were a man I could call you out for slandering my family with such a remark!"

"Your family loyalty is odd, to say the least. Not to mention misplaced."

"Think whatever you please." She walked past him. She wished she had chosen some other place to walk that day, but how was she to know Brandon would decide to come home just then? She hoped he had had a perfectly miserable time in London. For nights she had tossed in agony over whether he was making love to some other woman.

"If I catch him in another forgery, I'll have him arrested," Brandon called after her.

She kept on walking. She should have known such happiness as she had found by his side couldn't be constant. All her life she had expected to remain unmarried and relatively alone. She just hadn't thought it would be so painful.

21

Mario was quite proud of himself. Not only was he to
have a steady stream of Verdi paintings to sell, but he
wouldn't have to paint them himself. Certainly there
would no longer be the danger, however slight it had
been, that someone would know he was selling copies,
because now each would be an original. Of course
Teresa could try to double-cross him by telling Salvatore or Lord Kincaid, but Mario felt that was too remote to be a concern. His brother was powerless to stop
him, and Teresa had far too much to lose to let Lord
Kincaid find out she and her father had been duping
him.

He couldn't help but chuckle to think of Teresa as a
viscountess and a forger. What strange twists and jests
life provided! For the next three weeks Mario was
almost happy even in the classroom. He had found he
taught best by giving an assignment and ignoring his
students until it was time to gather in the work. The
boys were little the worse for it, since not one of them
had a grain of talent to start with, and the dean of the
school was none the wiser. Mario collected his pay and
let the classroom take care of itself. If it weren't for
needing a job to explain his having money, he would
have quit it altogether.

After supper, it had become his habit to go to the
White Swan for companionship. True, the clientele was
a rowdy bunch in general, but Mario had made friends

there. Even though he could now afford a better pub, he preferred the familiar haunt to the challenge of making new drinking acquaintances.

The White Swan stood near the edge of London, not far from the remains of an ancient Roman road. At one time a Roman outpost had provided the customers for a public house on this spot. That one was long since gone, though a part of the tiled floor remained at one side of the bar. The wall surrounding the courtyard had fallen down long before, along with the establishment's respectability, and neither had been resurrected.

As he approached his familiar haunt, Mario heard the muffled roar of a sailor belting out the refrain of a seafarer's song. The Thames was nearby and crewmen from the ships that crowded the river, moving their cargoes in and out of London, were often in the pub. Mario enjoyed talking to these men and hearing their tales of adventure. He was generally accepted by them as a comrade, though he never went to sea. None of them knew he was a painting instructor or had anything to do with as soft a subject as art. In the White Swan, Mario was a bit of a mystery. Some thought he might be a highwayman, and Mario was pleased to let them think so.

Lifting the worn latch on the door, he let himself into the smoky haze of the noisy room. The odor of stale beer, old hearth ashes, and unwashed bodies assailed his nose. Accustomed as he was to the pungent aromas of oil and turpentine, Mario didn't mind. These were men—real men. Not the quiet, scholarly sort who had frequented his father's house, but the kind who would rather fight than give an inch, and who referred to women and religion in the most demeaning of terms.

"Mario!" a huge man called from the bar. "Over here!"

Mario waved as he joined the big man. "Tom! I had no idea your ship was due back now."

"We had the devil's own time of it. Storms from here to the Canaries and back again. At least it blew us on at full speed." Big Tom jerked his head to summon the barkeep. "An ale for my friend."

Mario smiled. The best thing about Big Tom Wilson was that when he was drinking he would buy ale for anyone who would stand by his side. Mario tossed down a liberal gulp.

"We seen this girl on the islands like you ain't never seen the likes of before," Tom said conspiratorially. "A young one, maybe thirteen or fourteen. They ripen early on the islands. You ain't never seen no young girl built like that!"

Mario leaned forward in interest. He seldom had much use for women in the flesh, but he thoroughly enjoyed vicarious thrills.

"Me and old Jobe and Blue Tooth seen her walking on the beach all by herself, and we followed her. Jobe, he wanted to take her on board the ship. Said we could all use her till we reached port and sell her to a brothel. Sounded like a good idea to me, but you know Blue Tooth. He can't think past the end of his nose. He was all for using her then and there and leavin' her behind. Well, she was headed away from town, so we followed her and . . ."

Mario drank in every lurid word. As Big Tom's tale continued, his voice sank lower. By the time he described what had taken place on the beach, he was speaking in a harsh whisper, and Mario's eyes were glittering with borrowed lust. Mario swallowed hard and unconsciously shifted on the hard stool. Big Tom had a way of telling a story that made his listeners almost believe they had been there. "Damn!" he murmured when Big Tom drew back with a gap-toothed grin. "Damn!"

Big Tom chuckled. "She weren't hurt all that bad. Like I said, girls grow up fast on the Canaries."

"Did you bring her with you?"

"No, Blue Tooth talked Jobe out of it, and I didn't want to fool with it by myself. We could have got a pretty penny for her, though. Like I say, she was real young, and a beauty."

Mario wet his lips with his tongue. "You don't see girls like that around here, and if you did, you couldn't have them for the taking."

Big Tom winked at him. "You ain't looked in the right places."

Mario took another drink. He wasn't really interested in having the experience firsthand. He had learned he enjoyed the fantasy more than the reality.

Mario looked around the room. "It's busy here tonight."

"A lot of people got paid today, I reckon."

A sandy-haired youth came in the door and looked around as if he were new here. Mario's eyes narrowed as he recognized him as the boy who worked for Salvatore. He motioned to the bartender. "Is that Hal Lunn over there by the door?"

"Aye. He's been in the last couple of nights. If his pa knew Hal was here, he'd have his hide. Old Henry don't hold with drinking." The barkeep wiped a glass on his grimy apron. "Old Henry used to be a rouser before he got religion. Don't ever see him anymore."

Mario nodded. He couldn't care less about the boy's father. Teresa was supposed to bring the first of the paintings to him at the White Swan tomorrow night. If the boy saw her, he might tell Lord Kincaid. Teresa was much too prudish to frequent such a place without a good reason.

He scowled down at his nearly empty glass. Of all the places for Hal Lunn to sow some oats, this was the most inconvenient one he could have chosen. He knew of another place near here where they wouldn't be seen, however. It was called Maximus Bridge after some Roman commander, and was almost never traveled after dark.

"What's this?" Salvatore asked his daughter as he held up an unfamiliar canvas. Teresa was getting ready to remove the landscape she had done in secret for her uncle when her father had unexpectedly joined her in the studio.

"A landscape. I thought you would be in bed asleep by now."

"I heard a noise and came to see what it was. Teresa, I never saw you working on this."

"I did it at night when I was unable to sleep."

"But it's not like anything you usually paint. This is more like one of my compositions. I could almost believe I had done it!"

She took the canvas from him. "It's just a painting, Papa. Go back to bed."

Salvatore shook his large head. "Something is wrong here. Why would you paint at night after working in here all day? Even you must rest sometime, *cara*."

"I said I haven't slept well lately." She studied the painting at an angle to the light, then touched the white of the clouds. It was completely dry, which was fortunate, since she had to deliver it that night.

"Are you really so much in love with Lord Kincaid?" he surprised her by asking.

Teresa faltered, but she kept her eyes averted. The last three weeks had been nightmarish for her. "Yes," she said at last. "I love him with all my heart."

"All of it, *cara mia*?"

She searched his face for a hint of why he had broached the painful subject. "He is like my other half, Papa. The sun doesn't shine when he isn't around."

"There is your art to consider," he protested. "What about me and my name?"

She turned away and said in a small voice, "My love for Brandon is greater than my love for art, but I have refused him. Your reputation is safe."

Her father's deep sigh sounded sad, not relieved. "I knew someday you would find such a man. It's right for a woman to want to have her own household and to raise a family."

"I'm not just a woman, Papa, I'm an artist as well."

"Yes. I haven't forgotten."

Teresa turned to face him. "Why bring all this up again? It's over and done with."

Salvatore picked up the rubber ball he used to strengthen his fingers and absentmindedly squeezed it over and over. "Maybe we were wrong, Papa and I. Maybe we should never have encouraged you to paint. It's just that you were so good!" He went toward the door. "I'm tired. I'm going to bed."

"As long as you need me, I'll never leave you," she reassured him.

Salvatore turned, and through a sad smile he said, "Your mama once told me the same thing."

As Teresa watched him leave, she thought how old he looked. His face was lined with anguish and regret. Perhaps his reputation was safe in the art world, but he knew the truth. He had been unable to reach the pinnacle she had attained, and that had broken him.

She sat down in a chair and closed her eyes. In her success she tasted defeat. She dearly loved her father, but in giving him fame she had ruined him.

Two hours later she got up and started taking the tacks from the canvas and frame. She was anxious to be done with all this. Mario would get this painting because she hated the sight of it, but it would be the last. The sale of this óne would take him to Venice or wherever he chose to go, but she would never give him another. She had had Hal change all the locks the morning after Mario's surprise visit, so he couldn't get back in. If Mario told Brandon, then so be it. Brandon might not believe him, since he knew her uncle was guilty of forgery himself. He might think Mario was making it up to save his own skin.

She rolled the stiff canvas into a cylinder and tied it with string. She hated the idea of going to the White Swan, but she had no choice. At least all this would soon be behind her, and she could be rid of her uncle forever.

Teresa was in such a hurry to leave that she didn't see the note for her that Katie had put in her room.

Salvatore still couldn't sleep. He loved his daughter and wanted her to be happy, but he knew artists seldom were. There was a fire that burned in them that drove them to an impossible perfection, and all the really great ones knew they could never attain their dreams. In the end they all were constrained by two-dimensional paintings or by the stone they carved. Artists couldn't create life, and for the ones that burned with the fire, nothing less was enough.

Salvatore had lived with that maddening drive all his life, as had his father, and he had seen the same in Teresa's eyes. Knowing she was doomed to some degree of disappointment, could he force loneliness upon her as well?

He had not been a good husband to her mother. His first love had always been his art. His canvases had received his best and truest passions, not Eva Maria. And Eva Maria—a passionate woman—had suffered from his detachment. Had she turned to a lover, as he suspected? After all these years, he was no longer certain. Time clouded so much. He wondered if Teresa had inherited Eva Maria's passion and ability to love. If so, to deprive her of a husband would be doubly cruel.

Salvatore knew he rarely had such clear thoughts and insights these days, and he clung to them. While he was still capable of seeing matters so clearly, he decided he should go to Teresa and give her his blessing to marry. That was much more important than maintaining his hold on a reputation that wasn't rightfully his. He would not confess what he and Teresa had done, but would insist that he be allowed to retire due to complications from his illness.

He went to the studio, but saw at once that it was empty, though Teresa had left the light burning. That was unlike her, but she had been upset for weeks. He moved a stretcher frame to one side and wondered why Teresa had assembled it if she hadn't stretched a canvas on it. He concluded that was a wandering thought, and pushed it from his mind. Teresa was the important thing just now. He could puzzle over the stretcher frame later.

He paused outside her bedroom. He could see a crack of light under her door, but heard nothing from inside. Softly he tapped. "Teresa?"

When she didn't answer, he became apprehensive. Eva Maria had once threatened to kill herself. With alarm rising, Salvatore shoved into the room and looked about. It, too, was empty.

A note in a white envelope lay on the bed. A suicide note? Salvatore's fingers trembled more than usual as he picked it up. He tore it open and held the letter up to the light. There was no need to look at the signature. He had seen that cramped hand all his life.

By the time he had finished reading the note a second time, his face was blotched red with anger. In one strong hand he crumpled the paper and threw it onto the floor. Teresa had gone to meet Mario at Maximus Bridge! The painting of the landscape had been for Mario!

Anger suffused Salvatore's brain, causing his precariously ordered thoughts to cloud and churn. Eva Maria had been said to have a lover, and the rumors had all named one man—his brother, Mario. An animal growl emerged from deep in Salvatore's chest and his hands clenched into fists, released like talons, and clenched again.

Without pausing for a coat, he stormed through the cottage and slammed out the front door. He knew the way to Maximus Bridge, though he had never been there at night. Fortunately, a waning moon high in the sky gave just enough light for him to see his way. Mario was waiting at the bridge. And Eva Maria was not in her room! With a roar of angered pain, Salvatore ran through the night.

Brandon had rarely been in a worse temper. For

three weeks he had been irritable, and at times he had lost his temper such as he had never allowed himself to do before. All his adult life Brandon had prided himself on being calm and logical. If something needed his attention or went awry, he fixed it with cool dispatch and proceeded unruffled on his way. His name had been synonymous with genteel behavior among his friends and acquaintances. That was before Teresa.

She had turned his world inside out, sprinkled it with gold dust, then had gone on her way. Worst of all, there was no logic to support what she had done. He shouldn't have fallen in love with her in the first place, since in Barbara he had had a perfectly good candidate for a wife. True, Barbara had proved to be false, but he hadn't known it at the start. Brandon was quite sure his own parents had loved each other, though theirs had been an arranged marriage and they had seldom shown outward affection for one another. They had been perfectly matched, and well-suited to each other. Yet he and Teresa were as dissimilar as oil and water.

Then, when against all logic and discretion they had become lovers, she had refused to marry him. Unbelievable! The simplest reasoning would have dictated that it be the other way around.

To further confuse matters, she had finally agreed to marry him, then backed out again, and would give him no explanation at all. Brandon was confused, and he detested confusion. He was much happier with a serene, orderly life. Or was he? Since Teresa had abandoned him, he had had so much serenity around him that it was driving him to distraction. He had even started a deliberate argument with Colin simply in order to vent his frustration.

In his sitting room, Brandon slumped in a chair, staring at his two renditions of *The Harem Girl*. How had he let Teresa convince him not to pursue his investigation of Mario? If the man were left unchecked, he could do irreparable harm by glutting the market with fake Verdis. While it might be foolhardy to have the man arrested and thus cast doubt on the authenticity of every Salvatore Verdi painting in existence, Mario should certainly be warned not to continue his fraudulent activities. Brandon didn't believe for a minute that Mario would quit forging paintings just because Teresa asked him to stop. He might, however, if the warning came from Brandon.

Brandon took out his gold watch and clicked open the face. The hour was late, but London was still awake and bustling. Especially the pubs. When Brandon had had Mario watched, he had been told that Mario frequented a tavern called the White Swan, which stood between the old Maximus Road and the Thames. Brandon could no longer bear doing nothing. Thus he resolved to ride to the tavern and personally tell Mario to stop his forgeries.

He returned the original *Harem Girl* to its place on the bedroom wall, then strode out to call for his horse.

Teresa had ridden the pony that was used to draw the supply cart. It was a rough mount with no easy gait at all and had such a tough mouth that only a rider with considerable strength could control it. Keeping the pony more or less on the right path was hard enough without having to protect the rolled canvas from wrinkling.

When she reached the White Swan, Teresa was seized with fear. What if one of the rough-looking men in the yard tried to accost her? She had never been near such a place in her life. She saw a couple of women going in, but she knew they were prostitutes by their gaudy clothing. She groaned.

She was earlier than the appointed time, and it occurred to her that her uncle might not even be there. Waiting for him in that dismal place was out of the question.

After some deliberation, she tied the pony to a tree in the dark and crossed the shadowy side yard to look in one of the pub's small windows. She had never seen such a group. Smoke hung like a thundercloud in the low rafters, and the people seemed to be a jumble of different cultures and races. This was a crowd better suited to a dock than a tavern several blocks from the Thames. The people had only one trait in common—they were all rowdy.

Keeping in the shadows, Teresa curiously watched the goings-on; then, when the crowd shifted, she saw her uncle seated at a scarred table. Her expression hardened. She might not want to go in there, and she hated Mario for making it necessary, but she would do what she had to do. She was no coward.

Squaring her shoulders, she went around the corner and across the dimly lit front yard. The men lounging outside the door all noticed her approach. Two of them, a huge man with an unkempt beard and a tall one who was even dirtier, came toward her.

Teresa felt as if she might faint, but she didn't dare. When the two tried to block her path, she glared at them and tried to push past.

"Not so fast, my pretty," said the tall one, smiling to show a discolored tooth. "Where be you goin'?"

"My uncle is waiting for me inside," she snapped. "Step aside."

"Your uncle, is it? She says she's looking for her uncle, Big Tom."

The burly man grinned. "I ain't never heard one called that afore. We'd be glad to be your 'uncle.' Wouldn't we, Blue Tooth?"

"Aye." He reached out to push the hood from her head to better see her face.

Teresa didn't pause to think. She sank her teeth into Blue Tooth's hand and dodged past him into the pub.

"We'll be waiting for you," Big Tom said. "You can't stay in there all night, uncle or no uncle."

Her heart was pounding as she made her way to the table where she had seen Mario. Was there a back door? She didn't dare go past those men again, and she doubted Mario would be of any help. "Teresa!" he gasped when he looked up to see her. "What are you doing here?"

"Come now, Uncle Mario. I know you haven't forgotten what night this is." She shoved the rolled canvas at him. "Here is the landscape. There will never be another for you!"

Mario pushed it back into her hands as he looked around the room. "Not here! Didn't you get my message?"

"I've seen no message. Are you going to take this or not?"

"Someone might recognize you and realize what is happening," he hissed. "Take this back and meet me at Maximus Bridge in half an hour."

"What? You brought me into this den of thieves for nothing?"

"Lower your voice! This is no place for such unguarded talk."

"I'm not going to any bridge, especially not that spooky place. You can take this now or not have it at all. Use the money from it to buy a ticket to someplace far away, because if I ever see you again, I'll go straight to the police!"

"I told you to lower your voice! Meet me where I said."

"How am I to get there safely, Uncle Mario?" she demanded. "Two ruffians tried to attack me when I was coming in here, and I don't dare go past them alone. Isn't there a back way out?"

Mario glanced toward the door and saw Big Tom and Blue Tooth grinning in at them. He recalled the tale Big Tom had told of the island girl and others like her. He didn't want harm to come to Teresa, but he knew he couldn't stop men like these. "There's a back door behind the end of the bar. Give me time to slip out that way, then you follow."

"What? You're going to leave me in here while you get away? Uncle Mario!" She glanced toward the front door to see the bearded man coming toward her. Her breath lodged in her throat. "Uncle Mario?" she whispered. When she looked back, he was gone. "Uncle Mario!"

Big Tom reached her before she could move, and caught her arm in a painful grip. "Not so fast, my pretty. Mario never mentioned a niece to me. I think maybe he ain't your uncle at all."

"Let me go!"

"Me and Blue Tooth, we know better what to do with girls like you than Mario does. You come outside and see what we have to offer."

Teresa jerked back, but Big Tom held her in a way that threatened to snap her wrist. Fear left a coppery taste in Teresa's mouth, and she felt icy cold.

"Turn her loose at once," a familiar voice said.

Teresa looked up to see Brandon, and she felt as if all her bones had turned soft. "Brandon!" she gasped in relief, not questioning how he came to be there.

"I said turn her loose," Brandon repeated in a calm but commanding voice.

"Well, now, I don't think I want to do that." Big Tom sneered. "I seen her first."

"Actually, you didn't." Brandon drew a pistol from his pocket and pointed it at Big Tom's chest. "I did."

"What are you going to do with that gun?" Big Tom demanded as he backed up.

"I'm going to blow a hole in you that's big enough to put a ramrod through. Unless, of course, you release the lady."

"Hell, you can have her. Ain't no woman worth getting shot over."

Brandon held out his hand to Teresa, and together they backed through the crowd.

"There's another one," she whispered. "A tall man with a dark tooth. There he is."

Brandon motioned with his pistol and waited for Blue Tooth to come into the room. Then he led Teresa out into the night. "What in hell were you doing in a place like that?" he demanded when they were safely hidden by darkness.

"Nothing." She knew she couldn't tell him anything that he would believe.

"You came here to meet your uncle, didn't you?"

Teresa's head jerked around in surprise. "What?"

"Don't play the innocent with me. I know Mario frequents this place." His arm went around her as he ushered her farther away from the pub, and his fingers grazed the rolled canvas. "What have we here?"

Teresa wanted to throw the canvas away in hopes he couldn't find it in the dark, but Brandon was too fast. She could feel him glaring at her even though it was too dark to see his eyes.

"A painting, I believe." Brandon took it from her and pulled loose the string that secured it. Stepping from under the trees into the moonlight, he stared down at the dimly lit picture. Silently he raised his head and looked at her.

"It's not what you think!" she said.

"No? Tell me what I think."

"I'm not siding with Uncle Mario to supply him with paintings!"

"Amazing. That's exactly what I was thinking." His cold, emotionless voice chilled her to the bone.

"No, Brandon, it wasn't like that at all!" She knew he would never believe her.

"Does your father know about this? I assume he doesn't, since you were in a place like the White Swan. What do you do? Wait until he's asleep, then smuggle his paintings out for your uncle to copy? What an interesting family you all are. And you nearly took me in."

"They are my paintings!" she blurted out. "Uncle Mario found out I'm the artist and not Papa, and he was trying to blackmail me! I brought him this one, and told him to use the money from it to go far away from here or I'd have him arrested."

"Of course you did. Then why do you still have the painting?"

"He wouldn't take it! He said for me to bring it to Maximus Bridge and give it to him there."

"Dammit, Teresa! Give me credit for having some sense! No one would be foolish enough to believe a story like that!"

"But it's true! All the paintings you've assumed were Papa's have been mine. The early ones were Papa's compositions, but I finished them. Since his illness, he has been unable to paint at all, and I've done them all myself."

"Including the royal portrait? Several people saw your father painting the prince and princesses," he pointed out sarcastically.

"Yes! They saw Papa sitting behind an easel, but they never saw him actually paint. He has such a tremor he can hardly hold a brush to the canvas."

Brandon shook his head in dismay as he rerolled the canvas and thrust it back at her. "You astound me. I discover you defrauding me in the most obvious way, and you try to work your way out of it by claiming to be the artist. Amazing."

"It's true! We didn't mean to deceive you. We thought Papa would be able to paint again after he came to England, that his melancholia would lift. Then he got sick, and after that he shook so badly. I—"

"Teresa, spare me your lies." Brandon's condemnation was evident not only in his words but also in the tone he used. "I can prove you're wrong merely by handing your father a brush."

"You wouldn't! If Papa even thought I had told you, he might die!"

"Men are generally hardier than that," he said. "He might be hurt to know what his daughter and brother have been up to behind his back, but I doubt the shock would be lethal. You really had me fooled on the trip to Venice." He paused as if unable to continue.

"But I love you!"

"No! Don't ever say those words to me again!" He grabbed her as if he would like to break her in half, then stared down at her in the moonlight. After a long moment he released her and stepped back. He didn't speak, though he glared at her in the silver light. Then he turned on his heel and stalked away. Only a moment later Teresa heard the hoofbeats of his horse as he headed away in the darkness.

Struggling to maintain her balance as her head swirled, she made her way to the pony and mounted. After looking for a minute at the roll of canvas, she threw it from her as far as she could.

As the pony was eager to return to his stall, the trip was a quick one. Teresa was glad her mount knew the way, because she couldn't see past the tears in her eyes.

She had to tell her father. Although she dreaded it, she had to prepare him before Brandon confronted him. After she released the pony in the stall and fed him, she went to the house.

The lights were on just as she had left them, but there was no sign of her father. Teresa hurried through the rooms, checking again, but Salvatore was gone. Back in her bedroom, she noticed a crumpled paper beneath the foot of her bed. After straightening it, she discovered it was from Mario. She vaguely remembered he had mentioned a message. It said to bring the painting to him at the Maximus Bridge rather than the White Swan.

Teresa's eyes widened. Her father must have found the note and read it! And he must be on his way to the bridge to confront Mario!

Teresa ran up the stairs and awakened Katie and Hal, then grabbed her cloak and ran down the slope to Hawthorn. The note would have been more than enough to send Salvatore into a rage, and she had to have help.

She pounded on the door for what seemed forever before a sleepy Fitch, who had a dressing gown wrapped over his nightshirt, finally opened it. "What's going on? Is it a fire?"

"Where's Brandon?" she cried out as she pushed past him. Running up the stairs, she screamed, "Brandon! Brandon!"

His room was empty. As she dashed out onto the wide landing, Colin burst out of his room, his shirt unbuttoned and stuffed askew into the waistband of his trousers. "Teresa?"

"Colin, you have to help me! Papa has gone to meet Uncle Mario at Maximus Bridge and he may be in danger!"

Colin grabbed his coat and ran after her, asking for details as they raced toward the horse barn.

22

Salvatore was still breathing hard when he reached Maximus Bridge. Wild-eyed, he looked all around, straining to see in the dim moonlight, but found no one. They must be here somewhere! Mario and his Eva Maria. The past crowded upon Salvatore, and he was again in Venice searching for his lovely, elusive wife. Perhaps he had left her alone too often, but she was his wife! He resolved when he found her this time to get her with child. His father had said this was a sure way of keeping a wife faithful. But where was she?

He pushed aside the bushes that were brittle with cold. She was hard to find these days. Often he caught glimpses of her in the studio or on the slope leading to Hawthorn or in the ruins of the bleak castle beyond the woods.

Salvatore blinked in confusion. Why would Eva Maria be here in England? Wasn't she dead? A dread thought! He pushed it aside. She was here. Eva Maria had said she would never leave him.

Charging here and there, he searched for her. The cold permeated his body, but he paid it no heed. He had to find Eva Maria and get her to safety.

Mario! That was the threat! Salvatore tried to force his muddled brain to recall exactly what the note had said. Something about the Maximus Bridge and a painting. Surely Mario wasn't using Eva Maria as his model— she had promised she wouldn't pose again for Mario.

Salvatore didn't trust his brother. Mario's eyes were too alert when Eva Maria was present. Mario had little compunction and no moral strength.

Through the darkness Salvatore saw a figure approaching. It was Mario! Salvatore had somehow reached the bridge before the tryst had come to pass.

He edged into the deep shadow of an oak and waited, scarcely daring to breathe. Mario came nearer, his steps unafraid, as if nothing could harm him. At the end of the bridge he stopped and looked down at the silent black water. A chill seemed to pass through him, for he shivered. Salvatore's lips drew back from his teeth in the semblance of a grin. She was late, as usual. Eva Maria had never been punctual.

Mario turned away from the bridge and peered back the way he had come. Salvatore was puzzled. Wouldn't he expect her to come from the other direction, which led to the cottage?

After standing there stiffly for a moment, Mario paced in the patch of moonlight. Several times he paused and peered through the inky night. Salvatore's grin widened. She wasn't coming! His Eva Maria was faithful after all.

Stealthily Salvatore stepped out of the shadows, and when his brother turned to face him, Salvatore was rewarded by the startled look on his face. "She isn't coming," Salvatore said in Italian.

"What? What do you mean, she isn't coming? How do you know?"

"She is true to me. She will never come to you again."

Mario frowned. "I know she said as much, but . . . she told you?" Amazement rounded his eyes.

Salvatore shook his head. "There was no need." He was pleased to hear that Eva Maria had told Mario she wouldn't meet him again. But didn't that imply they had been meeting before? His grin faded and disappeared.

With a scowl Mario faced his brother. "So you found out about the paintings. I told Teresa to be careful!"

"Teresa?"

"What did she do? Let you catch her painting that landscape?" Mario paced again to the bridge, then returned. "She can't stop, you know. Not ever. Now that I know which of you is actually the master artist, she has no choice but to supply me with paintings!"

Salvatore stared at Mario as his brain began to clear. "Paintings?"

"Of course! What else are we talking about? Is your mind so foggy from your illness that you've already forgotten why you're here?" His voice was filled with scorn.

Salvatore glanced around. They were in England, not Venice, and Eva Maria was long since dust on the cemetery island of San Michele. Teresa! The threat was to Teresa, his beloved child! Fury leapt to life in Salvatore, and he took a menacing step toward his brother.

Mario edged away. "You can't begrudge me a living. Papa would never forgive you for that!"

"Papa is dead! Eva Maria is dead too! It's Teresa that you would harm!"

"Me harm Teresa? Don't be a fool. I only want her paintings."

Salvatore thought of the countless paintings of violets and roses and still lifes that Teresa had done over the years. Mario could have no possible use for these. He was lying! He wanted to steal Teresa away just as he had tried to steal Eva Maria. This time there was no father to stand between the brothers.

With a cry of rage Salvatore lunged at Mario. His iron grip bit into Mario's arm, and the momentum carried them almost to the edge of the deep channel.

Mario at last realized the danger he was in and began to fight back. The brothers were equals in age and build, but Salvatore had the greater strength. With their eyes locked in mutual hatred, they struggled. As they wrestled, the ground became soft under Salvatore's feet, then marshy. He knew they were too close to the icy water, but he was intent on vanquishing the brother he had hated for so long. "You took my Eva Maria!" he ground out as he fought.

Mario's eyes grew wider. "That was a long time ago!"

"I should have killed you then!"

Fear gave Mario a burst of adrenaline, and with a twist he ripped free from Salvatore and pushed him over the edge. An angry cry rent the air as Salvatore felt himself falling, and with a last swing he found and locked onto Mario's ankle. Mario struggled to maintain his balance and kick free of his brother's death grip, but the bank was muddy. With a scream, Mario followed Salvatore into the icy water.

Mario struggled frantically in the frigid blackness, but Salvatore's grip was relentless. The water was deep and so cold that Mario's muscles became rigid from the shock. As Salvatore sank lower, so did he. The river swept them deeper, locked together, and when the current caught them, they were dragged to the bottom.

Teresa and Colin rode as hard as the horses could carry them. Moon-washed grasses blurred beneath the iron-shod hooves as the horses galloped at full speed through the night. They reached the bridge and reined to a plunging halt.

"Papa?" she cried out. "Papa!"

There was no answer except for a cold wind that rustled the bushes. "Maybe he isn't here yet," Colin suggested.

"He must be! And Uncle Mario has certainly had enough time to get here!" She slid off the horse and tied it to the nearest bush. "Papa?"

"Tell me again, more slowly," Colin said as he dismounted. "Why would your father come here?"

"Uncle Mario was blackmailing us," Teresa said in a rush of words. "He sent me a note to meet him here, but Papa evidently read the note before I got it."

"What have you done to give your uncle opportunity to blackmail you?"

Teresa paused. There was no reason to lie about it

now. As soon as Mario showed up, he would tell everyone. "Papa isn't the artist—I am."

"You!"

"Brandon saw me at the White Swan trying to deliver the blackmail painting to Uncle Mario."

"You went to the White Swan! Even I wouldn't set foot in that place!"

"I met Uncle Mario there to deliver the painting. I told him there would never be another and that he was to leave us alone in the future, but he wouldn't take it. Maybe he was afraid some of those scoundrels would steal it from him if they knew what it was. Oh, Colin, it was a dreadful place!"

He stared down at her. "Brandon was there?"

"Yes! I don't know why, but he was. I guess he came to confront Uncle Mario; I don't know. He got me out safely, and I tried to explain it all to him, but he wouldn't believe me!"

"Maybe he didn't understand. It's very confusing, you must admit."

"He understood, but he said I was lying. He accused me of slipping Papa's paintings to Uncle Mario to be copied."

"Incredible!"

"We already knew Uncle Mario was forging paintings, but I had nothing to do with that."

"And you say you're the artist, not Signor Verdi?"

She nodded miserably. "Papa is good, very good, but first he was so melancholy over Grandpapa's death that he couldn't paint. Then he had the brain fever, and it left him with a tremor. That's when I started doing the entire painting."

"Amazing!"

"Brandon will never believe me. After this I'm sure we'll be sent away. Oh, Colin, I'll never see Brandon again!"

"I'll try to reason with him."

"He won't listen. You don't know how angry he is." She walked to the end of the bridge and gazed in the direction her father would have come from. "Where could he be?"

Colin looked down at the trampled grasses, silver in the moonlight. Silently he followed the bent grass down the slight slope. The mud was smeared around as though there had been a scuffle, and he could see the clear imprint of shoes. Colin stared at the black water. "I think we should go back to Hawthorn."

"Go back! I can't go back until I find Papa."

"Teresa," he said reluctantly, "there's a chance they have already been here."

"And gone?" She looked around, but failed to draw the conclusion Colin had. "Yes, they must have. Papa must have returned to the cottage while I went to Hawthorn."

Colin wasn't so sure of that, but he didn't tell her of his fears. If he was right, she would know soon enough. "I'll stay with you until he's found."

When they returned to the cottage, Katie and Hal both stated that they hadn't seen Salvatore since they had gone up to their rooms after dinner. Teresa wanted to go back to the bridge, but Colin stopped her. "We just came from there and your father was nowhere to be seen. I think we should stay here and wait."

Hesitantly she agreed, and they began their vigil.

Near dawn they saw Brandon returning to Hawthorn and Colin went to tell him of his suspicions.

"Drowned!" Brandon exclaimed.

"I saw footsteps at the edge of the water, and signs of a struggle. You know how cold it was last night. If Salvatore fell or was pushed into the water, he might not have been able to save himself. The river is deep there at the bridge."

"Yes, I know. Drowned! I don't believe it!"

"He didn't return home all night."

"How do you know?"

"I stayed with her."

Brandon looked away. "How is she?"

"I didn't tell her what I think happened. There was no reason to alarm her if I was wrong."

"No. No, that would have been cruel."

"Brandon, go talk to her. She's told me the most fantastic story!"

He smiled humorlessly. "That's exactly the word for it—fantastic."

"I believe her. Why would she lie about something that's so easy to disprove?"

"Why would she do most of the things she has done?" Brandon snapped. "She's never made any sense! I wouldn't expect her to do so now."

Colin frowned at his elder brother. "What are you going to do?"

"First of all, we have to find Signor Verdi. Those tracks could have been left by anyone."

"Not many people use that road, especially not after dark."

"That's just superstition about its being haunted."

"Probably, but it still keeps people away."

Brandon put his cloak back on and sent Fitch to have a fresh horse saddled. "Gather up some men and have them come to the bridge. Maybe Signor Verdi was injured and is still alive."

"I doubt that could be the case. It was as quiet as death out there."

"You always did have an overactive imagination," his brother said.

"I hope that's all it is."

Brandon glanced back at Colin. "You stay with Teresa. If her father shows up, come tell me. If he doesn't, well, she may need you."

"No, she needs you," Colin said bluntly.

"She has never needed me."

"You're wrong. Teresa loves you."

"Did she tell you that?"

"Not in so many words."

"I thought not. I don't know what they are up to, but

Teresa and her uncle have played me for a fool. I intend to find out if her father is also in on it."

"Are you going to send them away?"

"I have no choice." Brandon's face was stiff with suppressed emotion. He wanted to run to Teresa and hold her so close to him that nothing could come between them, not even his suspicions. Instead he would have to send her away and never see her again. The thought wrenched his insides. Whether Salvatore was guilty or not, Teresa most certainly was, and he knew Salvatore would never consent to stay without her.

He didn't trust himself to speak again, so he hurried from the house. The groom soon had a fresh horse readied for him. Brandon mounted and rode away in the direction of the Maximus Bridge. He didn't let himself so much as glance at the cottage.

When he reached the bridge, he saw what Colin had discovered the night before. The dry winter grass was bent and broken, especially from the side of the bridge to the water's edge. There were several clear imprints of men's shoes that could have been made by two men who had stood there, then wrestled in the mud. In the shallows of the water, just before the bottom dropped sharply away, he saw an indistinct print. Someone had gone into the water and hadn't come out.

Dreading what he might find, Brandon looked under the bridge and several yards downstream. He could see why people avoided the place. Even in broad daylight it had an eerie feel, though no one had ever seen the phantom Roman that supposedly haunted it. Brandon straightened his shoulders. There was nothing to be gained by letting his imagination run wild.

With great care he searched the bushes and nearby woods for any sign of Salvatore. Soon he was joined by a group of men Colin had sent from Hawthorn, who helped him search the nearby woods. By noon it was agreed that the river was the only place they hadn't looked, so Brandon led the search party down the bank.

Within the hour they found Salvatore and Mario's dead bodies entangled in a raft of brush near the turn in the river. Brandon helped pull the men from the water, and he was the one to pry Salvatore's fingers off Mario's ankle. None of the men felt like talking as they tied the two bodies to a horse's back and rode home.

Brandon sent one of the searchers to fetch an undertaker, then escorted the brothers back to Hawthorn. The most difficult task he faced was his ride up the slope to the cottage.

Teresa was in the parlor, her face drawn and white when Katie let him in. Colin stood expectantly when Brandon entered the room, but Teresa seemed to draw further into herself. Her eyes were large and dark as she gazed imploringly up at him. Colin looked down as Brandon began to speak.

"We've found your father and your uncle," he said in a low voice. "I'm afraid you must prepare yourself for the worst."

"They're dead," she said almost inaudibly. "How did it happen?"

"They seem to have fought and fallen into the river."

"Papa could swim. He was a good swimmer!"

"The water was cold. I imagine he lost consciousness quickly." He saw no reason to tell her that her father had obviously pulled her uncle in with him.

"Uncle Mario too?" she asked.

"Yes. I've sent for an undertaker, and I'll see to it that everything is done properly."

"I want to see him."

Brandon and Colin exchanged a look. "I don't think that would be a good idea. You can see him later."

She forced him to meet her eyes. "Uncle Mario killed Papa?"

Brandon drew a deep breath. Why hurt her with the knowledge that the opposite had happened? "We will probably never know for sure."

Teresa stood and walked on rubbery legs to the window. Cold air leaked in around the panes, but it was no match for the chill she felt inside.

"The world has lost a great artist," Brandon said to ease her in her loss. "All the art world will mourn him."

Teresa lifted her chin with pride, but it still trembled.

Colin looked at her, then at Brandon, and left the room. Brandon wanted desperately to go to her and hold her, to comfort her, but he couldn't. To put his arms around Teresa would be to tell her none of her duplicity mattered, and he couldn't do that. She had never loved him. Perhaps she was incapable of loving anyone. Faced with the death of both her father and her uncle, she stood ramrod straight, neither crying nor fainting.

After a long moment Brandon turned away and left the room. Colin tried to detain him, but Brandon had to get as far away from there as possible before he embraced her and threw away what little self-respect he still had.

Colin followed him to the manor house and tried to reason with him, but Brandon, usually the most patient of men, refused to even be civil. "Dammit," Colin burst out in exasperation, "she needs you!"

"Did she say that?"

"She doesn't need to say it. Anyone with half a brain could figure it out. Her father and her uncle were all the family she had left in the world to take care of her. I gather there's an aunt that she doesn't like and some cousin she barely knows, but no one to whom she can go."

"She has a palazzo in Venice. I've seen it myself, and it would definitely be no hardship for her to live there."

"How can she live alone?"

"She has two servants there to care for her."

"Servants aren't the same as family, and they must be paid. How is she to live?"

Brandon poured himself a brandy as he said, "I'll arrange for money to be sent to her. She won't lack for anything."

"It's not like you to be so unfeeling!"

"No? I've always been told I'm too cool in my emotions."

"Not like this. This is different."

"Colin, don't badger me." Brandon glared at his younger brother. "You know how Teresa and her uncle were duping me. Maybe her father as well, for all I know."

"I don't believe it," Colin said flatly. "Teresa wouldn't do that."

"Then *you* marry her."

"She won't have me."

Brandon gave him a level look but didn't comment.

"At least go to her and hear what she has to say."

"I've heard her story. She told it to me outside the White Swan. Now, there's a fine place to find a lady! If I had any doubts about what sort she is, that should have shown me! The White Swan!"

"Her uncle forced her to meet him there. She must have told you that."

"I don't believe her. She had a painting to give him. I intercepted her before he could. Otherwise he would have had another Verdi to copy."

Colin hesitated before he said, "Teresa says she painted the Verdi canvases."

"A prime example of her lies. What woman could handle a brush with such passion? I've seen her paintings of flowers and such. They're good, but they aren't of the same quality as *The Ladies on the Altana* or *The Fisherman of Chioggia*."

"She says she painted the flowers in such a way as to cast no suspicion on the Verdi canvases."

"Naturally you believe her. Do you also believe that King Arthur sleeps with his men under Glastonbury Hill and that fairies dance in the moonlight?"

"That's hardly the same thing."

"I know art, Colin, and I say no woman who paints violets is capable of turning out the *Diana*. No one has that versatility."

"I believe her."

"That's because you aren't as knowledgeable on the subject as I am." He tossed down a stinging gulp of brandy. "The White Swan! Can you imagine Lady Barbara in such a place?"

"I can't imagine Teresa there either."

"Nevertheless, she was."

Colin frowned. "Then you won't go to her?"

Brandon remembered the way the sunlight caught in Teresa's fragrant hair, the feel of her warm and healthy body in his arms, the music of her voice and laughter. Silently he shook his head.

"I've always considered you to be reserved," Colin said with suppressed anger, "but never before now did I think you to be heartless."

Brandon listened to Colin slam out of the house. Heartless? He couldn't be that, for his heart was breaking in two.

Late that afternoon, after the undertaker had finished his work on Salvatore, the somber hearse stopped in front of the cottage. Teresa, dressed in her only black dress, opened the door to the man's knock. In the back of the house she could hear Katie crying as she dyed other dresses into mourning hues.

Teresa silently watched as the undertaker's assistants set up their trestles and draped a bier with a black cloth, then brought in the coffin. The undertaker opened the casket for her and stepped back.

She stared down at the calm features she had loved so much. Except for the death of her grandfather, she had had no contact with mourning at all. She was unprepared for the wrenching pain at seeing her father so still in death. Until now she had thought it might be a mistake.

A noise at the doorway drew her attention. The assistants were struggling to bring in the second coffin. Teresa stopped them. "Don't bring him in here."

The undertaker's professionally solemn face gaped. "But, Signorina Verdi, what are we to do with him?"

"I don't care what you do, but he won't lie side by side with my father. Not when he was responsible for Papa's death."

"I know you're upset, signorina. Who wouldn't be? But as I understand it, this is your own uncle."

"Yes, a fact my father deplored. Surely there is some other place to put bodies until they can be buried."

The assistants looked at each other and shifted under their heavy burden. "Signorina Verdi, this is highly unusual!"

"I suppose it is, but he isn't coming in here." She refused to budge from the doorway.

Colin, who had been in the studio, came to the door in time to hear her words. "Put him back in the hearse," he told the men.

"I won't have him buried with Papa, either," Teresa added.

Colin saw the pain in her eyes. Having to refuse to accept Mario's body, even after all he had done, was hurting her. To the undertaker Colin said, "Find a decent cemetery in town and bury him there. Send word to Hawthorn to let us know where he lies." Colin fished some gold coins from his pocket. "This should cover your extra trouble."

When the hearse had rumbled away Colin said, "We'll put your father in our family plot if that's agreeable with you."

"Has Brandon give his permission for that?"

"Yes."

She nodded. "Papa would rather be on San Michele beside Mama, but that isn't possible. However, in his recent state of mind, I'm not sure he would realize the difference if he were alive to see. He was never the same after his illness."

She and Colin went into the parlor and stood looking down at Salvatore. "He should have been great," she said at last. "To me he was."

She lifted her eyes and gazed through the window and beyond it to the sprawling bulk of Hawthorn. She wanted Brandon so much she actually hurt. Where was he if he loved her? Was his love so insubstantial that he could forget her and shut her out of his heart so easily?

With her sewing scissors she snipped an iron-gray lock of her father's hair. Carefully she placed it in her mourning brooch and snapped shut the lid.

"I'll watch with you," Colin said. "You shouldn't be alone."

"Thank you," she said with a wan smile. "You're a good friend, Colin."

"I would be more if you'd let me."

She reached out and touched his arm in a sisterly caress. "I need a friend just now." She had heard that a numbness settled in when a loved one died, but she was still locked in pain. Guiltily she realized her pain was as much for the loss of Brandon's love as for her father.

23

All night Teresa, Colin, and, for a while, Katie and Hal sat with Salvatore. For Teresa it was a time for endings, for remembering the good times and the bad, for saying her last farewells. Katie interspersed her time in the parlor with sewing black bands for Hal's arm and black trim on Teresa's bonnets and clothing, as well as on her own.

By morning Teresa was exhausted physically and emotionally. Colin went to Hawthorn to dress for the funeral, and she lay down on her bed for a badly needed hour of rest. Before it was time for the undertaker to arrive, Katie came in and helped Teresa dress in one of the newly dyed and freshly ironed black dresses.

Teresa moved automatically, grateful at last for numbness. A hush lay over the small cottage and everyone moved silently, as if they were in church. No one spoke unless it was necessary, and then only in a whisper.

The undertaker arrived and solemnly removed Salvatore Verdi to the hearse. Teresa stood in the misting rain, staring at her father's coffin through the glass windows of the somber black coach. The four perfectly matched black horses, each with black harness and a black plume on its head, stirred as though they were anxious to get the job done.

"I never liked black," Teresa commented to Katie before looking away.

Soon Colin arrived with his carriage for Teresa and

the others, and they followed the hearse down the winding path that had first carried Teresa and her father to the cottage.

"Papa had a premonition when we first came here that he would never again see Venice."

Colin covered her cold hands with one of his. "Brandon sends his condolences."

"He isn't coming?"

"I'm not sure. We had words. I don't know if he will or not."

Because Salvatore hadn't set foot in a church since Eva Maria's death, except for Antonio's funeral, Teresa had seen no need for a church service. Because she was Catholic, however, she had asked that the parish priest hold a graveside service. Since it wasn't a Catholic cemetery, and therefore unhallowed ground, the priest had been reluctant, but due to the circumstances he had finally agreed.

The hearse stopped inside the iron gates of the Hawthorn cemetery, and Colin tied his horses outside the fence. Only the corpse and its attendants were allowed to ride inside. Teresa and Colin, followed by Katie and Hal, went in the ornamental side gate.

The air was thick with mist that veiled the massive manor house and surrounding grounds. Teresa could feel the damp permeating her cloak, making it heavy on her shoulders. Her black bonnet shielded her face, but the mist dampened her skin and she found it difficult to breathe.

The priest performed his duties, and the coffin was lowered into the moist earth. Teresa scarcely heard his words. She was more aware of the small sounds: the creak of the lowering ropes, the snort of one of the horses, the click of the side gate. Turning her head, she saw Brandon step into the enclosure and stop.

Tears welled in her eyes, and she clasped her hands tightly to keep from going to him. She felt Colin stiffen beside her, and she wondered what words had passed between them.

Although she didn't understand why he had so completely turned his back on her in her time of need, she still loved him.

Brandon looked at her through the mist that clung to his eyelashes. Even in dull black mourning, she was incredibly beautiful. Though tears stood in her eyes, she seemed strong and serene and completely without need of him. Colin had led him to believe Teresa was on the verge of collapse, but she certainly gave no sign of it. He would happily have gone to her and given her support and protection. But as usual, she seemed to need neither.

If only he didn't love her so damned much! She stood there, not leaning on Colin or Katie, and looking as unmoved as if this were merely a church service. What kind of woman could do that? It only served to show how little true emotion she was capable of feeling. She had never loved him; she had only used him. He ached to go to her.

Teresa hesitantly turned back to the grave. The priest had finished and everyone was looking at her. Bending, she picked up a bit of dirt and tossed it onto the coffin. Wiping the mud from her fingers onto her black handkerchief, she turned away, for she had no desire to watch the undertaker's men fill in the grave. Her heart was already too sore.

As she crossed the enclosed walk between the older graves, the undertaker stopped her. "I've arranged to have the other Mr. Verdi laid to rest in St. Matthew's churchyard. Is that suitable to you?"

Teresa nodded. She had no idea where St. Matthew's might be, but it didn't matter. She would never go there.

She looked over the few yards of wet grass to where Brandon still stood. As before, he made no move toward her and his face was unreadable. Had he only come to see her grief? Teresa turned to Colin. "Please thank your brother for allowing a burial place for my father. Tell him I will leave the cottage as soon as possible."

Colin looked at Brandon, who had easily heard her words. Turning back to Teresa, he said, "Where will you go?"

"I have my palazzo in Venice. Perhaps I will go there."

Brandon pivoted and walked through the gate and back toward Hawthorn. The gate clanked shut behind him.

"He's hurting as much as you are," Colin told her. "If either of you would give a bit . . ."

"He couldn't possibly be hurting, because he has no heart," she said in a stiff voice.

The next day Colin rode to the White Swan. He couldn't picture Teresa coming here even under the most dire threat. Colin felt uneasy being there, even though he was a strong man and quite capable of defending himself.

Inside he found only a few men who looked as if they were more or less permanent residents. The smell was potent and the bar was filthy. He went to the scarred counter and motioned for the barkeep to come nearer. Colin was reluctant to put too much distance between himself and the door. "Do you know Mario Verdi?"

"Aye. He comes in regular," the man said suspiciously. "What's it to you?"

"Does he talk to you?"

"Run out on a debt, has he? He don't talk much to me." He turned to a table. "Big Tom! Come tell this man where he can find Mario."

Colin watched the huge man stand up, and hoped he wouldn't have to fight his way out of the bar. Unlike Brandon, Colin hadn't thought to bring a gun.

"You a bill collector?" the bearded giant demanded.

"No."

Big Tom studied Colin derisively. "They all deny it. I ain't seen Mario for a couple of days."

"I didn't think so. I'm wondering about something

he did a while back. Do you know anything about him
blackmailing someone?"

Big Tom's squinty eyes narrowed. "How did you
know about that?"

Colin was glad to discover the man's intelligence wasn't
in proportion to his physical size. He smiled. "Bartender, give the man another ale."

When Big Tom's beefy hand was wrapped around the
glass, Colin said, "I know Mario, and he was bragging
about how he got money from some relatives of his. I'd
like to get in on it too."

That seemed to satisfy Big Tom, because he nodded.
"He said he had something on his brother and that he
wouldn't have to work no more when it come to pass. I
never knew Mario worked anyhow. He's out here most
all the time."

"Did he say what he had on his brother?"

"Naw, not a word." Big Tom's face split into a grin.
"I seen somebody what claimed to be his niece, though.
Mario never mentioned having a niece, let alone one as
pretty as that. Come in here looking for him, she did.
Had something rolled up, about the size of a ship's
map. He wouldn't take it." Big Tom's expression lowered. "I had in mind to get something on her too, if
you follow me. But I was stopped."

Colin managed to smile. This man was scarcely more
than a beast. He couldn't bear the thought of him
trying to touch Teresa. Colin almost hoped he would
have to fight the man. "But the blackmail—he told you
nothing?"

"Not him. Mario wouldn't tell nothing if he could
profit by it hisself."

Colin took another coin from his pocket and slid it
toward Big Tom. "Thank you. You've been most
helpful."

He left before Big Tom could pocket the coin and
demand more. Mario must have been mad to have
Teresa come here! As he started to mount, Colin saw a

discolored cylinder of canvas lying beneath one of the nearby bushes. He picked it up and unrolled it.

The rain had not damaged the oil paint, though the canvas was wet. The landscape was undeniably the work of the same artist who lived in the cottage. Whoever that was. Now that he knew Mario was involved in blackmail, and he had found the missing painting, he was even more inclined to believe Teresa's story.

He rerolled the canvas and mounted his horse. Somehow he had to get Brandon to see Teresa and ask her to prove her claim. Since she wouldn't have him, Colin wanted her to have the man she really loved.

Brandon was in his sitting room staring at the copy of *The Harem Girl,* just as he had been since Salvatore's funeral. Colin came in uninvited and shoved the rolled canvas at him without a word. "What's this?" Brandon asked as he unrolled it. "Where did you find this?"

"Exactly where Teresa said she discarded it—outside the White Swan."

"You went there?"

"I also talked to a big man who must have been the one you threatened to shoot. He said Mario had told him that he was blackmailing Salvatore."

"Why would Mario tell anyone?"

"How should I know? Maybe he couldn't hold his liquor."

Brandon was quiet as he took the canvas to a marble side table and flattened it to dry.

"Don't be such a stiff-necked fool that you ruin your life and Teresa's," Colin said bluntly. "Go to her."

"She wouldn't have me."

"You're wrong. She loves you."

"Dammit, she and her uncle were forging paintings! I can't just go to her and make up as if it were only a spat!"

"I'm telling you she's innocent, and not only that, I think she is the artist, not her father!"

"I don't believe it."

"If it's not true, why would she be so foolish as to

throw away a painting that Salvatore would be certain to miss? All you have to do is go to her and have her draw you a picture. She can prove it in minutes."

"And if she can't? Colin, I loved her! I can't go crawling up there and ask her to prove this to me. If she can't, she'll laugh at me. I'm the leading art critic in London! I can't admit I don't know whether the Verdi canvases were done by my protégé or his daughter!"

"Then what are you going to do? Let her leave without a word? Lose her forever?"

"I know exactly where her palazzo is. I can find her again."

"I never thought you'd be this foolish, Brandon."

For a minute Brandon scowled at his brother. Then he said, "There's one other place to look for proof. Come with me to Mario's rooms at Ramsden. Let's see what canvases we find there."

Teresa looked out her window at the slow-flowing stream. She had wanted to see it in the snow, she thought inconsequentially. She had seen so little snow in Venice.

Turning away from the window, she went to the bag that sat on her bed. As Katie was folding the last of Teresa's clothing into it, she wept silently.

"Don't be sad, Katie. It's best that I go away."

"I can't help it, Miss. I'll miss you."

"I'll miss you too." Teresa touched the walnut-black of her folded blouse. It had been pale blue, one of her favorites. Now they all looked alike. A sudden thought struck her. "What date is this?" she asked.

"It's the tenth, Miss."

"Why, you were to get married this afternoon!"

"I know, but after Signor Verdi's dying and all, I told Allard it would have to wait."

"Nonsense." Teresa firmly shut the fabric bag and lifted it from the bed. "You two have waited long enough as it is."

"I can't marry and the house in mourning! It wouldn't be right!" Katie's eyes were round at the idea.

Teresa put her hand over Katie's. "Papa is gone, and even if he weren't, he would tell you to do the same. Life is for the living. You and Allard marry this afternoon as you had planned, and bring some happiness back."

"But what about you, Miss?"

"I won't be here. So you see, there's no reason for you not to marry."

"Where will you go? Back to Venice? That's a fearful long trip for a woman to make alone."

"I'm not afraid, and my mourning will be protection enough. Hal will take me to the docks and see me safely aboard. I have money to pay for my passage, and some more besides."

"I had hoped you'd stay longer. The funeral was just yesterday."

Dismally Teresa said, "I had hoped I would stay forever." Then, pulling herself up, she added, "Will you put flowers on Papa's grave now and then? I won't be here to do it myself."

"Aye, Miss. You can trust me to do that."

Although it was earlier than she had planned to leave, Teresa asked for the cart and pony. Now that she was packed, she couldn't bear to stay any longer. If she did, she might do something foolish, like unpack again or run down to Hawthorn and make a simpleton of herself.

One last time she walked through the cottage and studio, then through the winter-brown garden to the stream. She was leaving so much behind: her dreams, her hopes, her heart. Teresa lifted her chin and returned to the cart.

Hal was quiet all the way to London, and she was glad he wasn't talkative by nature. As they rode through the bustle of the crowded city, Teresa said a silent good-bye to all the intriguing streets and shops that she had never had time to explore. Now that the time had come to go, she found she really didn't want to leave England at all. She loved the misty greens of the trees and the watercolor hues of the sky. Above all, she loved the open spaces such as the grounds of Hawthorn. Venice held nothing of the sort for her. Then she recalled the last time she had been in Venice, and how Brandon had held her in his arms all the cold night and how they had made love until the world sang.

Teresa's mouth was tight when Hal stopped in front of the loading dock where the ship that would take her to Venice was moored. For a moment she stared at it, then resolutely got out of the cart. "Thank you, Hal. I can manage from here."

"I ought to see you aboard, Miss," he objected.

"There's no need. There are plenty of workmen about to see to that. I want you to take this coin and buy Katie a nice wedding gift for me. You'll do that?"

"Aye, Miss." His plain face broke into a grin.

"Good-bye, Hal. I'll miss you."

"Good-bye, Miss," he said awkwardly. "It's been a pleasure to serve you."

She watched until he was gone, then looked back at the prow of the ship.

Brandon and Colin went up the dark steps to Mario's rooms. Overhead a baby cried and a small dog barked. The smells were better left unquestioned. They found the door locked, as Brandon had expected, but he broke it open with a shove of his shoulder.

The front room was cold and reeked of damp ashes. The scanty furniture was of a seedy quality, but the canvas on the easel glowed like life itself.

"See!" Brandon said to his brother as he jabbed his finger at the copy of the *Diana*. "I told you he was forging the pictures!"

"I never questioned that. I said only that Teresa is innocent."

"How else could he have copied the canvases unless someone let him?"

"I have no idea." Colin looked in the back room, which contained only a sagging bed, a scarred dresser, and several pictures leaning against the damp wall. "There seems to be only one forgery. Salvatore would never have painted these others."

Brandon glanced through the perfectly symmetrical compositions. "These are all Mario's. I recognize most of them from when I was here before."

Colin went back to look at the *Diana*. "It's remarkably similar."

"Yes, he was good at being dishonest. That doesn't clear Teresa's name, however."

"I don't see any other paintings here that indicate she was giving them to him. Even if there were, they might have come from Salvatore and not her."

Not bothering to remove the tacks from the canvas, Brandon took out his pocketknife and cut the canvas from the stretcher. He folded it, then stuffed it in the fireplace and lit it with a lucifer match. "At least that's one that won't show up unexpectedly."

"Here, now," said a voice from the doorway. "What're you up to?"

Brandon looked up as flames curled the canvas into brown ashes. "Are you the landlady?"

"That I am. And who might you be?" She waddled into the room, bringing with her the smell of garlic.

"I've come to inform you that Mario Verdi died of drowning two nights past."

"Dead, is he! He still owes me two months' rent!"

"You're welcome to his things in recompense," Brandon said. "There are paintings in the other room, and some clothing, I would expect."

"Ain't nobody else going to claim them?" she asked suspiciously. "I'm a honest woman, and I don't take what ain't mine."

"No one else wants them." Brandon and Colin crossed the room and left as the woman began shuffling through his things.

"At least see Teresa," Colin repeated. "Talk to her. If you loved her, you owe her that much."

Brandon was quiet as he mounted his horse and rode with Colin toward the edge of town. He was amazed he could miss anyone as much as he missed her. No matter what she had done or why she had done it, Mario was dead now, and it was finished.

"Perhaps she said she did the paintings to protect her father somehow," Brandon said. "I hadn't considered that."

"It's possible. Teresa is loyal to a fault."

"But what could she be trying to hide?"

"Ask her."

Brandon touched his heels to his horse's side. "I will."

They rode directly to the cottage and dismounted at the gate. The garden looked dismal with all the flowers bitten back by frost. Only the hedges gave the house an aspect of life. Brandon strode up the short walk, anxious to see Teresa now that he had made up his mind to do it.

Katie, wearing a pink dress, opened the door and stared up at the lord of the manor. Remembering her manners, she bobbed a quick curtsy.

"Why aren't you in mourning?" Brandon demanded.

"I'm . . . I'm on me way to get married to Allard Beck. Remember how you said we could? Miss Verdi said I should go on with it."

"Did she now! Where is she?" He walked past the maid. "What sort of woman doesn't observe mourning for her own father?" he demanded of Colin. "I'm telling you there's no way to understand her!"

Colin looked around sharply. "I don't see any of her things."

"No, sir, that's what I was about to say," Katie spoke up. "She's gone, and that's why I'm to go ahead and marry Allard."

"Gone!" Brandon wheeled to face her.

Katie backed away. "Yes, my lord. Hal drove her

down to the ship a good two hours past. He's already back, packed up, and gone to his ma's. I was coming after my things just after the service." She added, "Miss Verdi was so thoughtful as to send me a bride gift of a teapot. And it's a fine one too."

Brandon wasn't listening. He was going through the house, searching from room to room, and finding nothing. Katie hurried after him. "Miss Verdi gave her father's things to Hal. They're too big for him, but his ma can alter them. I hope that's all right."

"It's fine," Colin said. "Run along now or you'll be late."

"Yes, sir." She gave Colin a bob and cast Brandon a doubtful look before hurrying away.

"She's gone!" Brandon said in stunned disbelief. "Did you know she planned to leave so quickly?"

"She said she would go as soon as possible." Colin looked in the studio.

"I know, but I assumed she meant in a few weeks, months perhaps. To leave like this at the start of winter, with her father barely in the ground! It seems, well, odd."

"Odd!" Colin exploded. "You've treated her like a leper, never bothering even to listen to what she had to say that could explain this tangle, and you think it's odd that she not stay around to be further mistreated?"

"Mistreated! I've never mistreated a lady in my life!"

"What would you call it?"

Brandon glared at his brother, but he had no good answer. He had, in fact, been churlish toward her.

"It's no wonder she ran back to Venice," Colin continued, his voice filled with anger. "After the way you've thrown her aside, she could do no less! My God, Brandon, are you so self-righteous you can't let yourself love a woman who obviously adores you?"

The words stung Brandon's ears, especially since he knew they were true. "I love her too, dammit all! I can't understand her, but I love her! Colin, you don't know how hard this has been for me!"

"No, but I know how it's been for her, and if you weren't my brother, I'd call you out over it!"

"If she loved me, why in the hell did she run away?" Brandon demanded.

"She's a proud woman. I imagine she was trying to save face."

Brandon sank onto a chair. "God, Colin! What have I done? I've driven away the only woman I've ever really loved!"

Although Colin still glared at Brandon, he lowered his voice. "Go after her. Tell her you love her and bring her back. What difference does it make if she says she's an artist or a blacksmith, if you love her?"

Brandon jumped to his feet. "I'm going to the docks. Maybe she hasn't sailed yet!"

Hours later Brandon returned empty-handed and took up residence in a chair beside the fireplace in Hawthorn's back parlor. "I couldn't find her. Her ship was already gone. Another won't sail until this same day next week. I've told Fitch to have Robert get my things ready to go then."

Colin could tell from Brandon's slumped shoulders and glum expression that he was feeling miserable. Knowing that Brandon loved her and that she would have, in Brandon, what she wanted, helped ease the ache in Colin's own heart. "When you find her, listen to her. Talk to her."

"What do I say to her?" Brandon asked as he stared at the flames. "What can I say that will erase all the pain I've caused her?"

Drawing a deep breath, Colin leaned his head against the chair's back and closed his eyes. His face was lined, as if the words cost him a great deal. "Just love her, Brandon, and let her love you. That's all she wants."

"How did you get so wise, little brother?"

Colin managed a smile. "At least one of us had to understand women."

Brandon left for Venice full of high hopes and eager

for the journey. A month later he returned in a howling snowstorm. Teresa wasn't with him.

When Colin met him in the drawing room, he was shocked. Brandon appeared to have aged years in the short time he had been gone. His face was drawn and lifeless. "I couldn't find her, Colin. Either the Valores didn't know where she is or they wouldn't tell me. It's as if she simply vanished."

The brothers settled in to wait out the longest winter they had ever spent, each day hoping for news that didn't come.

24

Spring came late the following year. Mitchell had received his doctor-of-medicine degree as planned, but had stayed on to work with one of his professors who was especially interested in the diseases of the poor. Being away from England for the extra year had been difficult, but he had gained valuable experience that he would need in his own practice. Now it was time to return to his homeland, and Mitchell packed with as much excitement as he had shown on arriving there. He had enjoyed his studies, and he liked the small German town with its wreath of mountains, but he was eager to get on with the humanitarian goals he had set for himself.

Most of his life had been spent in classrooms, but Mitchell hadn't objected. He was of an inquiring nature and found studies enjoyable. He had always felt that of the three brothers, he and Brandon were the most alike, although he was much more idealistic. He had often wondered whether Brandon might have been less prosaic in his approach to living had it not been for the responsibility of Hawthorn. Then there was Colin, who seemed to have no sense of direction in his life at all. How he could be content to be blown about by the winds of fate was a mystery to Mitchell.

Mitchell smiled as he thought how he had missed them both more than he had ever admitted. He was looking forward to living near them again.

As his coach wound its way toward the train in Munich, a spring rain whipped through the mountains. Even the rain fell differently here. Mitchell longed for England's gentle showers. No one had bidden him farewell, and Mitchell was glad. He hated good-byes and would do almost anything to avoid one.

The train trip through Paris to Calais was uneventful, though as the miles passed, his longing to be back on British soil became even greater. England! He could already smell the lavender and roses and see the rainwashed cobblestones of London.

The English Channel was rough, and Mitchell found his newly acquired degree in medicine was needed among the seasick passengers, though he could do little to relieve their suffering. But no doctor could have done more, for it was a perverseness of nature that the most common maladies such as seasickness and sniffles were the most elusive of a cure.

Although the ship's destination was London, it was blown off course, and the captain felt fortunate to find dock at Harwich. So did Mitchell. Although he was a good sailor, the constant pitching of the ship, combined with the stench from the illness belowdecks, was beginning to affect him.

Since no one was expecting him at Hawthorn at any particular time, Mitchell disembarked and took a room in an inn to wait out the storm. So much for England's gentle rains, he thought with a wry grin spreading across his strong features as another squall lashed the windowpanes and wind rattled the casements.

The storm raged for two more days, and Mitchell was glad he had left the narrow cabin of the ship. He planned to finish the last leg of his journey by land and enjoy the sights of his homeland after the harsh German winter.

When the storm finally abated, Mitchell hired a horse and rig to take him to London and made arrangements for its return. He was in no rush so he took the road that ran along the channel. At midday he stopped to eat at a small dining establishment in Clacton-on-Sea.

Through the window at his table he noticed a tiny art gallery tucked between two taller buildings. After he finished his meal, he would go there and buy a gift for Brandon. After all, his brother had been reasonable about Mitchell's decision to practice medicine in London's slums. Mitchell had expected much more opposition from him.

He paid for the meal and strolled outside. The sun was nudging its way from behind a bank of clouds, and a few spring flowers could be seen in the window boxes of houses and businesses alike. A velvety emerald moss filled the spaces between the cobblestones at the edge of the street where traffic was light, and although the channel was out of view, he could smell the tang of the sea.

The small art gallery was well lit in front by large windows, but was shadowy in the rear. Mitchell walked down the single corridor that ran from front to back in the narrow shop, studying the oils and pastels and watercolors. He was accustomed to the prestigious galleries he had frequented with Brandon, and was disappointed at the quality of the art displayed here.

Just as he was about to leave, the gallery owner heard him and came out of the back room. "Can I show you something in particular?" he asked to stop Mitchell from leaving.

"No, no, I was only looking."

"Don't be hasty, young man. You've not yet seen my best."

Mitchell paused. London was still a long way off, and he had seen nothing in this shop to hold his interest.

The owner chuckled. "You're just passing through, aren't you? I can always tell folks that are passing through. Hurrying about like Old Nick was at their heels. These pretties here are just for the undiscriminating. I've another painting in the back that would appeal to quality like yourself. My name's Pollard, by the way, Ian Pollard."

Mitchell gave him a sidelong look. "Why would you keep your best works in the back?" He was beginning to wonder if the man planned to lure him away from the window and do him some harm.

"Bless you, I don't keep it there. It's in the back because I've not had time to hang it properly." He motioned and waited for Mitchell to follow him.

Curiosity overcame his better judgment, and Mitchell went with the man into the office at the rear of the shop.

The owner scurried over to a canvas that stood on the floor, face to the wall, and lifted it with a flourish.

Mitchell's eyes widened. He wasn't the connoisseur that Brandon was, but this painting stood out like a diamond in a bowl of pebbles. He took it from the man and carried it back to the front, where the light was better.

The scene was of an inn yard. A pair of matched horses stood impatiently as the carriage was being loaded. Several small boys and a spotted dog ran across the packed dirt yard as a barmaid gave the coach driver a suggestive smile.

"I've never seen anything to equal this!" Mitchell said in amazement. "At least not outside a museum!"

"The artist is a crippled lad by the name of Benito Cioni. He was broken up in a shipwreck and decided to stay here."

"Could I meet him?"

"I'm afraid not. His health is real poor, especially when the weather is so wet. His wife brings in the canvases and collects his money when they sell. And they sell real well," he added proudly. "Clacton-on-Sea saw a fortunate day when the Cionis settled here."

"Could I meet his wife, perhaps? My brother is rather influential in the art world, and I believe he would be interested in Signor Cioni. It could be profitable for you both."

Pollard laughed and rubbed his hands together. "We might be able to arrange a meeting. Is your brother staying here?"

"No, no, he's in London. I'm here alone."

"I guess I could arrange for him to meet with Signor Cioni. She refers to him that way, his wife does, them both being Italians and all."

Mitchell nodded. Brandon hadn't been fond of Italian artists after his dealings with the Verdi family. Although Brandon had never confided in him, Mitchell suspected he was rather fond of Teresa Verdi and had been deeply hurt when she left without a word. Perhaps meeting this Benito Cioni would restore his fondness for Italian painters. With a smile, Mitchell said, "They aren't from Venice, are they?"

"No, no. They come from a place called Rimini. Near Florence, I think she said."

"That's good. I'll take this painting, and if you'll give me your name and address, my brother will contact you."

The man hurried about wrapping the painting, and when he finished, he scrawled his name and address on the brown paper. "There. You can't misplace it that way."

Mitchell smiled and nodded a farewell. If nothing else, the trip to Clacton-on-Sea would be good for Brandon's sprits. His letters recently had been so melancholy that Mitchell was concerned.

Pollard watched him go and his smile grew even wider. This could mean a great deal of publicity for his shop. An art critic from London could bring in tourists by the droves. Pollard had no doubts that the critic would be impressed by the paintings; everyone was. If it hadn't been for the Cioni canvases, he wouldn't have managed to stay in business this past year.

He puttered about the shop, rearranging things by moving the older of his paintings toward the back so passersby would assume they had sold.

Within an hour Pollard heard his door open again.

This time he saw a woman silhouetted against the bright sunlight in the windows. As he approached her, the light caught her face and he recognized her. "Signora Cioni! What a surprise to see you again so soon."

"I've come to take back *The Inn Yard*. I can't . . . that is, my husband has decided not to part with it after all."

Pollard's smile wavered. "Why, it's gone, signora. I sold it not an hour ago."

She came nearer and pushed the dark hood back from her face. Her black hair was braided in a neat coronet and her golden-brown eyes were worried. "Already? It's sold already?"

"Yes, that's right. I sold it to a man passing through on his way to London. But that's not the best news! He said his brother is a famed art critic, and he's buying the picture for him. If the brother likes it, he'll contact your husband."

Teresa caught her breath. "What did this man look like? Did he have light brown hair and green eyes?"

"No, he was dark. I didn't notice his eyes, but I think they were gray."

So it wasn't Colin after all. Teresa relaxed a little. "What was his name?"

"He didn't give it, and I didn't think to ask. I gave him mine, though, wrote it down for him. He can find me, and through me, you."

"Yes," she said absently. How many art critics were there in London? "You're sure his hair was dark?"

"Nearly as dark as yours. Why?"

"It doesn't matter. I thought I might know him, but that would be too great a coincidence."

"You should be more excited!" Pollard chided her gently. "Don't you see what this could mean to your husband? If his art catches the eye of a critic, he could have shows in London and get all sorts of publicity. It could make him a small fortune."

Teresa glanced at him, then looked away. "He wouldn't want publicity and showings. Signor Cioni's health isn't good, as you know."

"I know, bless his heart, but it would mean more money for you and a better name for my shop. Signor Cioni wouldn't have to go to the shows if he wasn't able. You could go in his place."

"I couldn't leave him that long," she protested. "It's impossible."

"Well, we'll work out something, I'm sure. I'll bet he's happier about this than you are. How is he today?"

"Not well. Not well at all." She pulled the hood back over her head in preparation for leaving.

"Poor man. It's all the rain, I expect, and spring has been long in coming. He'll perk up as warm weather gets here."

"No doubt. Thank you, Mr. Pollard," she said as he counted out the money for the painting. She put it in her reticule and drew the strings closed.

Holding her cloak tightly about her, Teresa went back outside. A London critic! Surely it couldn't be Brandon. The description wasn't right for Colin. In her concern she almost forgot Brandon had another brother, one she hardly knew at all. She had no doubt the critic would like *The Inn Yard*. It was one of her best efforts. She wished she had stayed with selling the back stock of violets and daisies and still lifes. Even though *The Inn Yard* was in her own style rather than in Salvatore's, it was too similar for safety.

She went down the winding streets, keeping her face concealed in the hood in case this mysterious stranger was still around. Her walnut-hued clothing blended with that of the other poor women passing on the street, and bundled as she was, she might have been any age at all.

Once again she was going to be "discovered," this time as Benito Cioni. She had been far more pleased the first time. Now she would have to leave the snug house she had begun to like. There could be no publicity because there was no Benito Cioni.

Her house sat in a small yard in what had once been the edge of town before Clacton-on-Sea had spread in that direction. She let herself in the low gate and crossed to the house. Around the corner of the house she could glimpse the sea. She had taken this house because its shape and yard reminded her of the cottage at Hawthorn and the back view was vaguely reminiscent of Venice.

She went in her house and picked up her cat. It blinked its golden eyes and purred as she scratched it under the chin.

"We may have to move, Luna. We may no longer be able to live here." The black-and-white cat blinked in commiseration, as though it had understood her soft words. "But listen to me. What makes me think he cares at all where I am?" She went to a window seat and sat down with the cat curling in her lap. "It's been a long time now. Over a year. By now he's forgotten all about me. Maybe he's married or is engaged to someone else."

The cat hopped down and stretched. Teresa unfastened the frog that secured her cape. "Yes, no doubt he has forgotten about me."

She let the cape drop onto the cushion behind her. "But he will not have forgotten Salvatore Verdi. I must move, but to where?" She smiled down at her pet. "You should learn to talk, Luna. Otherwise it's as if I'm talking to myself." She stood and hung the cape on a peg. Loneliness had been terrible for her. Never having been alone before, she had found the silence unnerving at first. Then one night she discovered Luna sitting on her doorstep as if she owned the place. Since then the house hadn't seemed quite so empty, and Luna had become an affectionate companion.

To her neighbors Teresa was the widow of a man lost at sea. To Ian Pollard she was the wife of a cripple. Thus she kept her identity secret and explained the absence of a man in her house. A couple of men had tried to get to know her better, but she had sent them on about their business. Teresa loved Brandon and there was no room in her heart for anyone else. Besides, love had hurt her so much, she didn't want to relive the experience. After a while, even the women in town had left her alone, and that was how Teresa wanted it. She couldn't afford to have anyone see one of her petulant, stormy canvases.

From time to time she took a painting to the small out-of-the-way gallery. Almost no one went there, so there was little chance of her work being recognized by anyone who would see its similarity to that of the famous Salvatore Verdi.

For a long time she had sold only the flowers and still lifes she had done, but they were slow to sell. In desperation for money, she had invented a husband who was unable to walk or receive guests, and sold some of her more powerful canvases as Benito Cioni. But even Pollard hadn't seen her most impressive works. Since leaving Brandon and losing her father, Teresa's talent had reached new and unexpected heights.

Taking *The Inn Yard* to the gallery had been a mistake. It had hung on her parlor wall since she came to Clacton-on-Sea and had haunted her with its memories of the trip with Brandon and her father. That trip had been one of the last of the happy times before Salvatore became ill and permanently disabled, but above all, it had been a time of love between Brandon and herself. She still recalled all too well the day on the cliff in Scotland when he had kissed her with the passion of a sea storm. It was this aching memory that had prompted her to sell it. Once it was gone, however, she missed it too much. The painting had been a link with Brandon and the love they had shared.

Love. She touched the obelisk of crystal that he had given her that day at Hawthorn. She still loved him so much. Love wasn't at all what she had expected it to be. True, when she had been with Brandon, the emotion that closeness evoked had felt like the source of life itself, but now she saw its nether side. Love unshared was painful in the extreme.

Although she wasn't hungry, Teresa gathered a half-loaf of bread she had baked and some cheese. She knew she had to eat. As she pulled a chair up to her table, Luna hopped up on the one beside her. At least, she consoled herself, she never had to eat alone. Alternating bites between herself and Luna, Teresa let her thoughts drift through her misery.

Brandon must not have loved her, she concluded for the thousandth time since leaving Hawthorn. If he had, he would have listened to her explanation. Common sense should have told him that she wouldn't have exposed Uncle Mario as the forger if she were also involved. Brandon was so proud of his logic, and yet he couldn't see something so obvious.

Or was it that he was simply so closed-minded that he couldn't conceive of a woman being able to produce the Verdi canvases?

"We're better off without him, Luna," Teresa said with a sigh. "I just wish I believed it."

After she ate and cleared away the simple meal, she took out her mortar and pestle and began grinding chunks of ocher into powder for her paint jars. Buying the paints already powdered was a luxury she had had to forgo. Her strong hands pressed and mashed the lumps into dust as she thought.

There was no need to leave yet, she tried to tell herself. First of all, she had nowhere to go, and second, no money to pay to have her belongings carted away. The money Ian Pollard received for her paintings barely covered her needs for food and painting supplies, much less the money she needed to send to the Valores for their faithful service. Besides, this art critic might not see the value in her art, or the man who made the purchase might simply have lied about his connections. People often told harmless lies in order to puff up their own importance.

"We'll stay a bit longer and keep our eyes open," she informed the cat. "If there is word from this art critic, we can leave then. In the meantime, I should try to sell another Cioni picture and get enough money to move, in case we have to leave quickly." The cat hopped onto the window seat and curled up for another nap.

There was always her palazzo. She could go there if she had enough money for the trip, but once she was there, what could she do? She couldn't possibly sell her paintings there because everyone knew her and her family. She would have to hope she could marry someone who would allow her to paint, even if it were only flowers, and who wouldn't sell her family home or turn the Valores out onto the street to make room for more tenants: No, the safest thing was for her to continue her self-imposed exile and send them money so they could live out their last years in familiar surroundings.

She wondered if she could develop another style and sell paintings in nearby Colchester as well, but she discarded the idea. She would run a greater risk of someone's discovering who she was. Besides, she had no horse and therefore no easy way of getting the paintings to another town.

She uncorked the jar where she kept the ocher powder and poured in the dust from the mortar. As she replaced the cork to keep out the dampness, she wondered how she had ever put herself into such a muddle. It seemed as though it had been a lifetime ago when she had stood in the studio in Venice and altered her father's painting almost on a whim. So much had happened since then. She was no longer so naively confident that everything would work out for the best.

25

Brandon watched the first flakes of snow drift silently down, then disappear on the muddy brown walk and pale yellow grasses. The morning room was warm from the crackling fire in the hearth, and he heard the steady hum of lowered voices and hushed steps that meant Hawthorn was running smoothly. A faint click of glass against silver meant Fitch was removing the morning coffee tray, but Brandon didn't turn to look.

Up the slope he could see the tiny cottage. No smoke curled from its chimney, and the windows were as dark as the gloomy day. The gardener still manicured the shrubs and tended the gardens in their season, but the house was lifeless. Brandon felt the same way.

He heard Mitchell's step behind him and looked back to say, "It's a good thing you got in last night. It's starting to snow."

"Again? I thought we were through with it."

"Spring is later than usual this year. We've had a hard winter."

"All the way home I imagined kingcups and speed-wells and anemones. All I've seen are crocuses and a few primroses."

"You know how capricious spring can be."

Mitchell came around to stand by Brandon. "You've lost weight. Have you been sick?"

"Nonsense."

"Yes, you have. I noticed it when I arrived last night,

but I thought it might be a trick of the gaslights. It's true, though. Perhaps I should have a look at you."

Brandon gave him a faint smile. "Save your medicines for patients who need it. I'm not sick and don't want to be your guinea pig."

Mitchell didn't look convinced, but he said, "Look at this, then. I brought you a gift." He went back to the door to retrieve a flat, rectangular parcel.

"You shouldn't have done that," Brandon said as he took it. "You'll need your money to set up your practice."

"Our banker tells me I have more than I thought I should have in my account. You never told me you were my benefactor."

"I told Grimes not to tell you. It seems you can trust no one these days." He pulled away the heavy brown paper and held the canvas at arm's length.

When after several minutes Brandon still had said nothing, Mitchell ventured, "I thought it was nicely done. Of course, I don't know much about art, but I like the picture."

"Nicely done indeed." Brandon looked down at the author's signature, half-expecting "S. Verdi" to leap up at him. Instead he read "B. Cioni." Another Italian. Could that perhaps explain the strong similarity? "It's excellent. I've never heard of this Cioni."

"He's a local man in Clacton-on-Sea. A cripple."

"You met him?"

"No, but the gallery owner was full of praise for him. It seems he was a sailor by profession, but was badly crippled in an accident and has settled there in town."

"A sailor?" Brandon was familiar with sailors who could produce delicate scrimshaw and wood carvings, but no sailor had created this scene. Oils took years, even a lifetime, to master to this degree. "It seems unlikely that a sailor would portray the courtyard of an inn rather than the sea."

"Maybe he turned against the sea after his injury."

Brandon stood the painting on the sofa and pulled a chair around to face it. Now that he studied it, he saw more action in it than in the Verdi canvases. Salvatore always portrayed great moments on the brink of happening. This artist had presented the action itself as it was occurring.

There was something about the picture that tugged at a distant memory, but kept eluding him.

"This is the inn at Clacton-on-Sea?" Brandon asked.

"I have no idea. I was only passing through and stopped for a meal. The gallery caught my eye and I went in. As soon as I bought the canvas, I left town."

"The one in the picture doesn't strike me as an inn one would find on a seashore. I would have placed it farther inland."

Mitchell shrugged. "Perhaps Signor Cioni traveled by coach before he became bound to his house."

"He doesn't travel now?"

"His wife brings the canvases to the gallery and collects his money. I gather the poor man doesn't get about at all."

Another shadow of memory teased Brandon. A reclusive artist from Italy whose only contact with the outside world was through a woman. "He's not from Venice, is he?" Brandon asked, half-joking.

"No, from Rimini. I assumed you'd had your fill of Venetian artists. By the way, any news from Teresa?"

"None." Brandon leaned nearer the painting as he examined the brush strokes.

Mitchell shook his head as he said, "I thought more of her than that. Colin is ready to deify her."

"Colin would deify anything in a skirt."

"You're wrong. I talked to him for quite a while after you had gone to bed. I think he was rather in love with her."

Brandon didn't answer for several minutes. "I suppose we both were."

"Too much reserve can be a bad thing. A woman needs tending like a delicate plant—with kind words and little attentions and so forth."

"I sent you off to become a doctor, not a gardener or an adviser to the lovelorn."

"I assumed you already knew that old saying about faint heart never winning fair lady," he said with a smile.

"My heart wasn't faint. She was a forger along with her uncle, and when their deception came to light, she took to her heels!"

"Colin had a slightly different version."

"Colin would. To him, life is just one big romance." He bent over the canvas, studying the manner in which the brush strokes feathered into each other. "Amazing!"

"What is?"

"Look how the brushing is done in the barmaid's hair and the mottling of the doorway behind her. I've seen that technique only in the Verdi canvases."

"Is that unusual? They just look like brush strokes to me."

"Painting techniques are as individual as people's signatures."

"Verdi couldn't have painted it—he's dead, and so is his brother. Besides, the gallery owner knows Signor Cioni and is familiar with his work."

"Maybe, just maybe," Brandon said thoughtfully, "this Signor Cioni studied art under Salvatore Verdi before he went to sea. That would explain his ability. And *maybe* he studied under Antonio Verdi, as did Salvatore and Mario." Excitement was building in Brandon. He paced quickly to the window and back again.

"I've bought another Venetian painting? I'm sorry, Brandon. I know how you feel about them these days."

"Nonsense!" He paced to the door and back. "There's a chance, though a slim one, that I may be able to trace Teresa through this Signor Cioni!"

"How? Why would he know where she is?"

"I said it's a slim chance. If Cioni and Verdi studied under the same master, they may have friends in common. A friend who might have taken Teresa in when she left here. Or maybe he knows about some relative

that I never heard of but that Salvatore Verdi could
have mentioned to Cioni."

"I thought you had given up looking for her."

"I've never given up. It's been over a year since she
left, and I was beginning to lose hope, but I've never
quit trying to find her. I've even enlisted a man in
Venice to watch the palazzo and report to me immediately if she should appear. I've visited the Verdi palazzo
myself several times, and I write to the Valores as often
as I wrote to you, but there hasn't been a word. Catherina
Valore admitted she receives money from Teresa, so I
know she's alive, but Catherina won't or can't tell me
where the money comes from. Teresa must be in Italy,
perhaps even in Venice itself, but I couldn't find her.
They stick close together against outsiders, those Venetians. It's difficult to tell what they may know and what
they simply won't tell."

"But you think this Signor Cioni may know where
she is?"

"No, that would be too much to ask. Especially since
he's here in England and not in Italy. But he may be
able to put me back on track."

"You really care for her, then?"

"I love her." Brandon met his brother's eyes. "I was a
fool to let her go. I knew it at the time, but I let my
damned pride get in the way. I thought I could remain
aloof until matters calmed down, and I could then
approach my decisions with logic. I never dreamed she
would bolt the day after the funeral!"

Mitchell eyed Brandon with great compassion. "I hope
you find her. I always knew she was an unusual lady,
and she must be unique, if she can stir you to this much
passion after a year and more."

"She is unique indeed," Brandon agreed tightly. "And
I'm going to find her if I have to search for the rest of
my life."

The snow was a light one, only filling the ditches and
capping the fence rails. The roads stayed clear enough

for travel, and Brandon had little difficulty reaching Clacton-on-Sea.

He took a room at the best inn, one that bore no resemblance at all to the inn portrayed on the canvas, and left James Owens to care for his team and coach and Robert Flynn to look after his belongings. He hoped to find a lead to Teresa, and with both Flynn and Owens along, he could leave from Clacton-on-Sea to find her and not have to journey back to Hawthorn.

After a short search he located the gallery owned by Ian Pollard and let himself into the dim interior. The building was old and dark and not well-suited to an art gallery, but Brandon suspected the rent was cheap. That could be a distinct advantage, judging by the quality of paintings Pollard had on display. Only one had any value at all.

It was a small canvas for an oil, and the subject was simple. It showed a wooden dock silhouetted against the shimmering dawn, with a black-and-white cat perched regally on the old planks. A simple subject, perhaps, but the cat was handled with no simpering sentimentality, and the opalescent water seemed to ripple, its transparency such that Brandon felt he was actually looking into the water's depth. The sky was a tender color with only a hint of the blue it would become. He could almost fancy that the sky was brightening as he watched. Before he was near enough to read the name, he knew it was signed "B. Cioni."

"Ah," said the proprietor, coming forward, "I see you have an interest in *Dawn*. It's lovely, is it not?"

"More than lovely. How much is it?" The price the man quoted caused Brandon's eyebrows to raise. He hadn't expected the man to ask so little for such a magnificent work. As he counted out the money he said, "I am Lord Brandon Kincaid, of London. I would like to meet this artist."

"I'm Ian Pollard, at your service. As for meeting Signor Cioni, I'm afraid that's out of the question."

"My brother met you recently and purchased a scene of an inn yard. He told me Signor Cioni is crippled."

"Yes. I recall your brother. A nice man, very agreeable indeed. That's right. Signor Cioni's health is quite precarious, and he doesn't venture out, even in a cart." He leaned nearer to speak, even though they were alone in the store. In an undertone he said, "I believe he has suffered a facial disfigurement as well as the loss of his legs, for otherwise he would surely go for at least an occasional cart ride."

"You've not met him yourself, then?" Brandon asked in surprise. "How extraordinary!"

Pollard shrugged. "I'm a lonely man and live a quiet life. I don't get about much myself. If a body wants privacy, he's welcome to it, I say. It's a pity for his wife, though. She's a pretty little thing, or might be if she weren't so drab and sad."

"But this Signor Cioni. Can you tell me who his master was?"

"Not I, Lord Kincaid. I never asked. I'm so proud to get his paintings that I never questioned where he learned his art."

"Where can I find his home? If Cioni won't see me, surely his wife can answer my questions."

"No, my lord, I can't tell you. Even if I knew, which I don't, I couldn't see clear to tell you. Like I said, Signor Cioni is a private man. I couldn't send a stranger to his door, not even your lordship."

"Then when will Signora Cioni be in again?" Brandon asked with growing impatience.

"Don't know, exactly. She don't come regular. Maybe tomorrow, maybe the day after. She will likely step in by next week at the latest."

Brandon groaned, but he knew he had reached an impasse. There was nothing to do but wait and see if he could intercept the man's wife. "Can you tell me what the signora looks like?"

"She's a bit shorter than average, I would guess, and dark like most of them Italians. She always wears a hooded cape that's sort of a rusty black like they get after a while. All her clothes are dark, come to think of it. I guess that's their custom or something."

Brandon thanked him and left, the painting under his arm. There must be a hundred women in Clacton-on-Sea that fit that description.

Teresa longed for true spring and warmer weather. The last unexpected flurry of snow had left her depressed. Her father had been dead over a year now, and by custom she should be discarding her mourning. However, she didn't have enough money to buy new clothing, and she still mourned for Brandon. Time hadn't lessened the pain of her broken heart; it had merely settled into an endless, empty ash.

Luna lay on the warm bricks of the hearth, her appearance one of pure comfort. Teresa sometimes envied the cat. As long as Luna was full and warm, she was perfectly happy. Teresa knelt and stroked the soft black-and-white fur. Luna's purr increased, and she rolled her head back to let Teresa stroke under her chin.

With a smile Teresa picked up the cat and put her out the door, then crossed the room to get her cloak. If the painting of Luna on the dock at dawn hadn't sold by now, she would be hard pressed for money. Although she lived frugally, she had not had any money come in since the sale of The Inn Yard. At times she wondered if Ian Pollard was honest in the amount he gave her for the sale of her paintings. There was no way for her to ask without offending him, and she didn't want to jeopardize her relationship with her only source of income. Luna was able to supplement her own food by handouts from kindly neighbors, but Teresa had to depend on fate to send buyers to the ill-appointed gallery. At least, she consoled herself, at Pollard's there was little likelihood of anyone seeing her canvases and linking her to Salvatore Verdi.

The wind was brisk, but she thought she smelled a

sweetness of flowers in it. Surely spring couldn't delay much longer. Stepping carefully over the uneven cobblestones, Teresa took the shortest way to the gallery.

"Signora Cioni," Pollard exclaimed as she came in the door. "I have good news. The *Dawn* sold."

Teresa let out her pent-up breath in relief, but tried not to show how worried she had been. She always had to appear confident in order not to shake Pollard's faith in the Cioni paintings. The man knew so little about art!

Pollard gave her the money, and although it was much less than she had expected, Teresa's fingers closed over it quickly, as if she were afraid it might disappear.

"Perhaps if I bring two, maybe three canvases next time," she said hopefully, "you might sell more?"

"No, no. You can see how little space I have. All these others are by local artists, and I couldn't afford to offend them."

"But my husband has several that are quite good, and it's so difficult to guess which one might sell over the others. If your customers had a choice—"

"It would only confuse them," Pollard said with jovial briskness. "Only confuse them. Bring me a small canvas, about the size of *Dawn*. The big ones take up so much space. I have a small shop, you know."

Teresa closed her lips to bite back her reply. Whoever had heard of buying an oil painting by its size rather than its subject matter and quality? She was sure her father and grandfather were rolling in their graves over this blasphemy. "Very well," she made herself say. "A small one." That meant another of her wildflowers or still lifes, she thought. Her more important works weren't small at all.

As she turned to leave, Pollard said, "I have more good news."

She looked back at him and waited for him to quit wringing his fingers and speak.

"Do you recall the man I told you about who bought

The Inn Yard? Well, his brother was here two days ago. He's the one who bought *Dawn* in fact."

Cold dread mingled with excitement as she tried to still her emotions. "Lord Kincaid was here?"

"Why, yes, that's his name. I didn't realize I had mentioned it. As a matter of fact, I don't believe I did! How did you know?"

"I guessed," she said in a flat voice.

He looked at her suspiciously. "You haven't had correspondence with him, have you? It's customary to go through the gallery, meaning myself."

"I know what is customary." She wondered if the pompous little man really believed he was the agent for all her paintings and not just the ones he had exhibited.

"Yes, well, I just wanted to remind you. He's still in town, by the by. He was in again yesterday. Says he must meet your husband before he will leave."

"My husband never accepts visitors, Mr. Pollard. Surely you told him that."

"Of course, but he wants to hear it in person. He's staying at the Bear and Staff. If you could send around a note saying that all your dealings must go through me, I'd be much obliged to handle it all for you."

"Yes. I'm sure you would." Teresa put the money in her reticule and drew the strings shut with a snap. "There was something else I was to tell you. My husband says the climate here is too damp and he plans for us to move."

"Move! Move where?" Pollard exclaimed.

"Back to Italy," she improvised. "We miss the sunshine."

"Nonsense! Why, the sun shines here. Bless me if it don't!"

"Not as often, nor as brightly," she said with detachment. "You may tell Lord Kincaid we have gone and left no forwarding address."

"But . . ."

"Good day, Mr. Pollard," she said as she walked from the store. Where could she go? There wasn't enough money in her reticule to buy the week's bread, let alone to move!

She had no fears that Brandon might think the Cioni and Verdi canvases were by the same hand—he would never consider the possibility. No, she had been "discovered" again. But where to go? Colchester was the nearest town of any size. It would have several galleries and the anonymity of sheer numbers, but it was too far for her to walk and push a wheelbarrow of belongings—she could never hope to rent a cart. To leave her paintings behind was impossible. Frimon and St. Osyth were closer, but they were both so small that a stranger would be remarkable. She doubted either had the type of art gallery she needed to make her living. Nor was there time to find a position as governess, which was the only occupation open for a woman of her education and breeding. Teresa would starve in the streets before she considered selling her body to any man who had a coin.

Brandon sat in a small café across the street from the gallery, sipping his coffee and glancing up occasionally from his paper to watch the door of the gallery. The article was a lurid account of the deaths of several people in a boating accident, but he pretended to read it in order to have an excuse for continuing to occupy the table. When he had gone to the gallery the evening before, the owner had implied that he was Cioni's sole agent and had hinted that Brandon was taking liberties in even wanting to meet the man. Brandon didn't care what scheme Pollard had cooked up to bilk his artists, but he was determined to meet Cioni and see if the man knew of Teresa Verdi. Since seeing *The Inn Yard*, he was almost obsessed with the idea of finding one of Antonio Verdi's students.

He almost missed seeing the woman leave the shop —he hadn't seen her enter. She shut the door and walked briskly away, her hood pulled close about her face.

Brandon leapt to his feet and tossed a coin to the waiter. Abandoning his paper, he hurried out the door after the woman.

She looked like dozens of others he had seen in Clacton-on-Sea. Her cape had the faded appearance that black fabric takes on after numerous washings and exposure to sunshine. He couldn't see her face at all, only part of one hand that gripped the edges of her hood against the wind. She seemed a little shorter than average, but all in all she wasn't anyone he would notice in a crowd. He almost lost her twice as she threaded among the people on the street. For some reason, however, Brandon was positive she was the woman he had come to find.

His long legs could have easily overtaken her, but he held back. If she really were that protective of her husband, she might not let him accompany her home. Even if he couldn't meet Cioni face-to-face, Brandon hoped to question the man through the mediation of his wife.

The crowd thinned as they neared the edge of town. The houses here were of a poor quality, almost what Brandon would consider shoddy. It wasn't a place where he would have expected to find an artist of Cioni's ability. He wondered if Pollard might be keeping a larger share of the sale price than was customary. On the other hand, there might be medical bills or children to feed, and Pollard wasn't charging what the paintings were worth.

A black-and-white cat sat in the road as if waiting for the woman, and she bent to pick it up. Brandon's steps faltered and he stopped. There was something about the way she moved, even hidden in the voluminous cloak, that was hauntingly familiar. For a moment the woman stood there cuddling the cat, and a gust of wind brushed the hood aside long enough for Brandon to get a glimpse of her rounded cheek and a profile of her nose and chin. Teresa!

Brandon felt all the air leave his lungs. It was Teresa!

The brief glimpse had been enough for him to recognize the features he loved so well. Still carrying the cat, she entered one of the small weathered houses.

Brandon's first instinct was to run after her and take her into his arms and pour out all his love for her. Then reason won out and he remembered she was now named Cioni, not Verdi. Pain knifed through him. Teresa had married. What else could she honorably have done? She had had no one to take care of her, so she had married. A woman like Teresa would have no trouble finding someone eager to marry her. He was a bit surprised she had married a cripple, but perhaps he had not been so when they wed. More remarkable, she had found an Italian who was also a great artist. She had been gone from Hawthorn for well over a year. Evidently her life had been full. He swallowed hard to control his emotions.

He turned to walk back the way he had come, but he couldn't leave. Not without at least one more glimpse of her face. But did he have the right to show himself and bring up what must be unpleasant memories for her? On the other hand, maybe she would be pleased to know her father's grave was being well-tended and that Katie had planted a small yew tree at its foot in remembrance of him. Teresa had been fond of Katie—maybe she would be happy to know that Katie now had a plump baby boy, or to learn that Mitchell was home from medical school, or that Colin was the same as always.

Why was he trying to fool himself? He wanted to look into her eyes and hear her voice one last time.

Brandon drew a deep breath and retraced his steps. After a pause, he went into the small yard. The cat sat in the window watching him, and Brandon recognized it as the one in the picture he had just bought. That seemed to confirm the rest of it for him: Teresa living in a place like this and married to a cripple. Teresa married to *any* other man was insupportable!

Jealousy tore at him. Crippled or disfigured as he

might be, this Signor Cioni lived with and had a man's rights over the woman Brandon loved! Torturing thoughts ripped through him. Just how ugly and deformed was this man? Teresa might well have been forced into marriage with someone in order to support herself. Was he cruel to her? Although Brandon could hardly bear to know, he had to find out.

Rather than knocking on the door, he stepped around to the window and stood at an angle so he could see in past a bush and not be seen by anyone inside.

Teresa's cloak was hanging neatly on a peg on the wall. The house was scrubbed and polished, though the furniture was of a poor quality. Two easels stood at one end of the room, each with a canvas in different stages of completion. A glance was enough to tell Brandon that both were masterpieces far too grand to enter Pollard's insignificant gallery, and, in fact, even surpassed the Verdi canvases.

She sat at the battered table and counted a small number of coins from her reticule. The worry etched on her face made Brandon ache. Was that all she had received from his purchase of *Dawn?* After a while she got up and went to the cabinet to get a small wedge of cheese and the remains of a loaf of bread. He expected her to feed this to the cat and prepare a supper for her husband and herself, but she surprised him by ripping off a mouthful of bread and eating it as she sat back down at the table.

Brandon frowned. Something was wrong here. He silently stepped away from the window and made his way around the corner to the back of the house. Here the narrow yard dropped down to the water's edge and a rickety dock. Brandon saw that the colors in *Dawn* had been those she remembered from Venice, for this dock would see only western sunsets.

He found a small window and with a great deal of compunction and self-loathing looked in, expecting to find a husband, but saw no one at all. The small room held a bed, a chest, and a straight-backed chair. Nothing else. No husband of any shape or form lingered there. Yet Brandon had been told quite definitely that the man was unable or at least unwilling to leave the house.

He leaned against the wall to think this over. Again he recalled Teresa's preposterous insistence that she, and not Salvatore, was the artist. Such an idea was impossible! Yet someone in this house was capable not only of artistry but also of greatness.

Doubt crept over him. Surely he had not thrown away their love and happiness because he had been too stubborn to see the truth! It wasn't possible!

Slowly he went back to the first window. Teresa had finished her meager fare and had wrapped a smock about her. Although she had always been slender, he could tell she had lost weight since he had last seen her.

His eyes widened as she tapped some blue powder onto the palette, added a few drops of oil, and began to mix it with a palette knife. When the consistency and shade were right, she selected a brush from a crockery jar and began laying bruised blue shadows onto a tumult of glowering storm clouds.

Brandon stepped back, feeling as weak as if he were recovering from a serious disease. Teresa was the master artist—just as she had said!

He went back to the door, but didn't bother to knock. There was no reason for a door to bar him now. He pressed the latch and it swung open easily. He was met by the warmth of the fire and the heavy odor of oils and turpentine. He stood silently in the doorway, then closed it behind him.

Teresa's eyes widened as she realized she was no longer alone. With a strangled cry she leapt to her feet and spun about to face the intruder. For a long moment she couldn't speak or think or even breathe. Brandon! So often had she pictured him standing here, with so much love in his eyes, that at first she thought that this Brandon was a chimera, a mere illusion.

"I've come to take you home," he said.

"I am at home." She lifted her chin defiantly. "My name is Cioni now. Teresa Cioni."

"It doesn't matter what name you're using. You'll soon be Lady Teresa Kincaid, Viscountess of Hawthorn."

"You're . . . you're too late," she said fearfully. "I'm married. My husband is in the next room. Surely Mr. Pollard told you I'm married! Leave, please, before you upset poor Benito!"

Brandon crossed the room in lithe steps that reminded Teresa of Luna on a hunt. He took the brush from her and placed it on the tray of the easel. "There is no 'poor Benito.' "

"There certainly is! He's—"

"I looked in the back window."

She stared at him speechlessly for a moment. "These are his canvases! He must have—"

"No, Teresa. These are your canvases. I was a blind fool, but I see that now. *The Inn Yard* seemed familiar, but I couldn't figure out why. Then I finally remembered I had seen the place myself in York, just as you did. More important I saw your unfinished sketch of it. And I have just now been watching you paint this one."

"I never thought the Viscount of Hawthorn would stoop to window peeping like a common boy of the alleys!"

"Neither did I, but I'm glad I did. Otherwise I would have believed that story about your being married to some unfortunate artist. I could have lost you forever. You are indeed the master artist you claimed to be."

She could only gaze up at him, her arms aching to embrace him, her heart crying out to be filled with his love.

"Teresa, I was wrong. I love you," he said sincerely, "and I want you for my wife."

"I—"

He silenced her with his lips, then spoke. "I don't know what I'll do if you refuse me again."

She smiled slightly. "I was about to say 'I love you and will be honored to be your wife.' "

For a moment he tried to control his passions, but then abandoned the effort. She was his and he was hers, as truly as if their names had been written in the stars.

Hours later they lay on the narrow bed, too happy to care that it was lacking in comfort. Brandon stroked her skin, still rosy from their fevered lovemaking. "You're so dear to me," he murmured. "The past months were a living hell. Never leave me again. Promise it."

"I do promise. I never knew I could be so unhappy! At first I hoped there would be a baby so I would have a part of you with me. Later I was glad there wasn't because I've had so much difficulty making enough money to keep even myself."

"Why didn't you come back to me?" he asked. "Didn't you know I would take you in?"

"As what? A charity case? A criminal? I thought what we had between us was gone forever. It nearly was."

"No, only you were gone. The love stayed and waited for you."

"I never stopped loving you," she said. "Not once. I hoped you had found happiness with someone."

"I never hoped that about you."

"Well," she admitted with a smile, "I never wished it earnestly."

"And now the nightmare is over. You and I can return to Hawthorn and live happily ever after, as they say in the romantic novels."

"Not quite." She eased back so she still lay in his arms but could look into his eyes. "I won't give up my art."

"Of course not."

"No, I'm not talking about those insufferable daisies and violets and bowls of fruit. I mean I won't give up my real art. My large canvases."

Brandon pulled her close. "Darling, I've never had an eagle, but if I had, do you think I would clip one of his wings so he couldn't fly?"

"What does that have to do with me?"

"You mean more to me than an eagle ever could." He lifted her small, square hands that held so much strength, and kissed them. "You are the one I have always searched for—not only my perfect mate, but a master artist on a par with Titian, Tintoretto, Winterhalter."

"Winterhalter!" She jerked her hands away. "I'm better than Winterhalter!"

He laughed. "I was trying to keep you humble. I see it's useless. No, Teresa, there will be no question of your not painting whatever and however you wish. I'll have one of the rooms with a northern exposure made into a studio for you."

"I do wish there had been a baby," she sighed.

"There will be. Just give it time."

"Perhaps if we have a son right away, in a few years I can paint my pictures under his name. Or maybe I could invent a brother, or . . ."

"We'll work out the details later, darling. Right now I only want to love you."

With a happy sigh Teresa gave herself over to him. The hours spun toward dawn like gossamer waves of silver and gold.

Epilogue

Hawthorn had never looked more lovely. The tender flowers of spring had given way to the burst of vivid summer. Even the long slope behind the manor house had cooperated with a carpet of blood-red poppies that nodded with each passing breeze.

Teresa brushed aside the lace curtain, and as she looked out onto the drive, the sunlight glinted on the wide gold wedding band on her left hand. "I don't see anyone yet. What if no one comes?"

With a smile, Brandon reassured her. "You weren't this nervous on our wedding day. They'll come."

"That was different. There were only the two of us, Colin and Mitchell, and Katie. What if your friends won't accept me? What if they don't approve of what we're doing?"

"Nonsense. If my friends don't accept you, we'll drop them from our social list and cut them dead in public."

With a nervous laugh she said, "Don't tease me, Brandon."

"I wasn't." He went to her and put his arms around her from behind. Teresa settled back against the comfortable breadth of his chest. "I don't want to be friends with anyone who won't accept you. If they reject you, they reject me. None of them will, though. How could anyone not love you? I'm more concerned that I'll have to fight endless duels over your honor."

"Brandon," she said with a laugh, "how you do run on!"

He nuzzled her hair. "Remember our honeymoon?"

"No woman ever forgets her honeymoon," she said. "It was perfect." Her eyes grew dreamy and she unconsciously put her hand over her still-flat stomach. Later, when they were alone again, she had an announcement of her own to make.

"I'm glad we went back to Venice," Brandon said. "We had already seen most of the sights, so we had plenty of time for more important things."

"What a rogue you've become!" She turned, laughing, to face him. "I love it."

"From now on I'll take Colin's advice and keep my heart on my sleeve, where he says it belongs."

"He never said to wear it on your sleeve, just to take it out of the box."

"I have no middle ground. Don't be surprised if I develop a habit of kissing you openly in public gatherings and holding your hand on the streets of London."

"I wish Colin had instructed you earlier. We could have saved months of grief." She hugged him close and rested her cheek over the steady thud of his heartbeat. "I wish Papa could have seen this day."

"If he were still alive, this occasion might not be happening."

She looked back at the window. "But, what if no one comes?"

"They'll come. After all the excitement I've generated among gallery owners and buyers and art critics, Hawthorn may not hold them all."

"Brandon, I'm so nervous. What if they hate the paintings? What if our plan is ridiculed?"

"Impossible. These people are connoisseurs of art, not bumpkins. Look. Here comes the first carriage."

Teresa's heart was pounding as she smoothed the ivory flounces of her gold satin dress. Her hair had been perfectly coiffed by Hawthorn's best lady's maid. Her hands were covered by fine lace mittens that left the fingers bare, and on her right hand she wore a ring of topaz and diamonds that matched the brilliant necklace at her throat. Her eyes had taken on the gold from her clothing and jewels. Teresa knew she looked quite presentable, but she was as nervous as a thief.

She kept her head high to prevent her chin from quivering with fear and stayed by Brandon's side to form a receiving line for their guests. Not only was this the first gathering she had ever hosted as his wife, it was one of the most important she would ever attend.

Behind the first coach came another, then two more. Not only were these people knowledgeable, they were punctual. Teresa had a moment of deep trepidation when Lady Barbara Weatherly arrived on the arm of Lord Ashford Benchley. After almost two years they still weren't married, and it was rumored that Lord Ashford was cooling toward her. Lady Barbara gave Teresa a lightning glare that was there and gone before Brandon and Ashford could see it. Curiously, Teresa felt more confident afterward. The worst of the confrontations was over.

The guests milled about in the great ballroom where Teresa and Salvatore had come soon after their arrival. Teresa had a sense of *déjà vu* as she looked at the draped canvases on the raised stage area at the far end of the room. Her thoughts went back to the trepidations of that night. They were shallow compared to what she was feeling now.

When all the guests had arrived, Brandon offered her his arm, and they made their way to the stage. With a smile and a reassuring wink, Brandon left her by the short steps in almost the same place where she had stood to watch her father's paintings being unveiled.

"May I have your attention?" Brandon called out over the murmur of conversation. "As you know, I have discovered a new talent, the equal of which I have never seen."

Teresa's hands were like ice and she felt her stomach churn. What if this didn't work? What if . . . ?

"This artist has painted since early childhood," Brandon continued.

"Who is he?" a jovial voice called from the crowd. "Don't keep us in suspense."

Brandon smiled as if he were thoroughly enjoying himself. Teresa felt clammy all over. She glanced toward the nearest doorway and gauged how long it would take her to run through it. "This artist has studied under the great Antonio Verdi, just as did the late Salvatore Verdi."

"Where do you find these geniuses?" someone else asked good-naturedly.

"This one dropped into my lap, and I almost missed the opportunity altogether." Brandon moved to the first easel and uncovered *The Inn Yard*. Murmurs of appreciation ran through the crowd. Next he swept the velvet covering off *Dawn*. Again the crowd sounded their approval.

"These two canvases were my introduction to this master," Brandon said, drawing out the suspense. "The others are the more recent canvases, one of which was completed here at Hawthorn."

With a quick movement he revealed the painting of a tumultuous storm breaking over a seaside town. Several women took a step backward from the force of nature captured on canvas; the men all stepped closer. The next canvas, an enormous one, portrayed the downfall of the Garden of Eden, Adam shown with a primitive defiance mingled with awe as he sheltered a frightened Eve from the destruction of their paradise.

No one spoke.

Teresa put her hand to her throat as if to steady her pounding pulse. Suddenly applause broke out, and a wave of profound relief poured through her.

Brandon's smile broadened as he heard clamors from a dozen throats to know the name of the artist. When the uproar died down, Brandon said, "The name of the artist? I can do better than that. Ladies and gentlemen, may I present the one with the master's touch herself, my wife, Lady Teresa Kincaid, Viscountess of Hawthorn!"

Again there was stunned silence, but Brandon's eyes met hers and Teresa drew upon his strength. Slowly she mounted the steps, and he took her hand and drew her to his side. As their eyes spoke to each other, thunderous applause erupted throughout the ballroom.

"I love you," she whispered.

Brandon boldly pulled her to him and kissed her with all the love a man could have for his perfect mate.